The inheritance

The Inheritance

sahar khalifeh

Translated by

Aida Bamia

The American University in Cairo Press

Cairo • New York

Translator's Note

Although a translator does not need to justify the choice of any of Sahar Khalifeh's novels, I feel somewhat compelled to explain the selection of *al-Mirath* ('The Inheritance'). As the world moves toward globalization and U.S. society becomes increasingly multicultural, Khalifeh's novel seemed an appropriate response to some of the issues faced by offspring of mixed marriages. The protagonist, Zayna—product of an American mother and a Palestinian father—is confronted by situations of the sort that arise in culturally diverse families, regardless of the country of origin of the parents. A constant search for identity is shared among the children of such families, who are torn between two worlds and struggle to adapt to one or the other. For immigrant families from developing countries, the challenge of living in the United States is significant even when both parents belong to the same culture. For children pulled in two different directions, with each parent trying to assimilate them to his/her culture, the difficulties can be insurmountable. Khalifeh addresses many of those issues in *al-Mirath*.

The novel explores some of the consequences for Palestinian women of the year of the Nakba (1948), when men found themselves unable to sustain their families. Young women just out of high school stepped up and gladly chose to work in distant lands, assuming the role of the breadwinner. Many of these women helped brothers and sisters acquire higher degrees and succeed in their professional lives, but their siblings, in turn, often paid scant attention to the young women responsible for their success. Often these women sacrificed their futures to guarantee that of their siblings, turning down marriage proposals to provide for their families. It is this poignant aspect of the first generation of Palestinian young women that Khalifeh artfully portrays, delving deep into the psyche of that generation through the character of Nahleh and providing a frank and often raw description of her experience and feelings.

With the same directness, Khalifeh takes a highly critical look at the post-Oslo conditions in Palestine, unreservedly delineating the mistakes and the shortcomings of the Palestinian Authority.

The translation of the novel was challenging to say the least, due to the extensive use of Palestinian dialect, even in narrative text, contrary to the practice adopted by many Arab novelists of limiting the spoken language to the dialogues. Khalifeh's style in *The Inheritance* is characterized by very long sentences and complex meanings and expressions that do not always find their match in English. Despite the temptation to rewrite the novel, I have stayed as close to the original language as possible while preserving the intended meaning. In this spirit, I have often made use of very long sentences in English and, at times, seemingly interminable paragraphs as I have sought to reproduce the mood of the Arabic style. I have tried my best to recreate the high-spirited and sarcastic undercurrents that run throughout the novel, an important aspect of Sahar Khalifeh's inimitable style. I have chosen to include Arabic words in the English translation to convey a deeper sense of authenticity in a novel concerned, among other things, with cultural heritage.

Those words are explained in a glossary at the end of the book. In the same spirit, I observed the Palestinian dialect in the transliteration of colloquial words. Therefore, for the reader used to saying 'kunafah' instead of 'knafeh,' I beg patience and understanding. I hope I have imparted at least a small sense of the beauty and flow of the original language. If I have failed, the blame rests entirely on me.

part one

without Heritage

I went to the West Bank looking for him, looking for them, searching for my own face in the land of exile. I wanted to know how it would look. I had received a letter from a man saying that my father was somewhere; in other words, that he was still alive. He said that he was my father's brother from Wadi al-Rihan.

A huge gap separates Wadi al-Rihan from New York and Washington. I had always visualized Wadi al-Rihan as being the opposite of New York, as a small clean town inhabited by simple people, good-hearted and nature-loving, not like New York. Whenever I heard my father talk about the place in the evening, I would run down the stairs, shouting "We're going back home, we're going back, we are going back." But we never did because my father ran away or, to be accurate, I ran away.

The story began in New York, when my father came from his village and married an American woman, my mother, and as a result acquired a green card and became a resident alien. Then came the divorce, predictably, then the grocery store and other wives and an army of children. Before he had the grocery store, my father sold small items, which he carried on his back, going from door to door. He sold all kinds of merchandise, regardless of its origin, as products of the Holy Land. He would fill small bottles with water and sand and call in the streets, "Holy water and holy sand from the holy river. Do you know Jordan, Madam? Holy water and the baptism of Jesus Christ. Is there a baptism in your family? We have many baptisms in ours, we get baptized every day." Then my father would add, "I am from Jerusalem and I have brought water from the Jordan River."

He had trouble speaking English but managed to communicate in a typical Middle Eastern glib manner. He would display his wares—shiny clothes, pins, and threads—and say to the American housewife, "Look, lady, how beautiful it is! This caftan is hand-embroidered in Arabia, far away, do you know Arabia? The land of sand and camels, dates and incense, gum and the Qur'an. Do you know Mecca?"

Seduced by the exotic appearance of the man and his merchandise, she would answer with great enthusiasm, "Oh! Mecca! Arabia! Of course, of course, let me see, let me see."

"Easy on them lady, look at this and this and this."

Then, as if by pure coincidence, he would happen upon something of little importance, an old, faded photo of Husayn I. He would ask her, "Do you see this, lady? It is my father's photo, he was a great prince, but died. A Bedouin tribe seized his emirate while I was still a young boy. I ran away to Jerusalem, then to Cairo, and later to Marrakech. From there I took a boat to America. Do you see, lady, I am a poor beggar while my father was a great prince!"

The lady would stare at the photo with eyes wide, seeing a noble face, a white beard, and a large turban on his head. Deeply moved, she would repeat, "Oh dear! Oh dear!"

My father would say again, broken-hearted, "Do you see, lady, I'm a poor beggar while my father was a great prince."

"No, no, never!" the lady would object. Her eyes moving between him and the picture, she would comment, "No, no, never. You're not a beggar."

Looking at him again, she would stare at his black eyes and his glittering dark mustache and whisper to herself in amazement, "His father was certainly a prince, he looks like a prince too. I'll bet anything you're a prince!"

At this very moment he would wrap a piece of silk around his head and, standing in front of her, ask flirtatiously, "Like so?"

Visibly moved, the woman would exclaim, "Oh! Goodness me, I can't believe it! I'll bet anything that you're a true prince!"

He would move toward her, saying, "You too are a princess, a sultana, the goddess of beauty and charm, by God Almighty!"

He would then take another piece of silk, tie it around her waist and swear, by the Prophet Muhammad, master of all Prophets and Messengers, that she looked exactly like Sheherazad, with all her majesty and glory, that she was even the jewel of all Arabs and Muslims, amen. He would swear three times that he would divorce his wife if he were wrong. He would repeat it over and over again, each time saying, "Let's try this one again, one more time, one more time."

This is how he was able to sell Hong Kong merchandise as products of the Holy Land made by former "princes" such as himself. In a few years he was able to open a grocery store in Brooklyn containing everything one could imagine.

He was naturally successful, not because of his knowledge of English and his fluency, but rather because of his eyes and his mustache and his ability to make up stories and invent dreams.

I was born to inherit all this. I became a well-known writer in the field of human civilization; in other words, I am an anthropologist. Yet, before becoming what I am now, I made use of my father's tricks. The story began when I felt the pain of my budding breasts. My stepmother said that that was a hereditary chronic illness in the family. The illness progressed to the point that it made me peep through keyholes and windows that were ajar.

One day, while I was standing on the roof spying on two lovers kissing in the dark and learning from them, my father caught me red-handed. I had no choice but to invent a story about me fasting and waiting on the roof for the call to prayer. I asked him innocently what time the sun set for iftar, the evening meal at sunset on a day of fasting, in order to break my fast. I explained that I was waiting for Bilal's call to prayer.

Bilal was our senile and clumsy neighbor who said he was trying to convert America to Islam by making the call to prayer every day, five times a day. My father looked at me, perplexed, but chose to believe me. I convinced even myself and almost choked with tears from pangs of hunger. I said in a strangled voice, "I'm hungry, I'm so hungry!"

At night I heard my father reprimand his wife, saying, "Show some mercy—the girl is killing herself with this fasting! See how small and thin she is! Is it acceptable that she prays five times a day, fasts the whole month of Ramadan and makes up for missed days?"

My stepmother turned in bed making the springs squeak under her huge weight, and said to my father, "Isn't that what you want her to do?"

He replied anxiously, "Me! And also to make up for the missed days!"

She said angrily, "What? What missed days? Why? Pray tell me do you think that your daughter really fasts? She eats like a horde of locusts. She could gobble me up in a single bite as though I were an appetizer. Before lunch she gobbled up seven ears of corn at one go. I tried to stop her but failed. My God, how stubborn she is and unbearable. She is headstrong, a liar, crazy; she never tells the truth. May God protect us from her. I'm afraid she'll do something like Hoda and embarrass us in the neighborhood."

Hoda was the daughter of our neighbors living in the same complex. Like me, she was half-American. She became pregnant at fifteen and we all saw her father run after her in the street like a raging bull, carrying his longest knife. My father tried to stop him, but couldn't. Finally, with the help of two neighbors they were able to prevent him from killing her. My father constantly said, whenever he had the chance, "He should have killed her, she sullied his name, stained his honor, and humiliated him among his people. Had I been in his place I would have gone after her to Hell."

Hoda was able to escape, however, and took refuge in her American grandmother's house. We did not see her in Brooklyn again, but we heard rumors. Some said she had kept the baby, others said that she had given him up for adoption. Still, others said that she had had an abortion. Regardless of all the rumors, everyone agreed that Hoda's father was no longer a man since he had not washed his honor in her blood.

I heard my father mutter, from his bedroom, "God forbid, God forbid. She said that she was waiting for the call to prayer while I stood there like a billy goat. All I needed was a turban!"

The following morning my father announced the news, "To hell with America and the Americans. That is it—I'm going back home."

He was sitting in front of the grocery store with two of the neighbors, smoking a water pipe. I stood in a corner, watching them expectantly. As I heard the words "old country" I jumped for joy and almost flew up the stairs to the second floor. The words "old country" were music to my ears, as melodious as the long stretch of a mawwal. It was like a miracle, a story similar to that of Aladdin and the magic lamp, with its magic words, 'shubbayk, lubbayk,' one of father's stories, enveloped in smoke, incense, and butterfly wings.

I pushed open the door and shouted, "We're going back home, we're going back home!"

My stepmother came toward me holding a big wooden spoon that she waved threateningly, "A liar goes to hell, you will go to hell and melt like a candle."

I started crying but repeated, stubbornly, "We're going back home, by God Almighty. I heard my father say it with my own ears. Go listen to him."

She hesitated for a few seconds, then rushed to the window, looked below, and heard my father saying, "What are we waiting for, friends? Haven't we had enough of America and its trash? We all have boys and girls, do you want your daughters to be loose like American girls? Do you want to protect your girls, keep them pure, and bring them up strictly and marry them well?"

The two men nodded approvingly, and my father became very emotional. He shouted in a voice that could be heard at the end of the street, "There, one really lives, brothers! There you speak Arabic, eat Arabic, drink all-Arabic coffee. Everything is Arabic! If you need help, you find a thousand hands stretched out to help you. If you need money you can take it from a friend, no banks, no checks, and no headaches. At the end of the day you can sit in the cafe for hours on end, then go to the mosque or to the diwan. There, people are genuine Muslims, even the Christians are good-hearted and know God exactly as we do. We worship God in a mosque and they worship Him in church. There's not much difference. As for here, God Almighty protect us from what is here! Is there anything here, please tell me?"

One of the two men growled, "Hah!" and my father shouted, "Well, well, we all gorge ourselves. I eat and you eat and everyone of us eats to the point of saturation. But pray tell me, the Americans in Saudi Arabia, what are they doing there? Are they defending the Kaaba? Are they being baptized in the River Jordan? Or do they perform the tarawih prayers? Do please tell me what are they doing there?"

The two men shook their heads without saying a word, provoking my father's anger. He shouted at them, "Don't shake your heads like Bilal! Just tell me what they're doing there?"

One of them exploded, saying, "They eat our food and take us for a ride! This, in a nutshell, is what they're doing there. We Arabs, on the other hand, are as stupid as mules and donkeys, and deserve more than that. That's what they're doing: they're screwing us openly and shamelessly."

"God forbid," commented my father.

The other retorted, "They're screwing us? I'm the one doing the screwing. I don't spare anyone, white or black, and I screw them all."

My father shouted, "That's the intention—you screw their daughters and they screw yours. Isn't that the plan?"

"God forbid!"

The first man shouted, "I won't let anyone touch a hair on one of my girls!"

"Well, what about Hoda?" my father asked, "What happened to her?"

The three men bowed their heads for a few minutes until my father ended the discussion, saying, "I want my daughters to be brought up as Arabs, clear and transparent as a candle. I want them to marry Arabs and Muslims, according to the Prophet's teachings. I want them to be impregnated by Muslims. To hell with America—I'm going back home."

My father didn't return home, however. He opened another grocery in New Jersey, bought a new house, and married a new woman. Then he ran after me in the street, holding the longest knife he had. I was fifteen years old, and pregnant.

My language was lost before I was lost and so was my identity. My name and address followed suit. My original name was Zaynab Hamdan, and with time it became Zayna. My father was called Muhammad Hamdan and with time I was left with neither Muhammad nor Hamdan. My father's birthplace was Wadi al-

Rihan and mine was Brooklyn. As Zayna I was caught between two languages and two cultures—my father's Brooklyn and the West Bank on one side and my maternal grandmother's American culture on the other. I was later left without any culture and lived in a vacuum. My father's songs, the Qur'anic verses, and the praises of the Prophet were meant to protect me from the negative influence of American culture. Obviously, they did not. There was a simple explanation for this: I didn't understand the meaning of the words and I didn't respond to the melodies. There was also my new stepmother, a person who considered the ability to speak English a sign of education, good upbringing, and civilization. Her own English was poor, however, and so was her upbringing. She pronounced *p* as *b* and the *k* as a strong guttural sound. She would say, "abble bie," "panana sblit," and "bark your car in the barking lot."

As for us children, we were able, thank God, to distinguish a *p* from a *b*, but were unable to put together a single meaningful sentence. Our conversation consisted of a strange mix of the two languages, so strange that our American guests wondered whether we went to school to learn reasonably correct English or not. Our relatives didn't hide their dismay that we did not join the Arab club and learn decent Arabic. To counter such criticism, my father would ask me at the end of each gathering to prove to our honorable American friends my mastery of the English language. I would spend part of the evening standing on a chair, surrounded by bottles of araq and plates of mezze, and the cheers and laughter of the visitors as I recited the verb "to be," then the verb "to have," followed by "Twinkle, twinkle little star" and "Row, row, row your boat." I used to end the show with the American national anthem, accompanied by the loud singing of all the guests. The noise would be so loud that our new neighbors would call the police and the fire department. The scene was repeated with our Arab relatives. I would stand in their midst and stun them with my knowledge of Arabic grammar, enumerating many defective verbs and conjunctive particles, reciting the laudations of the Prophet, and *tala'a al-badru, al-Hamd*, and the Fatiha—the first sura of the Qur'an. I would end my performance with an Andalusian muwashshah accompanied by the enthusiastic participation of all those present. By this time dawn had come and the police officers would have returned to the apartment to escort our relatives out of the building and possibly out of New York.

I can't really claim that my childhood was miserable. On the contrary, it was filled with excitement, fun, and good food. With the exception of my difficult interactions with my father's wives, my unfulfilled dream to return to the homeland, my hope to receive a phone call from my mother in Los Angeles, which never came, and a single visit with my grandmother without one of my father's wives spoiling it, it was a breeze.

I enjoyed living with my father, who was as dear to me as my soul and the light of my eyes. He was a good-hearted man, full of memories, anecdotes, and funny stories. I still remember him when he used to gather us around the large wood-burning stove on New York winter nights and tell us old jokes while grilling chestnuts, drinking araq, and eating mezze. He used to say that he was a child of the world. He had toured the globe, seen everything, and heard it all. Nothing surprised him or shocked him anymore, and yet, at the mention of the name of a relative or a friend in Beirut or Damascus, he would be overcome with emotion and cry.

He liked sad songs. He would listen to them and move with the rhythm, flapping his hands as if flying. Then he would get drunk, relax, and shout after each rhyme, in appreciation, "Allah! Allah!"

I would observe him quietly from my place, my tears flowing down my face. The tears, the rhymes, and the stories kept me from feeling totally ostracized from my family.

Whenever I remember the knife and that final look, I recall the tears of longing and the dream of returning to the homeland, a wish that was never fulfilled. His words still ring in my ears, "It's true that I'm a worldly man, but I have never dishonored anyone or betrayed the trust of any person. Every woman I've been involved with I have known according to God's law. I've never taken people's opinion lightly. All my life I've cared what they said and thought of me. Listen to me, Zaynab, the most important things in life are a good reputation, the fear of God, and the Day of Judgment. It's possible for a person to live without this and that, but if you forget God, He forgets you, and if you ignore God's words you won't remember people's words. That's how life is, and that's the way the world works. Life is but a lesson, an exhortation and a path. Life is a message, a message of love and forgiveness. What is life Zaynab?"

I would answer him, with tears running down my cheeks, "Life is an exhortation, Daddy."

"What else?"

"Life is a test, Daddy."

"What else?"

"Life is a path."

"A path to where? Toward whom?"

"A path to the afterlife, to the Prophet and his Companions, and the believers, both men and women and the pure men and women."

"Great, my daughter, great, great. May God protect you in this world, smooth your way and cover it with good intentions and good deeds. Come sit beside me and eat this. Be careful with the mezze and don't spill the araq. What's wrong with you my daughter? What's wrong?"

When I became pregnant the first person who came to my mind was my grandmother, Deborah. Maybe because Hoda had sought refuge with her grandmother, I did like her, and maybe because my grandmother was in the habit of sending me every Christmas, a fruitcake and a card decorated with candles. She even had sent me on another occasion, a bear as big as a baby. It was the first time I ever had been given a big toy. My father didn't like the bear and said that it was a boy's toy. He took it away and threw it very far. That's what he told me, but actually he had done nothing of the sort. Ten years or so later I found the bear in the attic among old things belonging to my mother.

When I found out that I was pregnant I went up to the attic and jumped up and down ten times on the floor. Afterward, I felt tired and sat down amidst old things covered with dust. I was alone in the dark except for the bear. I put it on my lap and began sobbing on its tummy. I was afraid my father would find out about my pregnancy and would kill me as he had once threatened to do. He did try to kill me when he learned of my pregnancy, but I ran away from my home in Brooklyn to my grandma's house in Washington D.C.

I lived a normal life in her house; in other words, I had no life at all. There was a huge difference between my life in Brooklyn and my life in Washington, where my life with Grandma was quite different from the life I had lived with my father. Whereas he had loved having fun, my grandma never drank and never dreamed. Her kitchen was sparkling clean, as white as a pharmacy. Everything in it was organized and kept in jars that revealed every grain and every seed. She had placed a label on each jar with numbers and letters. If there were more than one jar for the same product, she would write, sugar 1, sugar 2, sugar 3, or English tea, Australian tea, Chinese tea. Although my father had his own system of keeping things, her kitchen was more organized than our grocery store. He could find anything you requested in a few seconds, from a strange collection of garlic hanging from the ceiling to dried fish to sausages to onions to pickled turnip to eggplant to dry mulukhiya, to araq from Qurtas to tomato paste and orange-flower water. He would ask the buyer questions without waiting for a reply, "A kilo of mixed nuts? A kilo of black olives? Three yards of rope? A kilo of coffee with cardamom? Just relax, the world isn't going anywhere, why do you keep running, life isn't a race. Have you become like them, running like a horse without a bridle? Take it easy and enjoy life. Why run, why crowd your time? With whom are you competing? Can you go faster than life or death? Let me tell you this, the fastest is death. My God, how fast and close by it is, closer than the eyebrow to the eye! Trust in God and sit here. Drink a cup of coffee and smoke a water pipe. Let me tell you a story, come on, sit down, I won't let you leave, by God you won't go. I swear I'll divorce my wife if you leave, what's with you, man? Do you want to destroy my family and give my children a stepmother? I have gone through four wives and you haven't found one yet? What do you say, let me find you a bride. I know a girl from a good family, beautiful like a full moon and to your taste. She has a green card and you would obtain your citizenship without delay if you marry her. She has a waist that moves like a spring, and a couple of killer green eyes, may God be praised. She's as plump as a duck and her cheeks are like apples. She's young and as delicate as a twig of peppermint and you can shape her the way you want. Would you like to see her? Stay here then, she'll soon return from school. You're welcome here, give me a minute and I'll have everything ready for you in the blink of an eye."

One second becomes one hour and then you stop counting, and you don't feel the time passing, not because the service is slow, since he usually prepares your order as promised, in a wink, but because of all the stories, the tales, and the laughing while listening to tales from the Arabian Nights, 'Antar and 'Abla, al-Shatir Hassan, and Bilal the Stupid, to the news of the neighbors, the scandals, the politics, the price of gold and silver, the merchandise ads, the apartments for rent, the cars, and the tires. Didn't he say that he was a man of the world? A totally different world!

The confrontation between my father and my grandma came to a head after I got pregnant and took refuge in her house. I had been with her for a week when he came to see us. We were in the kitchen baking a cake when Grandma saw him from the window; she immediately pushed me to the storage room. He came into the kitchen, and Grandma tried to talk to him but he didn't answer her and began searching the place for me with the eyes of a hunting dog. He looked much older and darker. I didn't think he would really kill me, he loved me deeply, and I didn't believe him capable of doing such a thing. I hadn't lost hope in spite of my grandma's incessant warnings: "Didn't you see what happened to Hoda and to the others? Weren't they young girls? Didn't their parents love them?"

I held my breath while watching him through the holes in the door. His face was gloomy and his eyes were bulging. I saw him push my grandma away, and when she tried to use the telephone he snatched the receiver from her, pulled out the wires, and shouted in a thundering voice, "Nothing doing! Don't interfere! It's over; consider her dead. She must pay for her mistake. I must wash away my shame and hers."

My grandma tried to convince him that I wasn't there but he refused to believe her. Instead, he went to the sitting room and began breaking everything in his way, kicking things and shouting at the top of his voice, until he reached maximum anger. Whenever that happened, which was rare, he would turn into a ferocious beast incapable of reasoning or grasping the true meaning of events. He wasn't the father I knew but a total stranger.

He returned to the kitchen holding the big bear in one hand. I crouched back in fear and apprehension, causing a jar to fall and break. In a second I found myself at his feet. He dragged me into the kitchen, my body covered with pieces of glass, jam, and blood. He pulled my hair and shouted at the top of his voice, "Daughter of a dog, by God I will suck your blood!"

I held the hem of his trousers and begged for mercy. He met my pleas with heavy blows to my stomach and head. He pulled my hair and yanked my face up, asking with eyes afire, "Who is the bastard responsible for this?"

He was drunk and stunk of araq, the smell making me vomit. My father began to shake me as if I were an empty sack, and then shouted, "Who is this bastard who soiled my honor with mud?"

I couldn't utter a single word as I was gradually losing consciousness, but I was aware of his movements and felt that my end was near. I closed my eyes tightly and felt his kicks to my chest, while waiting for his knife to fall. Suddenly we heard a crack like a bomb exploding. It shook the whole kitchen. I felt the muscles of my father's legs tighten, then he collapsed on the floor. As our eyes met for a second, I saw in his amazement, extreme pain and surprise. I looked toward the door, where my grandmother stood holding a hunting rifle in her hands. She whispered, hissing, "Move and I'll blow your head to pieces."

Her face was calm, while her eyes moved left and right.

"Drop the knife right now," she told my father.

He replied, rattling, "Daughter of a dog." Then a second bullet hit the table near him and it fell on him.

"Zaynab, come here, quickly," said my grandmother. But I was dazed and couldn't move. She turned to my father and said, "You've seen what I can do, Hajj, throw away your knife." He did as she said, using his left hand while pulling his wounded arm to his chest.

"And you, young lady, move, go to my room and call the police, fast."

I climbed the stairs, but I didn't dare call the police. A mixture of guilt, shame, fear, pity, and loss froze my thinking and paralyzed me. I sat on the edge of the bed and looked out the window. Fall was nearing its end and the leaves were falling from the trees, a few remaining on the branches. I whispered, wondering, "What did I do? What will I do? What's next?"

A gloomy feeling took hold of me and I felt a strange calm. I was unaware of time passing but I finally went downstairs and heard him say to my grandma, "You're the cause, you made her leave. You destroyed my family and broke my heart. You're neither a woman nor a man."

She replied quietly, "Calm down, Hajj, let me clean your wound. Hold this for me, put your mind to work, and let's talk quietly. Zaynab is staying here. You can go to your people and tell them that you acted like a man and killed her. Don't play games or go to court or do anything else. You know what will happen. You tried that once before, so don't try it again. Forget Zaynab like you forgot her mother."

He answered her, crying, "I have not forgotten her and I never will."

I, too, never forgot him and lived with my grandma for many years. I later forgot my mother and my son, but I never forgot the sight of my father crossing the hallway with his arm tied to his neck and his back bent under the weight of thousands of years of shame. I shouted at the top of my voice, "Forgive me, Daddy."

He turned and pointed to the skies with his sound arm. The road was desolate as he walked heavily, his head hanging, a bandage attached to his neck, and dragging his feet through the dry, fallen leaves.

I shouted, feeling quite guilty, "Forgive me Daddy! Please forgive me!"

He motioned once more with his hand and disappeared down the road, forever.

Life with my grandmother passed quickly. Events raced by and I can't recall the details except for two events that haunted me day and night. The first was giving up my son to an adoption agency and the second was meeting my mother for the first time. Between the two events my grandmother taught me how to deal with life. At the beginning I proceeded carefully, like someone walking in the rain trying not to get wet. My Grandma continuously repeated to me, "Make success your aim because if you fail, people will feel sorry for you, but they won't respect you or befriend you. If you want to keep your son, take him only if you are able to support him."

From then on, I became a winner in everything I did, whether sports or academics. At first I thought I was doing all this for my son, not for me. I thought that my success would make me strong and would make it possible for me to get him back. The reality was different, however. The more successful I became, the more I wanted to succeed. Success meant proving myself, but it made me lose touch with the rest of the world.

I became aware of people only when I wrote about them. I saw them as nothing more than competitors, individuals to beat. I had no time for love, emotions, family ties, or friendship. No one counted except Grandma Deborah and me. Eventually, Deborah melted away and disappeared, leaving me alone following my path, with a forlorn heart. I was all alone, no one with me and no one supporting me. I saw nothing but my shadow and even my steps stayed behind me. My questions remained unanswered. I had no time to talk with others, no time for memories or feelings. I did nothing but run.

I changed completely. I lost my unique personal characteristics. I didn't feel nostalgic for the strange stories and tales of my childhood. I didn't laugh or have fun, and I no longer enjoyed eating with others. I learned to eat sandwiches on the go. I learned to live in silence and spend my days alone. I became accustomed to spending long hours in social gatherings without songs and music. There was nothing strange about this life because my grandmother was serious by nature, and so were my university colleagues and others I met. They were kind, but each was for himself, and all moved in their own orbits. I learned from them, locking myself in a glass cage and keeping people and emotions outside.

It was comforting to live that way. It was agreeable and our conversations were superficially pleasant. There were no fights, no blame, no frictions, and no aversions—and how could there be with such high walls erected between us! In this social setting, so different from the one I knew when I lived with my father, we neither touched anyone nor were touched.

Yet, despite all that peace, under that pleasant and innocent surface, something cold was growing inside me, making me shiver on the hot summer days. At night,

I would switch off the lights and withdraw to my grandma's rocking chair, spending hours in the dark feeling my enthusiasm for life draining away. Whenever my grandma returned late from one of her meetings, she would sit beside me and read the day's newspapers. Out of consideration for her I would usually relinquish the rocking chair, except when I felt a cold chill around and inside me. Then I would remain seated in the rocking chair oblivious to my surroundings. Grandma would feel sorry for me and say, "You must have had a long day, poor thing? Did you?"

If I didn't respond she would continue, "Poor thing, she works so hard!"

She would remain in her seat for an hour or longer, and before she went to bed I would hear her say, "Oh! My God, what has happened to America and Americans! What has become of us?"

The "us" was painful to me. What does "us" mean? Who is "us"? "Us" Americans? I am not American.

"What are you then?" Grandma asked me one day as I said those words.

I didn't say I was Arab because I wasn't. Who am I then? Despite my mother's citizenship, my birth certificate, my school certificate, my books, my accent, my clothes, and everything about my life, I was not truly American. The depths of my mind were inhabited by visions and pictures, love songs, those Arabic mawwals moving like the passage of a breeze, the scent of violets, the fragrance of memories, all leaving behind a honey-sweet solution in the heart. Memories would rush in like a swarm of butterflies, hovering in the room until the morning, filling the darkness with the fragrance of jasmine, rare incense, Arabic coffee with cardamom, almonds and cinnamon, mahaleb and nutmeg, grilled bread and chestnuts. The butterflies would glide like the sails of a boat, a waving hand, a flock of pigeons. My ears would respond to a remote voice calling and singing, *Amaneh ya Layl,* 'I trust you, O night.' I would plead in my longing, "Forgive me, Daddy, forgive me." I would spend the night watching the flames change into ashes. Grandma's hand would then reach to me in the dark and shake my shoulder, whispering, "It's nothing but a dream Zayna, just a dream."

"No, I'm not dreaming," I would tell her.

"No Zayna, it's nothing but a dream," she would repeat.

A dream? A dream? What about the little girl and all the anthems, the songs, the laughter, the pleasure, the food and drink, the mezza and the araq?

"It's only a dream, Zayna, nothing but a dream," she would say, then return to bed.

I was probably depressed. When she grew weary of my condition she consulted a psychologist who immediately identified it as a case of homesickness, nothing more. She shook her head approvingly, and added, "Of course, it's normal, a young mother of a young child."

She took me to see my child. He smiled, but when I approached to touch him, he withdrew his head and cried, fearful.

"Do you feel better?" she asked.

"I feel nothing at all," I said.

My grandmother was surprised but said nothing. On the way back to the apartment she tried to explain that it wasn't normal to be indifferent and that a mother is expected to feel something. She went on lecturing me until she was tired of the whole issue. While she was talking I wondered whether human beings are expected to feel or not to feel, and whether that child felt something or felt nothing. If a child can feel, what does he feel—is it boredom? Love? Fear? Is he homesick? Does he recognize his mother on his own or is he taught to recognize her? Does he know that I don't feel?

To be fair to her, I must say that my grandmother was patient with me. She invited my mother to visit us from Los Angeles. I was getting ready to meet her in the hall when she came up to me from behind. She laughed and cried and said, to justify herself, "I was young."

She wiped her tears and continued, "I couldn't handle him, I couldn't put up with their traditions, their food, their drinks, and their skin color! They were strangers and their habits were strange to me. I couldn't bear it."

I didn't open my mouth and kept looking in the mirror.

She pleaded with me, "Don't blame me!"

"Why should I blame you?" I said.

She asked, "Do you love me?"

18

"I don't hate you," I replied.

"What about love?"

"Yes, what about love?"

"You don't love me then?"

She felt stupid and I was extremely bored. She went on talking, crying, and sobbing. I was about to lose my temper, and I finally shouted, "Lady, please tell me, how can I love you when I don't know you?"

She replied, reproachfully, "But you love him?"

I didn't utter a word.

"Though he tried to kill you!"

I didn't defend him or myself.

"He tried to kill you!" she repeated.

I didn't look at her and kept looking in the mirror. Finally, I told her, "Lady, I don't blame him, I don't blame you, I don't blame anyone. I only wonder."

She whispered in amazement, "She only wonders, she wonders!"

When she reached her car, she waved and I waved back. I watched her until she disappeared from my view.

My academic life was barren, tasteless, and emotionless. My mother died and I inherited her property. I had two apartments—one in Washington, one in San Diego. I acquired two cars, attended yacht and swimming pool parties, and diplomatic receptions. I was a member of three different health clubs. I did aerobics and enjoyed Jacuzzi baths, massages, and saunas. And yet, despite this life of luxury, I felt deprived. Aware of my feelings, my grandmother would ask me, "What are you missing? Aren't you successful?"

Yes, I had succeeded, I had, and what a success! I had received an award for the best research at the university, I had become chair of the anthropology department, but I wondered what next? I was in my thirties then. In ten years I would be in my forties, then fifties, then sixties, I would retire, then die. What happens after death and even before death? What would be left for me to do in my sixties? How would I be? Would I be a carbon copy of my grandmother? Make jam and bake cookies, join a charitable organization and go to church every Sunday? No, I never had gone to church and I wouldn't begin now. I was neither Christian nor Muslim. Concerned, my grandmother repeated constantly, "You need an ideology, you need faith."

What faith, I wondered? When I was young and I still had the strength to debate and ask questions, I couldn't bear the idea of celestial justice. I was firmly convinced that what happened to me was no more than clear proof of the absence of justice. Even if justice existed it was not necessarily celestial. Because of this I never entered a church in my life except to attend a wedding or a funeral. I would cry at the sound of church chanting, but I would rush to wipe the tears away. I didn't want anyone to see my tears, and I never cried in public. This was the secret of my success—I was strong, and I neither cried nor broke down.

As time passed, the gap between my past and my present grew narrower. I was extremely homesick, and frankly, longed for my past. Fulfilling myself through research was only a substitute. As for my true feelings, what had broken inside me was an old wound that no longer bled. It was the deep dirge that reminded me constantly of the past and the wailing of the soul. The only solution was to admit that I wouldn't settle down and find peace until I returned to my past, to what was lost.

I returned to New York for the first time since I ran away, to our grocery in Brooklyn. Everything was different, everything had changed, and our store was no longer a grocery, but a huge white building that looked like a palace. It had a high fence, large, bushy trees, and a dark Arab concierge. He asked me what I wanted. I said I was looking for my father whose grocery had been in the spot where the palace now stood.

"When was this?" he asked, a look of surprise in his eyes. He said he had lived in Brooklyn for many years and he knew many grocery owners, but he had never heard of Hajj Muhammad. He suggested that I go to his father and ask him because he was an old man and might remember.

I walked in the back street trying to recall signs and events. This is where I had lived and where I'd been fashioned. I saw the riverbank and the intersection, the west side and its trees across the river and the courtyard where young black boys played their music. An old man dozed on a chair, wrapped in his coat. Everything was as I remembered it in the neighborhood, except for my father, the grocery store, the line of shops, and the neighbors. I reached the house described by the young man and knocked at the door. A woman who reminded me of one of my father's wives opened the door. She said in a friendly voice, "Yes, madam. Abu Faleh is there, sitting near the window."

She smiled and pointed to the window, causing her gold bracelets to clank.

He was sitting on a rocking chair facing the western window, a crocheted blanket covering his legs and a cotton Arab skullcap on his head. Behind him, the skyscrapers looked like a line of piled matchboxes and Legos. The contrast between the background and the man was striking. Here was an old man with ancient features sitting against a background of modern buildings and columns.

The woman whispered, "The whole day he goes in and out of sleep. He is old and forgets people but remembers things centuries old. He remembers the fig tree, the village jar-shaped oven, Hajj Muhammad, and the mayor, but he doesn't remember me. What would you like to drink, coffee or lemonade? For God's sake, don't say no, what's happening, have we become Americans? Believe me, even if we stay in America hundreds of years we won't be like them. You said your father used to live here? This happened long ago, before I married this old man, so wait until he wakes up, and perhaps he will tell you. He might remember and then again he might not. You have to be patient. What shall I give you, a lemonade or a Pepsi?"

I sat on the sofa, in the corner, under the traditional photo of the head of the household, Abu Faleh. He was in his youth then, wearing a waistcoat and a tarbush, the traditional Turkish headgear. Squeezed under his photo, near the edge, there was a torn picture of a number of young men with hats and mustaches. In the dark corner where I sat was a table with an embroidered cover, plastic flowers, and pictures of numerous grandchildren. There was a picture of a bride, a photo of a college graduate, and one showing a young man flanked by an old man and an old woman. Standing in this order were two young boys, a young girl, and then a young boy, a 1920s Buick with a man wearing white shoes and a tarbush, standing in front of it, one foot on the ground and the other on the running board. A prayer rug hung on the opposite wall. It looked like a painting, showing the Dome of the Rock and some Qur'anic verses.

Abu Faleh woke up, drank some lemonade, yawned, and paid no attention whatsoever to me. The woman nudged his back and said, "Hey, Abu Faleh! This woman has come all the way from Washington to see you. Talk to her. Did you know someone who had a grocery in our street, near the bakery?"

He mumbled, surprised, "Which bakery?"

She winked at me and whispered, "God protect you, it's no use."

She nudged his back again, saying, "Do you remember Hajj, or don't you? He might be in the photo with you all, here. Look at it, dear, you might find him."

I took the photo and examined it. He could have been this or that one, but he was neither this nor that one. They all looked like my father, but none was my father.

The woman said, "Your Arabic is so-so; is your mother Arab or foreign?"

My voice broke as I explained, "She died a long time ago, I can't remember. When I was a kid, I could speak it well. My father used to tell us stories, all kinds of stories. Sometimes he would talk about Jerusalem and sometimes about another city, I can't remember what it was called. I truly don't know, it was either al-Ram or al-Tireh, and possibly Abu Dees. I really don't recall. It was a different name every time, then Jerusalem, always Jerusalem, the tannery, Bab al-Khalil, and Musrareh."

The man mumbled, sighed and said, "Oh, the old country! My heart yearns for those days!"

The woman stared at me, as if to encourage me, and said, "Talk some more, let him hear you."

I searched my memory for a souvenir, a story or a picture and found nothing but a hazy vision of a photo hanging in the living room and others hanging here and there in my memory, photos of places, the courtyard of the Aqsa Mosque, the Dome of the Rock. I saw stone tiles, silver columns, sweet basil, and refreshing ablution water as cold as melting snow pouring through the tap on hot days. I saw my father moving in circles, carrying his usual basket and bound Qur'ans decorated with mother of pearl. I saw copper kohl containers shaped like peacocks and their dipping sticks shaped like wings. There was amber, mother of pearl, carnelian rosaries, and caravans carved in olive wood, as well.

The man mumbled again, repeating, "Jerusalem, Jerusalem, Oh the old country! My heart yearns for those days."

His wife said, playfully, "Hey Abu Faleh, would you like to go back to the old country to bless our pilgrimage, receive benedictions, and discover who we are after a long absence?"

He mumbled, surprised, "What is left for us to find? Our children have grown up in a foreign country and have left us alone in this house, with no one except the Everlasting."

"God is with us," the woman replied, getting emotional. She regained her composure, and said enthusiastically, to spur him on, "Come on Abu Faleh, you ought to thank God. We did our duty and a little more. Your children are successful and you and I wish for nothing more than good health."

He turned to me and said, "The most important thing is health, my daughter. In this country we are worth nothing without health."

He rocked his chair, his eyes wandered and he smiled slowly, saying, "In the old country, whenever a horse fell ill we used to stay with it, we did the same for a donkey. We would talk to it, sing for it, as if it were a family member or a neighbor. Here, however, there is no family and no neighbor. Each one minds his own business. You said that your father lived here? What was he doing? What was his name, his surname, and from which region was he?"

I searched my memory once more for the name of the city but I couldn't find it. It was mixed up with many other names I had heard from the beginning of time. My father, on the other hand, was present—his shadow was here, his sadness and that look!

"He lived in Brooklyn," I said, "and our house was located where the palace now stands. My father and his neighbors used to talk about America and the Americans and said that the old country was much better."

He rocked his chair and moved his head approvingly, "Of course better!"

"Do you remember, Abu Faleh?" I asked.

"Who can forget?"

"And my father, don't you remember him?" I asked.

"Which one of them?"

"He had opened a shop here," I explained.

"We all did."

"He used to live here," I added.

"We all did."

"It was where the palace is now and where your son Faleh works."

Feeling sorry for me his wife interrupted, saying, "Come on, Abu Faleh, the lady has come all the way from Washington!"

"Even if she had come from Mexico, I don't know," he said, looked far away, then turned to us and said, "If she knew his name, it might be possible."

"His name was Hajj."

"Who was not a Hajj?"

"His name was Muhammad."

"There were at least fifty Muhammads," he explained.

"He had a grocery."

"Thousands had groceries," he added.

I got so close to him that my head reached his knees, and my voice quavered, "Is it possible, Abu Faleh, that you don't know?"

He stared at me from behind his thick glasses, his eyes looking like two small fish lost in two glass containers. Squinting his eyes and pondering he said, "Do you want me to know?"

"You must know?"

He stared deeply and an expression of sudden understanding appeared in his eyes. He laughed maliciously and said, "There was a man who had a daughter who made a mistake and then ran away. From that day on he disappeared leaving no trace."

24

I felt as if a shower of cold water were pouring over my head, but I persisted, "Well, and then?"

"Some say he went to the old country, others say he went to Canada, and some say he lost his mind and died."

"How can I find out?"

"Only God knows."

"But how can I know, Abu Faleh?"

He turned toward the window and resumed rocking his chair, lost in the world of his silence, while I repeated my question to him, "But how can I know, Abu Faleh?"

The only thing I heard was the squeaking of the wood and the rocking chair. I gathered myself and stood up. I looked at him for the last time hoping for some indication or sign. All I saw was a debilitated old man, looking across a window, with buildings stretching all the way to the horizon, a dark, limitless sky, and the street below rumbling with cars. I had reached the door when he called me. I stopped and turned, my heart pounding. I listened with apprehension, "Tell me my daughter, truly, in God's name, aren't you Zaynab?"

I looked at him, and he stared at me, and the two fish moved at the bottom of the bowl. I felt cold seeping into my bones and I left, oblivious to everything around me.

I went back to the spot where our house used to be and where the palace now stood. I looked for Abu Faleh's son, the palace concierge, but the gate was closed. I sat on the bench waiting for him. I looked beyond the bridge and beyond the sea at the port. This is where my family had arrived in boats that had carried thousands, spewing them forth without mercy. This is where they had stepped down, and if they went back they would have returned from here. Where was my father, then? Had he immigrated again? If I were to see him I would ask about his life and his health. If I only knew where and how he was living now. If I only knew how life had treated him, whether it had helped him retain his memory or whether the hand of time had changed his appearance, like the palace and the garage that were built on the land where our house and my father's shop had stood.

I heard Faleh inquiring, "You're back?"

I summoned my courage and told him that I had lost the beginning of the thread, I had lost my family and my father. I didn't know where they were or what I could do now.

part two

This inheritance

I received a letter from my uncle saying what amounted to, "Come quickly before the thread breaks and you lose your claim to the inheritance."

I lost no time thinking things over, but decided without hesitation. I felt at that moment as if I were standing before a window whose curtains were hiding the symbols of the country I had long dreamed of seeing. There was the affection of the family I had lost in my childhood and the warmth of my connection to the roots for which I had long searched in vain. So I gathered my things and left. I took an indefinite leave from work, explaining to my dean that I would not return to Washington until I had found my family and reconnected the severed stem to its roots.

I took the first plane to Ludd's (Ben Gurion) airport in Israel and from there I went to the city of Natanya. I crossed the Green Line in an Israeli taxi that took me to the outskirts of Wadi al-Rihan. The taxi driver left me at the entrance of the town, refusing categorically to get close to the crowded streets of the city. So I carried my suitcase down a narrow, deserted asphalt street filled with potholes, curves, and weeds. When I reached the first populated street, the windows opened and shut quickly; faces hid behind curtains but followed my every move. I was puzzled by the silence and the deserted streets. There were no cars, no children, and no pedestrians. Everything was still. The dogs in front of the houses did not bark and the cats walked slowly and lazily under the shining sun. The smell of garbage and manure combined strangely with the scent of eucalyptus trees, filling me with sadness, oppression, and a captivating nostalgia. Images of the past and childhood memories from Brooklyn began to surface, events that had taken place and others that I had imagined and believed to be real. My eyes wandered in all directions in the street that was jammed with buildings lined up without harmony. I was searching in vain for the charm of this country I had long dreamed of seeing, but I found only emptiness, silence, and clutter. The stillness was unexpectedly broken by the squeaking of a worn wooden door that opened without warning. The faces of mischievous children peered behind it, disheveled and curious. They stared at me in silence, daring, and cold. When I reached the end of the street a young girl shouted sharply, "Shalom, woman," and the other children echoed her, "Shalom, shalom."

I was overcome with feelings of sadness and estrangement.

I stood in front of a blue-gray iron gate and a wall covered with dark green climbing plants and flame-red flowers. Behind the walls I could see acacia trees, and despite the midday sun, jasmine was still giving off a fresh scent that mixed with the smell of recently watered grass. I rang the bell, and a few minutes later I heard a soft voice saying gently, "Just a minute, just a minute." The door opened to reveal a fair woman's face, a short woman with bold eyes and a dignified smile. She was still in her nightgown and housecoat, with curlers in her hair. She glanced at me from behind the door, and I saw that she was holding a broom and a garden hose. She looked at me and smiled apologetically. As soon as she heard my heavily accented Arabic she understood who I was and rushed to welcome me, throwing the door wide open, repeating, "Zayna, Zayna!" She set aside the broom, threw away the hose, and reached out to take my suitcase, insisting on carrying it despite my objections. She kissed me warmly, as if she had known me for years.

The tiled floor was still moist from the washing and the recently watered plants, and the flowers glistened in their containers. The air was filled with the smell of cleanliness, the scent of jasmine, and other flowers. A fence separated the narrow entrance from the land around the house, and I noticed a garden with more flowers, trees, beehives, and flying butterflies behind the house. I was amazed at the difference between the inside and the outside of the house, as all along the road I had seen nothing but garbage, walls splattered with white and black paint, paint covering writing on the walls, streets filled with scrap metal, sewage, and more garbage. Inside there was an abundance of water, flowers, and overwhelming cleanliness. I later learned that this is the way things are in this country, or rather these countries.

Excited, the woman asked as she welcomed me, "How did you manage to pass during the curfew? Didn't they see you, didn't you see them? And you walked? It's bizarre, truly bizarre!"

I told her about my trip and the mean taxi driver. She laughed, explaining that taxi drivers fear stone throwers. She added that the stones are thrown at Israelis only, recommending that I be careful lest people suspect me of being one.

Why should people be suspicious of me? Am I not a brunette and aren't my eyes chestnut black, like all Arabs?

She turned and looked at me from head to toe and smiled ruefully, saying, "It's true that you're a brunette and that your eyes are chestnut black, but your clothes . . ."

The mystery behind the "shalom" was then revealed and I resolved to become aware of the way other people saw me.

She took me to the guest room. When she opened the locked door, the air felt heavy, still smelling of furniture, tobacco, and the weight of time. The brown furniture was arranged in a cluttered line like the buildings in the street. Despite the abundance of fresh flowers in the garden, there was a plastic bouquet of roses. The walls were covered with Qur'anic verses with golden frames, cross-stitched embroideries representing a Spanish dancer, a young child, and a red rose. A dining table and six chairs, an engraved desk with a large mirror, and a tea trolley stood in the other half of the room. I had the same feeling I had experienced in Abu Faleh's house in Brooklyn.

Nahleh and I sat near the wall in the garden to avoid the blaze of the sun and the garden bees. We were getting acquainted. She was my distant cousin, single and unemployed. She used to be a teacher in Kuwait, but she was expelled like everyone else because of the Gulf War. She passes her time with embroidery, knitting, washing the floor, and sweeping. I, on the other hand, am a university professor and a writer. Wasn't I afraid of writing? Of being read by people? she wondered. But I was American, brought up as an American, and Americans are different. She had heard that American women have a different way of life—much like men, they take strange jobs, marry and divorce easily, and have boyfriends. Nahleh was certain that I would do nothing of the sort because I am an Arab, the daughter of an Arab, and one is guided by one's origin, as people say. But America is very beautiful, isn't it? Tell me about it.

I asked about my distant uncle, her father, and learned that he was a farmer. He had a farm where he planted seedlings, raised bees, and sold honey in small jars under the brand name 'Honey of the North.' My uncle's health was declining now; he was diabetic and allergic to flower pollen. He takes injections in the spring, traveling to Germany for his treatment. Five years ago he had a stroke and forgot the matter. He regularly visits his three sons, one of whom lives in Germany and two in the United Arab Emirates. The first is a civil engineer and the second a chemical engineer; the third son works as a lawyer for a powerful sheikh. A fourth son is in the candy business. He has a factory in Nablus and lives there with his wife and children. The fifth son was the real problem, as he was the victim of a small mine explosion during his resistance years. It had destroyed his foot despite the treatment he had received in Moscow and the U.S. Thanks to the intervention of an Arab member of the Knesset he had managed to return to the West Bank. But what about my father, I wondered? She looked away, then at the clock, and said anxiously, "Your uncle will tell you the story. He'll be back in an hour at the most."

He did indeed return an hour later accompanied by his wife, Shahira. My uncle was in his early seventies and his wife in her mid-fifties. He was tall, with a beautiful figure for a man his age and with his health problems. His hair was thin and he wore eyeglasses, a set of false teeth, an American shirt, and a Swiss watch bought with Gulf-earned money. He talked, breathing heavily, and his greeting was warm and lively. He shook my hand with a granite grip. As for Shahira, who was not the mother of the children, she was fair and plump and had green eyes.

She spoke only when necessary and looked adoringly at her husband, approving every sentence he pronounced, constantly saying, "Alright, as you wish, Abu Jaber, and may you prosper." She sat under the walnut tree, cleaning okra and stuffing grape leaves, filling the refrigerator with goodies.

I loved him immediately. He was strong and generous. I later observed him with other people. He looked them straight in the eye, laughed boisterously, and tapped their shoulder, repeating, "God be praised, welcome, welcome, you are here in your home, sir. What would you like to drink, coffee, tea? Come here under the walnut tree; it's the best place in the whole world." He sat there with his friends from evening until nightfall, then bade his guests farewell and walked them to the gate.

I sat with him under the walnut tree and listened to him saying, "God be praised, by God you have grown so much. This world is truly strange. Have you eaten? Did you have something to drink? Did you wash your face and hands, are you well rested? The top room was ready for you two weeks ago. It is a beautiful room, we painted it anew, added a small bathroom and a sitting area on the terrace, a wonderful place to relax and see the shore and the sea lights. At night, when silence covers the place, you can even hear the surge of the boats. What can we do my child, this is our destiny, we lost the country and the relatives, and each one of us lives in a different place. This is our lot in life. Well Nahleh, has your cousin tried your jam yet? It is quince jam that Nahleh makes herself, the most delicious quince, the most delicious jam made by the most beautiful Nahleh. What about you Zayna, is your name Zayna or Zaynab? Zayna is nicer and easier to pronounce. Go ahead Zayna, tell me your story from the beginning."

We sat under the walnut tree until midnight. We ate, drank, and had a dinner of cheese, za'tar, olive oil, olives, and Nahleh's jam. I told him about the university, my work, and my grandmother. As for my mother, she disappeared in California and we lost touch, completely. I said to him, "My grandmother died, my mother died, and my father will soon die, and I know nothing about my family except memories and now you all. Tell me uncle, who are you?"

The house filled with visitors, family members, and neighbors; every single chair in the house was brought to the garden and placed under the walnut tree. My uncle's wife's cousin came with his wife and daughters and other relatives and neighbors. My uncle's wife's cousin is a realtor who struck gold recently, living a wild land-buying rush. This cousin's urbanized peasant wife wore a dress with ruffles and a kilogram of gold around her neck. Each of his thickset daughters wore an ounce of gold around her neck, a miniature gold Qur'an, and a golden mashallah.

There was also Grace's mother, known as Umm Grace, after her first son's name, and her daughter Violet, a hairdresser and Nahleh's colleague and best friend. She had been a teacher with her in Kuwait and had been expelled with compensation. There was my cousin's wife from Nablus as well, my cousin the toffee and candy maker. She came with her five children and her suitcase, because she wanted to spend the night. Late in the evening my cousin Mazen, the youngest, the land-mine victim, came. His older brother, the father of the five children and the owner of the toffee and candy factory, made an appearance as well.

My uncle sat leaning against the walnut tree, and before him stood the barbecue, the big copper tray, and the water pipe with Persian tobacco. He sat on his throne in a glorious and grand manner and said, addressing his words to the realtor, "Zayna is American, ya Abu Salem. Her mother and grandmother are American and she is like those Americans, who are smart and capable, with many sources of income. God be praised! She has a house in Washington D.C., and one in New York, a yacht, a helicopter, and maybe half a dozen cars."

I opened my eyes in total surprise, since I didn't own a helicopter, a yacht, or half a dozen cars!

The realtor commented, indifferently, "God be praised!"

My uncle resumed the conversation saying slowly and proudly, as he squashed the Arabic dessert, the knafeh, between his hands, "God be praised, she takes after her father! He was smart, ya Abu Salem. America attracted him at a very young age. We never heard from him again until people told us about him. He was mentioned during all our gatherings. God be praised! The man who used to carry the basket for the Christians in Bab al-Khalil, became somebody!"

Umm Grace's melodious voice rose, in objection, "What's wrong with the Christians, ya Abu Jaber?"

Realizing what he had said, my uncle looked at her from under his eyeglasses, then turned toward Violet and said quickly, "They're the best of people, they're all that is good and blessed."

He then turned to Nahleh and asked her to bring him some clarified butter.

Umm Grace continued to mumble; I followed the action and the signs in order to understand. Umm Grace is a fair woman, of medium build, with short hair dyed lighter than its original color. She was wearing a short-sleeved summer dress with a white belt and an extremely clean American collar. Everything about her was elegant and orderly and carefully calculated, which made her look quite distinguished and neat among the other women. Compared to the rustle and frills of the realtor's wife and my uncle's wife's long robe decorated with gold and silver thread, Umm Grace looked like a Parisian woman, as did her hairdresser daughter. Violet looked like a queen in the midst of the crowd consisting of Nahleh and the realtor's heavy daughters wearing all their gold. It was not only their elegance that distinguished them, but I sensed that they were different, somehow artificial, with an exaggerated politeness and sweetness in articulating their letters and words to the point of affectation. I could not put my finger on exactly what distinguished them from the others, but they seemed different, curious. Trying to understand, I asked, "Did my father go around with the Christians?"

My uncle stopped squashing the knafeh and said, reluctantly, "He worked for them, that's where he used to work."

Umm Grace replied with studied terseness, "He worked as a messenger for a number of souvenir shops."

I noticed Violet's hand nudging her mother's, as if to stop her from saying more.

Curious, I persisted, "You said he went around carrying a basket?"

My uncle replied gloomily, changing the subject, "This comes later, it is enough ya Abu Salem. Life is so strange! My brother came and went and wandered left and right, but returned to die in his homeland!"

Then he looked around him and asked for the cheese.

The realtor inquired, without looking at me, as if I were not present, "Did he have other children?"

My uncle said, sadly, "He had many more! But poor man, praise be to He Who taketh away and giveth, she is the only one who has survived." He added, "Bring the knafeh tray."

Everybody watched him in total silence, as he moved the knafeh from one tray to another. I looked at the color of the knafeh and at everyone's face, including my uncle's face, and wondered whether my father was as dark as them? Was he tall, as tall as them? Did he resemble them? I couldn't remember the details; my father's features had eluded me. They had become gradually distant and then had disappeared. So had he.

The realtor asked, "What does your brother own? Did he leave any real estate?"

My uncle muttered, still busy turning the tray of knafeh, "Blessed be God, he has plenty. He owns a great deal, a piece of land on the way to Nablus that is worth thousands."

The realtor stopped blowing the water pipe and puffed saying, "Hem . . . m . . . m . . . ."

My uncle continued, "He owns also a hill on the way to Sinjel, worth one million and maybe more."

The realtor shook his head, mumbling, again, "Hem . . . m . . . m . . . ."

"He owns also two dunums on the road to Jerusalem, near the airport. When the problem is resolved and the airport opens, God willing, its value will climb as high as an airplane," explained my uncle.

The realtor turned to me, looking at me intensely as if discovering my human value for the first time, then said, "May God be praised, by God, your brother produced quite an offspring!"

He continued to stare at me for a few seconds as if trying to decide whether, as a woman, I was worthy of all this inheritance. Then something occurred to him and he said, maliciously, "What about you Abu Jaber, do you get anything?"

My uncle raised his head and looked in amazement as if surprised by such a strange and unusual question, "What would I get?" he asked.

The realtor moved the tube of the water pipe left and right, then pointed it toward my uncle and said, "You must get something, according to shari'a and the law."

The room was semi-crowded, making it difficult to determine the identity of the motionless body stretched out on the bed. There were my second cousins, a blonde woman who looked like a movie star, and an ugly nurse with a mustache. My cousin, the father of five, was sitting with his back turned to the blonde woman, while Mazen, the land-mine victim, stood behind the patient's head arranging the IV tube. The nurse watched Mazen, as if he were the one in charge and she were a guest. The blonde woman sat on a small chair near the bed, holding my father's hand, the one which did not have tubes attached to it. As is customary, my cousin, the father of five, didn't shake my hand lest he soils his ablution. Mazen didn't shake my hand because he was busy adjusting the IV and the blonde woman didn't shake my hand because she was holding my father's hand.

My uncle greeted them all and shook his head in the direction of the blonde woman in lieu of a greeting, then pushed me toward the bed, nudging Mazen's shoulder to make room for me to see my father. I saw nothing but the skeleton of a human being with two large eyes, skin and hair, or rather some remnant of hair. His eyes were motionless and expressionless. He did not blink at all. I bent politely to kiss him and was amazed to find out that he was breathing. He smelled of baby powder, disinfectant, and urine. I felt dizzy. I was ill at ease and nervous. My feelings were dulled and I didn't know what to do, what to say, and how to conduct myself. I stood in my place and watched him in silence. I saw nothing in my father's face that revealed that he recognized me or was even aware of my presence. I continued to watch him, emotionless and motionless. I stood aside to regain my composure and catch my breath, then looked around me to scrutinize the faces of the visitors.

My uncle took me by the shoulder and sat me down in a chair, while he sat near my father and began talking with the others, asking the nurse questions about my father's food, his clothes, his daily baths, and his medication. The blonde woman said, "This hospital is not suitable."

She looked around her waiting for a reaction from the others, but no one replied or acknowledged her opinion. A few seconds later, my uncle whispered, "This is his wife, his new wife."

His new wife! I looked at her carefully. She was my age or slightly younger, blonde, fair and heavily made up in a strange way. Then I looked at him, this sick man, incapacitated, paralyzed, motionless, a handicapped man, truly handicapped. That is what my uncle had written in his letter to me. He also said what amounted to, "You'd better hurry and claim your inheritance." So, this is my inheritance!

The woman spoke in a harsh voice that seemed inconsistent with her make up and her efforts to be amiable and fashionable, "The hajj spoke today and called me mama and I said yes."

The father of five shook his head without commenting, but Mazen said politely, "Really?"

My uncle remained silent, watching my father, and I watched them and him. My cousin, the father of five, growled, saying, "There is no power and no strength save in God, the Great, the Almighty. I ask for God Almighty's forgiveness, I ask for God Almighty's forgiveness."

He sounded angry, and there was a certain rhythm in his tone. It did not appear that he objected to God's will, but something else seemed to have provoked his anger and made him ask for forgiveness. Was it me? Was it the woman? Or was it both of us? The woman said insistently, "I wish we could transport him to the Maqased hospital. The Maqased is a much better hospital."

My uncle replied, kindly but firmly, "No, my daughter, he must stay here with his family. His daughter has come from America to see him."

The woman looked at me with eyes that expressed reproach, as if blaming me for depriving her of an opportunity to be the only one in charge of that dear man's health condition. I sensed that she was weak, disoriented, lost, and not very bright. I felt sorry for her. Mazen said politely, "This hospital is close to us and if something should happen we would be by his side."

38

She moved restlessly in her seat and said begrudgingly, "Every day I come here and each time the road seems longer."

As no one answered, she looked at me, complaining about the trouble she endured, "The trip to Jerusalem has become a journey."

I stared at her and shook my head, speechless.

She said, unthinkingly, "Are you his daughter?"

I nodded my head in assent. I examined her and she examined me. I didn't like her, but for some unknown reason I felt sorry for her. She was the type of person who leaves one cold and scornful. She probably knew that and tried to make up for this shortcoming by wearing short clothes, coloring her hair, and wearing heavy makeup. The colors of her clothes matched, and revealed a certain taste and class, a good social standing. She was not cultured, however, and did not seem very bright. What did I expect from my father?

At this very moment my father's features became more familiar to me, more real. I saw the streetwise grocery man, a man who became rich because of his exile and his situation, because he worked for a long time overseas. He married an American woman who was my mother, then another and another and then this woman. He owns property estimated at thousands of dollars, and perhaps up to two or three million. I am here to claim my right and she is, too, and so is my cousin, maybe my uncle as well, according to shari'a and the law.

The woman stood up, pulled her short dress and shook her long, blonde hair. My cousin who had asked for God's forgiveness mumbled, "May God Almighty forgive me, may God Almighty forgive me."

The blonde woman said, "I'm going to the store. Does anyone want anything?"

No one replied, so she looked at me, making me feel sorry for her again. I said, "Thank you."

She left and they looked away. As she closed the door behind her and I heard the sound of her heels become fainter and fainter, I whispered to my uncle, "I don't understand."

He whispered, examining my father intently, "I don't understand either. When we met him he was alone and when he became ill they said: this is his wife."

Mazen said, smiling, "It doesn't require any explanation. She is here for the inheritance."

The other cousin growled, "By God, over my dead body!"

I looked at one, then the other and the other, then returned my gaze to the forgiveness seeker. He was a big man with a narrow forehead, thick eyeglasses, slicked-back hair, and a mouth where saliva gathered around the lips, turning slightly white and hard. He was the only one among my five cousins without an education and a formal degree. They were all educated and cultured, with titles and in important positions, whereas he was only a craftsman.

My uncle had bought him a candy and toffee making machine and rented a big store in Nablus because of the city's large size and its market. They called the machine and the store "Al-Hana Factory," implying that toffee was a symbol of bliss in Nablus. There might have been another reason for the factory other than bliss, as I believed it to be a way to commercialize my uncle's honey. Despite its good quality, my uncle's excellent honey was not selling well in the face of competition from Israeli honey. By suggesting that his son make a kind of candy filled with honey, he guaranteed the sale of his honey.

The honey candy sold well only at the beginning of the Intifada, when people complied with the call to boycott Israeli products. My cousin made money at that time and controlled the market, but he lost customers when he started cheating, replacing pure honey with a mixture of sugar and honey. As the amount of honey decreased and sugar increased, the candy became as hard as granite and tasted like castor oil. My cousin began complaining again. He doubled his prayers and ablutions, and his towel hung continuously on the balcony railings. His wife was struck with chronic liver disease as a result of her numerous pregnancies and inflammations.

My uncle held my father's hand, patting it and talking to him as if he could hear, see, and interact with him. He told him, "Well Muhammad, do you see Zayna? Here she is, she came to see you."

He then signaled me, took me by the arm to bring me closer to my father's eye level, but my father's look remained vague, his eyes resembling unfocused fish eyes.

My stepmother returned from the store while I was alone with my father. The others had gone to check the candy factory and buy a few things while I stayed with my father, observing him. I chose to stay beside him to discover my true feelings. I wanted to sense the bonds of the past, to my memories and the subconscious yearning of the heart. My memories were mixed—a medley of photos and an amalgam of emotions. When we were apart, the memories were distant; now that we were close, the human current that bound us together was interrupted. How could I feel the current without talk, without a look? A person's eyes are his measure, his knowledge, and the mirror of his soul. The man stretched before me was not my father, only a body. Had he smiled, moved, revealed emotions in his eyes, I would have said, "We have arrived." This man, however, this nearly dead man with a glassy look, was the past, or the voice from the past in the present.

When my stepmother entered the room and saw me staring at my father, she began to cry. She thought that the shock of seeing him in this condition had paralyzed me. She took her place near him, held his hand, kissed and coddled it, and warmed it around the wrist near the artery and the pulse. She raised her eyes and looked at me, and her face, now free of make-up, revealed a lusterless, dull complexion. She suddenly looked old, making me feel sorry for her, for him, and for myself.

We sat in the balcony chewing gum and watching the people go by. As usual, the city looked beautiful to me from afar, but up close, what devastation! There was something noble, uplifting to the soul and the heart on the horizon, but people there lived in the bottom of the valley.

She gave me a piece of chocolate and said simply, "This piece is filled with hazelnut."

I looked at her in amazement, an amazement that was close to admiration for a type of person that fascinates me, one who does not lose themselves in dreams, explanations, interpretations, and meanings; a person who lives without favors and goes about life without prattle, but chews gum, talks clearly, and calls things by their name. She opened her purse, took out an envelope containing photos and said calmly, as if she had not been crying a few minutes ago, "Look at this one."

I took the picture and looked at it. There she was with my father, in a romantic moment. They were at a New Year's Eve party surrounded by light and decorations, glasses of araq, appetizers, and beer, wearing conical hats covered with curled paper ribbons.

I compared my father in Brooklyn to the man I saw at the hospital and to the one in the photo. My father in Brooklyn was the father I knew, whereas here at the hospital he was only a corpse. The man in the photo was a living man but he wasn't my father—he only looked like him, a man with a different gaze. The man in the picture was elegant, a businessman with glasses, an expensive suit, and colored hair. He looked twenty years younger than my father; he was laughing and had one arm around Futna—her name is Futna—and in the other hand he held a glass of araq. She was drinking beer and wore a dress revealing her shoulders and neck and hardly covering her nipples. She wore huge earrings, a grape bunch hanging under her conical hat. She looked beautiful and happy, and he, too, appeared happy. She said, smiling, evoking the past, "We were engaged in this photo. Do you see my engagement ring?"

All I saw was a diamond ring with a stone bigger than a hazelnut. She was wearing a matching bracelet. He had gold-rimmed eyeglasses and straightened teeth and did not look at all like a grocer, but like an important businessman, an immigrant who had returned to his country. I asked absentmindedly, "What kind of work was he doing?"

She turned to me surprised, with a question in her look that she left unasked. Instead she showed me a new photo and said, "He was a landowner. Look at this photograph, it was taken in Jericho on the rose and strawberry farm. Do you see these roses? Five dunums of roses and lilies and ten dunums of strawberries and oranges."

I looked at the picture and saw my father wearing a hat, sunglasses, a T-shirt, white pants, and tennis shoes. He really and truly looked like a returning immigrant—in other words, he looked like me and I looked like him! Futna looked like someone dressed for a party, with a golden belt made of chains, a necklace, and gold earrings. Her short skirt fit tightly around her thighs, ending a few inches above the knee. She was leaning on his shoulder and holding his hand firmly. She explained the circumstances surrounding the photo, "We took this picture during our honeymoon. After our trip to Switzerland, we returned to Jericho and remained there until summer when we returned to Wadi al-Joz.

"Wadi al-Joz ?" I asked.

"Yes, Wadi al-Joz, in Jerusalem. Your father could live with me in Jerusalem because of his American passport. Don't you know Jerusalem? Come visit me there for a few days. I live alone and I have no one except this man. If anything happens to him, I'll lose my mind."

Then she gave me another photo and explained, "This one was taken in the Nile Hilton. Have you been to Egypt?"

I shook my head, while staring at her clothes and my father's, the movie-star surroundings, and the lights. Then came another photo.

She explained, "This one was taken there, in Haifa. Look at this, see their art! The rascals, they're smart! Your father used to say that after Beirut this was the place to be. Beirut is the best in clothes and elegance, then comes Haifa. Look at your father—see how he laughs, see how happy he is! When I married him he was tired, and after our marriage he felt better, he even thought of having children."

Without thinking, I asked, "At his age?"

She shook her head and hand as if she were reprimanding me, then said, "Why not, what's wrong with it? Men older than he have children. It is I who didn't know what was wrong with me. I tried treatments, but unfortunately, I have had no luck. Once he recovers, God willing, I will make it up to him. But to be frank with you, Zayna, I'm surprised that your father never even mentioned that he had a daughter."

I didn't reply and occupied myself with the photos, going through them once more, looking at my father surrounded by flowers in Jericho, my father shopping in Haifa, my father in Jerusalem in front of the Dome of the Rock, my father drinking, my father eating, my father clapping for Melhem Barakat's singing, and finally, my father dancing.

She said, staring at me, absentmindedly, "You are a girl, however!"

She then turned her head the other side and mumbled, "Had I been lucky I would have made it up to him and given him a boy."

I turned toward her in an effort to understand. She looked at me and lowering her voice, she said whispering, conniving, "A boy protects the inheritance. Without a boy your uncle inherits. Do you understand what I'm saying?"

Umm Grace invited me to Violet's birthday and warned me not to mention anything to Nahleh. I assumed, therefore, that I was the only one invited, but when I got there I saw Mazen on the balcony, surrounded by greenery and potted plants. He was relaxed, as if in his own house. Then in came Violet, her friends, a bald man and another good-looking man with white hair and piercing eyes. He stared at me intensely and asked, "How is your father, I hope by God's will he is doing well?"

He began telling me the story of his acquaintance with my father when he worked as an errand boy at the souvenir shop and how he fell in love with a nun who left the convent for him. "She was as beautiful as a full moon; she had translucent skin, and her eyes were the color of the sea. She came from a village near Jerusalem where there are Roman and Crusader ruins. She had exceptional blue eyes, the most amazing the districts of Dabbagha, Musrareh, and Via Dolorosa had ever seen. We used to line up on both sides of the street whenever she went by; we would hold rosaries and incense and chant. Some of us thought of joining the priesthood to emulate her."

He then raised his cup, "My glass to Muhammad, by God your father was a man!"

Mazen laughed and said to me, "Have you heard what your father used to do? Have you heard? Are you like him or different from him?"

At this moment Violet called him, so he left me alone to mull over his question. How could I know the answer? I never knew my father well enough to provide an answer. I was young and here I am a grown-up, coming back to gather the details of his life like someone collecting grains of sand.

I sat in the corner, by the fern and the fertilizer, and looked out through the glass window. The mud resembled henna and the hose was spraying droplets of water in the evening sun. The air was fragrant with the smell of flowers, mud, the linula viscosa and mint. My relatives were all in the living room singing a song with a monotonous, sad rhythm. I remained there sipping wine and gazing at the golden sun.

The light was oscillating, and I felt my head stretching upward while my body was swimming under the effects of the wine, the music, and the shimmering light. Suddenly, in the middle of the confusion and the clamor of people's voices, rose the sound of a guitar and a melodious voice. There was total silence except for the guitar and the cooing of a woman, whose singing sounded more like praying, an invocation. She was imploring, pleading and repeating pledges for love to last till death. She was pleading with love to remain because sleep was resisting her, abandoning her eyelids and leaving her with a burning heart. The words of the song were naïve, heavily charged with feelings of love and tenderness, reminding me of the romance of the fifties and the sixties, of Frank Sinatra and Nat King Cole. Those were lost days and emotions that had escaped and hidden far away in a harbor between train stations and theater stages, while we stayed stiff, surviving only through touching. But people here are still genuine like fresh fruit, untouched by the manipulation of the experts' hands. She repeated, accompanied by her guitar, "I am yours forever, be mine."

The guests were still, no one moved except to utter an "Oh" every now and then. Listening to those words—"I am yours forever, be mine"—I started crying for no reason, and I did not hold my tears back or try to understand the reason I was crying. I knew at that moment why I had returned. It was to be revived, to feel my heart beat again. Here I was able to recover my feelings and to experience my father's world. Here singing is different and talking is different; here they love from the bottom of their hearts, and their hearts are offerings on the altar of selflessness.

I stood there watching this scene and the feelings of the most melodious voice. She was beautiful beyond description. Her world was fabulous, while her voice wavered in a space between clouds and darkness, like a foggy light. Hearts were moved, emotions were released, eyes were moist, and suddenly from the midst of darkness and the depth of the fog my cousin's voice without warning, shouted, "God of humanity! We lost Beirut!"

We walked together that evening, an October night with heavy fog covering the roads and fields. The house wasn't very far, but my cousin Mazen, whose emotional wounds had been reopened, was distressed and wanted to walk a little to calm down. I walked by his side in silence, complying with his wish, and occasionally stealing glances at him. It was a dark night and the street lamps were swathed in fog. All I could see of him was a tall and large ghost, with little hair and a beautiful head. He looked elegant, like a baron or a cavalier. He was impressive despite the limp caused by the land mine. He usually was able to conceal the limp and the wounds, but alcohol tore off his masks and uncovered his bruises. We had no serious discussion during the walk. He had lost his concentration, and his talk was all foam, froth, and bubbles on the surface, keeping his inner feelings hidden. Sometimes the froth revealed bleeding wounds, Beirut being the most painful memory, his first and probably his last. There was something deep inside him, deeper than the wound of the country. I wondered whether it was the wound of manhood lost in the battle, the wound of the mind groping about in the whirlpools of infinity? Was he a human being without depths, without wings? Was he smart? Had he failed? Had he been a spoiled child? There were unfathomable secrets in the depth of the self that I didn't understand, but that I continued to gather in order to understand what it meant to be a human being.

He mumbled absentmindedly, "After Beirut and its lights came Wadi al-Rihan! This prison called Wadi al-Rihan, this oppression known as Wadi al-Rihan, this desperation, those people, the misery and the backwardness of Wadi al-Rihan. My soul is there, I was there, how did I get here?"

Trying to bring him back to reality, I said, "We are here now, in Wadi al-Rihan."

He muttered the words of a drunk, "The way we were in Jinsnaya and the rose hills."

"Jinsnaya?" I asked.

"Jinsnaya is over there, with Maghdousheh," he responded.

I said, "Lebanon is lost."

"And Salma, too," he muttered sadly.

"Who is Salma?" I asked gently.

He said, as if talking to himself, "Beirut's Salma, Jubran's Salma, Salma from the Lebanon of the seventies. But Salma's Beirut is lost and Lebanon is lost and today we are in the nineties. Guevara returned to the bottom of the valley, carrying a rock that Sisyphus had pushed to the point of exhaustion. You have come back as we did; you'll soon discover that we have lost our dreams in a stolen market and that the seventies aren't the nineties and that we're getting older."

I looked at him and saw a head swaying with every step he took in the silence of the night. I began to experience his feelings; his pain and fears were transferred to me. They made me swallow the silence and refrain from asking questions or digging up memories that would bring back stories. I didn't want to hear what he had just said or remember that this valley was Wadi al-Rihan, a stolen market that we had lost, that the seventies were not the nineties, and that we were getting older.

My cousin went to his room, leaving me alone in the night, a dark night, an oppressive night. I heard him bang against the furniture, then collapse on his bed and drown in silence. I kept walking around the house trying to calm down and restore my heart to its regular rhythm. My thoughts were torn between pity and fear. Should I feel sorry for him or fear him? I wasn't sure. I was even more confused when I heard his story from someone else and from another point of view. Coincidentally, I heard the two versions of his life story on the same night.

While he told me the story of Beirut and the revolution, she sang the story of a house and children, the ingratitude of the boys and the worries of the girls. His was a love story, and hers was a story of hunger for a loving touch. His was the story of a leader and a rock, and hers was about small concerns of a schoolteacher who began her life a radiant woman and ended a spinster. A spinster? A spinster! A flat word that conjures selfish personal worries and a barren woman, one like the fallow land, unappealing and uninspiring, like a land without rain.

Her room was lit and she was sitting on the edge of the bed, with a photo album placed over the comforter. She wasn't looking at the album but staring at the mirror. She stood as stiff as a statue in front of the armoire mirror. She remained there motionless for a few minutes, while I stood near the door observing her without curiosity. The impact of my cousin's story made me withdraw from the atmosphere of the house, from Nahleh, and even from myself. The world he had evoked had transported me to Beirut's echoes, the departure of the ships and the port. We had seen them on television, we had seen them carrying guns and olive tree branches, and wearing kufiyehs. We had seen them after a heavy bombardment and a sky bristling with lights and bombs. Much had been said, much had been written about them, and meeting upon meeting had been held. Then had come the departure of the ships and the caravan on television, just like in films, like at the movies, like in a play.

She spoke to the mirror, angrily, "What a shame! What a shame! Is this what it has come to?"

I watched her from behind the shutters that were kept ajar, standing behind them under the cover of night. She repeated her words as if she were talking to me or talking to someone who could hear her, saying, "Is this what it has come to?"

I thought she was talking with someone or on the phone, but she was sitting on the edge of the bed, fully dressed, wearing her dressy shoes. She was looking at the mirror, totally dazed, repeating those words over and over again. I raised my arm and knocked at the shutter, but she didn't turn toward the sound and continued to stare at the mirror, repeating, "Is this what it's come to?"

I knocked once more and whispered, "Nahleh, Nahleh, what's wrong with you?"

Then she turned very slowly to me, still dazed, her eyes wide open in a strange way.

"Nahleh, Nahleh, what's wrong with you?" I asked again.

She didn't answer and continued to look at the mirror, seeming somewhat disoriented. I rushed to the door, then through the hallway to the living room and, finally, to her room. I pushed the door, entered and said, "What's wrong? What's wrong?"

She didn't reply, remaining motionless. I took hold of her shoulders and shook them, but she didn't respond or look at me, only turned her eyes toward the wall. She just repeated, almost nonsensically, "Is this what it's come to?"

I put my face close to hers, and asked, "What's wrong? What's wrong?"

She turned to me and said straight into my face, "Is this what it's come up to? You two hide from me?"

Hide from her? We, hide? Who is we? Mazen and I?

She went on repeating bitterly, as if the matter were a crime or a catastrophe, "You ran away and went to the party."

I immediately sat on the floor, overcome by her words. This reasonable woman with an honorable history in the family, who spent years away from home in Kuwait, earning a good salary, winning her father and her brothers' respect, was sitting here during the night, looking like someone who had just buried a loved one simply because she didn't go to the party, because we didn't take her with us? She looked me in the face and said with suspicion in her eyes, "It was Violet's birthday, wasn't it?"

Then she added with deep anger, almost hatred, "It was Violet's birthday and you didn't tell me."

I didn't reply but looked down, trying to understand the situation from her point of view. Then I remembered that when Umm Grace invited me she asked not to tell Nahleh. I understood that Violet and Umm Grace didn't want Nahleh at the party. Could the matter really justify this dire response?

I said apologetically, trying to comfort her, "You did not miss anything, the party was boring."

She shook her head right and left, still gaping, "Don't say a thing, this isn't the point. I don't care about the party or Violet's birthday, or even Umm Grace and her stories about Grace, America, Santa Claus, the Christmas tree, and everything she says to prove that she is important and high-class. Neither she nor her daughter is high-class. Her daughter is a hair stylist, nothing more. So why does she act haughty and important—because she's a hair stylist? Because she's celebrating her birthday? Since when do hairdressers celebrate their birthdays? High class? That is like Americans and foreigners—so stupid and inappropriate.

Even if she celebrates thousands of birthdays, she'll still remain Umm Grace—Sarah the nurse, whose life was like that of a maid, sleeping in the hospital. Who does she think she is? She doesn't invite me? Don't I have anything better to think about than Violet and Umm Grace? How ridiculous would it be for me and you to stand with them before the cake, blow out the candles, and sing 'Happy Birthday!' My God, we're becoming civilized and important! That's what it's come to! Happy birthday? Did you all really sing? And you too—did you sing or didn't you?"

I didn't answer her, listening to her anger in total consternation. What lay beneath that deep resentment? Was it Violet? Or the party? Or was it Mazen? There was something hidden deep within her that hadn't yet surfaced. All this foam and froth was only the surface.

She insisted, "In God's name, tell me, did you sing with them or didn't you? Tell me, tell me."

I couldn't help but smile. Despite its tragic and its mysterious aspects, the situation was funny. She stretched her arm and grabbed my skin above the shoulder, saying with deep hatred, "Don't smile and pretend not to understand. You understand Arabic better than I do and you understand what I'm saying and the whole story."

I stopped smiling and looked at her innocently, "What story? I don't understand."

She stared at me suspiciously, and said, "No, you understand very well, but you pretend not to understand. You understand that Mazen is bedazzled by her, by them all. He goes there to drink, eat, and enjoy himself. He acts like a sultan there, sitting on the sofa, laying back and listening to our Arab singers Fairuz, and Umm Kulthum singing *al-Atlal*. He acts like he's an important man and speaks in riddles. He's completely foolish and tactless. He's unemployed, doing nothing with his life, and he acts as if he were Guevara and Layla's Qays.

"Is this what I get in life, is this what I spent my youth for—living in exile! Is this why I gave him hard-earned money and sweated in Kuwait! Is this what I end up with? He and they, all of them, all squeezed me like a lemon and then left me behind. They loved and hated, had relationships with more women than the hairs in their beards. They became engineers, with God's grace, while I worked in

50

Kuwait, being milked like a cow, teaching and bringing them up, but they paid no attention to me and did what they wanted.

"Each one of them has a large family, one or two wives, and I'm here like a billy goat, cajoling the stricken man, and spoiling the rotten Guevara. He pretends to be a freedom fighter, a fidai, and an intellectual concerned with the grievances of the whole world and yet he can't handle his own! Instead of going around courting and wooing women, making a fool of himself, he ought to look for a job that will provide him with an income. All he can do is write bad checks while I cover up for him as usual.

"All my life I raised them, paid their debts, and said amen. I used to say to myself, 'They'll be there for me when I need them; after all, no one is safe. I could become ill; I'll grow old, become senile, and they'll be there for me in my old age.' But here I am, with no one who cares about me or asks after me. They didn't care then and they don't care now. Goddamn me and them, it's a miserable life.

"I sacrificed my life and raised them with my work and now I can't find anyone to talk to me. Imagine, imagine, even Grace who was first unemployed and then worked as a waiter in Israel has become somebody. Every year he sends his mother and Violet a ticket to visit him in the U.S. When they're there he loads them with gifts and takes them everywhere, to Florida, to New York, to Disney World, and Epcot Center and other places I've never even heard of. Though I funded my brothers' education with my earnings and sweat in Kuwait, not one of them even thinks of inviting me on a trip. When they needed me they would send me letters and call me beloved sister, my soul, my eyes, you're the best of all women, the most understanding, you Nahleh, the most beautiful and kindest Nahleh, the best Nahleh, by God, I am hard up and I need some money. I would say all right, here you are my brother, take this. Money for this one and money for that one, the father hard up also, with a bad season and my mother ill, needing surgery and hospitalization, and the stupid brother wanting to become an industrialist, to make candy and chocolate. Guevara wanted to become a revolutionary, leave his university and wear jeans. Help us Nahleh, only one year to go, may God help you.

"But one year followed another, claiming a good part of my life. It is slipping away. I suddenly realized this and woke up to find myself old, with many years lost. I woke up and found myself old, without a husband, without a house, and no one to call me Mama. This is how it ended. Do you hear what I'm saying? This is the end for your cousin Nahleh, a forgotten cow in a barn, now that her breasts are dry. Go tell Guevara that instead of telling people about his philosophy and his worries, he ought to remember me, at least once. He never even once thought of my problems, do you understand what I'm saying? Go tell him."

I no longer knew what information to collect or what I had come looking for in my country of origin. In the midst of this overwhelming welter of people's problems and worries, I lost track of my objectives, which scattered in many directions. If I were ever going to organize my thoughts and understand what was happening around me, I would have to analyze the material, applying the methods of research available to me.

The first tool for understanding people is their language, their expressions, their news and conversation. Because I spoke broken Arabic, hardly adequate for my personal quest, I undertook to learn my native tongue using books and audiotapes. I began with classical Arabic, then moved to colloquial to understand the language of the street. In time, the spoken language proved insufficient for my research, which convinced me to return to classical, only to find myself lost between the classical and the colloquial. My preoccupation with people's worries compounded matters. I became aware of the gap between the classical language and people's worries, and the colloquial language and its capacity to understand people. In other words, classical Arabic offers no insight into people's worries because it is the language of the censor, the same censor who checks over politicians and the self as well. Thus what escapes the scissors of the censor is trimmed by the scissors of the self. As the language of censorship, classical Arabic lacks truth, while colloquial Arabic is feeble because it has neither commas nor question marks. I had difficulty figuring out what I was hearing, saying, and feeling. Was this the result of America's influence on me, my research tools, or the language of the people? Was it because I was lost between the two languages, the two awakenings, and the two time zones that I had lost warmth and emotions? Or was my past catching up with me?

This may explain why I didn't cry when my uncle announced the tragic news of my father's death. He said, saddened, "May you be safe, your father died."

As I didn't react, he put his hands on my shoulders and looked me straight in the eyes to make sure I had understood what I had heard. I turned my face away from him lest he see my own surprise at my lack of reaction, my inability to feel anything. I even wondered whether that man was truly my father.

Nahleh came in but didn't look at me, probably embarrassed by the memory of the birthday night, or she was afraid to mention the word death. She held me firmly and whispered to me sympathetically, "This is life, this is how it ends." She cried intensely, but I believe that she was crying not for my father but for her broken dreams, as I had in my youth. Then Futna came in and delivered the earthshaking news, that she was pregnant; it had been confirmed by her doctor in the Hadassa hospital. Everyone gathered around the deceased discussing the situation with gestures. My cousin Said, the factory owner, rubbed his hands nervously, and said with some anger, "By God, she won't get what she wants!"

I smiled and thought that the cunning woman had done it! I smiled to her discreetly, recalling our past conversation about the effect of a male child on the issue of inheritance. My uncle accepted the matter without comment, but opened the palms of his hands in a sign of submission to God's will and said, with affection and compassion, "God be praised, life is born from death!" Mazen finished his father's sentence with realistic gloom, saying, "And the dead is born of the living."

Nahleh, on the other hand, unable to hide her anger, could not help saying, "We've lived long enough to see people become pregnant through wishful thinking!"

The news spread as fast as the plague, transforming the mourning gatherings into noisy beehives, and people's whispers sounded like the buzz of flies as they repeated, "Futna is pregnant, Futna is pregnant." Some gulped, others stared, while Nahleh mumbled in the midst of the buzz, "We live and see."

My uncle's wife was as pale as saffron and her cousin got hold of my uncle in the kitchen where the sugarless, cardamom-filled coffee is prepared. He said words we didn't hear, but his whispers lasted for a very long time.

The news of Futna's pregnancy spread in the streets and houses. Women peered through their windows, salesmen stood still in their shops, talking, inquiring, gulping. Some objected, saying, "It's impossible, this is a conspiracy, she did it to get the inheritance, but Abu Jaber and his children are more deserving of it. As for his daughter, neither she nor his wife count—his daughter is from an American seed and his wife is a prostitute without a permit. One is a stranger and the other is a judgment, a judgment from God. What a shame!"

The family gathered in the sitting room after the burial and ate the traditional mansaf, mounds of rice and meat. Futna sat on the sofa in a focal place of the room and placed a cushion behind her back to support her. She was pale without makeup and her blonde hair resembled straw after her lamentations over her husband's death. The mourners sat quietly; we could only hear the clack of their prayer beads and their angry breathing. The loudest breathing, however, was my uncle's, caused by his stroke and old age, and Said's due to his excessive weight, the narrowness of his nasal passages, and a stomach stuffed to the rim with mansaf.

Nahleh, dressed in black from head to toe, inquired of Futna, "How far along are you in the pregnancy, may God protect you from the evil eye?"

Futna arched her back to reveal her pregnancy, but her belly was as flat as a tile. Neither deterred nor insulted, she said, apprehensively, "It's still at the beginning, maybe two months."

Said's breathing rose and his prayer beads fell to the floor, but he didn't say a single word. Unfazed, Nahleh continued her inquiry, "Maybe two months? But my uncle has been bedridden for two months and he was unconscious from his stroke for sixty days."

"Fifty-eight," corrected Futna.

"Oh!" said Said mechanically, while his eyes popped behind his glasses until they almost reached the lenses.

My uncle commented in his usual kind and affectionate way, "Poor Muhammad, in God's name, everything is a matter of fate. I wish he had lived to see the son he had hoped for. He married seven women, but they gave birth to girls only. Well, you might give us a boy that would carry his name."

Looking toward the window, Said repeated, "A son who inherits his name."

Staring at his son, my uncle said, "A son who would inherit his name and his money—it is his right, his own. All we wish for is safety and Muhammad's son."

Said shook his head nervously and repeated angrily, "Muhammad's son!"

No one commented, but Futna blinked and I continued to watch the others in excited anticipation.

Total silence fell on the place, broken by Nahleh's inquiring words, "I would like to know, dear Futna, why we learned of your pregnancy only after my uncle died?"

Futna looked at me, but I looked down and avoided looking at her and everybody else. I feared the situation would escalate, resulting in an investigation that would reveal the lie. I knew it was a lie, and the others did too. Yet, I was the only one to whom Futna had said a few days ago, "If things had worked better I would have made it up to him and given him a boy."

She had also told me, provocatively, "A boy protects the inheritance!"

How will dear Futna manage to go on living her lie and inherit the wealth? Pregnant? By whom and how?

I took her aside that evening and asked her, with genuine concern, "What will you do if they find out?"

She responded with unexpected force, asking defiantly, "Find out what?"

I whispered, choking with embarrassment, "That you aren't pregnant."

She stared at me and raised her hands to push her hair away from her face, then shook her shoulders and said smiling, "But I am pregnant!"

Losing my self-control, I shouted, "Okay, fine! But by whom?"

She turned away from me and raised her shoulders, laughing behind her hand, and said, "Pregnant by artificial insemination at the Hadassa hospital."

The mourning period ended a few days later. During that time family and friends drank barrels of sugarless coffee and ate mansaf, knafeh, and other delicious foods brought by relatives and neighbors. People sent trays of msakhkhan, lamb, bags of rice and sugar, whole cartons of cigarettes and matches. The kitchen was filled with food and merchandise and looked like a grocery or a restaurant.

I used to watch them sitting in a corner under the walnut tree during the good weather, or on the living room sofa, cleaning okra and green beans, or knitting with Nahleh, waiting for the baby to be born to divide the inheritance. The judge of the shari'a court ordered a freeze on the inheritance until dear Futna gave birth to the heir apparent.

"The heir apparent," said my cousin, the owner of the factory. Then he blushed and turned yellow and added, "And maybe an heiress."

"God forbid, the doctor in Hadassa said it is an heir not an heiress," exclaimed Futna, who had come to invite me to visit her in Wadi al-Joz.

I accompanied her to Wadi al-Joz, an area that is neither a valley nor has the walnut trees suggested by the name. It is an old neighborhood in New Jerusalem that was once beautiful and is now dirty. The New Jerusalem is not West Jerusalem, either, because the Israelis have West Jerusalem, everything is for the Israelis. West Jerusalem is filled with Ashkenazi Jews, men with side-whiskers, Sephardim, and the like. As for the New Jerusalem, it has only Arabs, Arabs from Hebron, Arab Jerusalemites, and riffraff Arabs who settled there after the high-class Arabs left, taking with them honor and noble descent.

I had accepted her invitation to go to Jerusalem for various reasons—and who wouldn't like to go to Jerusalem, especially me! I had many reasons to go there: first, because my father had worked in a souvenir shop there; second, because Umm Grace had told me that all the churches in the world were no match for even the smallest church in the smallest alley in Jerusalem; and third, because Jerusalem is always on our minds and in the news, in our poetry, and in the Chairman's speeches. Everyone talks about it, and its fame is legendary. Finally, Jerusalem is for tourists, and I am, despite my origin and my true religion, a tourist immigrant.

When my relatives heard my reasons for going, they were upset with me and considered me callous and weak in faith. They disapproved, and I understood that they expected me to explain my decision repeating the nationalistic slogans heard on Arab radios. Futna also told me, "In Jerusalem there are things to buy, shops, large streets and Hadassa!"

To make a long story short, I drove there with her in a white Mercedes, a 1990 model. Had it not been for my father's stroke and his death, she would have bought this year's model. On the way to Jerusalem she never stopped talking, telling me every story, large and small, about my uncle and his children, stories that would make your hair stand on end. She said, "Your uncle, may he go blind, has everything, money and ranches. He owns a huge ranch filled with bees and wasps and the Honey of the North is their honey. If he had taken good care of it and refrained from cheating, it would have been imported by Maxime's restaurant. Do you know Maxime's?" she asked me. She continued, "Your cousin, may he go blind, is so unbearable—he is not only unbearable but also a cheater. The Israeli candy is better and tastier than his candy. It's worth the price you pay for it, unlike your cousin's candy, which is as hard as a rock. Your cousin spits when he talks and breathes as heavily as a bull. May he go to hell. I would never have just shut up and handed over my rights the way he wanted me to. Who does he think he's dealing with? I'm a Jerusalem girl and from the Musrareh too! Even though I belong to a well-known, well-respected family, hard times forced us to live in Musrareh when we were kids. We lived in the family house; it was an old and uninhabited awqaf property. We cleaned it up and stayed there till we all got married. We learned everything there—we learned to fight, argue, and use very big words. My mother, who was educated by the nuns and who is very cute—you'll soon meet her—whenever she heard what we were saying she almost passed out. She would cry and ask my father, 'Do you want my daughters to be uncouth, rude, like street girls?' My father, who was handicapped and very sick, would try to comfort her, saying, 'They will marry one day, ya Amira, soon the girls will meet their destined men and find the suitable person.'

"My mother would shout, 'What well-born young man would agree to marry the girls of the alleys? Your daughters are street girls, how could well-born girls have become like this? Do you expect the Nashashibi or the Khalidi families to become our in-laws while we live in this house? Who among their children would marry our daughters?'

"My father would cry and sob and so did we. Then we got married to lowly relatives, one was unemployed, another penniless, and a third was crazy, drooling, and had a runny nose, too. What counted was that we married men from our social class, well-born men who made us live in hell. We ran away—I left and my sister did the same; my third sister went to Cyprus; the fourth was admitted to a mental hospital; and my younger brother became a man only when I married your father, who opened a shop for him. What can we do? That's life. I was humiliated and so were my mother and my father. I'll never return to Musrareh, even if it means killing someone."

I discovered Jerusalem at Futna's hands. Her east balcony overlooked valleys, olive trees, and the garden of a missionary university with walkways that led to wide stairs, residences, and blooming flowers behind large glass panels. I could see the Aqsa Mosque with its shiny dome and its minarets, the wall of Jerusalem, and its historical buildings from her west balcony and from the kitchen. I saw churches, bell towers, the cemeteries of various religions, dark-colored trees, white rocks, and a barren brown-gray colored land from the roof of her elevated house. Far on the horizon, where the western clouds appeared, I saw high and low buildings, a wall of strange constructions that looked like a hospital or a huge prison that Futna referred to as a "settlement." A settlement, she explained, is what my uncle, that spiteful, ignoble man, and his children, would like to do with the inheritance. She firmly believed that they wanted to put their hands on my father's real estate.

Futna directed me toward the east, then the north and the south, saying, "Look, look, do you see our tombs, our houses, our alleys, and our courtyards? Do you see the trees? We planted them. Do you see the Russian church? And the Roman Catholic convent? Here and there, it all belongs to us. Tomorrow, I'll take you to meet my cousin, who will explain history to you."

We visited him on a Friday evening, at the usual reception time. The living room was filled with relatives and other visitors. Before going in, Futna showed me the house library to prove to me beyond a shadow of doubt her cousin's knowledge of history. I noted the beautiful building, the courtyard, the pond, the fountain, the gazelle's head, the Persian rugs, and the lamps. The pond was made of marble and was surrounded by lions and snakes from whose mouths water flowed with force, making foam. There were also jasmine, lemon trees, and a climbing plant. The whole place was surrounded by a run-down wall with holes, and white columns blackened by age and history.

Regrettably, Futna's cousin was an ugly and uncouth man, though she thought he was a great man because of his culture, his education, the cigars he smoked intently, and the checkered cashmere vest he wore. On that day, however, he wore an ordinary tie with a bronze pin shaped like a black woman's head. His name was Abd al-Hadi and everyone addressed him as Pasha or Bey and other such honorific titles because he worked as an advisor or consul in embassies in a number of capitals. He was from an ancient city and of noble origin, heir to a house that testifies to his high rank. He was the pride of the family in his youth, a part he always played well. At his receptions there were always one or two famous personalities counted among the guests, as well as eminent family members, and young men and women. Traditionally, coffee was served at the receptions, first bitter coffee, then sweet coffee, followed by English tea with cakes and chocolate. The receptions were agreeable gatherings eagerly awaited by everyone, for which they wore their best clothes and their favorite perfume in the hope of finding what they were looking for: a position, a contact, or a means to reach both. There were sometimes educated, haughty young women hard to please, looking for a good catch, arriving with their parents and artfully and elegantly displaying their qualities, drinking tea quietly, without making noise, and mixing whispered Arabic and English words. The graduates of the Schmidt and Talita schools spoke German, but those who studied at the more reputable Zion School spoke French with an accent and broken Arabic.

The Bey, a man used to elegant circles, greeted us in a stylish and polite manner. He was distinguished in everything, despite his ugliness, his sagging jowls, a conspicuous gold bridge, broken yellow teeth, and a pale wrinkled skin. All in all, he inspired admiration or respect, or both at first, but his conspicuous bragging and unpleasant appearance soon undercut that impression. He had a body like a sheep, all fat and no muscle.

The Bey took us on a second tour of the library, looking at dictionaries and classical books such as the works of Avicenna, al-Ma'arri, Jean Paul Sartre, Oscar

Wilde, and Ernest Hemingway. He liked Hemingway's sense of adventure and love of traveling, his youthful life, his audacious and lustful nature—he was a man who, in the Bey's opinion, refused to be humiliated, preferring to die with dignity rather than debase himself, a true hero.

Futna nudged me lightly to draw my attention to the Bey's words of wisdom, while her eyes hungrily took in his world. She drew enough optimism from his sparkling personality to invigorate her and revive her belief in a kind and gentle life filled with precious moments that would erase the painful memory of her life in Ramleh. The Bey explained that Hemingway had influenced his decision to remain single and resist the pressure of traditions. A life of love, politics, travels to Spain and Africa, enthusiasm for hunting, trips, nightlife, and caféés caused the cousin to dream of an impassioned and adventurous life. He explained how he roamed the world and the universe in search of glory and experience, yet he sincerely had found nothing more gorgeous than the city of Jerusalem and the eyes of its women. The city was his first and last love and without it glory and history were meaningless. History started and ended in it, history and the secrets of the world lie in it. That's why we fight with our cousins in order to promote and inherit the secrets. That's the essence of our movement and theirs, two entities fighting over history and dignity and all kinds of glory and authenticity. Who will it be, they or we? Who will inherit the glory, the church of the Holy Sepulcher, the Aqsa Mosque, the Wailing Wall, and the church of the Nativity? Who will inherit Salome's square, the place where she danced and received John the Baptist's head on a silver tray, I wonder!

Futna nudged me again and whispered humbly, "Do you hear what he's saying? Now I understand."

I whispered to her while trying to catch every word in an effort to understand, "What do you understand?"

She covered her mouth with her hand and said, "I'll tell you later, later."

The Bey moved on to another subject, away from nostalgia and nationalism because tackling national subjects moves and upsets him. He believes that this generation has not lived up to the accomplishments of their ancestors. How can we compare with the past, with their history, with their sovereignty? Our revolution failed because we marched behind the beggars and the vagabonds. During the days of Hajj Amin things were different, the leadership belonged to the upper classes; their origin, social rank, and appearance were a source of pride for the people. Clothes are very important, but those who are not familiar with high society, the upper class, and elegant circles are not familiar with such matters. The way food is presented is very important, and so is eating with a fork and a knife, not picking one's teeth, or sucking bones in public.

Everybody laughed at the joke because they were adept with a fork and knife, and had never sucked a bone or even a piece of meat without hiding behind their napkins. Someone mentioned a certain ambassador who didn't know English and wore slippers; when he crossed his legs, his feet were in his guests' face; he was also in the habit of rubbing the space between his toes. He addressed Hillary Clinton, Benazir Bhutto, and even Mrs. Thatcher by saying, "How are you, beautiful?"

The Bey's guests usually laughed at such stories, but he wasn't amused because he found such situations embarrassing to him personally. They hurt the reputation of the Arabs. When he was overseas, in Washington, London, or Paris, he tried his best to give the Americans and the Germans the best impression of the Palestinians and to plant in their minds a new image, one totally different from reality, because reality, let it be said between us, is bitter. It's an undeniable fact that our people are backward and underdeveloped because they marched in a revolution led by ruffians. Who are our leaders but a bunch of thugs?

I stopped him at that moment and asked him about an article I had read in the *Washington Post* in which the woman writer had written, "The revolution is your revolution." No one understood what I meant because of my broken Arabic, which was described as *sukkar qalil*, 'semi-sweet,' in reference to the way Arabic coffee is drunk. I did not understand what the 'semi-sweet' meant, however. The Bey laughed at my comment, showing his bridge, a sight that made me pretend to have understood to put an end to his laughter, but he went on laughing and I could still see his bridge. He asked gently, with a sly politeness, "What, what did she say?"

Someone explained, teasing me in a charming manner, "She said, "Our revolution is your revolution, or rather, their revolution?"

The Bey said, laughing, "Wait a minute, let's listen to her, did she say our revolution is your revolution or their revolution?"

That same one, who was short and thin and wore tweed and glasses, replied, "Did she say our revolution in Amman or our revolution in Lebanon or our revolution anywhere?"

Someone else commented, "Or maybe the revolution in Washington!"

I didn't answer, but I continued to smile for this and that one, and I looked at each one of them, then around the diwan, and at the top of the wall, and at the gazelle's head, and the Aqsa Mosque poster hanging above the Bey's head and that of his family. I looked at the two swords above the sofa, at the fireplace, and a mother-of-pearl maquette of the Dome of the Rock, and camels carved of olive wood. Then he asked me again: "Which revolution?" I only smiled with pronounced politeness, while staring at the poster above the Bey's head, the two plated swords and the wooden camels.

When Futna's mother entered the room everybody jumped to their feet. Her son—the shop owner whose shop was financed by my father—his pregnant wife, and a young child, accompanied her. Futna rushed to her mother and cried a little, grieving for my father's death. She was seeing her mother for the first time after the mourning reception, which Sitt Amira had missed. Ill and with brittle bones, Amira walked slowly and carefully, and went out only in emergencies. Her visits to the diwan however, were something else. She never missed them because, according to her, they kept the family close and safeguarded traditions.

Amira is a regular of the diwan and so is her son Abd al-Nasser. She participates actively in its gatherings and listens to the discussions she deems very serious and earnest. A woman of her intelligence and personality, with a degree from Zion School received in the good old days, a woman who does embroidery and crochet and plays the "Moonlight Sonata" on the piano, a woman like her wants to stay in touch with what is being said in society's circles. Her father had joined the revolutionaries fighting against the British, then he fought with Hajj Amin in the revolution. She too contributed to their effort, knitting sweaters for the revolutionaries and giving injections, a skill she learned in her nursing lessons. She listened to Haykal's articles read at Sawt al-Arab radio station in the 1960s. She named her son Abd al-Nasser to show her strong belief in Arab nationalism and her support for the cause of liberation.

This explains the regular attendance of Sitt Amira at the diwan meetings regardless of the Bey's presence or absence and despite some negative factors in her life; she had married a poor member of the family, had lived in a waqf house in Musrareh, had long been humiliated at the hands of the Shayib family, and though no one gave her the time of day when she needed help, she had maintained her dignity. She firmly believed that attending the diwan gatherings gave a person a sense of belonging and importance and an awareness of one's origin and social consequence. Even if no one helps when one is in need, as happened to her, it's enough to feel that despite them she is a member of the family who is a Shayib from father to son; she married a Shayib, and so did her daughters. She had wanted those marriages, including Futna's to my father, and her son Abd al-Nasser's wedding, to have taken place in this gathering and in this diwan. My father had considered buying the diwan once but failed.

He had gone there to assess it and examine the furniture with the intention of buying it, but he had seen Futna, checked her over, gotten her, but he could not get the house, which had not been for sale.

Sitt Amira greeted me and offered her condolences, assuring me that if it were not for her health and the difficult political situation she would have done her duty in such circumstances. She would have visited us at home to comfort us, and she would have visited the tomb and read the Fatiha for the repose of my father's soul. But now that I was in Jerusalem, she would do the right thing, she said and winked at me. I didn't understand the meaning of the wink, thinking it was a sign of illness or old age. I later learned that a wink between women meant shared secrets, and the secret I shared with Amira was her hesitation to invite me in front of this army of people present at the diwan to avoid including them in the invitation. In any case, we visited and talked, reverting to serious conversation.

At the mention of Hillary Clinton and Washington, the Bey told us that he had worked in the American capital, attached to the embassy, for more than five years.

He told us that he had lived his life to the fullest, but that Arab women like me tried their best to hang on to him because he was a catch for a husband and they were without men or husbands. He couldn't explain this phenomenon. He inquired and investigated the matter and found out that the secret lies in Arab men, not Arab women. But what was the secret?

He turned to me unexpectedly, but I shook my head to express my total ignorance. Then the Bey volunteered that the secret was the virility of the Arab men that Arab women couldn't handle. I asked him, without smiling or fluttering my eyes, "Can an American woman handle one, then?"

He laughed, his neck shook, and his bridge shined as he repeated, "Ha, ha, oh only one? Oh!"

Futna exclaimed, "You naughty bunch!" while everybody laughed and I did too, amused by the laughter of the Bey, the sight of his jiggling jowls and pounds of flesh. Futna whispered to my ear, "Thank God I didn't marry him."

I whispered, "Why, did you intend to marry him?"

She replied hurriedly, covering her mouth with her hand, "I'll tell you later, later."

Sitt Amira reminded us in a powerful voice that contrasted with her tiny build and her delicate bones that such words should not be uttered in the diwan, in the presence of women and children. One of the women in the audience said haughtily, aiming her words at Sitt Amira and her daughter-in-law, "The diwan is not for children, because visitors do not usually bring children."

Abd al-Nasser blushed and so did his wife, but Sitt Amira did not blink. She was waiting for an opportunity to prove to the others that bringing her grandson to the diwan was not a sign of her daughter-in-law's modest social background or the result of a life of poverty and the Musrareh neighborhood. Her son Abd al-Nasser, thank God, was doing very well with a shop in Bab al-Khalil as large as two or three ordinary shops, and his name was mentioned everywhere, he was known to travel agencies and tourists. She turned toward me, then, looking serious, she asked Futna, "Did you take her to the tourist shops area?"

She inquired in all earnestness, as I was thinking about my father's early childhood as a messenger in a souvenir shop.

Futna whispered to me, "Your late father had very much wished to have a small souvenir shop before he immigrated to the U.S. My brother has a very big souvenir shop."

Naturally, she did not mention my father's funding of the shop lest I, as heir, add it to my inheritance claims.

On our way to the souvenir shop district, Futna told me two things: first, that the family—that is her mother, her father, and her brother—didn't know about her pregnancy and that she didn't know how to break the news to them. Her mother, despite her strong personality, was old-fashioned and very conservative about matters of honor. She feared God, and the artificial insemination in Hadassa Hospital would be contrary to the moral ideals that she had observed throughout her life in the holy city of Jerusalem. Woe to Futna when her mother learns the truth. She will unleash her fury at her.

The second thing Futna told me was about the time that preceded her marriage to my father and how she had been on the verge of marrying the Bey. Marrying the Bey! This was the second time she had surprised me and I said as much because the Bey was much too old for her. He could have been her father. She reminded me that my father was not younger than the Bey or her own father, and that she was, in case I had forgotten, my age or younger. This was true; Futna was younger than me in everything—age, looks, and maturity—but she treated me with a respect close to deference. My age was a factor, but being an American and speaking English, a language she didn't know, added to my prestige. Her mother spoke French and English fluently, and Abd al-Nasser, made good use of her language expertise as well as her ability to handle correspondence with Taiwan and the organization of the business. Abd al-Nasser had inherited his father's stupidity and laziness.

Futna, too, was not very bright, but Sitt Amira considered her smart because she had married my father and insured her life till death. She would have loved to have married a rich man herself, but she did not; first, because she was not fair and blonde like Futna, and second, because at that time she didn't know that money was important. And, finally, because her generation or those who inherited the family name among them did not view money the way they do now. Money, as her father, Hajj Ibrahim used to say, comes and goes, but origin, honor, and good manners are the measure and the scale. When Ra'fat al-Shayib proposed to her, Hajj Ibrahim did not hesitate to accept and neither did his daughter Amira, because in addition to being well-mannered and well-behaved, Ra'fat belonged to a good family.

We reached the souvenir shop district before noon. It was humid and rainy, and Bab al-Khalil was as usual swarming with tourists, activity, a few pedestrians, priests, nuns, and vendors of ka'ek, sweets, and lemonade. Sitt Amira was sitting in the middle of the shop behind her son's desk, reviewing the accounts, opening letters from companies, and getting ready to reply to them. There were piles of paper, writing pads, a fax machine, and a typewriter in front of her. When she saw us she came to greet us cheerfully, then asked the salesman to show us the most beautiful merchandise for me to choose whatever I liked and suited my taste for myself and my friends. She suggested, and then later insisted, that I buy mother of pearl crosses and a maquette of Jerusalem for my American friends in Washington and New York and an embroidered dress to wear in Washington that would represent Palestine and show Americans that Palestine has a civilization, as would be made obvious by this kind of embroidery.

Futna wanted to talk to her mother. "Mama, I want to tell you something but promise me not to shout," she told her. But Sitt Amira did not pay attention to her daughter; she was used to her endless, silly stories. Anxious, Futna looked at me for courage and said: "Mama, what I want to tell you is very important."

Sitt Amira continued to pour the coffee, then placed the cups beside us on the edge of the desk where she was sitting. She later said, with little consideration for her daughter's words, "All right, dear, tell me, tell me."

Then, addressing me, she said, "Here is your coffee, Zayna, I hope you like it. I bought the coffee this morning on my way to work and I asked the salesman to add more cardamom to it. Taste it and let me know if it's sweet enough for you."

Futna twisted and turned in her seat, pulling her vest around her sides, then looked at the empty shop and the street full of people and said nervously, "Mama, are you listening to me?"

Her mother took a sip of her coffee, raised her eyes, looked at Futna, and said indifferently, "Yes, I'm listening, of course I am."

Futna twisted and turned in her seat, feeling scared as the moment of truth drew near, forcing her to face the situation seriously and unequivocally, possibly for the first time since the artificial insemination. Here she was facing her mother, this exemplary woman, this role model, this capable and intelligent mother who had trained her children to speak the truth to her without maneuvers or trickery or any possibility of escape. This mother who had taught them the art of struggle for survival, is the daughter of Hajj Ibrahim, the well-born man, son of the guardian of the Haram al-Sharif and keeper of the keys of the Aqsa Mosque. She is also Hajjeh Ra'ifa's daughter, a well-known woman in the circles of charitable organizations and orphanages. Sitt Amira herself is the descendant of a noble family and, most important, was a student at the nuns' school. She learned refined manners and knows right from wrong, qualities that reveal the well born. Futna, who didn't enjoy a similar education, idealized her mother and believed firmly and unambiguously that Sitt Amira occupied a place one-degree below God. This was evident in the expressions she often used: "On my mother's life this and that happened; on my mother's life so and so said this; my God! What would happen if mother knew about this or that."

Sitt Amira glanced at me apprehensively and then turned to her daughter, clearly annoyed, and said, "I'm listening."

She then put down her coffee cup and sat as rigid as a statue. Futna, overcome with a crushing sense of fear, replied, "Mama, my God, what shall I say!"

The mother replied firmly, "Say it."

Futna asked her in a conciliatory tone, "Promise you won't get upset?"

The mother didn't reply but continued to stare at her. Futna looked around her again and said suddenly, as if spitting something from her mouth, tired of having kept it secret for so long, "Mama, I'm pregnant."

The pupils of the mother's eyes dilated as if someone suddenly had hit her on the head. She turned as pale as a corpse. Had it not been for the sound of her breathing, we would have thought that she was dead or that she had had a stroke or a heart attack. She didn't say a word. She asked neither how nor when, but stared, first at her daughter and then beyond her at mysterious spaces invisible to us, and possibly to her.

Futna broke the silence, saying, "I told Zayna and she didn't mind, mama."

The mother neither responded nor looked at me or at her daughter, but continued to stare and breath heavily.

Futna went on saying, "My late husband wouldn't have been upset," but her mother neither replied nor moved.

Futna began to defend her action as if her mother had accused her of wrongdoing, "Mama, why don't you answer me? I did nothing that would anger God. It was a simple surgery done at the hospital; the doctor wore gloves and a mask and was assisted by a female nurse."

Receiving no reply from her mother, Futna went on talking with greater enthusiasm, looking at me for moral support, "It's a very simple procedure, simpler than opening a pimple. It takes two to three minutes and does not even require an anesthetic. In other words, it's like a regular gynecological check up."

There was still no reply from the mother, causing Futna's voice to rise and quiver as she continued, "Oh Mama, why don't you answer me? I'm telling you, it's a simple procedure that many women have undergone before me, five or even ten years ago. It was done in America and Europe twenty years ago. If we don't do it here it's because we don't have enough doctors and first-class, clean hospitals. In Europe and in Israel, medicine is very advanced and so are we."

A bitter smile appeared on the mother's lips, but she didn't comment and went on staring at the empty space before her.

Futna's voice shook even more and its pitch rose almost to a shout as she said, "Mama, say something. You make me feel guilty, even though I didn't do anything wrong. What do you want me to swear by to convince you that I did nothing that would anger God? What can I say to convince you that I didn't commit a sin? Mama, it was only a simple surgery that took only an hour of my time. There was only the trip to the hospital, the procedure, and then the doctor said, 'Congratulations, you're pregnant.' It was like a dream, I don't even remember how it happened and how I did it! I have a hard time believing it myself sometimes, and I sometimes wonder, saying to myself: Oh my God! Is it possible that I am pregnant like other women! All my life I've wished for a baby, all my life I've dreamed of becoming pregnant. It didn't happen with my first husband, or the second one, but now I am pregnant from Hadassa, Oh God Almighty!"

The mother emitted a snoring sound that resembled the noise made by a sheep or a bull being slaughtered. Her head and chest shook as if she had received a strong jolt that made her stagger. The hand she had placed on the desk moved as a result, spilling the coffee and the water. Futna jumped toward her mother from across the desk to prevent her from falling, but the mother's head fell on the desk over the papers and the mixture of coffee and water.

Futna shouted like a crazed person, "What happened? What happened?"

I, in turn, ran to the telephone to call a doctor or an ambulance, but I quickly remembered that I was in Jerusalem, a foreigner in a foreign place, and I didn't know whom to call or what number to dial. So I went out to the street calling for help, but the people in the street were foreigners, even more so than I, and I saw no one but vendors, customers, and a large group of tourists.

I cut my trip short and returned to Wadi al-Rihan, escaping the artificial surroundings, Amira's illness, and her daughter's pregnancy. I went seeking my uncle's surroundings of sincerity and truth. I went looking for the blue sky over the cracks of his farm, the twinkle of lemons under the falling rain, and the plastic houses for the chicks where everyone hid whenever a strong westerly wind blew. I longed for the conversation we would have on the way to the fish market and the farm and Nablus, where my cousin the toffee maker lived; we would speak words that came directly from the heart, the broken dreams and the memories, some sweet and some bitter. Their hope was to find peace one day, and rest after a long struggle. My uncle looked at me and laughed and coughed, while I drove and spoke about my feelings of loss and my heart longing for rest. He commented on my words, saying affectionately, "My God, how cute you are Zayna! You were lost! You were seeking rest? What should I say? What would Nahleh say? What would Mazen say?"

He went on talking about his worries and those of his children, "Mazen is tired and burdens others with his uncertainties. Mazen goes from one house to the other, moves from one girl to another, between friends and cafées. When he talked about politics, we said fine, but what then? What would he do after politics and the headaches it causes? He has no work, no wife, no children, and no car, what then? What does he want to do with his life? He does not want to work with me cultivating the land, and he refuses to run a grocery that I'm willing to open for him. He doesn't want us to finance a project for him to provide him with an income. He produces nothing but words, he talks about politics, but says nothing about his work and his worries, and neglects his soul and heart. I would tell him, what then my son? Beirut is lost, Amman is lost, and Tunis too, and you're here today. Yesterday has passed and we're here today, what would you like to do with your life? Nahleh would wink at me asking me to stop, because of his heel. His heel has been mended with a piece of metal and the surgery was successful, and thanks be to God, he now walks like me and even better. He is two meters tall and maybe more and there is nothing he needs."

My uncle would stop to catch up his breath, then resume, agonizing over his son, "I've given up, Zayna. I can't say a word to him like a father usually would. I don't like his frowning. He's like a giant, and he's as proud as a prince. He's conceited and always has been. He's gallant and proud, and I always treated him like a prince. Everyone, his mother, Nahleh, and even the neighbors used to say that this young man was like a prince, but what then? We've had it with princes and politics, with the Nassers and the Guevaras. I always encouraged him to be active, to look after his own future, to search for his path, for something to do for the rest of his life, for the many years he had before him. He's over forty now, which means that he is a man, a man with brains, and those his age are married with children taller than themselves, and already in college. But my son, the good one, hasn't yet settled and has chosen neither the temporal nor the spiritual. He's in a daze and makes me dizzy. This has been going on for a long time and isn't over yet, making me wonder, what next? Talk to him, Zayna, advise him; he might listen to you and be convinced. He might find an idea in your words that would guide him."

I promised to help more out of pity for my uncle than from a belief that I could change his attitude. But my uncle continued, "Talking about America and life there, the hard work and the struggle of the Americans working like machines might awaken him from his dreams. He keeps saying that soon America, like England, will shrink and start begging. But it is we who shrank and our only worry is to find food. We face nothing but worries in our life. Can we continue to live now the way we lived in the past? The answer is obvious and one doesn't need second sight to see it. Why can't Mazen see it? In God's name, Zayna, tell him to open his eyes. The world has changed and Mazen Hamdan is a child of this world and he can't change that. He has to wake up and look to his own interests. Who is he counting on? He has to wake up and take care of himself. Whatever he does he is still Mazen Hamdan , not Guevara. Tell him that."

We went looking for Mazen, riding in the station wagon. We searched everywhere, at his friends' houses, in caféés, at the fish market, and at the municipality, but we found no trace of him. At the municipality they said he was in Nablus, and in Nablus we were told he was in al-Tur. There we were told that he was with Umm Grace and her daughter visiting a priest. The priest said that they had returned to Wadi al-Rihan. We finally gave up and returned home without further ado. We ate our dinner in the warmth of the kitchen, while my uncle's wife prepared tea with maramiyeh and fried goat cheese. Every now and then Nahleh would look in, wearing her nightdress and with rollers in her hair, and inquire mockingly, "The Bey hasn't come yet?"

We didn't answer her and went on talking about Mazen, his adventures, and his concerns. She came again and asked angrily, "Well, hasn't he yet honored us with his presence?"

My uncle raised his hand and asked her to keep quiet. She laughed and squirmed, and wondered whether it was she or Mazen that was annoying the group. She would then wink at me as if she were saying what she had told me hundreds of times already, "Notice the difference between him and me. When I am absent, no one cares. No one says that I've wasted my youth and life in Kuwait's heat, living alone in a foreign land. Now I don't care, even if heaven falls on earth, I don't care, even if the whole Hamdan family disappears, I couldn't care less!"

Our eyes would meet, I would smile at her, and she would respond with a cold, strange smile that I didn't understand. Ever since my father had died, or rather since she had opened up her heart to me that night and the following nights, her smile to me was full of reprimand, bitterness, and deep hatred.

Looking around him, my uncle whispered, "Nahleh has changed, changed very much. She has become cruel and stubborn and says strange things. She even wears strange clothes, laughs loudly, and chews gum! What's happened to Nahleh? That isn't like her."

I, too, was aware that Nahleh wasn't like that, had never been like that. She had changed and become this way, and she will continue to be this way until the day God provides her with a solution. She needed a solution that would save her from her reality—the reality of a fifty-year-old woman. That woman had once been beautiful, fresh, young, and full of love and feelings, then she had been hit with the realization that she was fifty, homeless, aimless, and unsatisfied. She controlled herself, considered her limited options, and tried in vain to adapt to her life. She started using make up, taking small, timid steps, and secretively applying small amounts of eyeliner. She used blush and put rollers in her hair every night. She started going to Nablus every Thursday and returning with piles of clothes and trinkets. She would spend hours in her room, trying on the dresses, the mascara, the eye shadow, the lipstick, the various creams for her skin, moisturizer, cleansing, anti-wrinkle, and neck and eye creams. Her father often wondered where she was hiding. She would spend hours in her room, trying on her clothes in front of the mirror, exercising to lose weight and listening to songs by Wardeh, Najat, and Umm Kulthum. Then she took up writing, she wrote in her diary and sometimes wrote poems that she didn't finish. She would fill one page, then another and another and then stop, not knowing how to end it or what to say. She would then return to her tapes and gymnastics, to Umm Kulthum, and to sighing. We would hear her sing with Umm Kulthum: "Give me my freedom, release my hands, I have given everything and did not hold back."

My uncle's wife would smile, and my uncle would shake his head looking at me as if to say, "Do you see what Nahleh is doing?"

Mazen would comment, "Nahleh needs a change of scene. Tell her to go on one of those long, package tours, or let her go visit her brothers."

I would smile and look away lest they realize that I knew how little her brothers cared. If it weren't for the Gulf War she would have continued to endure the heat and sandstorms of Kuwait, and no one would have cared.

On my advice, my uncle left the kitchen and went to Nahleh to let her know that he cared and that everyone cared and to tell her that her brother in Frankfurt had called to ask after her. My uncle's wife sat close to me and whispered, "I want to tell you a story but I don't want you to repeat it."

She told me that she had heard that Nahleh was having a relationship with her cousin, the real estate agent, and that he, a married man with ten children, wanted to take her as a second wife. Meanwhile, his children were going out of their minds, saying that they would kill him and her.

"Kill her, how?" I asked, terrified.

My uncle's wife mimicked the shape of a firing gun with her hand to explain, and said, "That's how they shoot."

Her hand truly looked like a revolver. I asked, surprised, "Do people have weapons? Don't they fear the Israeli authorities?"

She whispered with the same degree of fear, "His oldest son is a member of many organizations and is wanted by the authorities. People say that he's an important leader. Nahleh is crazy; she doesn't seem to care. They would kill her and him if they go ahead with their plan. There's no authority and no one would care. Life is cheap. Your uncle is coming back, no more talking; don't quote me."

She then went to the sink and poured the tea.

Nahleh was facing the woman who was rubbing her skin with the oils and creams she had bought from the perfume vendor in Nablus. There she saw women wearing long coats, their faces hidden behind scarves to conceal their identity and their presence in such a place. They whispered their requests to the vendor and he whispered back, while searching the shelves for all kinds of bottles. Then, in a mortar, he pounded stones that looked like amber, handling the powder with extreme care, pouring perfume over it and adding heavy, scented oil with a syringe.

The customers observed him from behind their veils and listened to him explaining, "This is for firming the skin, this is for blood circulation, this is meant to open the pores, and this to whiten the skin; they will make your skin feel like velvet."

The customers made no comment but continued to stare, breathing behind their veils. Nahleh requested the same products and was told that the qirat costs five dinars.

She inquired about its effect with the savvy manner of an experienced buyer. To her the vendor looked like a priest or a magician. The whole atmosphere was heavy and complex and secretive, as if someone was engaged in dangerous activities forbidden by the law. But what law? There was neither law nor police, not even a state to defend their rights. It was as if the end of the world were near, and everyone feared the future, feared they might wake up to a different world, in a country with roads emptied by curfews, with only guns, bombs, and loudspeakers, and the radio announcing the news, as usual. There might be a new operation at Hertsiliya and on the road to Jerusalem, a kidnapped soldier, a burned factory, and a Jewish farmer hit with an ax. His attackers would be chased by the army and the police, and the poor Arab workers would spend the whole day in the sun while people there, in Israel, would spit and swear and throw stones and shoot. The roads to Haifa, to Nablus, and to Jerusalem would be closed. Her father wondered what she did in Nablus, "Every other day you go to Nablus!" he said, "Yesterday conditions were crazy and every day there's a new operation. I'm afraid you'll get stuck there."

She replied, "I'd go to Said's house and sleep there."

She was lying because she didn't like Said or his wife or his children, and she found their house in Makhfiyeh disgusting. The name Makhfiyeh, which meant "concealed," reflected the wishful thinking of those who would have loved to keep such a nauseating neighborhood invisible. Nahleh's sister-in-law was filthy and her children were like worms. She had never seen dirtier kids. Even her brother was filthy and the stupidest one in the family, but he at least had a family, a wife and children, and a toffee factory, whereas she, Nahleh, the lady of ladies, the clever and smart one, the beautiful, elegant, and coquettish young woman, was unmarried. There were no young men left in the neighborhood who hadn't proposed to her, but she had turned them all down. Now there is a real estate agent, illiterate, with a big belly, his eyes always puffed, and headgear that covers half his face. But when he looks at her she melts immediately, and she feels things inside her, the same things she feels listening to her favorite songs. That was the time when she used to dream at night and wake up, her heart beating, dazed and sweating.

Poor woman, poor girl, this is what life does to her? But love has its ways, it brings back youth to the heart and mind. The mind becomes dizzy, and thoughts and beautiful visions like dreams fill her world. She stands, then sits, then sleeps, then bathes, then showers, feeling him, his eyes, his hands, his lips, and all his being, making her vibrate. She discovers love, warmth, and the sweet taste of life, the beauty of experiencing those sensations, this enjoyment. All this makes her forget the world and the long, sleepless nights and the subjugation and the worries, her fifty years and the graying hair and the changes in her body and the hot flushes. She's getting older and her period stops for two or three months and then returns, causing her great pain. The doctor told her that it was normal and that it will stop. Stop? Stop? The beautiful, elegant Nahleh would have no period. It has hardly started, then it ends! Fertility hasn't begun yet for her, she hasn't tried it a single time, not even one time, one time in her life!

She would listen stealthily to the conversations of women burdened by numerous pregnancies and deliveries, submitting to their husbands' disagreeable demands, forcing them to have sex against their will. Nahleh would smile to herself, and laugh at the women's silliness because they didn't know how to live, how to enjoy themselves and their sexuality. She, on the other hand, will fully experience these things because even songs move her and so does just thinking about it. His fiery, eagle eyes burn her, making her wet and overwhelming her with a burning sensation. She would circle in her room like a bee, listening to songs that stirred her, that set her on fire, then the telephone rings and a voice says come. She throws down the receiver, puts on her tight skirt, and goes. In the car he touches the silky and velvety skin of her legs, that velvety feel she had worked to create with the products made with the perfume vendor's stone.

Her father was deeply concerned and wondered why she went so often to Nablus—Nablus was hell. But she has known the true hell of the hot sandstorms in Kuwait, the hell of life in a faraway country, years of subjugation, of loneliness and desolation, the hell of the yearning heart, and the hell of the hot flashes. There was also the hell of the damned realization that the beautiful Nahleh, the diligent Nahleh, the elegant Nahleh, the best among all girls, had reached fifty. She lamented over her fate in disbelief that she had reached fifty, an old woman whose youth was totally gone or almost gone. She wondered about the ingratitude of life, about having reached fifty without having lived her life.

A neighbor told her that things were even better at fifty, the same one who used to hang the towel to dry in the courtyard in broad daylight after her lovemaking. The house was now empty and there was nothing to worry about. She had explained, "All the children were grown and each left doing his thing and the old man and I stayed behind. But he's not really old, a sixty, a seventy, and even an eighty-year-old man is not old. I too at fifty—I'm not old, dear Nahleh. Things are much better at fifty."

The neighbor laughed and so did Nahleh, who immediately went back to her room to rub her skin and listen to Najat and Wardeh's songs and wait for his phone call, inviting her for a ride.

When she saw him for the first time she was shocked by his height and his size, his sloppy wife with her double chin and her golden kirdan. His foul language appalled her, using words like an illiterate, ignorant man, a backward animal. His wife spent her days cooking and tending the sheep under the fig tree. Her father was a shepherd and she was used to the sound of the sheep, their smell, and their milk. She made cheese, cheese cream, and butter with the milk—a white butter that Nahleh liked and ate with sugar and country bread. When he heard her mention the white butter he told her, melodiously, "Miss Nahleh, you're more valuable to me than butter. I'll have your butter ready for you and my eyes too."

He looked at her keenly, which made her realize that he had two eyes, two lips, and a beautiful black mustache despite the black dye.

76

He is her uncle's wife's first cousin, born to a twelve-year-old mother and a father in his nineties with a large retinue of wives who filled his olive yards with progeny, prosperity, and country bread. She lived well, thank God, raising the child alone since his father died soon after his birth. The boy grew up among the vine trees like a goat, grazing like sheep in the midst of grass, radishes, and shrubs, while his mother tended the sheep with his half-brothers and his father's other wives. He spent his early childhood without education, and when he became an adolescent he started herding the sheep with the other shepherds, gathering mulberries and olives from under the trees. Then he was able to shake the branches with his stick and later married his first cousin, having sold a piece of land from his inheritance.

He bought a cupboard, a mattress, a radio, and bracelets shaped like a rope. He opened a shop with the remaining money and traded in oil, cheese, and olives until he accumulated enough money to buy land for almost nothing from the peasants and sell it at a very high price to the city dwellers. This is how he became rich and how his wife acquired two chins, two kirdans, and ten rope-shaped bracelets.

His children are in universities and organizations and attend conferences, and it is said that one of his sons is in the peace process delegation, acting as a negotiator. It is also said that another one is in the opposition, a third one is a sheep merchant. Two of his daughters are unmarried. The brave Nahleh is stepping in the midst of this large family, including a merchant who is a well-connected negotiator, a member of the opposition who is ready to die a martyr at a moment's notice for the sake of his beliefs and the liberation.

Love perturbs sane minds, however, and transforms a free woman into a servile slave to her feelings. It changes a man who knew no other woman but his unattractive cousin into a jealous man ready to sacrifice his life for love and the beloved. The beloved is a city woman, well born, educated, and composed, with two twinkling eyes, white skin, without a mustache or a double chin. She is fashionable, with legs that look like cheese under the nylon stockings, and a behind as soft as butter. She laughs coquettishly and talks softly. She makes jam like the one the English call marmalade. He ate the marmalade or the jam and felt elated, as if he were flying or dizzy. It tasted of the magic of high society. He made up his mind and waited for the right time, so when she said "butter," he replied generously, "You're more valuable to me than butter."

This is how the far-reaching love story began, and the rest is history.

When he touched her knee and her calf without any objection on her part, he was dazzled, his head burned as if in a blazing furnace. He was overcome with conflicting emotions: concern for and disgust with a woman who allowed a strange man to touch her unabashedly, and the memory of his childhood experience when he used to venture with the children of the shepherds to observe the sheep, the cows, and even the chickens, mating. For years he couldn't get enough of this. When he finally lost interest he lost his sexual drive and thought he had become impotent. He withdrew within himself, and centered his attention on his family, his children, and the mother of his children. He focused his efforts on making money and never had enough of it. But finally, he had. He wondered how this could have happened, though he had heard the elders and the sheikhs state that the human eye was greedy, but a handful of earth can fill it. He found out that the eye of the human being doesn't remain greedy to the end of life and can find satisfaction in less than a handful of earth long before death.

It was a strange experience, difficult to describe or explain. One of his sons passed his exams with honor, and that was great; another one landed a high position and married the daughter of a minister. That was fine too. The price of the land rose and he sold the meter for one hundred dinars, ten times the price he paid for it. What then? He bought a palace in Amman from a wealthy man who went bankrupt, then sold it for ten times what he paid for it. What then? His capital was in the millions, his children were distinguished members of society, and he owned land in Nablus, Ramallah, and Amman, and a magnificent palace in 'Abdun. But he continued to live in a house that was more like a shack, with a woman his age, but one who looked like the trunk of a Roman olive tree dating back to a time before Christ. She had made the pilgrimage to Mecca three times and was getting ready for her fourth trip. She had decided to don the hijab following her fourth pilgrimage. She usually wore a long gray or khaki, or maybe green dress made especially for her, utterly colorless and shapeless. She covered her hair with a white scarf, tightened around her forehead and jaws. It made them turn red and caused the skin to puff up.

The realtor was watching the singer Wardeh on television one day when his wife told him, "Hajj, after the 'umra, I will wear the veil, God willing."

He took a quick look at her and in one glance saw her puffed up skin, her cheeks, and her forehead. He muttered, while eating watermelon seeds, "Okay, okay."

She turned around to show him how the long dress looked on her. All he saw, however, was a barrel-like shape filled with fat, with a propeller, two oars, and two fans. She moved past him, displaced the air, which smelled of butter and buttermilk. He muttered and uttered God's name, asking for His mercy, then shifted his attention to Wardeh as she sang, "I like your company."

He felt oppressed. He felt as if a heavy stone were weighing on his chest, and he had a shrinking feeling at the bottom of his belly. The telephone rang, startling him, making his heart race as if a bomb had exploded and shaken the house. It wasn't a bomb but the voice of a realtor in Nablus telling him that a lot he owned was worth a quarter of a million dinars. It didn't matter to him whether the land was worth a quarter of a million or half or even ten million. What difference would it make in his life? Would this change the face of the earth, his feelings, or this woman standing before him? But was she a true woman? A female? A human being? Despite his money, his travels, his new house, and his rugs, his wife had a rancid odor and smelled of the country oven. Nothing had changed in his life despite the dining room bought in Jerusalem, the living room bought in Haifa, the television from Natanya, the Mercedes with a double antenna, a telephone, dark windows, a roof window, and a horn with three different sounds: a happy sound, a dancing melody, and an alarming sound like a police siren. Despite all his wealth, at the end of the day he spends the evening watching television with his two daughters who look like frogs and the "barrel" wife. Lately, he had been sitting alone to watch television; he had bought a new set and put the old one in the girls' room. His wife was busy finishing a khatma, a reading of the Qur'an, and getting ready to start a new one for his soul. She had recited a khatma for each dead member of the family and she was poised to start a khatma for the living members, for Salem, the oldest son, for Hamzeh the second son, for Marwan, for Saadu, for Mahmud, for the two girls, and, finally, for her husband. Yet, he didn't feel any better as he stared at the television, examining Wardeh's cosmetic surgery. She was very beautiful after her face-lift and the weight loss; she looked younger and more radiant than before. Her face was like a rose and her neck slender. He thought to himself, "How lovely Wardeh is, looking so young and energetic. That's the way to live, that's life for anyone who understands what living means, not like my life, worthy of cows."

He began to rebel against his life, his children, and his wealth. If he were told, "The price of land had gone up," he would reply, resentfully, "What do I care whether it goes up or down?"

If he were told that the dollar has gone down, he would reply, "Tomorrow it will go up."

If he were told that the price of gas has increased, he would respond peevishly, "Why should I rejoice? What is there in life to make me happy?" He would then take watermelon seeds out of his pocket and split them between his teeth, spitting the skin and yawning.

When Nahleh responded to his advances and asked for butter, he regained his energy and his will to live. Romance began in the Mercedes, on the trips to Nablus and al-Tur Mountain. He started thinking seriously about a different venue for their encounters, one that would be in agreement with the sunna, God's law.

Nahleh and Mazen were late, and my uncle was worried. He called Ramallah, then Nablus and Jenin, looking for them. He wondered where his children were at this time and in those days; he pondered about this life and time, when no one cared for a father, a brother, or a family, with people doing whatever they liked.

My uncle's wife winked at me and whispered in my ear, "Nahleh is certainly with the realtor."

I didn't react and went on watching the television news describe the latest guerrilla operation and the movement of the ambulances carrying the wounded to Hadassa hospital. The soldiers were leading disfigured Arab workers to buses that looked like cages used to transport animals to the slaughterhouse or the zoo, with bars and barbed wires on the windows.

My uncle's wife whispered again in my ear, "Mazen is certainly with Violet."

I didn't react but my uncle heard Mazen's name and said, angrily, "If Mazen were here he would have looked for his sister!"

I said, trying to calm him down, "Maybe Nahleh is with her brother in the Makhfiyeh."

Embarrassed, my uncle replied, "Maybe, maybe! If there were only a telephone at the Makhfiyeh!"

Then he muttered, angrily, in frustration, "I would like to know where Mazen is!"

My uncle got up and went to perform his ablutions, before reading the Qur'an and going to bed. I sneaked out from the kitchen door and went looking for Mazen at Violet's house. She didn't live very far—her house was in the same street, near the realtor's house. The backyards of the two houses were contiguous, separated only by a chain link fence and cypress tree. Suddenly, I heard a car engine in the distance and decided to hide behind the cypress trees. The car stopped a few meters away from the realtor's gate and two young men got out. I couldn't see their features in the darkness, but I heard one ask the other, "Are you going to say hello to your mother?"

I realized then that they were the realtor's children, and I understood that one of them was wanted by the Israelis. He hadn't seen his mother and sisters in many weeks. The wanted brother said, "I warned him but your father is as stubborn as this wall."

The other one replied, "You have guns."

The wanted brother hastened to reply, "Who said that my weapon is for such matters?"

Both stopped talking and a heavy silence fell on the place, all I was able to hear was their heavy breathing caused by the heated argument. I had the impression that they were continuing a conversation they had started long before they had arrived here. One of them said, impatiently, "Let's not quarrel again. Let's sit under the trellis until he shows his face."

They opened the small gate, entered through the garden, and disappeared between the trees. All I could hear after that was my heartbeat and my rapid breathing. I hurried to Violet's house looking for Mazen to tell him what was happening. He was the only one who had the means and the ability to intervene with the brothers and put an end to a deteriorating situation, to prevent a crime or a scandal.

When I entered the house, however, Mazen was in a setting quite different from the one I had expected. He was sitting on a sofa at the entrance of the house, surrounded by mezze dishes, vodka, and araq glasses. A man I had seen at Violet's birthday party was sitting with him. Violet didn't look cheerful and seemed rather shaken up. Mazen, on the other hand, appeared in high spirits and quite relaxed. In other words, he felt like a sultan. I sat on the edge of my seat, thanked Violet and her mother for the warm welcome they gave me, and tried in vain to point out to Mazen the importance of the matter that brought me to Violet's house. Violet's mother served appetizers and jabbered meaninglessly, while the man with gray hair and inquisitive eyes, made smug comments to the two women and me.

Violet was holding a remote control pointed toward a new electronic set that I hadn't seen before. She was willingly repeating parts of songs that Mazen requested with authority. It was clear that Mazen and Violet were in some way at odds or having a lover's quarrel, while the mother and the man were acting normally, neither interfering nor commenting nor smiling at anything they heard. Violet sighed every now and then, showing signs of impatience. She made comments that would have seemed casual and innocent to the inexperienced observer, but they were filled with riddles, double meanings, and the anguish of a heavy heart.

As he watched me with eyes shining from the effect of alcohol, Mazen said, "Look Umm Grace, see how beautiful my cousin is!"

Umm Grace laughed and said, affectionately, "God's blessings be upon her, she is very beautiful. I loved her the moment I saw her. She is pretty, thoughtful, and not at all pretentious. May God protect her from the evil eye."

Mazen wondered, "Why would she be pretentious?"

Umm Grace answered, affectionately, "Because anybody like her, with all she owns, Ma shallah, what God gave her, she is still humble."

Mazen laughed, then said, his jaws weak and his speech slurred, "What does she own, let's see?"

Umm Grace replied, looking at me and said smilingly, "She is beautiful and sweet, and she has common sense. She always speaks Arabic and isn't pretentious."

Mazen said laughingly, "Her Arabic accent is cute."

The gray-haired man said, smacking his lips, "It is very cute, nothing is cuter than that."

Mazen approved enthusiastically.

Violet looked away, upset with Mazen. She replayed the song she was listening to until she reached a specific part where the singer Najat says: "I implore you to leave, my love for the sake of our love."

Sure of his power over Violet, Mazen asked her to play *al-Atlal*. He then raised his voice joining the singer as she was saying, "Has love seen drunks like us?"

Violet looked at him sideways and whispered, "I want you to leave."

I understood from the covert struggle unfolding before my eyes that Violet, despite her known attachment to Mazen, wanted for some unknown reason to get rid of him and his love. I understood that Mazen, despite his Don Juan attitude, his moodiness, and his feelings of loss, wanted to keep Violet. It wasn't so much out of love or appreciation for her, but because she filled a void in his life and provided him with an environment he wouldn't be able to find in this semi-rural and conservative town. He had found it difficult to come to such a place after Beirut's open and pompous society. Violet offered him the best possibility here, in view of her somewhat higher social class, her education in a nuns' school in Bethlehem, and her training sessions in Beirut, Tel Aviv, and Cyprus. She knew how to talk, dress, and display Western manners. She was familiar with men's tricks, the relation between the sexes and the anxieties of love. As my uncle's wife and Nahleh explained, she also knew how to turn a man's head and reduce him to a toy in her hands. Mazen didn't seem to be a toy, however, but a sensible man who imposed himself and knew how to melt her heart with his games and his seductive black eyes.

He repeated while raising his glass before me and looking furtively at Violet, "You are so beautiful, cousin."

The graying man who made annoying comments said, "Thank you for saying that, I've never seen a more beautiful person."

Then he turned to me declaring, "Mazen is a very lucky man!"

I looked at him and understood the meaning of his words. He implied that Mazen's youth, games, and black eyes, his stories about the revolution, his body, his limp, and his sweetness had won me over. Not satisfied with Violet's love and companionship, he had turned to his beautiful, adorable, rich, and humble cousin!

The graying man turned to Umm Grace, and said, "Ya Umm Grace, isn't he a lucky man?"

Umm Grace moved her eyes between me and Violet, comparing the two of us for the first time. She said absentmindedly, "Yes, he's lucky."

Mother and daughter exchanged a look that filled me with doubt and made me wonder. I returned to my glass of wine, drinking and listening to the simple, clear words of the song written in plain standard Arabic. I understood them and began to react to their meaning. Umm Grace said graciously, "How are you? We haven't seen any of you in a long time. How is your uncle? And Nahleh?"

I looked at Mazen and suddenly remembered Nahleh's story, but Mazen was swaying on his seat, listening to the melody, pouring another drink and chewing slowly. He then said, in a commanding tone, without looking at Violet or using her name, "Bring some more ice."

She looked at him without comment, put down the remote, and went to get the ice he'd requested. He looked at her sideways and said, "Play *al-Atlal.*"

She moved slowly toward the tape player and sat holding the remote control in the direction of the set. The sound burst out, thundering and scary, from the loudspeakers. The room was suddenly filled with the roaring of the echo and the shock of the meaning. I didn't know why I felt a certain sadness, why I was emotional or for whose sake. Was it for the ruined love reduced to rubble? Or for the sake of a man lost on islands of salt? Or was it for the sake of this woman, this female with broken dreams and a bleeding heart? Or was I feeling a stranger in these surroundings, more alien than any of them, sensing something that I didn't understand but felt? My cousin exclaimed, obviously moved, "How did love become a piece of news, a subject of conversation like the weather!"

Nahleh was stranded in Nablus as the city was closed to all traffic, surrounded, and placed under curfew following the killing of a truck driver. A ferocious campaign was launched to arrest the culprit, but the perpetrator disappeared as suddenly as he had appeared. It was as if the earth had swallowed him, leaving the authorities no choice but to follow the usual procedure, which no longer scared or upset people. They had become accustomed to searches, curfews, strikes, road blocks, and the shop closures that caused fruits and vegetables to rot and garbage to pile up in the streets. Sewage pipes and drains ruptured, the sidewalks were destroyed, the asphalt and the buildings were damaged, revealing their skeletons and those of the people. They had gotten used to paucity and humiliation, and lived as if they were in the Stone Age.

Nahleh was not used to that kind of life, however. She was the product of Kuwait, a country where nothing was lacking or scarce. Despite the difficulties and the pain and suffering caused by the Gulf War, those earthshaking changes had come too suddenly to have become a way of life. There was a war, fighting, and expulsions; people suddenly found themselves in a different country and another reality. But their pockets were full, sparing them the compounded humiliation endured by their other compatriots for a quarter of a century or more. They left the comfort of Kuwait and spread out. The lucky ones went to the West Bank and continued to live a pampered life, among young people most of whom were not yet twenty, children of the occupation and the Intifada, who had endured prison life, beatings, hunger, unemployment, and need. Those who emigrated from Kuwait, despite their disgrace, were not humiliated because they had come from the land of affluence and wealth. They continued to see themselves the way people saw them, as providers who supported families, brought gifts to the West Bank throughout the years, and had bank accounts.

That's how Nahleh felt and that's why she couldn't adapt to the situation. She was resentful because of her age, a woman of fifty whose senses had awakened, holding on to a final chance, a last opportunity to escape her ordeal and the misery of repression, loneliness, and a squandered life. She was searching for a way to end her trips to the druggist and her pursuit of perfumes, creams, face lifts, and all the excitement they provided: the feeling of lust, the anxiety, the sighs, the dreams, the withdrawal from reality. She had gotten attached to specks of rosy clouds in a spring that was not hers but one that she was chasing, stubbornly. The realtor too was in a race to beat death in the way he lived his life.

Nahleh looked at her brother's wife, then turned her head away. She looked like a "bundle," a nickname the family had chosen. They also referred to her as the drum, the owl, or the cow, descriptions that seemed especially tailored for her. Whenever Said visits his parents, everybody says, Said has come with his bundle, or Said has come with his owl, or his drum. Those words were said casually, without a smile, in a matter of fact way.

The "bundle" was not a true bundle, but a mean street girl. Her father sold lupines and fava beans in the street. She suffered from an inferiority complex that caused her to be greedy and somewhat dishonest, especially toward the Hamdan family. She was a frustrated woman with a malevolent gaze; she felt crushed by the Hamdan family whom she perceived to be as powerful and glorious as the Turks, the Romans, and the British. She was conscious of their influential position in society while she, the bundle, had a real name, Ni'meh, whose meaning, 'blessing,' did not reflect her condition as a poor and lowly person. She used to accompany her father on his rounds, selling lupines in the street and chanting: "Here are the salty ones," while her father repeated after her: "Salty and delicious lupines, cheap and fresh, the product of the season."

As to why Said married her, it was because he was more stupid than she, though he was an industrialist at present, producing candy and toffee. He talked to people from the tip of his nose and dealt with them snobbishly and haughtily. His wife began spending a great deal of money after the factory was built. She spent a great deal on the family food, choosing only fatty foods such as tripe, and fried turnip with garlic and lemon. This explained the odors that invaded Said's house, which were more nauseating than the smell of public toilets.

Nahleh was naturally disgusted by the situation in her brother's house. She refrained from eating a single bite in Said's house. One can only imagine how she felt, trapped in the bundle's house, being served fatty food in the company of her crazy brother. She kept watching television, hoping for good news that would announce the end of the closure and the lifting of the security ring around Nablus. The speaker didn't say anything reassuring, and the news of the operation on the road to al-Ludd and the killing of the truck driver in Nablus added to her pessimism and anger. She wondered whether the day she was supposed to cross the threshold of the house that would soon become her own—a house of happiness, the realtor's house—would be a day of doom and gloom? Was this a bad omen, a sign of bad luck? Oh God, why? What had she done to deserve this punishment and face such hardships? Even the bundle was luckier than she. When the day she had been waiting for had finally arrived, the day she had hoped to begin to settle down, the world turned upside down with the killing of the truck driver! Why, God? Why all this? The worst part was being stuck in her brother's house. She wondered whether the situation would force her to eat and sleep in this disgusting house and to provide an explanation for spending the night in the Makhfiyeh. She was the author of this house's well-being, hadn't she given her brother ten thousand dinars to start the candy factory? She wondered why she felt humiliated in the company of the bundle, the girl who sold lupine, and salted fava beans and ate on a tabliyeh.

Her sister-in-law said to her seriously, but gently, "I set the mattress for you in the guest room. I lit the heater to warm it up. That room is cold and humid in winter because of its westerly location and its leaks. We never go there in winter, but in summer it's so wonderful, it's the best room in the house, cool and breezy, you feel as if you're in a plane."

She did in fact feel as if she were in a plane the whole night; the wind was blowing and shaking the door, the windows, and the television antennas on the roof. Everything sounded like the beating of hammers and the raging of demons. What a night! What a nightmare! She was scared and cold, surrounded by walls covered with maps drawn by salt, dampness, and black water moss that looked like crows. She was surrounded by the smell of mildew, which made her feel as if she were trapped under a mound of earth, inside a grave. Was this an omen, a sign of bad luck? She covered her ears and forehead with the comforter and the blankets despite their unpleasant smell and their dirtiness. They were Tarek's covers, her ten-year-old nephew, who spent his time in the street. His fingernails were long and dirty, as black as qazha, his shirt collar was disgustingly dirty, and his hair was always untidy and sticky, like that of a wet chicken.

Here she was lying, covered with a disgusting comforter; had her sister-in-law had any concept of good manners she would have given her a clean comforter and clean sheets, but she was an owl whose lowly origin gave her no concept of good manners. She loved food, however, and was generous in serving her guests. She would fill the table with all kinds of dishes, fried and battered cauliflower, eggplant pickled with walnuts and garlic, radish, lentil soup, bisarah, and pluck with parsley and heaps of onion floating in fat and clarified butter. The children would delve in the food helping themselves directly from the serving plate, their fingernails too long, their noses running, and their skin chapped from dryness and colds.

How disgusting and cold the house was! Can Nablus be so heartless! There are peasants, city dwellers, immigrants, and migrants in this city, but she, who is she? A migrant? Migrants don't own anything, while she does. She has a bank account in dollars and another one in dinars, a piece of land in the Makhfiyeh region and a second one in Jericho bought before the Oslo Conference. Yet, despite all that, she was humiliated in her brother's guestroom. She felt embarrassed despite his warm welcome, his generosity, and the greasy food he piled up on her plate, choosing a piece of delicious cauliflower, a pickled eggplant, and some breaded cauliflower that he insisted she should eat. He offered her red radishes, and many other foods until she was full and her stomach felt like a gourd. Then there were the gases and the trips to the bathroom. What an ordeal, she thought, by God, what a mess. She spent the night going back and forth to the toilet because of the food and the cold, the exhaustion and her anger at this bad omen. The house where she was expecting to live with the realtor must be an object of envy. He had built it for his children and their mother, then changed his mind and rented it to a Canadian professor teaching at al-Najah University. The professor transformed it into an Eden, built a cement wall around it and added iron bars that were almost as high as the roof. He covered them with climbing plants and ten kinds of mallow that bloomed throughout the year, even in January. She loved their sight, their beauty, and their colors, but wondered at the walls and the creeping plants. He explained that the professor was a specialist in agriculture who feared the Intifada, the stone throwing, and the young people. The professor wanted a safe fort that would protect his family from the abuses of the army, the children, and the neighbors. He worried about the neighborhood residents, their curiosity, and their interference in his life. They were watching them, his wife in particular, who wore shorts and girdles, and sunbathed. He built the walls to protect her from their gaze.

Following the visit to that house the realtor asked Nahleh, "What about you fair woman, do you have shorts?"

She laughed at his words, and he laughed pinching her in the back of the neck. She kept rubbing it until they left the house, the bad luck house, the one she begrudged.

Her stepmother said to her, "He built the house for her but she never lived in it. She still covets it. He's very stingy, he's never satisfied with any amount of material wealth."

Nahleh thought to herself, "No, he'll be satiated, I'll make sure of it." She remembered the story of the woman wearing shorts and sunbathing in her backyard. She thought that the sun would burn her fair skin, however, and that she'd look like a peasant. The realtor was attracted by her fair skin, as was obvious in his flirtatious words to her, "You fair one, you duck, you balouza."

Balouza, balouza, what a blessing, she will take care of her balouza, enrich it, embellish it, and improve it until she dies. But she won't die because she will live with all her senses, she will make up for what she lost in the past and she won't give up. If his children won't accept her, let them go to hell. If his wife will be upset, let her be upset. Her father will go crazy, but why? It will be a legal marriage according to God's commandments. Is it a sin? A crime? All the madhahib approve of it as long as there is a marriage contract. She will answer her father as she usually does, "So what?"

He remarried, although he is older than she. She was doing the same thing he did. She will marry and have a home of her own and a husband. What a pity, if she had been only ten years younger she could have become pregnant and given birth to a baby boy. But now it's too late, what a pity. Well, what could she do, this is better than nothing, as the proverb goes, "Better the smell than nothing."

Her stepmother told her, sounding her out, "Anyone who takes a second wife while married isn't a human being. Your father waited many years before he remarried and he did it because he was lonely. Your engineer brothers were in Germany, you were in Kuwait, Mazen was in Beirut, and Said had married and lived in Nablus, while your father was left alone at home. Destiny brought us together, it was a coincidence, and were it not for loneliness, he wouldn't have remarried."

Nahleh neither looked at her nor replied, pretending not to have understood or even heard her, making her stepmother carry on, saying, "A man who isn't good to the mother of his children isn't good to anyone in the world. Anyone who takes a second wife while married isn't a human being."

She felt like telling her, "Very well, I understand, enough, enough," but she didn't utter a single word and went on cutting the green beans slowly, pondering. She recalled her youth spent reading and educating herself during the 1950s. She tried to remember the names of the most prominent writers of that time, Khaled Muhammad Khaled, Rose al-Yusuf, and other thinkers. She was full of ideas, some forbidden, others permitted, some pure, others impure. She was conservative, strict with herself, and judgmental. She considered sacrificing herself for the happiness of others a great quality, and selfishness a vice. The love of one's country was, according to her, the noblest and the greatest feeling in the world, while the love of good deeds was part of her love for God and so was her love for her family. It brought about her parents' blessings, the utmost blessings in the world.

Nahleh lived for others, doing good deeds and showering her family with her love and affection. She gave to her family generously and promptly, never expecting anything in return. She believed deeply that giving was an expression of kindness and a form of payback. She gave her homeland what she could, donating significant amounts of money. Once she even donated a bracelet worth two hundred dinars and never regretted it. She wept for the wounded, the orphans, the failed revolution, and for Mazen, her lost brother who traveled aimlessly between airports and in the trenches. She felt that her donations were inadequate because while the fidai gave his blood and soul, she gave only a piece of paper. She cried and regretted not being a man so that she could join Mazen in his struggle for the homeland. She would have given everything and held nothing back, like him. She and Mazen were always different from their siblings, and her father used to say, "Nahleh and Mazen are not only brother and sister but they are made of the same stuff, God be praised!"

It was during those moments that Said used to ask his father, "What about us, what stuff are we made of?"

His brother the engineer usually replied, saying, "You are made of a special and unique substance."

A fight would usually ensue, which would soon settle down with everybody admitting that Nahleh and Mazen were superior to the others, made of a stuff that valued honesty and self-sacrifice above everything else.

Where was Mazen now? Where were honesty and self-sacrifice? "Both you and I paid for them, brother," Nahleh thought to herself, buried her head under the blanket, and cried bitterly.

Nahleh felt an even greater sense of suffocation on the second day with her brother's presence in the house due to the curfew. He gave orders and behaved like a sultan. He was insufferable as he sat before the television and began his list of orders, asking for coffee, tea and sweets, specifically 'awwameh and zunud al-sitt. He wanted everyone to eat with him. His wife went back and forth, moving with great difficulty, muttering angrily, "Damn this life, how disgusting it is. When your brother stays home I suffocate. He gives orders and bosses me around, reducing me to a shuttle at his service."

Then there were the children, Oh the children! The children of the genies and the devils must be quieter than them. They raised hell in the apartment and the building. Their mother, Ni'meh sent them out to play in the stairwell to get rid of them, but they littered the stairs with banana peels, pistachio skins, and torn pieces of paper. They tried to make a kite but didn't succeed: the tail got caught in the rail and when they tried to free it, one of them fell on the glass and broke the solar heating system's reflector. The young brother with a perpetually runny nose rushed in to tell on his brother, saying that Tareq had broken the tub on the roof. Said went crazy with anger, swearing at the children, at their religion and that of their mother and father. Back from inspecting the roof and still huffing and puffing, he sat on the couch and began complaining. He compared his wife to an owl and her children to dogs, like their maternal uncles. He ranted against a slow market and the dire economic conditions in the country.

"May God be praised!" said Nahleh, "I thought you were fine and the factory was doing well, with a lively market. What's happening? You're complaining like in the past. Is this more of the same old tune: my beloved sister, Nahleh, I need a few bucks? Well brother, no more of this talk. I'm not a stupid girl anymore, leave me alone, you've bankrupted me. Get off my back. You've milked me like a cow. I'm not the Nahleh of Kuwait, like you all I live on the West Bank now. I'm not even like you, you have families, wives and children, you don't need anything. It is I who has needs, so don't talk to me about compensation, my compensation is in a saving deposit account and won't be broken, no matter what you say."

Nahleh's words didn't put an end to his complaining. Both he and his wife went on talking. Nahleh didn't hear a word they said, she wasn't listening. She acted as the proverb says, as if she had an ear of mud and another of dough. She complained and told stories about the Gulf War, the aggravations of life in Kuwait and unemployment. She carried on, saying, "A spring that is not fed dries up, and brother, you are well aware of the situation on your father's farm and your brother Mazen's condition. As for me, I spend the whole day doing nothing, I'm not used to being at home, all my life I've worked and I've been active. Now I find myself doing nothing but housework, sweeping and cleaning, washing and making pickles! I'm about to explode, this kind of life is killing me. Am I going to stay home after having spent a lifetime working?"

Her brother looked at her with deep ire, angered by her tactic—instead of sympathizing with him and listening to his complaints, she reversed the situation, making him listen instead of whining. What a scheming creature, he thought to himself, but he didn't say anything. When it was time to eat, however, he didn't give her special attention as he had yesterday. He neglected to overfill her plate, refrained from giving her the best piece of meat, and the most delicious pie. He was gloomy, didn't talk, and opened his mouth only to eat, burp, and admonish members of his family. He threw disagreeable words at his wife, and addressed a litany of commands to his children, telling them to eat without making noise, to stay still and be quiet. He swore at them and threatened to smash their heads. He slapped one of the children, making him cry. The room was in an uproar for a short time, then fell into total silence, it felt like a grave.

What a gloomy place. What an atmosphere, thought Nahleh—a place more akin to a prison cell. Her sister-in-law was staring at her, angry but curbing her resentment. She blamed Nahleh for irritating her husband and putting him in a sullen mood. Had she offered to give him money to solve his financial crisis, he wouldn't have been so irritable and wouldn't have taken it out on his family. She was stingy and greedy despite all her money. Whom was she saving it for? She had no children and she won't have any. Who would inherit from her, her father with his failing projects or her womanizing brother surrounded by scandals? Had she had children she would have understood, but she isn't married and has no experience with children. She sits on a treasure leaving her family at the mercy of the sun and the rain. Our apartment is supposed to be a home, but is it really one? A room on the roof, even a concierge's room, a bird's nest would have been better. The apartment drips and floods and there's stone only on the façade, but the rest of the building is made of brick, which leaks all winter. Had she been kind she would have given her brother money to buy an apartment to protect him, his children, and the mother of his children. But the Hamdans are good for nothing, except feeling haughty. Damn this family, they think they are somebody, why? Because their name is Hamdan? So what?

That evening her sister-in-law did not make up the guest bedroom but told her, with a sullen face, "I left a mattress for you in the living room, and I have no more gas for the space heater."

So Nahleh spent the night in the living room and couldn't go to sleep until everyone went to bed and the television was turned off.

When Nahleh returned home to Wadi al-Rihan she experienced indescribable joy. First, she had escaped Said, his surroundings, and his disgusting family life, and then she was pleasantly surprised by the unexpected visit of her brother, the engineer who lived and worked in Frankfurt. He didn't seem happy to see her, however. She wondered what was the matter with him? Did he know about her story with the realtor? Had he been told about the compensation she'd received for her work in Kuwait, and had he come to tell her, like Said and all of them had done before, "Beloved sister, I need some money"?

Or was he here to study the situation in the country like other businessmen, and catch the worm before the veterans arrive? Of course he had, he had come to be the first to take advantage of the promising conditions for the future. The conferences of donor countries presaged great benefits for some. There will be those who give and those who collect as a result of such promises and generosity. A time of solace and manna looms at the horizon. All one had to do now was stretch out under a tree and wait for the fresh honeydew to drop into one's lap, in abundance. More important was the realization that one had returned to the homeland, the promised land, and the land of rendezvous. The returnees would usually bend down and touch the earth with their forehead, and declare before the cameras and the journalists with tears in their eyes, that the homeland was like the lap of a mother and without it they were nothing. They would stay with family members and be treated like sultans, eat msakhkhan, mansaf and tamriyeh, and knafeh on top of all that. Between invitations they would go to the city to study the conditions of the market and make sure that the family was holding its own. They would ask about the price of the land, the cost of a dunum, that of an apartment, the rent for a storage place, and a shop. They would ask about the down payment and be shocked by the amount, wondering why a storage that looks like a stable in a street that resembled a dump was rented for thousands of dinars. They wondered whether people here thought the returnees owned a bank,

94

or printed banknotes, rather than being humans. They had endured hardships, labored like everybody, and gave as much as anybody did. While some gave their blood, they gave money, and the revolution took away everything. Now, they wanted a share in the cake.

Incensed, my uncle said, with a smile, "A cake? A cake! Is this what the homeland represents for you? Is this what we've come to?"

The engineer said, by way of an explanation, "Father, why do you want to turn it into a tragedy? This is reality, this is life. Did you want us to give our money and our capital to the occupier? Ha, ha, ha, look who's coming!"

When Nahleh entered she hugged and kissed her brother. They exchanged news about Nablus, the security belt around the city, and the demeaning experience of being cooped up in Said's house with his wife and his unbearable children. She whined and sighed and praised God for her recovered freedom and leaving the house with her sanity intact. She had never seen children like them, filthy and lacking good manners. She wondered how he could live in such conditions, having been raised in a clean house.

"Let's not go on about him, let's return to our discussion of the market," said her brother. He then turned to his father and asked him, seriously, "If we want to start a project, such as building a factory, would you join us?"

His father replied smiling bitterly, "Me, join you? I have no money and no capital, I have nothing but my farm, and as God is my witness, the farm is not a help, but a source of worry."

The engineer replied in a realistic and intelligent manner, "Then sell it, and with its price we can build a factory, a very good factory."

His father shook his head and said sadly, "This is crazy, at my age and after all I've seen and endured for the land, do you want me to sell it on the open market? I would rather die. As long as I'm alive on this earth, this land will not be sold. This farm has been in the family from father to son, it belongs to us, to the Hamdan family, whoever sells it will incur my anger. I will curse whoever sells it from my grave."

Mazen said reassuringly, "No father, who would dare sell it? Kamal is only joking."

But Kamal turned to his brother explaining his intention, "No, I'm not joking. Good people, be realistic, nothing will pull this country out of its mess but industry and industrialization. You're holding on to the land as if it were something sacred! Let's see, what does the land bring you during the cucumber season or the cabbage and the tomato season? As for honey, the Honey of the North, do you sincerely consider it honey? It's far from being honey! You live here in this camp on the West Bank and you don't know what's happening in the outside world. People have gone to the moon and reached Mercury. They've built hydroponic farms and produced tons of vegetables through infusion. The sapling is placed inside a bottle and it becomes as big as this house producing a ton of cucumber, and here you are talking about the land of my ancestors, the Hamdan's farm. Forget the farm and all this nonsense, a small factory would be better, or if you want, we can have a farm with a greenhouse."

They all fell silent as if the raven of gloom had perched on their heads. What could they tell the engineer, that he was lying? He wasn't lying, he was educated and informed, he was well-traveled and knowledgeable about science and industry. He had specialized in chemistry and geology. They, on the other hand, were in this condition because they had lost touch with civilization. They knew that the outside world was either a paradise or a world of djinns, while they lived in a prison, a big prison. They had become like cave men after a quarter of a century under occupation and the years of the Intifada with the chaos it caused.

The engineer turned to Mazen and asked him, "What about you, would you join in?"

Mazen looked at him surprised, and asked, curiously, "Me, join in?"

The engineer replied, enthusiastically, "Yes you, who else, why won't you join in?"

Mazen explained, with a hesitant and stupid smile, "How would I join in? With what? I have neither money nor capital."

He turned to Nahleh, winked at her and said, "I didn't leave Kuwait with a compensation, either."

Nahleh replied, "Well, well, well, it's your turn, Bint Hamdan. We're back to the usual story: Dear sister, beloved sister, would you lend me money to get through this difficult time? Get off my back, you disgust me. None of you has a claim to the compensation. By God, I won't join such a group."

Mazen said laughingly, "Come back, come, why are you running away?"

The father and the two brothers laughed as well.

The following day, the engineer heard the same story from visitors who filled the house. He insisted however, wondering, "Is it possible, Father, that you refuse to sell a small piece of land that is two to three dunums in size?"

The father replied angrily and stubbornly, "I won't sell even half a dunum, or a speck of earth, or even a mint growing near the pond."

The visiting realtor started paying attention and began his calculations. Those words are worth thousands, what did they say, two to three dunums?

The engineer said enthusiastically, "I have already said that modern agronomy does not require dunums or hectares. You can plant the largest tree in a small bucket."

The father asked, surprised, "Since the land has no value why are the Jews killing themselves over it?"

The realtor asked, curious, "But why are you upset?"

Nahleh explained, gently, "They want Dad to sell, but he doesn't want to."

Her father heard her and replied, sharply, "I'm not a seller or a trumpeter. He who sells his land sells his soul, and I'm not selling."

Mazen intervened saying, "Alright, alright, Father, who said sell?"

The realtor understood and began shifting his eyes between the brothers and their beloved sister, between the father and his beloved daughter. In brief, the father wouldn't sell the land, which means that the deal wouldn't materialize. Why should he bother then? There was another deal, rather two deals in one, the factory and industrialization. This is a period of industrialization, when everyone was singing the praises of industry and industrialization. The West Bank would become the Hong Kong of the Arabs, and Gaza would be the Taiwan of the Middle East. All this would happen with industry and scientists. The engineer has the knowledge and he, the realtor, has the money. If he were to combine his money with the knowledge of the scientist, the industrialization project would be in his pocket. The realtor, son of a shepherd and a peasant, would become the owner of one factory, then factories, and later a prominent industrialist, with an educated wife from a prominent family who knows about perfume and caviar. He turned to Kamal and asked him seriously, in a sharp voice, "Do you want a partner?"

Everyone paid attention and silence fell on the place. He added, "I would be your partner."

Nahleh smiled smartly and whispered to herself, joyfully, "By God, he is a man, the best of all men, a planner, that's what you are, my man."

The news spread like lightning, like a fire in dry stalks. People were saying, "Abu Jaber's son and the realtor plan to build a factory as big as this country. Abu Jaber's son is like the Germans, he studied in Germany and is considered a genius. He was always the best in his class. He was ranked first in the high school exam and received a scholarship to study in Germany. When the Germans discovered his brilliant mind they kept him in their country."

People were respectful of countries that took care of their bright youth, but they resented the fact that their countries would be left with the garbage. They repeated constantly, "Those who have brains run away overseas, to study, work, and live, but for whom? For the others, and only the useless, the worthless, and the helpless stay in our country. But aren't we exaggerating? Look at Mazen, one of Abu Jaber's children, he was the best and most handsome of them all, he was called Mazen Guevara, Mazen Hamdan Guevara, his fighter's name. Enough about Guevara or Barara, we've had it with theories and meaningless talk, we want to breathe, to live, to have streets in good repair, we don't want streets that look like those of a stone mine or a fish market. Everything is broken, torn, and worn out. There isn't a clean street, a clean house, or clean air. This is no way to live. Let's see, does this genius engineer work like the Germans or is he more like his brother—full of himself and delivering only words? You say he's like the Germans?"

When the nature of the factory became known, people were astounded. They said, "By God! Are you kidding? I can't believe it, man, what are you saying? Is it possible? A recycling and sewage factory? Are you serious? A factory to can garbage? Can sewage be canned, as well? Like beer? You don't say! Oh man, God is great! A factory to can sewage, garbage, and scrap iron. Who buys it after that? Who eats it? Will the garbage be used as fertilizer and the sewage water for us to drink? Don't talk nonsense, is this all Abu Jaber's son is offering us? Is this what he brought from overseas, from Germany? A recycling and sewage factory? What a story!"

The news spread from house to house and from one caféé to another, and around the city stores. The conversation went this way, "A sewage factory and a shit factory, this is what Abu Jaber's son brought from Germany. It means that your shit comes back to you in a can like the beer can and you would drink it and get drunk from its smell. This is how Germans are, this is a science, sir. This world is crazy! What's worse is that the realtor was fooled by the project and believed the story. He's going around bragging to everyone that they're working for the future, for history, for the people and the country on the best project ever. But did the best project have to be a shit project? A project to can garbage and shit? Garbage in sardine cans and shit in sealed bottles! A factory for canning garbage!"

Kamal's problems didn't end with the people's comments. He faced serious resistance from the municipality, whose position puzzled and shocked him. When he applied for the permit the council was divided; half of its members agreed and the other half objected. Those who voted against the project argued that garbage was public property, like sewage, the sources of water and springs. If Abu Jaber's son was allowed to open the sewage, scoop from it and industrialize it, how can we guarantee that another engineer would not ask for a permit to open the springs and the water reserve! Water is, naturally, public property belonging to the municipality and to both sides of the government, the Palestinian Authority in power and the authority over its power, in other words, an authority that rules but doesn't govern. If a person satisfies the Authority, he might upset the power, and if the power is not pleased, it will not trust you or provide you with facilities to deal with the environment and its sewage. It won't even allow you to enter the municipality. As a result you would become entangled in multiple layers that would only lead to headaches.

To make a long story short, the counsel was internally divided, and Kamal, Abu Jaber's son found himself fighting a battle he didn't understand. He didn't know the reason for the delay in issuing a permit. In his mind things were very clear: everyone, on both sides of the political power would benefit from the reduction of garbage. The German-educated engineer truly did not understand the way things worked over here and what knowledge meant. He did not comprehend the logic of the bureaucrats, that of the administrators, the security officer, and all those entrusted with such matters: the protectors of the green line, the red line, and the color of blood, the blood of the Israelis. All that meant stepping into layers of interaction much more complex than the layers of the earth. Abu Jaber's son was familiar with the geological earth layers because he had studied them in Germany and received the highest grade in the subject, but he didn't know these other layers because he wasn't gifted in that art. Such gifts are either innate in a person or can be picked up from one's environment, then assimilated. Kamal's environment, as we know, didn't prepare him to work in this field because he was brought up by Abu Jaber and educated by the Germans.

The realtor, on the other hand, was qualified and had made his money using the system. He had bought the land from the peasants for almost nothing and had sold it at the price of gold. He had acquired experience and a good knowledge of people, both in the rural and urban areas. City people were of a different kind, there were the rich and the poor, the honest and the dishonest, but there were fewer of the former and more of the latter. It's possible to sort them out and discover their true intentions by waving of a dollar. It then becomes easy to buy and sell and acquire anything for a price.

The two partners sat in an office facing a computer, a fax machine, and a cordless telephone. Feeling grim, the engineer exclaimed, "I can't understand, I'm either crazy or retarded! It's only a permit, a plain, simple permit. Look at the quality of the offer, the machines, the sophisticated designs, even the Germans said that they were a masterpiece, but the ignorant council doesn't like them and says that they're incomplete. Incomplete! How can the designs be incomplete? Their brains are what's incomplete. They're ignorant, illiterate and corrupt."

The realtor stared at his partner with the piercing eyes of an eagle, those of a merchant and a real estate agent. He knew that he would face many problems with his partner because of his naivetéé and stupidity. Despite his university education and his brilliant project approved by the Germans, he was stupid and conceited, stupid because he believed that knowledge and maps alone suffice, and conceited because he described the members of the council as ignorant, as if it were a shame to be ignorant! Let's see who's ignorant! To test his partner, the realtor said, "Come with me to learn the art of real work."

The engineer looked intently at the realtor and saw before him nothing but a heap of angst, a legally blind old man, yet he was a man who could see well through his seemingly closed and malicious eyes. When he aimed his eyes at a target, he hit it with the force of a bullet. He wasn't that old either, his colored hair didn't indicate his true age. His erect stature exuded liveliness ever since he had fallen in love, so that he now appeared even taller than Mazen Guevara. His quick, hopping walk was definitely faster than Guevara's, forcing anyone walking with him to run to keep up. No one could keep pace with him as he climbed the stairs of the Custom Offices or the municipality.

The distinguished engineer thus found himself tagging along with the realtor, climbing the stairs of the municipality short of breath, moving from one office to the other and from hallway to hallway, shaking hands, saying, "Thank you," "Excuse me," "Whatever you want," and "Amen." This German university graduate was imitating the realtor, echoing his words like a parrot, saying, "As you like sir," "I owe you, tell me sir, what you want."

When the realtor would say, "There is an abundance of goods and people are supportive of one other," the engineer would echo his words as if dazed or bewitched, repeating, "People are supportive of one other." He would then see the banknotes roll above and under the table, in the hallways and behind the partitions. Then, suddenly, and without much ado he held the permit in his hand. He was extremely happy and ran down the stairs of the municipality laughing and shaking his head, saying to himself, "What a story! What a permit! What a people and what a municipality!"

The realtor watched him, smiling and feeling somewhat sorry for him, as he said proudly, "Let this be a lesson for you, Mr. Engineer!"

There was a frenzy of projects, everyone thinking of nothing else, talking and dreaming projects. The citizens and those relocated, and even the settlers thought of nothing else: how to seize the opportunity during this construction frenzy, in an atmosphere of peace and a general aversion for the poverty caused by wars, the Intifada, chaos, and broken bones. They were seeking projects with a guaranteed and quick gain. This was the question on everybody's mind as they rushed to be the first to seize a long awaited economic opportunity. They were impatient, repeating the same story everywhere: "We are fed up with words; today, only money talks. Let's see, do you have a project? Do you want a partner? Count me in."

Everyone was swept up in a whirlwind of activities, in projects needed by the country, whether they required cement, bricks, aluminum, or iron. There were housing projects, hotels, parks, restaurants, some small, some big, one for grilled food and chicken, and another for tikka and tandouri with spice, and tikka without tandouri and spice, a pizza restaurant, and an all-salad, falafel, ful, and shawirma restaurant. Why all those restaurants, people wondered? It appeared that the government had liberalized the import market and made it custom free. This meant that cement was available for all and so was aluminum, but it was better not to even think about a textile factory or dream of opening a canning factory. Where would one find a lot to plant and water to irrigate it? Even cucumber is imported nowadays and so are corn, zucchini, and okra. Everything is imported tax-free. Everything is open at present, everything!

People scurried to projects that specialized in providing services in tourism and food, with no other aim but financial gain. The dream of industrialization, the Taiwan of the East, Korea, and Hong Kong were things of a past filled with obsolete dreams. Others, in Moscow, Cuba, Iran, and Algeria had similar dreams that were like delusions at first, then turned into nightmares; let this be a lesson for the renegades.

Mazen surprised me with a new project. Pointing to his head, he said, "The project begins here."

According to him, the mind is man's treasure, the most valuable of our possessions. If it moves, we move, it is the leader. He told me stories about the effect of the camps on the minds of the youths, he said that education in the camps is the latest earthquake, and he wondered why we shouldn't try to shake people up? So we started planning for the project. It consisted of a large house or an old abandoned castle that we would renovate and transform into a cultural center, a home for intellectual and artistic activities. That same evening we told my uncle that we were looking for an old castle to bring the past into the present, to refresh people's memories through art and culture and prove that we were still there despite failures and a maze of losses. He looked at us and asked, bewildered, "Art and a stage? With spectators looking at us? Is this how low we have fallen?"

I immediately started working on the project. I found a castle, or rather a fortress, located on a forgotten hill between Natanya and Wadi al-Rihan, overlooking valleys and mountaintops. The place had been inhabited by a tax collector during Ottoman rule. We could see the lights of the sea, those of the port, the western fog, and the clouds of winter from its highest window above the stable, and from the soldiers' rooms and the guards' rooms. Fall was beginning to reveal itself on the hills and in the trees, we could see the apricot leaves looking like gold leaves under the sun before they broke and fell. Then came dust and wind from the west, blowing drizzle, accompanied by the warmth of the sea and the taste of salt. After the drizzle, the weather cleared up and the sun returned resplendent, covering the valleys in red.

We renovated the courtyards of the fort and redrew the partition of the open spaces in the hallways, the rooms, and the entrances. We transformed the stable into a theater, and the cells at the entrance of the fort became welcome stands and ticket booths. The roof above the wheat storage rooms and the soldiers' cells became a summer caféé and a cafeteria. As for the reception hall and the garden, they were reserved for musical performances, summer festivals, and poetry recitals.

Mazen commented on the project in these words, "They defeated us through the war but we will defeat them with our culture. This is a cultural struggle."

I smiled, as despite my doubts I had no other choice. What would I do other than go back to America and return to a life of estrangement? That was definitely not my choice.

Mazen said again, enthusiastically, "By God, this is cultural struggle!"

I smiled, exasperated by Mazen's ability to give things, events, and situations unusual names that sounded almost like advertisements or slogans lifted directly from a decree or a pamphlet. His stripping things of their innocence and freshness by giving them those names often disturbed me. Yet, when I remembered how he had been brought up, how he had lived, and how he had been defeated, I told myself to get control of my emotions. He has had the satisfaction of having lived the glories of the revolution and of having given to it generously. He didn't hold anything back. I don't care how he was brought up or how he explains things, what counts is his ability to give generously. Let him call things whatever he likes, what counts now is action.

We were dreaming of a grand opening with music, a play, poetry reading, folk poetry, and dance. We wanted a festival that would bring the notables of the country and artists from all over the world. We knew, however, that this dream couldn't become reality before the end of winter or the beginning of the following summer. It would take time to pave the mountain roads, to level the fields, to prepare the parking lots, the entrances, and the booths, as well as the halls and the cafeteria. All that required the efforts of hundreds of workers and technicians. Yet, in spite of the availability of workers due to the closure of the West Bank and the hiring of Koreans to work in Israeli factories to replace the Arabs, work didn't advance fast enough because construction materials were difficult to find. We were faced with many problems in connection with the telephone lines and the sewage pipes. Visitors created a problem as well, first my uncle came, then Nahleh, Kamal, Said, Umm Grace, and the realtor. Then there was Violet with her undecided and melancholic personality, besieging me with looks of doubt and anticipation at seeing Mazen springing back eagerly to action after his past apathy. Was I the cause of this enthusiasm? Was the work in this castle the cause of the interruption of his visits to her? Had I invented the idea of the cultural center to take him away from her? She didn't ask me these things in so many words but I could read the questions in her eyes. Then came the day of the confrontation, the day the accounts were settled, an unforgettable experience and one that opened my eyes about Violet, Nahleh, Futna, and myself, that is, my future here as a single woman without a man.

In the dusk of a dark day I sneaked from the back door of the house, far from the watchful eyes of the family, and went to Violet and Umm Grace's house. I passed by the living room and saw its large iron door wide open while the glass door was closed. When I turned the knob to go in however, the door opened easily. I found myself in the reception area, lit only by the faint sunset light that filtered through the glass door. It revealed white sheets thrown over pieces of furniture, hair dryers and a computer. I couldn't see much, but I felt that I was in an environment different from that of a rural town like ours. There was a touch of taste that had no relation to this northern part of the country and its semi-rural nature.

I heard the sound of a guitar coming from inside and I followed the melancholic tunes played in a slow, sad beat. I walked in the dark, guided by the faint light until I reached another glass door that was left ajar. It led to a small garden that separated the reception area from the rest of the house. There, I saw beautiful Violet from behind the door, sitting on a swing that matched the beach umbrella and the garden chairs.

Her face wore a grave expression and she was totally absorbed in her own world. I knocked lightly at the glass door to avoid startling her, but she didn't move. Her hand moved up and down in harmony with the musical notes. When I knocked a second time, she looked up and saw me but she didn't move or return my greeting as I waved to her. I pushed the door and entered slowly, walking quietly, as if crossing the halls of a church or a library that had an echo. I sat on one of the chairs in total silence and remained there for a few minutes without opening my mouth. I closed my eyes and almost fell asleep in the growing darkness, trying to escape an overwhelming inner sadness. I don't know how much time passed before Violet opened her mouth and talked to me. I don't know whether those were the first words she said or whether what I heard was the continuation of a conversation she had probably started before she'd heard me or, maybe one she had began inside herself. She was saying very slowly, "No, it isn't Mazen. If you had asked people whether Mazen was the reason, I have told you it's not he, despite what you've heard. I'm telling you, it's not Mazen, he was never the reason for my mood swings. The reason is inside me, I always build palaces in my dreams. When I go to the movies I imagine myself the heroine and if I see someone who resembles one in my imagination, I build up his image, which continues to grow until it fills my heart and my being. He becomes a giant and I move according to his wishes. I later wake up from my self-delusions and discover that those were my wishes, not his. I keep repeating the same mistake and I play the same role. Each time I'm left with a broken heart and a confused mind I tell myself: You are the cause and no one else. You build palaces and mountains in your imagination, you swim in a sea of delusions and drown in it."

She went on assessing her responsibility, "I cry for one or two months, I lament my luck and hate myself and others, until time heals my wounds and helps me forget. I find myself falling into the same trap over and over again. Because I endure so much and I'm so apprehensive, I often go on for a year or two and sometimes longer, without falling in love. I run away from everybody including, possibly, the right person. The nuns used to say that I was gifted, do you think I act this way because I'm gifted? But all girls are like me, even ordinary girls who never react to a beautiful sunset or to a beautiful melody. Do you think that Nahleh would conduct herself like me? I'll bet she would, though she pretends to be strong and a good girl. She too is guided by her imagination and illusions. Is her story with the realtor different from mine? She must be laughing at me, saying that I'm stupid, yet if she opened her eyes and saw herself and the realtor clearly, she would laugh at herself, she might even cry. I'm sure she'll cry a lot like me. I don't blame you for Mazen's indifference, nor do I blame Salma from Lebanon. Mazen Hamdan is responsible for his situation just as I'm responsible for mine."

She continued without giving me an opportunity to answer her, "I don't know why I'm telling you all this, you of all people. I know that Mazen is in love with you, or rather he thinks he is. Mazen falls in love with all the women he

106

encounters in his life, that's how he is. But Mazen can't relinquish his independence, even to you. He has to fall in love with every beautiful and intelligent woman and she has to love him back, he pursues her until she falls in love with him. When she does, he runs away, inventing stories that he repeats constantly until jealousy drives his victim crazy. I know that Mazen wishes he were strong, that he had the power of a magician to handle all the women he meets. The reality is completely different, however; in the area of women he's a loser on all fronts."

I opened my eyes to grasp the meaning of her words. She said, affectionately, looking at a chair as if watching a live person sitting on it, "He would sit there after sunset, and we would talk and listen to Fairuz or rather I did, since he prefers *al-Atlal* and always requests it. The first time he asked to listen to *al-Atlal* I thought I understood his message: there was Salma, Beirut, and the revolution, but now there is no Salma, no Beirut, and no revolution, they've become ruins. The singer would go on singing: 'Has love seen intoxicated people like us?' repeating the sentence many times and he would repeat it after her. Listening to her singing was like listening to him sighing. Every time I heard the song my heart would melt and I would feel drawn strongly to his world. I used to spend hours listening to the song and repeating its words, interpreting them in various ways, laughing, crying, wondering, and daydreaming, abandoning myself totally to his power.

"His song became my song, or rather my nightmare, he controlled me through it. Strangely enough, I felt as if every word she sang was addressed to me, personally. This is how Mazen was and that's how I interpreted his feelings. As I came to know him better I felt betrayed, cheated, and deceived, but who had deceived me and who cheated me? Do you understand what I'm saying?"

I shook my head without saying a word, but she didn't see me in the dark. She didn't wait for my reply but continued to talk uninterruptedly, "I want to go away, to America, to forget all this, not only Mazen. He was only part of the problem, which kept me away from life. I lived in a world where I have no friends, where there is no club or any way to meet people. All those I see at the beauty parlor are women, of course, and in most cases, housewives with no experience and no brains, or young newlyweds who, intoxicated with their happiness or confusion, do not say a word from the moment they enter to the moment they leave. Mazen was like an oasis in this desert, I held on to him like a drowning person holds on to a piece of straw. Mazen is indeed a straw, I knew it before he even returned to the West Bank, as his story with Salma in Beirut was known to everybody here. Yet, I fell in love with him and became attached to him, believing that with so much pressure and his new situation he would change and become more productive. All he did was break my heart, hurt me, and make people talk. He hasn't asked after me since the day he left, and my poor mother thinks it's because of you. It's not you or another woman, and it's not something happening now, this is how Mazen is, and he will never change. He's a defeated man and he's changed me into a defeated person."

I responded in a broken voice that sounded as if it came from another person, "Maybe, maybe."

She turned toward me, totally surprised by my reply and ran her hand over all the piano keys at once. The sound they made in the darkness was like the soundtrack of an action film. She echoed my words, saying, "Maybe? Maybe?"

She went on explaining, "Oh, this is exactly the situation, this is what I said and did. I told myself maybe I needed someone to stand beside me, maybe because I was alone and there was no choice, maybe because he was in front of me and close by, and maybe because I thought that time changes us. I thought he needed me because of his leg, he had no friends to talk to, friends who would understand him. Maybe, maybe, this is how we always think when we need someone; we say: When the conditions change, people change. No my dear, people do not change when the causes are internal, and Mazen is defeated, internally."

I said, regretfully, "Are you sure?"

She knocked on her guitar and said, "Of course I'm sure, I'm a hundred and one percent sure, but I only wonder whether his inner defeat caused his outward behavior or vice versa?"

I asked, confused, "How can we know?"

She answered, absentmindedly, "The future will tell, but unfortunately, I will be far, very far away."

Futna had come especially from Jerusalem to invite Violet and Umm Grace to a huge party in Wadi al-Joz. Futna's pregnancy was at an advanced stage, she was big and breathed heavily. Her face was covered with sunspots, making it look like a sieve. We advised her to hold the party at a hotel to avoid exerting herself, but she insisted, with undoubted sincerity, on holding it at her house. She intended to use her recently renovated terrace, covered with pots of jasmine, and her beautiful bamboo chairs and lamps. My father had planned this change before his death, he wanted to see all corners of Jerusalem from the terrace, but he died and Jerusalem revealed itself to other eyes than his.

Futna had insisted on inviting everyone to the party, including my uncle, his wife, and his children, except for Said and his wife. She also invited the realtor, his wife, and Nahleh. She was probably aiming at strengthening her position in the "Sewage Company," the joint venture between Kamal and the realtor, having bought thousands of shares. She probably wanted to win people's affection and appease emotions with the approaching delivery date for the heir, to facilitate the inheritance issue. She might have had in mind the establishment of a connection with Florida, through Violet, as America was a dream of hers ever since she had heard about it from my father. She had visited the United States and had fallen in love with it, returning with a number of suitcases filled with clothes, purses, Canon sheets, and feather comforters.

Whatever the reason, she invited us all to the party and announced very proudly that her famous cousin and some members of the Shayib family were invited as well. There will also be some young men and women, an organ and a guitar player, plus all her artist friends, those she knew from the time of her late husband. The party was expected to last till the morning. My uncle, as expected, excused himself tactfully, as did his wife and the realtor's wife, but the realtor planned on attending. Mazen sent his regrets as well, but Futna insisted and stubbornly requested his presence, calling him at all hours of the day, almost every day. She asked Nahleh, Kamal, and myself to put pressure on him until he finally condescended and agreed to join us. It was an opportunity for the Hamdan family to get out of Wadi al-Rihan, to breathe a little and visit Jerusalem after the closure. Ever since Jerusalem had been separated from the West Bank it had become like another state with borders, entrance areas, checkpoints, requiring identity cards, every sort of formality but a visa. There was something similar called a permit or *rishion* in Hebrew. Kamal had no problem entering Jerusalem with his German passport and so did I thanks to my American passport. Nahleh entered easily because she is a woman and the realtor did not have any trouble, probably due to his connections who could get him any permit from either the Arabs or the Israelis. He could even reach higher, to the Knesset if he had wanted to, but that wasn't his ambition. Rather, he needed the municipality, where he could obtain a permit for the car and its passengers.

We drove in the Mercedes, which had a telephone, two antennas, and three horns. We went together to the party with great expectations of enjoyment and entertainment. Kamel, guided by his German education and his good manners, refused to sit beside Abu Salem, leaving the place for either Nahleh or myself. He sat in the back and I ceded the honor of sitting in the 'seat of death' to Nahleh. It's strange that people here consider sitting in that seat a sign of great prestige, and I didn't want to deprive Nahleh of it. But, as she took so long to make up her mind, hesitating to move and insisting on refusing the invitation, Mazen jumped from his seat and said, firmly, "I'll sit in the front seat beside him."

Nahleh was shocked and so was I, because her brother's gesture was quite meaningful. It signified that the move was unacceptable and a source of possible trouble. It also meant that he was jealously guarding the honor of the family, Nahleh's honor. It might have been the expression of a sense of superiority over the realtor, as well. So, he opened the back door and said to his sister, with a frown, "Sit here."

We sat behind the driver, in silence.

Mazen was very uncomfortable with the party's atmosphere, the way it was arranged, and the formation of small groups of incompatible, disparate people. There was also the obvious upper-class ambiance that Futna had bestowed on the party, to be on par with her famous cousin. She laid the tables on the large terrace with a calculated bias. She placed her cousin's table and those of some of the notables, accompanied by tanned women wearing huge earrings reaching their shoulders, at the foremost point of the terrace. She surrounded them by pots of mallow, basil, and a large jasmine tree over a trellis that made the table look like a throne or a stage. Close by, sat Violet and Umm Grace, joined by a peculiar gray haired man, and a group of other elegant men and women, among them a well-known writer and a female journalist. There was neither trellis nor pots of mallow and basil around their tables, however. Then came the Hamdan table, which included Nahleh, the realtor, and naturally, Mazen, Kamal, and me.

We were at the other end of the terrace, far from the older people who spoke English as I did, the whisky drinkers and the cigar smokers. The realtor did not drink and Nahleh was half veiled, whereas Kamal drank only beer, Mazen vodka, and I, Pepsi. Futna served araq, tabbouleh, hummus, and ful for the artists and their fans, the organ and guitar players, and a large group of young men and women, most of whom were in black, while some wore khakis and jeans. They enlivened the party, sang and danced, then sat on the floor surrounding Violet as she played music. They cheered her on as she sang, they whistled, but then quieted down when she gave free expression to her longing for the distant beloved who disappears beyond the sea.

This is how Mazen found himself, for the first time, far from the center of attention, away from the lights. He felt so alienated and resentful that he considered leaving the party, but Kamal reminded him of a practical reason that would make it impossible for him to leave alone—he didn't have a permit to travel. It was thanks to the realtor and his Mercedes that he was here.

In an effort to lighten up the atmosphere Kamal turned toward the realtor and said, holding his glass, "To your health, Abu Salem," to which the realtor responded surprisingly quickly, "To my partner's health, to the best partner. If I didn't fear people's comments, I would have drunk to your health."

Kamal laughed wholeheartedly, and said maliciously, "You fear people but you don't fear God? Then take a sip."

He took the first sip then a second, a third, a fourth, and a fifth till he finished the first glass, then the second and a third one, while Kamal laughed and Mazen stared at him without commenting. I was watching the scene and Nahleh was smiling as she wished nothing more than to see a relaxed relationship between the realtor and her brothers. This was the first time they had sat with the realtor in public. The company he was establishing with Kamal, their partnership, and their visits to various offices and to the municipality were public matters, that wouldn't raise any suspicion. Here, however, in Futna's house, the Hamdan's daughter-in-law, sitting at a table where alcohol and mezze were served, things were different; it meant that the realtor had 'infiltrated' the family.

If Mazen, or my uncle, or even Said didn't like this situation, the Westernized Kamal considered the party a great success and took it upon himself to help Abu Salem bring down the walls that imprisoned him. He introduced him to some aspects of civilization and tried to shake the hold of traditions on him, pushing him to enjoy himself. He kept encouraging him to drink, one glass after the other, until Abu Salem was like a wet piece of cloth, and his eyes were as red as a ripe tomato. Kamal was in the same condition and they acted like foreigners when they get drunk in an evening organized by Arabs. He stood up and made a fool of himself, he sang and danced and clapped his hands. The singers, the artists, the organ and the guitar players were cheering him on until Futna's famous cousin noticed him and curious, he asked who was this pleasant American. Futna explained, proudly, "He's not American, he's German, he is Abu Jaber's son."

That was how Kamal joined the Bey and the notables' table. Minutes later Futna came to invite Mazen and me to join Kamal because her cousin, the eldest of the family, wanted to know the Hamdan family. I apologized in order to stay with Nahleh out of consideration for her. Mazen accepted the invitation concerned by Kamal's behavior under the influence of alcohol.

When Mazen arrived at the Bey's table, Kamal was talking about his project while the guests were listening to him with little attention, saying politely, "A sewage and garbage project, a nice idea."

Their haughtiness and pretentious attitude upset Mazen who was already infuriated by Violet's disregard of him. Under the effect of alcohol, he said sharply, "We need at least ten similar projects to cleanse ourselves."

Futna's cousin shook his head approvingly, and said, "By God, that's true, other people are improving their conditions, whereas we're regressing daily. There is no concern for social origin and respectable people are not to be found anywhere. This Intifada is killing us and now the Authority is adding to our worries!"

One of them said, in agreement, "Yes, it is the Authority, its true, you're right. . . ."

He wanted to take back what he had said, but he kept quiet and so did the others. Mazen noticed the calm that had fallen on the place, and looking behind him he saw the guests move toward a huge buffet, attended by waiters and maîtres d'hôôtel. One of them was standing behind the barbecue table serving grilled meat from the skewer. Futna came over breathless, and invited them, with insistence, "Please help yourselves, we're among friends here."

The Bey raised his waxy white hand, and said, "As far as I'm concerned, one apple would suffice."

She rebuked him, gently, asking, "Is this possible?"

She then turned toward Mazen and Kamal, saying, "By God, tell me, is it acceptable to diet in such a party?"

The Bey said playfully, "Instead of treating us to food and fat, why don't you treat us to a beautiful girl?"

Everybody around the table laughed, the brunettes whispered to each other, their earrings shook and the eyes of the males twinkled. Then Futna said, generously, "Your wishes are my commands, whom do you like?"

The Bey's eyes languished and he said maliciously, "You know."

Futna replied loudly, "You mean Violet!"

She immediately realized that Mazen and Kamal were present. She tried to recover and explain herself, saying, "It seems that he likes her voice, he finds it intoxicating. He thinks she's a true artist."

One of the notables whispered audibly, "She is like a smack of fresh cream!"

His comment annoyed one of the women, who said, "And you do nothing but smack your lips."

He stared at her and raised his eyebrows, saying maliciously, "I am with you till the morning."

Everyone laughed, Kamal roared and clapped his hands like a happy child, but Mazen kicked him in disgust and said, miffed, "Let's eat, come on, let's get some food."

Mazen stood up but Kamal did not because the Bey had asked him a new question, "Where in Frankfurt do you live? I stayed in Frankfurt for five months before I went to Washington. Frankfurt is a beautiful city, better than Berlin and Bonn, but the Germans are not likeable, although they are hard workers. They built their country after the war in a few years and their economy was second to Japan. They understand the meaning of life, unlike us. We have no people, no taste, no understanding, and no leadership. How are the elections proceeding? Who among you is running?"

Looking at Mazen, he asked him, to test him, "Will you run?"

Mazen answered gloomily, still standing behind Kamal, "No, I'm not running."

Futna's cousin shook his head in a way that expressed understanding, as if he were agreeing with Mazen on his position vis-à-vis the elections. He returned to the same topic to learn more about it, and said, "I agree with you and I understand you, but it's not conceivable either that we leave the country to the mercenaries. If every honest, clean, and respectable person from a notable family turns his back on the country, who will rule it? The riffraff and the swindlers? God protect us from their tyranny, even the Israelis have more mercy, mark my words."

One of the members of the group asked, "Do you think that it hasn't happened already?"

The Bey shook his head, as a sign of despair and regret. What could he say? What's the use of words? What is the use of action? He looked at Mazen and remembered what he had heard about his glorious past. He thought that, despite the difference in their directions, Mazen in this present situation was a partner and an ally and maybe more. Wasn't he from the same social class? From the same category? That of the devoted who gave a lot to the homeland only to be pushed aside by different circumstances and difficult times? They were placed on the shelf, collecting dust and relegated to history books. Is this what happens to families in the North of the country, in the middle, and the South? Even if they were farmers, property owners, and though they don't have good manners and education, they are nevertheless honorable people, with dignity, valor, and respectability, they would kill to protect their honor. As for the riffraff and the gangs, those who come from slums, are those revolutionaries? What a shame!

Kamal asked him, in all sincerity, "Are you running in the elections?"

"Me?" asked the Bey.

Then he stood up, pointed at himself with great pride and fear, and said, "Me, run? That's not possible."

Mazen asked him, maliciously, "Why won't you run, pray tell us?"

The Bey answered with regretful nobility, "Me, run? That's not possible."

Both men stared each other in the eye, examining one another with great curiosity and suspicion. As far as the Bey was concerned, this question raised old emotions that time and Abd al-Nasser, may his soul rest in peace, buried. He was great despite his fall, but when he fell he took us with him. There were nationalizations, insurances, then feudalism and the peasants, the factory workers, the factories that produced tin instead of steel. There were the farms of zucchini, the farms of fava beans, and mulukhiya instead of farms of cotton. What nonsense, what childish plans. No one but the revolution ruined us. Then he repeated painfully and regretfully, "May God forgive you, do you want me to run and spoil myself?"

Mazen turned his face away from him, looking toward the horizon and Jerusalem's night. The Western part of the city was shining in the night and lit the borders of the old wall, the dry valley, and the Jewish cemetery. He whispered to himself, "Who soiled it, and messed it up, who polluted its cleanliness? You're crying over its destruction now? We were young when you became important, and we followed you. Who but you, children of misfortune, destroyed it?" Then he tapped his brother on the back and told him to join him to get food.

Kamal was happy in this elegant ambiance filled with women's perfume and beautiful, slim women whose eyes twinkled in the night. He was drunk and happy and the Bey was nice to him, as he was planning secretly to form partnerships with him in the future. This was a time of projects, like the sewage and garbage project, a new and magnificent idea that might bring in millions. If it didn't bring in millions, it would bring renown, and renown brings followers, and this means power, authority, and the government. Kamal thus became the center of the Bey's attention and kindness, from questions to answers, to stories and commentaries until it became clear that the mutual admiration would end inevitably in friendship. Mazen found himself forced to accept an invitation to tour Jerusalem. He had tried to get out of it with various excuses, but the Bey had told him what amounted to these words: "Jerusalem belongs to us, and he who doesn't know it can't claim it; do you know it?"

Mazen had stared at him for a few seconds and said, defeated, "Alright," and accepted the invitation.

The realtor had drunk too much beer, and his bladder was about to explode. He was too embarrassed to admit it, however, for fear of being seen as a hillbilly, unaccustomed to parties and to the company of notables. He tried to control and distract himself by drinking more beer and touching Nahleh's thigh under the table, and moving constantly on his chair. Soon, he couldn't hold it any longer and nothing helped, neither the movement on his chair, nor caressing Nahleh's thigh, he felt instead like pinching and tearing something. He tried to blow and lean on one side then the other, driving Nahleh crazy. She wanted to cry but controlled herself and turned to me with a tortured look that reflected her endurance and confusion. She wondered what had happened to him, and whether drinking did this to people's brains, making them waver and quiver. Do drunks become sullen and violent, with an inclination to pinch and rip? Even his face was frightening, his sleepy eyes had grown bigger and more bulging, their color had turned into a strange turbid red, burning with an odd shine.

Though the realtor's eyes were filled with desire as well, caused by a lack of control and disregard for decency, Nahleh's inexperience made her see in his behavior a lurking danger menacing both of them. She knew that alcohol was a sin and would remain so, she used to hear about it and see it at the movies and on television, but she had never seen it personally or had been present at a drinking party. Alcohol had never found its way into Abu Jaber's house and she had never learned its rituals, its secrets. This was true of the realtor as well, since he was from a milieu that considered alcohol a sin, a forbidden drink in Islam. This was a first for him, and her brother Kamal was to blame; had it not been for his encouragement and challenge, Abu Salem wouldn't have done it and wouldn't have lost his self-control the way he was now, shaking like a sieve with eyes that looked like those of a hyena. How would she react if he were to begin to shout, sing, and dance like her brother?

Kamal was used to this kind of life, and frankly, he looked charming dancing in the middle of the terrace. As for the realtor, at his age with his suit and matching vest, and his dyed, lanky hair, what if he danced, or held her hand over the table when everyone was looking? What would her brothers do? What would Futna say, and the other people? Futna hadn't forgotten Nahleh's biting words when she announced her pregnancy during the mourning period. She didn't spare her in front of people, in the diwan gatherings and during the readings of the Qur'an. Would Futna spare her in turn, at this party? There was broken-hearted Violet as well, the woman she had criticized and gossiped about, the one she had called an idol worshiper, a piglet eater, and a consumer of forbidden drinks among other things. She had also said that a girl like her wouldn't be fit to be a daughter-in-law for the Hamdans even if she were covered with gold from head to toe. There was Umm Grace, whom she hadn't spared when the subject of a second wife was brought up. She had told her that if Christians didn't take a second wife, it was not out of decency or good manners but because their religion was too strict to allow them that. However, whenever they understood its rigidity, they changed their religion, converting to a more forgiving and flexible one, the way so and so did. Nahleh had also said that being in a polygamous marriage was better than being a widow or an old maid, referring both to Umm Grace and her daughter, who was over thirty and still unmarried—in other words, she wasn't marketable! What upset Nahleh that day was the reluctance of Umm Grace and Violet to explain the meaning of the look they had exchanged followed by a burst of laughter that had lasted almost an hour. There she was, facing her fate and possible dishonor, giving Futna and Umm Grace an opportunity of a lifetime to avenge themselves!

Nahleh felt a new pinch in her thigh and almost fainted. On the verge of tears, she looked at me and said, disconcertedly, "Tell me what to do with him, look what drinking has done to him."

I couldn't help smiling, but she started crying and was scared, not knowing what to do. She pleaded again for help, "What shall I do, cousin? I fear a public scandal! Look at him, poor man, his eyes are as red as smoldering embers and he seems unable to keep still."

I whispered in her ear, laughing, "Take him to the bathroom."

She sighed and the white of her eyes changed color thinking that I was making fun of her. She said in a moaning tone, "Please, cousin, for God's sake, this is no time for joking and criticism, he's about to do something scandalous."

I controlled myself and said, seriously, "Take him to the bathroom to avoid a scandal."

She was still bewildered, not knowing whether I was serious or joking. She looked around her to see if anyone had noticed the realtor's shaking and his odd comportment, but felt better when she saw people's preoccupation with the buffet and the conversation. She turned to me and said, "You too, cousin, are like them?"

I whispered, sincerely, "This is the effect of beer, take him to the bathroom, he'll feel better."

"How can I take him to the bathroom?" she wondered, "If Mazen sees me he would kill me, come with us, for God's sake."

We both walked with Abu Salem between the rows of people till we reached the bathroom. I stood watch at the door while they went in.

Mazen passed by, accompanied by Kamal. They were standing in line for the buffet and I did the same, disappearing in the midst of the guests. I saw Futna and Violet, then Umm Grace and the organ player, whose mother and father she knew. She also knew my father when she was young, studying at the nuns' school. He then left and so did Grace. Now it's the turn of her other children to go, Michel and Fouad, and she'll follow them. God Almighty, America is attracting everybody, they would all go if they could, and they wouldn't return. It's rather strange that I, unlike all those people, am coming from America and not going there!

He came out of the bathroom relieved and relaxed, feeling like a new person, young and filled with an overwhelming love for life. He will go out to the party now and enjoy it to the fullest in Abu Jaber's daughter's company, the woman with legs as white as milk pudding and a nape the color of butter. He will help himself from the buffet, then return to his table with a plate full of strange dishes, some of which he had never thought were edible. He had heard Nahleh tell Zayna the names of the dishes with which she was familiar. She knew their names and had their recipes copied in a notebook. She had collected them throughout the years, continually adding new recipes that she liked. He was staring at her, surprised and ecstatic as she mentioned the jams she liked and ate with butter, while looking at him to remind him that butter was the password between them. He smiled to her in his new state of relaxation, having emptied his bladder when it felt like a waterskin. For the time being he was very happy, looking at his reflection in the mirror, his new face, and smelling his first class cologne bought at the barber's shop near the mosque.

The barber had told him, "Rejoice ya hajj, this cologne came directly from Rome, it arrived only two weeks ago. Smell it, smell it, God is great, it's made of a mixture of orange and European jasmine blossom, quite different from our jasmine blossom, it's smaller in size and its leaf is as hard as wax. But hajj, God is great, the cologne smells like lemon blossom and even better. May God protect you, look how young you look after the coloring, what do you want me to say, people in civilized countries live to be ninety, and you being only seventy, you have twenty years and maybe more ahead of you, you must live them fully. You have money, you're prosperous and healthy, you're youthful, even younger looking than your children, excuse me for saying so. I wonder why nowadays, young people aren't so young looking and lack energy, brains, and stature. They look like worms and mice, though they eat like ogres.

"In our time food was scarce, we had neither cake nor steak, we had no mangos and guavas, but we used to dip a loaf of bread in a plate of olive oil, and felt as energetic as giants. I'm telling you, Abu Salem, olive oil is the medication of choice for all illnesses—for a stomachache, for a sore throat, drink oil. If your ear hurts, heat oil and pour it in; even skin, dandruff, sun spots, baldness, and asthma can be treated with olive oil. Today, however, they give you treatments that are very costly and inefficient: creams, ointments, and pills to swallow, some before the meals and others after the meals, and you keep paying money to no avail. It's all nonsense, trickery, and charlatanry just to get your money. Believe me, nothing is better than olive oil, it helps one regain energy and relaxes muscles. The human body needs oil to lubricate it like a car, it smoothes and softens the bones, the skin and the joints. Listen to me, every day, drink a cup of olive oil on an empty stomach and see how you will improve."

From that day on, Abu Salem never missed a day without drinking olive oil before taking his coffee and dipped bread in oil and za'tar. He stopped eating butter and sheep milk because fat was not healthy and could cause blood clots and blockage of the veins.

Abu Salem opened the door of the bathroom where Nahleh was standing in front of a large mirror. Perfume bottles, small bars of soap like pieces of Turkish delight, and a basket full of small elegant towels were displayed on a marble table in front of her. He didn't know why they were there or even how they were made, but Nahleh knew. There she was, standing before him, applying perfume and removing her scarf, revealing her hair rolled like spirals over her shoulders. When she ran the comb through her hair, this black waterfall, and shook her head in an elegant manner akin to a gazelle or a mare, he lost his mind and rushed toward her with a force acquired from years of drinking olive oil and the recent impact of beer. He dived into her nape while she struggled like a fish to free herself. Suddenly, the door leading to the hallway opened and Mazen saw the scene. Without thinking or assessing the consequence of his action, he grabbed the realtor and pulled him away from his sister. In a professional move he grabbed him, hit him, then threw him like a ball in the middle of the terrace where he landed in front of all the guests.

⟡

We were unable to sleep and dawn found us tossing in our beds like people overcome by fever. Our public scandal surpassed all other tragedies we had endured so far. The fact that it had happened in Jerusalem, among people we didn't know and we didn't expect to see on a daily basis or ever again in our lifetime, didn't help. We were sure that the story would reach Wadi al-Rihan by way of Futna, Umm Grace, and even Violet. It might be transmitted through other guests who would share the story with their relatives. Their relatives would tell other relatives and the story would reach the neighbors, the collective taxi drivers and the bus drivers traveling between Jerusalem and Ramallah, and those traveling between Ramallah, Nablus, and Wadi al-Rihan. It would then journey through the bridge to Amman, Lebanon, and all the way to Frankfurt.

Kamal was dazed and shocked by the bizarre event. He kept saying to his sister, "By God Almighty, ya Nahleh!" as he ate breakfast.

A scientific and organized mind like his found it difficult to understand how a grown woman, intelligent and refined, would establish a relation with an illiterate and uncouth man who had nothing going for him but money. His wife was as big as a Pullman bus, five times Nahleh's size. Kamal wondered if Nahleh had heard about the realtor's children and the number of people they had killed with their own hands on the pretext of cleansing the homeland. Many stories were circulating about family feuds and acts of revenge, which in the present condition of the country turned into strange tales of spying and killing for a price. He wondered whether the Abu Jaber children and the Hamdan family would be brought down by a realtor feigning to be young.

Kamal went on repeating to himself, "By God Almighty, ya Nahleh." He would then look around him, searching for a face that might have witnessed their scandal at yesterday's party. There was no one there but the hotel residents, including tourists and polite servants, who went about their business unperturbed by events, no matter how strange. He was obsessed with a feeling of shame that made him more conscious of his surroundings, and apprehensive of a new scandal, or even of seeing Nahleh's face that morning. But Nahleh was in her room, having refused to leave it to eat breakfast with the family. As for Mazen, he had not said a word since he had sent his famous punch. He had recovered his composure and had become aware of the gravity of his action. Although stupid Nahleh had made a mistake, his crime was more serious; had he been wiser he would have covered up the matter. He claimed however, that the shock made him lose his mind and that he had acted spontaneously, without thinking. He'd lost his composure, bringing shame on his sister, himself, and the whole family. Hadn't he learned discipline and organization from the party system? Hadn't he experienced more trying conditions during which he was able to control his reactions and his body muscles? Hadn't he had to repress his emotions in more difficult situations? Is it conceivable that he had lost his ability to control himself because he had left the Party, or was the situation more complex than anything he had been taught in the organization? Do private matters have a deeper impact on the unconscious than public matters, do they provoke in us uncalculated reactions impossible to predict? No one had told him or even assumed that Nahleh, in particular, would surprise him with this coup. Who would have thought Nahleh capable of all that?

One evening, Violet asked him, "Why do you accept conduct from me that you condemn from your sister?"

He didn't reply but turned his head and whispered, "Because Nahleh is above all other women."

He had discovered that after all these years he had been cheated and stupid. Nahleh was no better than other women or men or above sexual temptations. She probably was only interested in sex—what would otherwise explain her attraction to the ugly realtor? Nothing on earth could convince him otherwise. What would be the other possibility—that Nahleh was in love with the realtor? Why then did she hide when he fell on the floor and rolled like a sack under our feet? Would she have hidden and withdrawn far away had she been in love with him or felt sympathy for him? This sack-like man had stood up, leaned on others, stretched his crooked fingers in Mazen's face and twice repeated, fearfully, "It will be according to God's teaching and those of His Prophet."

People around him had been in shock, surprised by the event, while Mazen had stood alone at the door, his eyes fixed on the realtor, his head spinning and his stomach aching, with a desire to kill and vomit. Then, he realized, as he heard her crying behind the wall, that it was Nahleh, Nahleh, Nahleh. He'd left and soon disappeared.

Abd al-Hadi told them that he was a goodwill mediator acting on behalf of the realtor to ask for Nahleh's hand from her brothers. He pointed out to them Amira's opinion which was shared by others, that Nahleh's marriage to the realtor was in the Hamdans' interest. It was especially good for Nahleh because it would avoid a scandal. Mazen asked, quite shocked, "Does this mean that she will be the second wife?"

Kamal added, nervously, "Will she end her long abstinence by tying her fate to this old man?"

Mazen muttered, "He is also illiterate, ignorant, and a notorious usurer."

Abd al-Hadi Bey intervened to calm emotions, "Good people, let's stay on the subject, how can we deal with this mess?"

Kamal said thoughtfully, "We can talk to her and explain the truth about the man and about her own condition."

Surprised, Mazen asked, "Her own condition?" then added, "What would you tell her about her condition?"

Kamal pondered and stared, not knowing what to say, he had not even meant to say "her condition." He didn't know the reality of her condition. What aspect of that condition would he address? Why would he be the one to talk about her condition while in other countries of the world Nahleh should be the one talking about her condition, and in detail, as women do in conferences, magazines, and newspapers? There are many studies in universities, advisement centers, and support centers for raped, divorced, abandoned women, and old maids.

There are millions of single women in the West, but they're not considered old maids. They're a different kind of old maid; unlike Nahleh, they're free to move around, to use birth control pills and diaphragms, and to have numerous relationships. Each one of them has a boyfriend, or has had at least one at one time in her life. Did Nahleh ever have a boyfriend? Had she had a boyfriend she might not have looked at this monkey. He was as old as her father and even older, but he looked younger because of his tinted hair, his tip-toeing, and his waist-coated suits. She, on the other hand, was still attractive and lively, and if it were not for the scarf she wears, she would have looked more beautiful. If only she were in Germany, if Nahleh were in Frankfurt, things would be different. Kamal stared at Mazen and said seriously, "I must take her to Frankfurt."

Mazen stared at Kamal intensely, and remembered the comments that used to circulate about him: a bookworm, a genius, a man of brains. This is how he had been known before he left; people used to say that Kamal knew only his books and understood nothing else. Everyone felt sorry for this goodhearted young man who worked as hard as a donkey. They believed firmly that he was bright but stupid because of his excessive kindness. Years later, their opinion had not changed. They wondered why this 'stupid man' wanted to take Nahleh to Frankfurt?

Mazen smiled at him and shook his head as Kamal stood up and began to explain his plan, oblivious to the presence of their host, Abd al-Hadi Bey, practically an outsider. He said enthusiastically, "Listen Mazen, I mean it, Nahleh has not been anywhere or seen anything, and because she hasn't see the world she fell for this monkey. Had she left this rat hole and traveled abroad she would not have acted so stupidly."

Mazen stared at his brother, smiled, but didn't comment, which encouraged Kamal to carry on eagerly, "That's true of everyone else and our sister is no different. The problem is that we've gotten used to seeing her as an angel."

Mazen asked Kamal, inquisitively, forgetting the presence of their host, "Do you want to take her to Frankfurt to run around?"

Kamal stood still in the middle of the room, then turned to his brother, and said, "Why not? Let her enjoy herself."

Mazen shook up his head and rephrased his question, asking bluntly, "Do you mean to say that you want to take Nahleh overseas to help her let her hair down?"

Kamal stomped the ground and said angrily, "Good grief, how can you think that way? Haven't you lived abroad and run around? What do you call everything you did and tried?"

Mazen objected, saying, "It's different in my case."

But Kamal shouted back, saying, "No sir, your case is not different."

Mazen raised his hand and shook it in a gesture that expressed boredom and his desire to end the discussion. He had given up and decided to avoid such futile discussions that reminded him of his early youth in Beirut and Tunis. Here he was again doing the same thing in Wadi al-Rihan, in Violet's house, then in Jerusalem, in holy Jerusalem, at the diwan of the Shayib family.

He went on listening to the strange discussion between his brother and the Bey as the latter was beating around the bush, trying to formulate his questions in a roundabout way, asking Kamal, "Are you staying for the project?"

"Of course, of course," confirmed Kamal.

But the Bey insisted, "How will you stay if Nahleh goes?"

Kamal had a simple explanation, "She'll go alone. Nahleh is fifty years old and is capable of taking care of herself."

"What do you mean 'go alone'?" shouted Mazen, "Do you know what you're saying? Is it conceivable that after all these years and at her age we could let her travel alone? She'd die, she'd get lost, she'd lose her mind. What would you accomplish except to add to her heartaches?"

Kamal looked at him intently, and asked, "Is it I who has added to her heartaches?"

He was alluding to Mazen's behavior when he hit the realtor, causing a scandal for the whole family. Mazen lowered his gaze, and withdrew into himself, pondering past events.

Life tests us sometimes, and this was undoubtedly a test for Mazen. Almost thirty years ago, when he was in his late teens he had met a woman in a castle. They ate and drank while she played music and sang. He was dizzy and his mind floated as high as the stars and the cedar mountains. He thought he was in paradise surrounded by virgins, until he woke up one morning and saw the virgin without her paradise. She was sleeping on white, soft satin sheets, lying under him. He was shocked and couldn't understand what was happening to him. He was scared and shaken, seeing her in a different light, as a blood sucking ogress. He withdrew quietly, left the castle and ran to the sea to wash himself in the sea foam.

He saw her again, went back to her, then left again. He used his travels and missions as an excuse for his long absences that were more of an escape. He would dream of her, of being with her, and of being alone. He longed for the company of a young beautiful girl with braids, timid and halting in her walk, a young and innocent maiden, untouched, in the original wrapping. Such a girl couldn't be a member of the party, she would be too young to face frightening situations, too young to be enlisted, too young for politics and for the organization. The women enlisted in the organization were not young. They had been young once, but were soon torn open and changed, turning into a kind we didn't like except for passion and the nights of love, for a quick fling, the duration of a short couplet in a song heard in the pre-morning hours.

The mornings were a different matter, however, and things didn't look the same in the light of day. Daydreams and the depths of the heart were also different. He loved Salma to death, but he didn't die and he won't. He went back to her one morning and said, fearfully, "I'm sorry, things have changed."

She looked away, then walked away, having neither cried nor complained. He called her and said, trying to explain, "Those are the orders Salma, mere orders."

She looked at him and said these last words, "How could we believe that you were free!"

Salma disappeared, and Beirut was lost, and so will Nahleh, Beirut and Nahleh.

The two brothers agreed to avoid mentioning the incident to their father. They took Nahleh aside, tried to instill some sense in her mind and to open her eyes to the situation. They hoped to reach a satisfactory solution but things didn't turn out the way they expected. Two days after the incident Nahleh disappeared. She ran away to Jerusalem, first seeking the Bey's help, then she went to Amira. Her brothers looked for her quietly, but in the end they had to let their father know. As expected, it was a double shock for him as he considered Nahleh lost physically and mentally. He was shaken up and more afraid of scandal than for Nahleh's safety.

I was not surprised by the turn of events, as I had learned this lesson in my childhood and I had never forgotten it, and never will. To them, Nahleh was no more than a minor, a woman who had made a mistake late in life and humiliated them. That was worse to them than the dangers that threatened her. I found it strange to hear them talk about her as if she were a recalcitrant criminal. My uncle would sit at the table, his hands over his head or his eyes and say, mortified, "What did I do in my past? What have I done to you, Nahleh?"

He didn't look around him or even in front of him, but puffed and chewed in silence, and very slowly, swallowing with difficulty, clearly disillusioned.

Said's reaction was overblown, as he swore three times to kill Nahleh and divorce his wife if he failed. She shouldn't think that the world was free for her to do whatever she wanted, with no real men around to react. He turned to his father and brothers and shouted angrily, "You're the cause, you think you're real men? By God I will teach him and her a lesson." Then he turned to me as I was staring at him and said, "And you, you . . . ," but he didn't finish his sentence. He slammed the door and left.

I sat alone, watching them, thinking matters over and reconsidering our project. What project? Would I become like Nahleh here? Or Violet? Would the family become my grave? Is this the price of my inheritance? I wrote in my diary that the members of my family were merely detached pieces in a rusty chain. I had gradually discovered that their ties were not as strong as I had thought or as they wanted me to believe. Their relationship was part of the traditions and was only symbolic. They assumed that because a brother, a father, or a sister were blood relatives, they were their loved ones and dearest to them.

In reality, they lived in their own individual worlds and moved in their personal orbits. Nahleh's world was located somewhere there, in a certain place in this sphere, and so was her psychological world. Her bed at home was always empty, and when she returned every summer she filled it for a few weeks before leaving again. Years passed while she worked in Kuwait and returned as a guest, a summer visitor. With time, her bed in that room and this house became her home, whereas her family symbolized the homeland. Similarly, her colleagues who came from various Arab countries were closer to her than any of her relatives. They would gather around the television in the evening and talk about their dreams and worries, about their families and about working for the others, in this country.

They talked about the brothers and the fathers, the illnesses and those studying in the West. While the sister endured the toz, Kuwait's harsh sand winds, the brother was in Germany, Turkey, or Spain. After graduation he usually returned home with a beautiful wife and in gratitude he would send his sister a letter containing Maria's greetings and thanks for having such a brother. It is Kuwait that the western wife should truly thank, the country that made it possible for that brother to study in Germany. The supporting sisters were usually left with the photo of the brother and his bride standing in front of the wedding cake. It portrayed their happiness as he fed her a piece of the cake on a fork while she gave him champagne to drink. The photos from this or that brother filled the mirror with time, while the sisters remained without a photo.

What did Nahleh get from her brothers? She rejoiced for the married brother, the engineer, the scholar, and the hero, while she remained a mere schoolteacher in Kuwait, teaching the same lesson and receiving the same salary, transferring the same sum of money. Meanwhile, the graduating brother was married with a wife and children, but Nahleh had no children and no husband and no home of her own. Since Nahleh had no responsibilities it was normal that she continued to support the education of the second brother, and the third, and the fourth. What did she get for all that? The joy of the degree and the picture, the teachers surrounding her that evening asking for sweets to celebrate her brother's success? She would buy chocolate or knafeh, and play music to animate the party celebrating the brother's marriage. They would dance throughout the night and when Nahleh returned to her room she saw the wedding picture, the only thing left for her.

Futna called me from Jerusalem to ask about the family. She wasn't in the habit of calling to inquire about me or the family. As a matter of fact, she didn't care about the Hamdans. My relationship with her had remained friendly, but devoid of warmth. She belonged to one world and I to another. She asked me, breathless, "How is Nahleh?"

She didn't wait for my answer, however, and continued, saying, "You'd better come and visit us, come, come."

She was out of breath again, laughed, then repeated her invitation. I had my suspicions regarding the connection between Nahleh's absence and that telephone call. I tried to make her talk to find out more from her, but she avoided saying anything more. She laughed and added, maliciously, "If you want to know, come here."

I made the connection; it was clear to me that Nahleh was there. She must have gone to the Shayib family, having heard about their efforts to intervene to end the conflict. Abd al-Hadi Bey must have arranged matters, for some unclear reason, to move in his direction. He had learned from the realtor that the engineer Kamal Hamdan had asked him to break the company contract. The realtor would have welcomed the move had it not been for the high cost of license fees, registration, and the bribes he had paid. The respectable engineer was penniless and Abu Jaber had objected to the sale of a single acre to pay back the debt. Mazen, on the other hand, was a pauper, having nothing but his salary from the House of Culture and Arts. He was hardly able to pay his own debts, and the money wellspring, his sister Nahleh, had run away. In other words, the house was left without an emergency fund.

It was at this point that Abd al-Hadi Bey intervened and found the fatwa for the subject at hand: the realtor would leave the company and in return, he would marry Nahleh. It was agreed that the realtor's marriage to Nahleh would take place in Amira's house away from the eyes of the Hamdan family and to eliminate any suspicion about the involvement of the Bey. The realtor didn't swallow the bait, however, but pretended to agree in order to get hold of Nahleh. He was planning to turn his back on the Bey and the Hamdan family. Nahleh learned of the secret deal in the making and requested her future husband's share as her dowry, to embarrass the Hamdans. The Bey swallowed the bait and believed firmly that the realtor would end up by leaving and he would then get in.

When I arrived in Jerusalem I realized that the Bey had Nahleh and the realtor in his pocket, while Futna was taking photos of the signing ceremony. I saw the sheikh and the Bey, Nahleh and Sitt Amira, the photo of Abd al-Nasser and Futna's father on a wheelchair, hanging on the wall, while Futna breathless, stood behind the camera. I watched the scene and smiled, fearful!

Said pushed open the door and was met with huge clamor. He hesitated for a few seconds before entering to make out the details of the scene. His shaky eyesight resulting from his weak health and the strong outside light put him at a disadvantage. Nahleh shouted, and I gulped. She was faster than I however, immediately guessing the reason for his visit, judging from his look and the way he pushed open the door. In a split second she stood up and pushed a chair to delay him, then left from the front door and locked it. I was left alone in the kitchen, with the backyard door open while he stood before me in the light but didn't see me. As his eyes adjusted to the light in the room he said to me, angrily, "You're with her too? Of course, of course."

Then he entered the kitchen and began inspecting its content. There was a blender, a juicer, a microwave oven and a baking oven. He shook his head and repeated the phrase, "Mashallah, mashallah, God be blessed."

He slowly opened all the cupboards and broke plates, cups, and glasses. He pulled the china from the shelves, threw it to the floor and caused it to shatter into small pieces, which mixed with the spilled grains and liquids. He later went to the door and began banging on it, and shouting, "Open up, you whore, you bitch."

Nahleh asked him to leave and threatened to call the police if he didn't. She knew, however, and so did he, that there were no police because the country was in a state of chaos without a ruling government or authority. He turned toward me and said, "I'll kill her, you'll see."

He opened one of the drawers, searched its content, throwing everything onto the floor, till he found the biggest knife. He took hold of it and said while waving it in the air, as if trying it, "I'll do it with this, with this, do you see it? Does she think that there are no men in the family?"

Had someone told me that I would return to the past through the tunnel of time, I wouldn't have believed it. The past had become the present with no difference between the two except in the sound and the picture. It was the same scene and the same action. I said, trying to calm him down, "Take it easy, Said, sit down, we need to talk."

He stared at me for a few seconds then he moved away from me, hesitantly. I saw from his look that he wasn't really and truly angry, but only feigning anger because he wanted to do something and prove to the others that he was capable of doing something.

He went back to the door, banged on it as it groaned under his weight. There was silence on the other side, and I had the impression that Nahleh had run away and left us alone in the house. Said was stubbornly determined to act, and his anger was mounting. Every time he threw his weight at the door and then collapsed instead of breaking it, his anger grew and he got more upset, blaming Nahleh for the pain in his shoulder. He was sweating heavily and took a few minutes to rest, then returned to hitting the door with all his force; growling, he said, "By God, they'll both see what I'll do to them."

Suddenly, the door opened and I saw Nahleh standing with a huge gun in her shaky, trembling hands. She was pointing it at us but didn't say a word and went on staring at us holding the gun. The suddenness of her action startled him, he was panting and motionless. He moved toward her, causing the gun to go off. The world shook, I saw light, an empty space, circles, and shattered glass falling like snow, then I felt nothing but a sense of peace.

I wondered how I happened to be in this place, with its low ceiling, its ugly color, an old cupboard, and brown drapes. The view from the window revealed a green fog and tree leaves, while my uncle stood motionless, watching the fog, his head leaning against the windowpane. I was lying in a narrow, miserable bed and about to fall from it.

The door opened and I heard Nahleh say, "The doctor said that everything is all right, the wound is superficial and Zayna will wake up after the injection."

My uncle didn't respond or look at her, while I floated in the fog of the trees and the green leaves behind the windowpane. There were flying butterflies, a light drizzle, and a silence as thick as a heavy veil. I slowly left my body and the oppressive atmosphere of the place and saw rosy hills swimming in the light, a bright silver light and a sunny glare. My soul rose above the clouds and I began to fly. The door opened again and Nahleh said, "The tea is cold, would you like to drink coffee?"

He didn't reply and remained glued to the window giving me his back. The leaves were thick and so was the silence, the covers were white. I drifted back out like a breeze, swimming in the light. There were hills, a horizon, and a slight dark substance in the blue pit forming celestial shapes of unique beauty. What disparity between the two scenes, the internal and the external, between the view seen from the outside and the reality of the place. What a contrast. Silence fell and I went back to sleep.

I awakened to her sobs. She was sitting on a couch near the window while he stood at a distance, his forehead resting against the window. The fog was thick and the leaves were yellow. She was saying between her sobs, "I was defending myself, why don't you say something?"

He didn't answer and she withdrew into silence. I saw her standing by the door, looking at me, then at him. It was a strange look. I felt as if my heart were about to stop beating. I wanted to fly but I couldn't. I opened my mouth, then shut it, I closed my eyes but I didn't dream, I only managed to escape to the wind and the valleys, the almond hills and the art center. Mazen was there and people were coming for the inauguration. There was poetry, singing, music, and storytelling—beautiful stories that the world had told, while I lay down, resting, in silence.

I opened my eyes and saw Said sitting on the couch, the same big, old couch. He said to me, severely, "It's all your fault. She wanted to act like Westerners, like Violet, and Helga, and people on television. You saw and heard everything and you didn't once say, 'Have some consideration.' Had you said something she would have stayed put. Is it possible that she should do all this without being held accountable, why is it only us, only me that has to account for the slightest mistake? Why is Nahleh alone exempted? And now look what she's done, do you like it? Why are you silent?"

I didn't turn in his direction and he didn't look at me. I continued to swim in the silence and the colors of light, the white and the green and a shining light on top of the mountain and the depth of the valley. I saw the Art Center and the bulldozers. Nahleh announced, "Abu Salem is here, he wants to see you, do you want to go down to meet him?"

He didn't reply but I heard him take a deep breath. She closed the door, then I heard Said ask, "Do you want to go down? Why are you silent? Say something! Who should be held accountable? Had I done that how would you have reacted? If you want to go down, then go. If you want to patch things up with him do it, I personally don't care, to hell with both of them. If her brothers don't care, why should I; if her father doesn't care, why should I? Neither Kamal, nor Mazen nor you care, why should I care? If you don't want to talk, then sit down, you won't remain standing. Who are you punishing with your silence? I think you're punishing me and her with your silence. Why don't you answer? Say something, talk, move, sit here."

Said got off the couch to take hold of his father, but he pushed him with the back of his elbow, hitting his wound and causing Said to writhe from the pain. He screamed and tried to hide his pain but couldn't. He moaned and gasped and tears ran down his cheeks. He returned to his seat, breathing loudly. He dried his tears, then said, still in pain, "May God forgive you. You've always been like that with me, what have I done to you? I couldn't bear to see you standing, is it conceivable that I sit and you stand? Suppose I made a mistake, why did you remain standing and silent, you wanted to punish someone, who? I did nothing wrong, but she did. She fell in love and ran away with him and married him without consulting anyone. Aren't we men? Nahleh made a mistake but I didn't. All I wanted to do was to scare her into fearing us. That's how people are, one must instill fear in them. Only those who are afraid of you fear you. Why did we fear you when we were young? It's because we were scared of you. You used to scare us, your hand was faster than thunder. As soon as somebody said a word, a slap landed on his face, I don't know why. Until now I don't know why, what did you want, explain to me, I never knew what you wanted."

The father whispered saddened and dismayed, for the first time, "I wanted you to understand."

His son asked, "Understand what? What?"

The father shook his head in despair, mystified, and said, "That's enough, now is not the right time. Sit down and be quiet."

Said was furious at his father. He said, "You want me to sit down and keep quiet? All your life you've acted like this, all you ever said to us was, sit down and keep quiet, shut your mouth, and then? I don't know what you want? How do you expect me to understand if you don't say anything? How could I understand?"

His father said, desperate and despondent, "And you will never understand."

"Damn your religion," shouted his son for the first time in his life, deeply hurt. Once uttered, the slur burst forth like a projectile and it wasn't possible to take it back. Said cried like a child. His father turned toward him and commented, "I don't understand and he doesn't understand, neither of us understands."

He shook his head and stared at the huge man, his bull-like son and mumbled again, "God be praised! I don't understand!"

His son shouted at him, "What have I done? Isn't this what you want? Jaber is not around and Kamal has the patience of Germans, while Mazen runs around like her and more. You're getting old, who's left to take care of things? Tell me who?"

His father shouted back, "That's why you went after her with a knife? I wish I had died, I wish I had lost my sight, I wish I had buried you all before this day! My own children, Abu Jaber's children, going at each other with knives!"

The son replied, shouting, "But it was she who shot me!"

The father sobbed and said, "You fight against each other, against one another, sons of a dog? Against each other?"

He walked across the room, reached the door and left, alone.

Abu Salem's children, both boys and girls, were up in arms, and as the girls usually have nothing to fight with but tears, their brothers volunteered to do what was needed and made up for the difference. The news of the company shares that reached them was overblown. They were told that Abu Salem had written not only those shares in Nahleh's name, but the lots in the Ghor region, in Anabta, in Sabastiya, and in Nablus, as well. And so it happened that in the middle of the day, disguised men invaded the house, covered Nahleh with a burlap sack, as is done with traitors, and took her to a dark place smelling of blood and decay. They made her sit on the confession chair where traitors face the interrogators before they are tortured, then axed down.

When the news of Nahleh's kidnapping reached Abu Salem and he learned that she was a prisoner of the Black Tigers, he applied for an exit permit and went immediately to Amman. There, the city at least had a police force and an army, security, and a government, while here a victim would be buried without even a funeral. Abu Jaber's children had decided, when they learned about the matter, to hide the news from their father out of concern for his heart condition. As could be expected, Said, whose shoulder wound was still fresh, didn't sympathize with his sister but called her by the vilest of names and held her responsible for breaking apart the whole family. It was therefore understandable when the other brothers decided to rescue her from the clutches of the Black Tigers they excluded Said from their plan. They kept him in the dark as to their movements, the contacts they sought, and the promises they made to return the shares and the real estate to Abu Salem's children. They didn't know, however, how they would actually go about recovering those shares that were already registered in Nahleh's name. They didn't know whether the lots in the Ghor, Anabta, and Sabastiya were truly registered in Nahleh's name. They had the same doubts about his shares in the pumping company and his villa in Nablus. Was it even conceivable that Abu Salem, this weasel, this usurer, would do it? They asked me, but I denied knowing anything about the subject. Who would know what was in the register office but the Bey, naturally, which explains why they ran to the diwan to check with him.

Abd al-Hadi Bey feared the Black Tigers and consequently refused to say anything. Amira, on the other hand, heard about the incident and requested additional information. Accordingly, she made up her mind to support the Hamdans and stand by them in their ordeal. After all, it was in her house that the marriage contract had been signed, uniting Nahleh to the realtor.

"There it is then, he left her and ran away," said Sitt Amira, deeply moved and feeling guilty. Being the second wife in a family with many children has its price. Amira had known it all along. She had lived long enough to have heard many stories of crimes and scandals. This type of marriage was no joke and she should have known better, considering her age and her experience. Why hadn't she advised Nahleh? Why hadn't she, at least refused, the request of the Bey to have the wedding in her house and under her roof, with members of her family serving as witnesses? She was therefore responsible for what happened.

The search for Nahleh was launched while she was a prisoner in old Nablus. That place was like the underground, a world where buildings and rooftops intertwined and the labyrinths and narrow alleys were, in the middle of the day, as dark as the night. People living there were used to the humidity, the overflow of the sewer, the dirt, and the moss. There were beautiful but rundown old buildings and backyards, which constituted spots of light in the darkness. They overflowed with poppy, creeping plants, and the weeds of time, and those resulting from neglect or immigration. The old city was abandoned, or rather semi-abandoned.

During the Intifada the inhabitants escaped the confrontations between the army and the youths, the endless, daily forced entries that oppressed people. Many houses were blown up whenever it was suspected that young men were living in them. At the beginning of the Intifada people gave a lot, they committed unsurpassed acts of courage, and sacrificed a great deal. Everybody, without exception, got fully involved in the battle, but things lasted too long. The situation deteriorated slowly, however, and corruption caused people to withdraw their support. Nothing was left but bitterness and houses locked by order of the army and God's will. Nahleh was a prisoner in one of those houses, in a vault, surrounded by darkness and ghosts, and the memory of torture endured by heroes and collaborators.

Said asked, whispering and a little embarrassed by his attitude, "How did you know where she was?"

No one replied, as the Bey, Kamal, and Mazen were bent over a large map of the old city spread on a tea table. Kamal had brought the map from the municipality for the pumping company project. But it wasn't very useful without someone from Nablus to guide them through the landmarks of the old city and its secret spots. Said said, trying to cajole them:

"I know the city very well, I go there to distribute toffee, do you want me to show you around?"

Mazen looked at him and smiled, thinking that Said was trying to clear the atmosphere. Since Nahleh's kidnapping and the escape of the realtor to Amman, he had been trying to distance himself from any responsibility in the matter. He wanted to prove to everybody that the situation had changed because Nahleh was now held prisoner by outsiders, and he was her brother.

The Bey said, "In old Jerusalem, the Awqaf building is the entrance to the city."

Mazen thought about the idea and found it logical and practical. He said, while still thinking, "That's true, it's possible that this might lead us to the beginning of the thread."

Said was upset and said energetically, "We don't need the Awqaf, the imam, or any of this nonsense. I know all the grocers in the city and they, in turn, know the city well. I know someone who knows every corner, his name is Samaan. Do you want me to take you to him?"

His father became very angry and said, "Why all this beating around the bush, instead of the grocer and the imam of the mosque why don't we go to Abu Salem's house and ask to talk to his children? If they want the shares, we'll give them the shares, if they want her to be divorced, let him divorce her. Let them take the material gains and give her back to us."

Amira agreed, saying, "I agreed with the Hajj, why should we beat around the bush? I and the other women can pay Umm Salem a visit."

Mazen asked suspiciously, "And then?"

She replied with confidence, "She can talk to her sons, and this would be the beginning of the thread."

They all began talking at the same time, each giving his opinion, suggestions, and comments, creating a terrible hubbub. The Bey suggested the Awqaf and the imam of the mosque, while Said insisted on the grocer as a starting point, and Amira and their father wanted to tackle the situation in a straightforward manner. Finally, Amira put an end to the confusion, saying decisively, "Let everyone search in his own way and we'll see."

The group dispersed, each inclined to search in his own way, while Nahleh lingered in that vault, waiting for the Creator's mercy and the help of His creatures.

ᴇᴽ

Mazen tried to search for Nahleh following the Bey's suggestion, entering the city through the Awqaf building. Having studied and understood the idea, Mazen found it to be logical, because the imam of a mosque was nowadays, naturally, the beginning of any thread and even its middle. He knew the people and the city, its alleys and its secret hideaways. This is true as far as the poor are concerned, and today's poor are different from yesterday's poor. Those were the workers, the hired help, and the salesmen. They had read the manifesto and heard the sermons, then joined the organizations in large numbers. Today's poor, on the other hand, were fed up with sermons, slogans, and manifestos. They left the organizations, making the mosque their meeting place and their point of entry. So both men went there.

When they arrived, the imam had just awakened from his afternoon nap and was getting ready for the afternoon prayer. They didn't want to meet him in the mosque or in a caféé because they feared for their reputation, lest the news reach people's ears. What would they say if they knew that Mazen Guevara had visited the imam? Might they not think that Mazen Hamdan, Abu Jaber's son, a member of the political parties and organizations, sought the imam for an amulet or to predict his future? This is what went through Mazen's mind before he entered the imam's house. It explains the great secrecy that surrounded the visit, which he didn't share even with his father. Abd al-Hadi Bey was similarly concerned for his reputation and feared the Black Tigers.

After a slow, polite, and boring introduction by Abd al-Hadi Bey during which he tried to dispel suspicions about himself, the blind imam said, his eyes turned toward the ceiling:

"Son of Abu Jaber, we have heard a great deal about you, but we never thought you would be so audacious as to step over God's law and have your sister divorced from her husband."

The Bey interrupted him quickly, concerned that a misunderstanding would associate him with the apostate, Abu Jaber's son, and he would be accused of defying God's law. He said quickly, "Sidna, God forbid that it ever occurred to him or to me to dare God's law. Mazen is suggesting that each party takes what belongs to it: Abu Salem's children would recuperate their properties and the Abu Jabers, would get Nahleh back."

He then looked at the imam to assess the impact of his words. The imam moved his head to the right and then to the left, a habit he had developed throughout years of chanting the Qur'an and reading the dhikr for the dead. A few moments of silence followed, which Mazen broke with a clearing of his throat. He then asked, patiently, "Kindly tell us where they took her, if you know?"

The imam was clearly shaken, as if a serious charge had been made against him. He asked, "Know what?"

"Where they took her," explained Mazen.

"Where who took whom?" asked the imam.

"My sister, Nahleh," replied Mazen.

The imam said, "He who took her did not wrong her or you, it was all done in God's name."

Mazen looked at the Bey, embarrassed and angry. He was embarrassed to be in this place at this time of day, and angry at Nahleh for dragging the family into this hunt. He was furious at the Bey because he suggested this stupid, useless plan that would lead to nothing.

The Bey intervened, saying calmly, "Sidna, we came to you seeking your intervention."

Clearly displeased, the imam continued to shake his head left and right while his eyes were fixed to the ceiling, then asked, "Intervene for whom, by whom?"

The Bey answered patiently and indulgently, "Intervene with those who took her, Sidna."

When Mazen heard the word Sidna, which to him was a form of cheap imploration, he became even angrier and more humiliated. He considered running away from this situation that neither his mind nor his dignity tolerated. He was hesitant to do it because of Abd al-Hadi Bey, who had taken the trouble to come with him, to inquire and intervene. He stayed put, moving his long legs and watching the reactions on the faces of the two men. He felt doubly humiliated—for Abd al-Hadi Bey, who was embarrassing himself to save

Nahleh, and by the imam's attitude, pretending to be unaware of the purpose of their visit.

Abd al-Hadi Bey continued to use his subtle style and his patient diplomatic skills. He persisted, addressing the imam, "We came to you, Sidna knowing very well that you are able to deal with this subject and these surroundings."

The blind man ranted and asked, in total exasperation, "What surroundings and what subject?"

The Bey explained, "Nahleh's case and the group who kidnapped her."

"What group?" asked the imam.

The Bey lowered his voice and whispered, moving closer to the imam, "The Black Tigers, Sidna."

The imam responded, saying, "What do I have to do with the surroundings? I do not know black or white, I know neither a panther nor a ram, I have enough troubles of my own."

Mazen couldn't take it anymore, he jumped from his seat and said rudely, "All right, let's go."

But the Bey pulled him from his arm and said patiently, "Sit down, sit down, wait a minute."

He sat down, and listened to the conversation of the two men. The Bey was talking politely and kindly, choosing his words judiciously, saying, "You are among friends Sidna'l-Sheikh, and I promise you that if we find her we'll make sure to reward you for your help."

The imam didn't reply, his eyes were still fixed to the ceiling, but he wasn't swaying his head right and left. He was clearly weighing his words.

The Bey asked again, patiently insistent, "Well, what do you say?"

The imam asked, while pronouncing the name of God, trying to win time in order to think, "About what?"

Mazen jumped to his feet and spit out his words, saying, "What do you think of my lost sister whom we can't find."

A sarcastic and malicious smile appeared on the imam's face, as he asked, "Is your sister lost? Do you want me to make a talisman for her? Write an amulet or predict her fate? Maybe I should predict her fate."

"Al-salamu 'alaykum," said Mazen, taking his leave. The Bey tried to stop him, but failed. He shouted angrily, "Is this what it's come to? We've stooped to the level of writing amulets and predicting the future?"

He became suddenly conscious of his voice, realizing that he was in the street. There were no pedestrians due to the siesta time and the heat of the summer. He slowed down and waited for the Bey.

The women searched for Nahleh on their own. We held a meeting during which Sitt Amira told us what to say to Umm Salem and what to wear because our appearance would matter greatly. Our words must be transmitted literally to the kidnappers. It was important, therefore, to be conservative in appearance and refrain from exhibiting shapes, colors, and hairstyles. She said, "We don't want short clothes, or stretch pants, and no make up. Our words must be well balanced in order to convince them that we are respectable people. We will say that Nahleh will give up her rights, is it clear? Do you understand?"

Futna commented in her usual husky voice, "I wouldn't give up my right if I were her. What was written in her name was done by the realtor, that means it's hers."

Violet nudged me in a conspiratorial manner and said, "Is it her right or her price?"

Amira heard her, and said firmly, staring at her, "We shouldn't speak English either. Those people have their roots in Wadi al-Rihan. Do you understand what I mean?"

We didn't reply, but we smiled and looked around us scared and nervous because Nahleh's fate was in our hands. As a delegation of the weaker sex we were facing a situation that surpassed us because the matter didn't concern merely Nahleh's fate but the dire consequences of Nahleh's loss.

Umm Grace said, apprehensively, "Why don't we leave the matter to the men to solve? We, women, no insult intended, cannot face up to the situation. By God, if anyone says 'boo' to me I'll run away and hide like a cat."

We all laughed, including Sitt Amira, but she quickly regained control of the situation and said firmly, "No, ladies, we must be strong and should not let men feel vindicated. You must promise me before God, that at no moment you will forget that this concerns Nahleh. Nahleh's fate is in our hands, is that clear? Do you understand?"

No one answered, as if we had become totally dumb. Yet, moved by the situation, we all said Amen, and went looking for Nahleh.

Umm Salem entered the room swinging her fat, half a kilogram of gold attached to her neck and wearing half a dozen bracelets on her forearm. She welcomed us with a great deal of generosity and anxiety. The situation was indeed unnerving, and contradictory emotions were at play. She was mortified because Abu Salem had taken a second wife, but she was proud of her sons' tyrannical support. The most important element in this specific situation, however, was the realization that she had become the center of attention of all these women who had never visited her before. She was, unfortunately illiterate and didn't know how to dress, talk, or show off. She didn't know how to pretend and boast about her family and their achievements. She came from a family of peasants. Instead of a few sheep and a hen house, she found herself in a house filled with tables and sofas imported from Italy and polished by Abu Mas'ud, the neighborhood carpenter, to bring them up to par with Abu Salem's status. He added a gold string and satin and velvet cushions. There were trinkets made of mother-of-pearl and gold, and a musical cigarette box placed on the end table. There was a piano and a clock with a wooden bird that crowed every five or ten minutes. The curtains were made of pleated bold pink satin, with fringes and golden pompons.

Still breathless, Umm Salem welcomed them, saying, "You have honored us."

Then she sat down, apprehensive, looking sideways at Sitt Amira and Umm Grace. There was an old, ingrained enmity between her and Umm Grace because the latter was in the habit of showing off talking about America and planes, using strange words in English with the clear intention of humiliating Umm Salem and stressing her low social origin. As for Sitt Futna, her case was somewhat more complex, because, despite her blonde hair, her heavy makeup and her revealing clothes, she provoked contradictory feelings. In spite of her reprehensible

142

appearance she belonged to one of the oldest and most respectable Jerusalem families. The imam told them that they had been the keepers of the Aqsa Mosque key since the Ottoman rule, in other words, they were honorable people and from good stock. Moreover, her mother conveyed a sense of awe, with her large, bright and piercing eyes, and her personality.

Umm Salem repeated her welcome, saying once more, "You have honored us with your visit."

Sitt Amira began telling her plainly and frankly that the visit was meant for each party to get back its right, Abu Salem's children would recover their shares and properties, while the Abu Jabers would get back their daughter.

Umm Salem responded rudely, "The house in Nablus before anything else."

"Of course, the Nablus house too," replied Sitt Amira without hesitation.

"The gold and the lands in the Ghor, as well" added Umm Salem, loudly.

"The gold and the Ghor lands, too," echoed Sitt Amira.

"And the lands in Sabastiya and Qalqilya," said Umm Salem.

Sitt Amira approved, repeating, "And the lands in Sabastiya and Qalqilya."

"She must also be divorced three times," said Umm Salem, loudly.

Sitt Amira fell silent and began assessing matters in her head, wondering how Nahleh could be divorced! Was it in Nahleh's power to be divorced? The only one who could do that was her husband hiding in Amman, and even if he should return, would he consent to a divorce?

Amira said, quietly and clearly, in the tone of someone giving a lesson, "Forgive me Umm Salem, let's talk sense. We agreed to the property, the shares, the gold and the house, to the lands of the Ghor and Sabastiya. The divorce, however, is not a matter that we control, even the imam cannot divorce her, only Abu Salem can. In other words, it is out of our hands, it is a matter of shari'a, a matter of the law."

Umm Salem answered, somewhat rudely, "Don't go blaming Abu Salem now. He wasn't aware of what was happening to him, poor Abu Salem, someone must have concocted a magic potion for him, of the strongest kind. Neither the Sumerians nor the imam could undo it."

She then turned to Umm Grace, her face puffed and swollen, and said, "Not even the Orthodox priest could do it. The Sumerian said that the magic was done outside the country, far away and because of the distance it was difficult to neutralize it. I would like to know who did it since Nahleh hasn't gone anywhere or crossed the bridge ever since she returned from Kuwait?"

She looked at Umm Grace, then at me. Umm Grace smiled and whispered, "O my God! O my God!"

Umm Salem heard her and was upset, saying, "Listen, lady, you're in my house and that kind of talk is not acceptable here."

Umm Grace mumbled, fearful and intimidated, "Why, what have I done?"

Sitt Amira finally intervened to placate her and said, "Umm Salem, we are family and people help people. We women are more compassionate toward each other, while men complicate matters, if you do not mind me saying so. In other words, ya Umm Salem, you have men and the Abu Jabers have men too, and if men complicate matters where will we be, God forbid? You are known, ya Umm Salem to be pious, to pray and wish the best for everybody. Would you want to see Abu Jaber languish for any of his children?"

Umm Salem pondered for a while, lowered her gaze, and seemed hesitant, as she sincerely wished everybody well, being a God-fearing woman. She certainly wanted the best for Abu Jaber and every father and mother in the world. She was a mother too and an affectionate one at that. She loved all children, no matter whose they were, even calves and lambs, donkeys and mules. Whenever she saw a mother breastfeeding her baby she felt the milk in her own breasts, though she was in her sixties. Young ones, whoever they were, are pleasant to look at; what endears them to us is their need for their mother's affection. She found baby monkeys, frogs, rats, and snakes very beautiful. When she was about to open her mouth to talk, the door opened suddenly and her daughter entered to serve coffee.

She was about thirty years old, tall and full figured with flat feet. She was wearing a printed dress shaped like a sack that hid her early pregnancy. She sat down and looked around her then said with a thick, hoarse voice, "Welcome."

She stared at us directly, with large, protruding eyes, examining each one from head to toe. She went on staring boldly for some time until unexpectedly, our eyes met. Slightly embarrassed, she repeated her welcome in a thick voice that sounded more like an insult.

144

Sitt Amira resumed her control of the situation, asking, "Ya Umm Salem, what do you say?"

Umm Salem didn't answer her but she turned to her daughter and explained the purpose of the visit, saying, "They're here to intervene for Nahleh. They're willing to return the lots and all the shares."

The girl asked, very carefully, "And the house in Nablus, your house?"

Umm Salem shook her head approvingly, "They say the house too."

The daughter inquired as her suspicious, antagonistic eyes swept the room, "How can we guarantee that? My brother says that we won't let her go until she signs away her rights."

I asked with a great deal of curiosity, "You mean she hasn't renounced her rights yet?"

The woman stared at me with her protruding, antagonistic eyes, but didn't reply. She then looked at Futna who exclaimed spontaneously, despite her mother's admonitions to curb her reactions, "By God, she is brave!"

The daughter's look hardened, but she didn't comment. Instead, she swept the room with an angry look that seemed to project flames. Sitt Amira rushed to take hold of the thread and redirected the conversation to Umm Salem, who was the lesser of two evils. She said to her, "Ya Umm Salem, you are the baraka, a blessing, you are the one who can solve the problem."

Her daughter roared unexpectedly and said sharply, "How can she solve it, and why should she?"

Sitt Amira blinked, she didn't expect the high-pitched tone of the voice and its enormity, but she didn't flinch. She froze and her face turned plaster white. She said very politely, "I know that Umm Salem will solve it because she is good, she is kind, and has a big heart."

But the daughter asked, angrily, "Is it because she is kind that you want to corner her?"

Sitt Amira blinked a second time and said in a seemingly calm voice, "My daughter, this is not decent talk, we are here in good faith."

The daughter shouted, saying, "If you had good faith you wouldn't have come to us. I know why you've come here."

She regarded us with cold sarcasm, provoking our resentment and disgust. She seemed to be shaking off the long accumulated feelings of subjugation that she had possibly suffered, even before her father remarried. She said, "You came to take our pulse, you came to find a way to expose us."

Her mother chided her mildly, saying, "No Rawdeh, this is a shame! They are our guests!"

The girl shouted back, saying, "If they knew what shame meant they would have brought up their daughters well and taught them not to steal men. They would not have taught them shameless manners and exposing their merchandise in the street. It is well-known that men are small-minded and their eyes dazzle at the sight of flesh, painted nails, and blonde hair."

Unconsciously, Futna looked at her nails and her knees began to shake, while Umm Grace turned to her daughter and whispered, "Lets go."

Sitt Amira heard her and said, firmly, "No, don't leave, no one will leave."

Then she turned to the girl and told her firmly and without hesitation, "You have the right to talk and insult us, because we are your guests. Say all you have to say, don't omit anything, I'm listening to you."

The girl waved her hand nervously and returned to her vulgar talk, saying, "Who told you that I was waiting for you to tell me whether you were listening or not? Well, honorable lady, you came here to talk about polite and good things, but what did you say to the harlot who took my father away from us? Did you tell her it was shameful? Did you tell her it was a sin? Did you tell her: fear God, the man has a wife and children, that he is sick and half senile? She has stripped him of the little brain he had left. She used such powerful magic to win him over that even the Sumerians were unable to undo it. Where did you have it prepared? Nahleh has not left the West Bank since she returned from Kuwait. One of you must have set it up outside the country, then given it to her."

Violet jumped from her seat and pulled her mother. The girl laughed hysterically, at her, "Oh, oh, oh, oh! In God's name! Are you embarrassed to hear with your own ears what you have done? Does a person like you feel any shame?"

As she was leaving, Umm Grace wailed and banged the door behind her, saying, "Oh mercy, Oh mercy, what a trap!"

146

Abu Salem's daughter stood up and moved toward Violet. She opened the door and shouted at her back, "Ya Sitt Violet, does a person like you know what is shameful? Go hide somewhere. The stories about you and Mazen and others are known all over the country. Had you and your mother been able to get hold of him you would have taken him away like Nahleh took my father, you would have helped yourselves."

She then turned to Futna with one hand resting on her waist, and revealing her belly, while she waved the other hand, saying, "And you miss, when will the blessed one arrive? When will he claim his inheritance?"

Someone said, "Shut up, girl."

It was Futna who had shouted those words, having lost control. She added, "Excuse me, I mean keep quiet. I didn't say anything because we're guests, but it is apparent that you're rude and that you have no manners."

Abu Salem's daughter stood in the middle of the room, and rudely, showed them the door saying, "Go away, leave, leave."

Futna replied, smugly and stupidly, "I won't leave, let's see what you can do about it"

The girl replied, laughingly, "Oh, oh, oh, oh! By God! Do you think that I'm as kind and stupid as my mother? I'm not like her. I'm like you and I don't care. My husband divorced me when my father took a second wife and signed his fortune away to her. In other words, I'm neither fearful for the baby I'm carrying nor concerned about my husband divorcing me, or my father disinheriting me. I have nothing to lose. If you don't leave on your own I'll drive you out by hitting you on the head with this shoe."

Amira stood up and said in a shaky voice, trying her best to get out of this trap with the least possible embarrassment and scandal, "All right, all right, we're leaving, let's go, Futna."

Then she turned to me as I sat dazed, and said, "Get up, get up Zayna."

We left hurriedly with the insults of Abu Salem's daughter following us. When we got far away from her, Futna said breathlessly, "What a vulgar person, ill-mannered."

Sitt Amira said, patiently, "Let it be, let's think calmly."

We walked for a long time in the alley and saw faces looking at us from the windows and from behind the doors. We heard words such as "children of Abu Salem," "Abu Jaber's house," "Abu Salem's daughter," "the Black Tigers" and "kidnapped her." We paid no attention. We were still haunted by everything we had just experienced: Abu Salem's daughter, Violet and Umm Grace's escape, Futna's stubbornness and her defeat, the calm of her mother in the storm, and the words and the insults we had heard. Futna was steaming again, saying, "What a vulgar, ill-mannered person."

Suddenly, she stopped in the middle of the street, oblivious to people's presence and said to her mother angrily, "I would have taught her a lesson if you hadn't intervened!"

Her mother replied patiently, "Don't be odious, walk straight."

Amira continued walking straight and slowly, then turned to her daughter and reprimanded her, "Walk straight in front of people, they're all watching us."

She then walked slowly, her shoulders straight and her head raised.

Sitt Amira could not sleep despite her apparent calm and self-control. Her sense of the enormity of the situation, her humiliation, and shock robbed her of sleep. She spent the night reviewing the events of the day, what they had said, and what she had said. The words uttered by Abu Salem's daughter made her reconsider her position. They implied that she was divorced because of Nahleh's marriage to Abu Salem, and because of the loss of the inheritance. She felt that her father had forgotten her because of Nahleh. She would lose custody of her baby when he reached the age determined by the law. The poor woman would end up without support and without a family. She had no husband and no father, and she would soon be without a child, and without an inheritance, all because of Nahleh and her marriage. This means that the harm Amira caused to Nahleh by marrying her to Abu Salem was now doubled because of the divorce of Abu Salem's daughter.

How had she, Amira, been trapped in this way? How had she been fooled by this illiterate man, she the educated woman who had attended Sahyun school. He hadn't even had to try hard to convince her of his purpose and his good intentions. Even the Bey hadn't made a special effort to convince her, she had convinced herself because she believed that the protection of a woman, her marriage, and her reputation were the most important things for a family, a means to safeguard its honor. Now however, after this experience, she wondered which family should be protected: Nahleh's family? Nahleh and Abu Salem's family? Do Nahleh and Abu Salem form a true family? Were they married to form a real family? A seventy-year-old man, illiterate and backward, a hillbilly, and a fifty-year-old woman, educated and somewhat refined. He is a real estate agent and a usurer who adores money while Nahleh comes from an honorable family; she had everything she needed and her brothers are true men, educated and respected, they're not after easy money. In other words, Abu Salem belongs to one category of people and she to another, there is also the fact that he is as old as her father and possibly older. What was the purpose of this marriage anyway, to build a family and protect Nahleh? And now Abu Salem had escaped and Nahleh is being held in an unknown place.

The Hamdan family was truly in a terrible situation. They were worried about Nahleh and their reputation in society. They had become the center of attention and their story was being told everywhere. If they were to abandon Nahleh, they would cause a scandal and would be considered as weak as women, but if they were to follow her and get entangled in her problems, they would risk destruction in their confrontation with the Black Tigers.

Whose honor was at stake here—the honor of Abu Salem's daughter or that of al-Hamdan's daughter? The honor of Abu Salem's family or that of Hamdan's family? How could she, Amira, the lady of ladies, as she was always referred to in the family, the intelligent, well-born, and virtuous woman, have failed to understand matters from the start? It was only now that she understood! Only now! What made things worse was the fact that her own daughter was in the same situation. She too was like Nahleh and even worse. What she did was uglier, the ugliest thing a person could do, to become pregnant through artificial insemination in a Hadassa hospital! It was deceptive and immoral. Were those the moral values of the young and the old nowadays?

Amira ignored the matter, hoping that it would be forgotten or that it would disappear altogether. But it was alive and well, growing in her foolish daughter's belly. Oh how silly, spoiled, and stupid she was! She is her daughter after all, but the artificial baby she is carrying has Jewish blood. He will be a grandchild to the Shayibs before God, before society, and before the law. Though he will carry a name different from theirs, he will be one of them, he will be part of her and will be her grandson. This baby is the child of circumstances—were it not for Hadassa, Futna wouldn't be carrying a Jewish baby, were it not for the events, the conditions, the defeat, and the Jews, were it not, were it not . . . .

She collapsed, crying desperately because she had discovered suddenly and after all those years that the souvenir shop and today's concerns had made her forget yesterday's worries, her concerns about the Israelis, about the world and about history. History was one single connected piece and now it was shattered into pieces. It was a song she had often sung with Umm Kulthum, repeating her words with all her heart: "I love it with all my soul and my blood." She felt she was floating above the world, over the mountains of Jerusalem rising high above the clouds, above the Rock and the Dome, higher and finer. She had repeated with Umm Kulthum, euphoric: "I wish every believer loved it the way I do, the way I do." She had felt that her love for Jerusalem was like her love for Egypt, for Khan Khalili, and Bab al-'Amud, both had been born of the same father, the same progeny, and the fetus in her daughter's belly then, was not only a descendant of the Shayibs or of Jerusalem alone but of Abd al-Nasser. When Amira gave birth to her son she had been asked, "What will you call him?" She had answered lovingly, as she listened to Umm Kulthum, "Nasser, of course!"

That was the name she gave to her son Abd al-Nasser; what would Futna call her son? Hadassa? Kahana? Shlomo? That means that her son, Abd al-Nasser, will be Shlomo's uncle, but Shlomo what, Shayib or Hamdan? It doesn't matter, if he is Shlomo Hamdan, he will still be a grandson to the Shayibs. Whatever is done, even if he is called Muhammad or Mahmud, he will be her grandson and Hadassa's child.

The secret is well kept, however, and no one in the world knows about it. It will remain buried in a deep valley like a drop in the sea that days erase, the way the memories of yesteryears are forgotten. That's how life is, it makes us forget what we don't like, we overlook things, we bite the wound, we make believe and then forget. With the passing of days we forget our sorrows and dreams, and we forget reality, because reality changes and never stays the same. With time she'll forget the secret or pretend to forget it and with time she'll get used to him because he's part of her, and he'll grow up with her.

She will raise him the way she has raised all her grandchildren, the way she raised Abd al-Nasser. She will take him with her to visit the tombs of the Shayibs on feast days as she does with her other grandchildren. He will evoke their memory and read the Fatiha for the repose of their souls and those who preceded them and recall that the Shayibs were once the beloved of God, the beloved of Jerusalem and its cherished children. She will forget the past event because the secret is in a deep well, in a remote valley. She will give him an Arabic name, a pleasant one that reminds her of the Shayibs and their glory. She will either call him al-Amin or al-Ma'mun, or al-Nasser, or al-Mansour. What does the poor boy know, he is innocent and can't remember where he came from, and no one in the world will know where he came from, not even him, because he will be the descendent of the Shayibs and the heir of the Hamdans. Her daughter will thus give birth to a secret that will not be known to anyone, while she, Amira will remain Amira al-Shayib who will go on as she has so far, without stopping. She will reprimand her daughter saying, "Walk straight in front of people, their eyes are watching us."

When Kamal, the engineer, accepted the plan his brother had concocted with the grocer Samaan to rescue Nahleh from her captives, little did he know that he would be involved in unprecedented negotiations. It was like the dialogue of the deaf. When Said learned from the women that Nahleh was refusing stubbornly to give Abu Salem's children a general proxy, he came up with a solution to the crisis. He said that the moment Nahleh sees her brothers she would give them the required proxy because they are more worthy of representing her. Abu Salem's children must know that Nahleh has men ready to back her up. When he discussed the idea with Kamal on their way to the detention center of the Black Tigers, his brother stopped and said in disbelief, "Do you want me to be in charge of the proxy, never! If you want to do it yourself, go ahead, but I won't."

Samaan the grocer rebuked them, whispering, "Quiet, lower your voices, this isn't the time for this kind of talk."

The three men crossed over through the sewage of the city, and Kamal was up to his knees in it. He felt dizzy from the overpowering smell of the urine and was suddenly struck by the thought that this mixture needed millions of liters of clean water for treatment. Where would he get so much water for his project? Then he remembered what he had heard at the municipality, people explaining that the Oslo Agreement did not provide them with a share in the water. They would have to pay, in dollars, or in stocks and bonds, for the water they needed. But the capital invested would hardly cover the cost of the equipment, the buildings, the pipes, and the cost of digging and drilling. And what about the cost of clean water brought from Tiberias or even the River Jordan? What is the solution then? How will this mixture be treated? Why hadn't he realized before now that the sewage of this country is not as beautiful as that of Frankfurt or Berlin? In Frankfurt the sewage isn't disgusting like this frightening lethal stuff. If you hit it with your shoes it hits you back like rubber because of the shortage of water. What will you do then, Kamal? What was the use of all the efforts when the source of life was missing?

He stood still in the dark, but Said called him, frightened, "Come quickly, or we'll lose our way."

He then recalled that Nahleh was still there, captive, while he, his brother Said, and the grocer were on their way to her, carrying with them through this mixture, the hope of her freedom.

The scent of chamomile and lemon blossom wafted in the air as the moon shone on the walls and the tops of the houses. Seen from this angle of the courtyard, Andalus was more like a dream. Kamal was overcome by a sense of elation and guilt, as only a few moments ago he had been knee-deep in the oozing liquid, having forgotten the other dimensions to this country and this people, its shining moon and chamomile and lemon blossom.

He had forgotten that there were people above the ground and a sky over the ground and higher than life. What will he take away from this life but kindness, good deeds, and the love of virtue? What would he get from this world and from a life in exile? He had worked many years in exile, in sophisticated laboratories that looked like space stations, he had been given all the advantages, but he had never felt like one of them. The Germans gave him a house, cars, and a bank account, health insurance and a pension, yet every morning as he rode the university bus or the metro, he felt his loneliness and an estrangement that never stopped growing. It was as if a huge tree with crooked branches and black roots had wrapped itself around his neck, his entity, his forgotten dreams, and his nostalgic heart. Something down deep inside him called out to him at times, while he worked, drove his car, or listened to a new Arabic song that a colleague had brought back from home. He would go on listening until he forgot that Helga was his wife and that he would grow old with her at his side.

This is not nationalism however, and attachment to the nation and the land had never been his concern as it was for Mazen. He had always felt that the world was work and that work was the essence of life. He had believed that life was his laboratory and his laboratory was everything in life, it was its temple. He adored work and gave it his best, it elated him and he experienced the blessings of overcoming his limitations and his constraints. This process had taken years and had been preceded by hunger and a loaf of bread for a meal. When he had achieved everything he had striven for, he had been struck with a different kind of hunger, a hunger for an activity that would light up the earth and a desire for a country whose cleanliness did not depress him.

Oddly enough, the shiny garbage bins in Frankfurt had moved him, filling him with a sadness he had not been able to understand. Was it jealousy? Was it regret? He had not been able to tell, but he had been amazed by the peaceful feeling he had experienced in his car while driving through country roads outside Frankfurt, smelling the dung, the grass, the roots of trees, listening to Fairuz singing for the green mountain, the breeze, the pine trees and Baalbek's roses. He had then felt the scent of Wadi al-Rihan fill his nostrils, spread through all his limbs and restore his heartbeat. He had wondered about all the longing, the sadness and the ability of his heart to love. How could he have forgotten, while working in his lab and on his daily jog, that he still longed for those horizons, for the shade of the evergreen cypress and the narcissus? Strangely, everything looks better from a distance, more colorful, greener, more delicious, and more melodious. The narcissus here was smaller than the European narcissus but it was more beautiful and more delicate. Mint, chamomile, lemon blossoms, and fruits tasted better here. People in Germany complained about tastelessness caused by genetic modification—was this the reason then? The explanation is that in a world dominated by shades of color, and despite his fairness, he was black under his skin. His heart beat to the rhythm of the flute and the taste of dill eaten under the trellis and the fig tree.

One of his colleagues had told him once, after a trip to Syria and Egypt, "People there are better than us, they have voices, scents, and dreams, whereas we have lost our voices. We're surrounded only by the noise of machines. We have lost our capacity to dream and we smell only of deodorant and cologne."

Looking at his calves, Kamal smiled as he remembered the smell of the sewage and the suffocating smell of carbon dioxide. He felt a certain sadness and thought to himself: Better than them? Then he saw Said climb on Samaan's shoulder, hold the rails of an upper window, and heard him whisper fearfully, "Nahleh, Nahleh."

A tear fell from Kamal's eye and he thought to himself, "This is what I came for!" Even Said was risking his life and his safety for a lost sister who had shot him in the shoulder; who, over there, would do the same? There, everyone was by himself, an isolated, forgotten island. Except for your wife and the children, you have no one and nothing to count on but yourself, your money, and your work. If you slow down even for a second, the wheel and the machine will crush you. Over there you're like a beast attached to a wheel in perpetual motion; you don't have the right to be sick or feel tired, you don't have the right to be bored or to rest. You aren't allowed to make a mistake or give in to your moods, to be compassionate or emotional.

He wiped a tear away and shook his head. He'd thought he was a scientist with no emotions, but here he was crying like a woman. Like a woman? Yes, like a woman, like Nahleh. He recalled the tenderness he'd felt when he rested his head on her chest. He searched for it in exile and sought worldly things in their world.

He was supposed to have been struggling for our world, what had happened? Where had he taken a wrong turn?

He had written to his father saying, "Father, their world is merciless."

He had received an angry reply from his father who wrote, "Don't make the mistake of coming back. I have enough dealing with Mazen and his problems. Here, we have unemployment and war worries. Please, please, for my sake, be wise and do not make rash decisions."

He stayed wise until age fifty, but now that he was getting older and entering middle age, the age of despair, he wanted to recover his ability to feel. He wanted to live among people who were not born in tubes, to eat fruits free of chemicals, to sit at caféés and on sidewalks, and to eat knafeh and tamriyeh. He wanted to forget his life in exile, he wanted to do the right thing.

Kamal heard threatening words, warning him to remain still and keep silent, he then felt the tip of a knife thrust in his back. There was commotion, shouting, and Said was swearing loudly. Kamal tried to run in a different direction but he was hit on the head and lost consciousness. When he awakened Nahleh was standing near his head, crying quietly. She was dipping tiny pieces of paper in water and placing them on his forehead. Their eyes met but she whispered to him, "Hush, don't talk, rest."

She sat down, lifted his head, placed it on her lap, and caressed his hair. He looked around the place and in the darkness he could see a small bulb hanging from the ceiling. The old stone walls were black, revealing signs of fumes. The ceiling was dome-shaped and had long windows with wide sills and frames. There was a circle that looked like a pool in the middle of the room, an iron chair and chains stood in the center. Nearby, a large piece of iron that resembled a hanger was suspended from the ceiling. There were torn ropes everywhere, on the chair, over the barrel, and over the distant platform.

Kamal asked Nahleh, compassionately, "Is this where they tied you up?"

She didn't reply but pressed her hand on his chest and whispered, "Hush, don't say a word, just rest."

He was silent for a moment then remembered something and asked her, "Where is Said?"

She replied, cautiously, whispering, "Maybe they took him, I haven't seen him. Just rest, don't say a word."

They fell silent. But he said again, affectionately, "Said was here, he came for your sake, rest assured that we all support you."

He felt her fist stiffen, then she began to cry, while rocking him like a baby. His tears gushed again like a woman's tears, but he didn't try to hide them. When she saw his teary eyes, she said surprised, "You're crying? Is it possible, you, Kamal crying? I never dreamed or imagined that I would see you cry one day, not you."

He asked, lightheartedly, making an effort to smile, "Aren't I human?"

She looked at him intently and said, "You certainly are, but you're different from the rest of us, you've always been different."

He asked her, curious, "What do you mean 'different'?"

She got a distant look, rocked him again, then fell silent for a while, before saying in a broken voice, "I don't know, I don't know, maybe because you have always been distant."

"Me, distant?" he asked, surprised.

"I mean that you were always alone. Jaber and Jamal were the oldest, Mazen and Said were the youngest, I was close to my mother, whereas you were always alone with your books. You were the best in your class and the children called you bushnaq. You used to play football as well, you were either with your books or playing football."

Nahleh turned his face toward her and asked him, "Do you still play?"

He felt sad because he'd spent a lifetime without play. He had squandered years of his life running, but now he felt eager for change. He was searching for himself and wanted to live. He wanted a woman that fired his emotions, a project that motivated him and awakened his abilities. Look at Mazen, he took risks, fell in love with many women, braved death, and roamed about in foreign roads, airports, and world capitals. Mazen was adventurous and lived his life, but what about him, what had he taken from life? What had he given? And now, when it's time to give and take, he finds himself in this place, what's this place anyway?

156

He asked his sister calmly, without showing fear, "What is this place?"

She whispered, "It's an old soap factory that they took by force and transformed into a prison and a torture chamber."

He raised his head and asked her, "Were you tortured?"

"No, no," she said, "don't worry, just two or three slaps. Your sister isn't just anybody. By God, I will not sign and give away my rights. They wanted me to sign away everything. They believe that their father has signed all his fortune to me but, by God, he only wrote the shares in my name, nothing else. His children don't believe me, I swore to them by God and the Prophets and the Messengers, but they still didn't believe me. One of them looks like an imam, the other looks like you, as tall, but dark-skinned. Those two are nice, but the third one is like a beast. He used foul language and was quick to slap, a slap that makes your head turn and twist, like a wheel. I don't know how I got into this trap! Their father left and didn't care about me, he's too scared to come back. What a coward! Is this how virile men behave?"

Kamal smiled at the description and remembered Abu Salem at the party when he had rolled at their feet after the punch he received from Mazen. But he quickly remembered that he was in prison with his sister and that they wouldn't leave until she signed away her rights. He wondered where Said and Samaan were, then said, pitiful, "Poor Said, I wonder where he is?"

She didn't respond and wondered how it could be that Said had come in person to rescue her from this prison. She asked, doubtfully and somewhat surprised, "Is it possible that Said came for my sake? Is it true?"

"Why not?" asked Kamal.

"Well, don't you remember the day he came after me?" she asked.

"Of course I remember it, how could I forget? Truly however, it was he who brought me here. Without him I wouldn't have done anything. It's thanks to him that I came. I wonder where he went," said Kamal.

She whispered in disbelief and amazement, "Is that possible?"

Then she looked at him and said, "I can't believe that you came either!"

He looked at her, casting back to his memories, remembering what Nahleh had meant to him. He recalled a winter evening when their mother was very sick, and the doctor was called. When he entered their mother's room he took Nahleh with him, while his father stayed with them in the living room, reading Qur'anic verses and praying for God's forgiveness. Nahleh went back and forth in the house, without a moment's rest. She was still a teenager, but was acting like a mature woman, cooking, washing clothes, cleaning the house, and looking after her sick mother. She was the true mother in the house, while Mazen was the spoiled child and Said, poor Said, was the black sheep of the family. One day Kamal had asked his father what it meant to be the black sheep of the family, and their father had said, "It means the rotten fruit on a tree, and Said, the bull, is that fruit."

Kamal had then turned his head and seen Said listening to his father, expressionless. Had he heard his father's words? Had he understood them? Was he sensitive enough to react? Kamal had told his father, "Dad, Said heard you say the rotten fruit of the family."

His father had shaken his head and said, despondently, "What can I do with him? I have enough to handle with worrying about his mother and Nahleh. Look at the poor girl, look at her, the whole day she's as busy as a bee, while you all spend your time playing in the alley."

Kamal had asked if he could help, feeling guilty and lost. His father told him, "Don't do anything, just pay attention to your studies. I want nothing from you but for you to succeed in your studies and make me proud, not like this one . . . ."

He had pointed at Said, while Said had sat looking at him, his mouth open, his eyes expressionless. At this moment Nahleh had come out of her mother's room and said, in shock, "Mother is dying!"

Mazen and Said had started crying, but Kamal had run to his room, taken his book, his ruler, and his coloring pencils, and stood near the windowsill reviewing his lessons. He hadn't understood what he was reading but he'd kept on reading. Nahleh had entered the room and hadn't seen him; she'd sat on the edge of the bed and cried. When she saw him she smiled and said, feeling sorry for him, "Don't worry, Mom is fine." But he had left the room and stayed by himself.

Kamal asked her, curious, "Did you like me when I was young?"

She said, hurriedly, and simply, "Of course! Why do you ask?"

"Did you have time to love me?" he asked.

Surprised, she explained, "Yes, of course, you all meant the world to me."

"And do we still mean the world to you?" he asked.

She didn't reply and kept silent. He thought she didn't understand or hear him. He repeated the question, "Do we still mean the world to you?"

She shook her head and said, confused, "I don't know brother, I don't know where my head is and where my feet are anymore. The world isn't what it used to be. My mother passed away and you grew up, my father remarried and I got used to life in Kuwait, away from home. When I returned to Wadi al-Rihan I felt lost, I had nothing and no one special. The world has changed, this is how things are and this is how all people feel. You certainly aren't the same person you used to be. Sometimes I look at myself and wonder whether I was once young, and if I ever lived in this house. I can't believe that I spent more years in Kuwait than I did in Wadi al-Rihan. When I left the house I was nineteen years old and when I returned I was fifty years old, a quarter of a century spent away from you. The world can't remain the same, people change. Remember how you were and what you have become. You were reserved and you used to blush whenever someone spoke to you. Look at you now, may God Bless you, you talk and joke and laugh, you dance and sing and act crazy, you don't care. You've changed and I too have changed, at least I think I did."

He thought about what she'd said and asked, "I dance and sing and act crazy? How do you know?"

She laughed for a brief second then held him tightly, and said, "I saw with my own eyes, I saw you, I saw you."

She remembered that this had happened during the unfortunate party at Futna's house. She feared he would remember the events including the punch he had received, while she stood near Abu Salem. She couldn't believe that she, Nahleh Hamdan, daughter of Abu Jaber, with an impeccable reputation, well-born and wise, had conducted herself in that manner. Couldn't she have found a more suitable place to express her love than the bathroom? She stood facing the sink, in front of the toilet seat, with a man as old as her father, a man who colors his hair and has a partial in his mouth, a man who doesn't know his head from his heels. He knows where his head is, he really does, but not where his legs are and what comes above them. It's truly sad and disgusting. Is this what she had hoped to experience? Why people say it is heaven and love is like a fire with flames and volcanoes? Is it because Abu Salem is a pitiful man and she a fifty-year-old woman? Did he become ugly and old in her eyes after she signed the marriage contract? Or did it happen after the marriage was consummated? Had the situation been different, she would have run away, but where to? To her brothers or back to her father and the women in Wadi al-Rihan? She said regretfully, "Sometimes I wish Kuwait had remained what it was and I hadn't returned here. I wish what has happened hadn't happened."

He raised his head but felt dizzy and placed it back on her lap. He asked, resolutely and seriously, "Would you like to go to Frankfurt to stay with Helga?"

His offer took her by surprise, it was the first time he had invited her to visit him. She felt relief and joy, like a short-lived glimmer of light. But she was quickly overcome with a sense of fear and apprehension, as they both were in a prison and he was there because of her. How could she visit him? There was also the project and the company, would he stay here or return to Frankfurt?

She said, saddened, "What would I do in Frankfurt, and even if I wanted to go, how could I?"

"Do you mean this prison? We'll get out of here, eventually, in a day or two, in ten or twenty days, we'll get out of this prison. When we get out would you like to go to Frankfurt? Tell me, what would you like to do?"

"What I would like?" she asked.

"What I mean is, do you want to stay with that man?" he asked.

She replied, hesitant and uncertain, "Isn't he my husband? Even if he fled for his safety, he's still my husband and I'm his wife, and a wife has to endure hardships."

"That's nonsense," said her brother, "all this talk about patience and endurance. As if you haven't had enough. What do you want with him? What do you like in him? How have you fallen in love with him?"

She turned her face away and said sadly, "I don't know, brother!"

He was overcome with resolve and lifted his head, this time without feeling dizzy. He faced her, saying firmly, "When we leave here you must divorce him and go to stay with Helga in Frankfurt."

But she objected saying, "Divorce him! How can I do that? Do you think that divorce is easy?"

He said, firmly, "Don't worry, leave it to me."

She exclaimed, concerned, "No, my brother. Do you want me to get a divorce at my age, what would people say? Do you want them to question my reputation? Do you want people to say that I married him for the inheritance? Or do you want them to say that I married him just to have a taste of him?"

He asked, perplexed, "What do you mean 'to have a taste of him'?"

She lowered her gaze, embarrassed or sorry, or both. She seemed to regret having said what she had. But he insisted, asking, "Tell me, have a taste of what?"

She didn't reply, saying tersely, "Forget it."

He finally understood and saw the connection between her words and the situation. He said excitedly, "So what, let them say what they want! Is it a shame to have a taste of him? Is it a sin? And what if you did? What business is it of anyone whether you had a taste of him or you didn't?"

"Enough, my brother," she said sighing heavily, adding, "Don't burden me with more anguish and worries."

"I don't understand why you behave like this," he said.

She looked at him inquisitively and defiantly, then asked, "Why can't you understand? How different from us are you?"

He stared at her, but his eyes were roaming in the depth of the place and probing her words. He repeated, absentmindedly, "Me, what about me?" He blinked and said repeatedly, "Me, what about me? I don't know, tell me."

She smiled to him as she noticed his bewilderment and his inability to figure things out. Defiant and conniving, she said, as if revealing a secret, "Haven't I told you that you were never like the others, you were always different?"

"How different?" he asked, curious, as he was beginning to see that he was not like Mazen, Nahleh, Said, and all the others. Was it because of Europe? Because of Helga? Because of chemistry and his work in the lab? Was it his sense that the human being was made merely of matter, feelings, and emotions? The human being working in a lab was nothing but chemistry, Freud, Margaret Mead, civilizations, values, borders, and references.

What could he do to be like the others, to become one of them? What could he do to get close to them and bring them close to him, to change them, to open their minds to the world, to civilization, and to history? How could he explain to them that people are both unique and similar? The human being is the child of his civilization, he eats and drinks from it, he sucks its milk, its values, and it shapes his personality. He eats, drinks, relieves himself, loves, makes love, and marries according to laws, but the excrements are the same everywhere, and the digestive system is the same, the mouth and the orifices are the same. Why then do we worship an orifice or an organ when science has proven that man is in majority water, excrements, gases, and metals? He is a mere tube with an entry hole and an exit hole, and what exists and what doesn't depends on civilization and values. How could he explain to her and to the others that their world was the true one, the world of the individual, that life is the life of the individual and the value of the individual depends on what he accomplishes, not what he rejects. He went back to his original question and asked her, excited and insistent, "So what? Is there any shame in having a taste of him? What business is it of anyone whether you had a taste of him or you not?"

She exclaimed, perplexed, bored, and in pain, "Enough my brother, please don't add to my worries."

He stared at her as she stared at him and whispered, insistently, "You must go to Frankfurt."

The door opened with a loud squeaking sound, causing the two prisoners to freeze, though the door was on the first floor, and they were on the second. The night was coming to its end and dawn had not appeared yet. Nahleh jumped to her feet and whispered, "It might be them, Abu Salem's sons."

She then moved closer to her brother and remained still.

Kamal thought that the time for action had come and wondered what he would do. Yesterday Nahleh had told him that one of the sons was pious, which means that he had a conscience, while the second one had studied in Budapest, which means that he was educated. He was ready to discuss the matter with them and reach an agreement. The first step was to remove his sister completely from this environment and send her abroad, show her a different world. That plan would certainly suit Abu Salem's sons, offering them a radical solution to all their problems. It would put an end to a silly marriage, return their father to his family, and guarantee the fate of their inheritance—what more would they want?

Kamal made up his mind, therefore, to greet them and offer suggestions that would put their minds at peace, thus erasing any doubt they might have. They might even be happy with his offer and feel grateful to him, shake his hand in a friendly gesture, and part as friends, or even partners, since all of them had the same aim. They could take Nahleh's shares and thus truly become his partners.

Nahleh moved away from the stairwell and said, hysterical, "Said is with them, why? What does that mean? Maybe? Maybe?"

She was beating her cheeks with quick, repetitive slaps, and moving in a circle like a moth caught inside a lamp. Kamal sat on the window seat because he felt dizzy again, and was shaken mentally and physically by the surprise. He wondered why Said was with them, why he had returned with them and was behaving like the leader of a campaign? Had he struck a deal with them? Or had the grocer Samaan betrayed him and handed him over in person to his enemies? Was this possible? He remained quiet while his sister clung to him waiting for matters to clear up.

Said stepped forward and introduced them to each other, "This is my brother Kamal, the head of the project, and here are Salem, Hamzeh, and Marwan, and Samaan whom you already know."

Kamal stretched his arm to greet them one by one, holding to the window seat with one hand and pressing his sister's shoulder with the other. The three were silent, their faces stiff and expressionless. Samaan, on the other hand, was moving about, looking for something and appeared familiar with the place and with the people. Kamal felt that he was on their side, working for them. He brought an empty jerry can, turned it upside down and said to Salem with great respect, behaving like a modest employee toward a high ranking government official, "Please, sir, sit down, sit here."

Salem sat down facing Kamal, and in an oblique position in relation to Nahleh. He said gently, "Hello and welcome, this will be the beginning of a friendly acquaintance between us, God willing. Listen to me and praise the Prophet, we want nothing but our due rights. My father is getting old and is becoming senile, he doesn't know how to conduct himself. To make a long story short, the real estate belongs to the family and is its source of income; the Sabastiya lands, those of the Ghor, and all other lots must all be returned, as well as our shares in the company. We understood from your honorable brother (pointing at Said) that you intend to do the right thing and return everything to us, is this true?"

Kamal answered very carefully, "Yes, but . . ."

Salem smiled and said, amiably, "We too have conditions."

Kamal hurried to ask, aggressively, "And what are your conditions?"

Salem stretched his hand in a generous gesture and said, half mockingly, "No, sir, you first, you're our guests."

He then looked furtively at Nahleh and turned to Said, saying, "You're our guests, our relatives, and our neighbors, and I wish we had met in better circumstances and in our homes. We apologize, we hope with God's will to come out of this crisis with a reasonable solution and remain friends, and even partners. Let's hear your conditions."

Touched by his words, Kamal said, "This is a reasonable beginning, presaging good things."

Salem echoed his sentiments and said, truthfully and sincerely, "May God guide us and you, let's hear your conditions."

Kamal thought quickly and firmly and went straight to the point, "My sister must be divorced immediately, now and on the spot."

The Abu Salem brothers froze and so did Said, whose jaw dropped. A heavy silence followed, immobilizing Salem's prayer beads. One could hear the silence of the night and Said's heavy breathing.

Salem said staring at his adversary's feet to avoid looking at him and Nahleh: "I don't understand."

Kamal repeated his words, slowly and clearly, "We want Nahleh to be divorced from your father first of all. We want the divorce immediately and on the spot. What about you, what are your demands, let's hear them?"

Surprised by her brother's request, Nahleh whispered to him, "No, my brother, what are you saying?"

Then Said murmured loudly, "This is not what we agreed upon."

Kamal ignored his sister's words and repeated his condition, "My sister must first be divorced because it is a vile and unlawful marriage."

Nahleh whispered again, in a weak, sad voice, "No my brother, it's not unlawful, it was according to the sunna, according to God's law and that of His Prophet."

The brothers sitting in the background smiled and the grocer turned his head to hide his smile, while Said went on mumbling, "This isn't it, it isn't it, no, no, not like that."

Kamal ignored him again and said firmly and very clearly, "Our second condition is that no one is to represent Nahleh, she is an adult, not a child. Our intention is to put an end to this story and set things right. I promise you that everything will go back to its rightful owner. Nahleh has nothing but the shares and even the shares will be returned to you, I vouch for that. We can remain friends and, if you'd like, partners as well, what do you say to that?"

Salem was silent and still, his eyes were fixed on Kamal's shoes. His brothers sitting in the background were also silent and didn't interfere, but Said intervened firmly, feeling fidgety in his seat, and said, "I'll tell you what they said."

Kamal scolded him and said, "No, don't tell me, I want to hear it from the gentlemen directly."

Angry, Said continued, "But they said . . ."

Kamal interrupted him again, saying, "Enough, Said, let's hear from the gentlemen, what's wrong with you?"

Salem raised his hand gently and slowly, and said seriously and clearly confused, "We're truly surprised. We had come with clear conditions but I'm surprised and I can't come up with a clear answer alone. May I consult with my brothers for at least half an hour?"

Nahleh whispered in her brother's ear and said, "Now they will go and forget about us."

But Kamal told her, hurriedly. "Alright, alright, we'll see."

Salem looked at his brothers, then at Kamal and got up saying. "Give us only half an hour."

He walked away and joined his brothers. They went down the stony stairs to the lower floor, while Said stayed with his brother and sister, and the grocer stood at a slight remove. Said looked at Nahleh for the first time since the bullet pierced his shoulder and experienced mixed feelings. She was his sister and the woman he had defended before God and before the people a few days earlier. He had braved dangers to save her and if it weren't for God's mercy and His protection, he would have been hanged in this place or another one for an action he didn't approve of. He was overcome with a feeling of disgust, hatred, and vindication. He said harshly to his sister, "You were just married and now you want to be divorced? Is this what we've come to, as if we need more scandals and gossip?"

She replied weakly and somewhat evasively, "It is not I, not I, I didn't say I wanted to get divorced."

Kamal looked at her without uttering a word. He continued to watch them, all the while thinking about the conditions that the Abu Salem's sons would offer. He wondered about the malicious grocer sitting in the corner listening to every word they said.

Nahleh turned to him and said, "Why did you bring up the divorce, Kamal? Do you want me to get a divorce at my age? What will people say?"

Said stood close to her, having somewhat calmed down, feeling that he would be able to come to an understanding with her, after all she was the cause of all the problems. Kamal has Western ideas and can't understand them or his sister. Nahleh, on the other hand, despite her shortcomings, has more common sense than he. He told her, gently, "Listen to me sister, Kamal lives abroad and thinks like a Westerner. Our brother thinks that divorce is a simple matter, no my dear, it isn't a simple matter."

She answered, submissively, "I know that it isn't a simple matter, by God I know."

He told her, seriously and almost whispering, "I talked with Abu Salem's sons and I found them to be decent and simple people."

The word "simple" struck Nahleh and made her pay attention. The term meant many things—it meant showing compassion and giving them little importance. It

166

also meant accepting difficult conditions on the pretext that they were simple and decent. Furthermore, it meant that Said was stronger than they and as a result she too was stronger because they were simple. She was all eyes and ears as she listened to him whispering to her, as if he trusted her alone with his secrets.

"Are you listening, my sister?" he asked her.

She replied, attentively, "Yes, I am."

He explained, "That is why, my sister, we have to deal with them according to their limited mental capacities."

She asked, cautiously, "What do you mean deal with them according to their limited mental capacities? I don't understand."

"I mean, and my brothers and father agree with me, that the lands belong to them and the house you live in is their mother's house and the company is theirs too."

Kamal intervened, saying, "No, sir, the company in particular is not theirs, they only have a share in it and so does Futna, but the rest is mine. Have you forgotten? Please explain to me how you reached Abu Salem's sons while I was driven to this place? Who arranged this? Who planned it? Who plotted and executed the plan? Can you explain that to me?"

Said was embarrassed and began to stammer. He said to his brother, "Who do you think I am? Like you my brother, I don't know what happened. When I woke up I found myself in a strange room and Samaan was with me, isn't that true, Samaan?"

Samaan shook his head without uttering a word. Said resumed his explanation, "What's important now is to let you know what they told me. They said that they want nothing but a power of attorney. Nahleh has to sign a small paper before a clerk and everything will be over."

"What power of attorney and what clerk?" asked Kamal.

Nahleh shouted at Said in a strangled voice, "Do you understand what you're doing?"

He stared at her angrily, remembering how she had caused all these problems and scandals. He wondered how she dared to speak. He said crudely, "Let's continue, if you don't mind."

He ignored her completely and turned to Kamal, assuming that she couldn't understand men's talk and serious topics. He said to his brother, "Listen to me

Kamal, they're good and reasonable people, they want nothing but the power of attorney. They even said that they would accompany her to the office of the notary public and would act as witnesses."

"What office and what power of attorney?" asked Kamal a second time, angrily.

Nahleh was wondering on whose side Said was, but he chided her and asked her to shut up.

She replied, defiantly, "What! What are you saying? Isn't it enough for me to deal with Abu Salem's sons, do I have to deal with you too?"

His resentment had reached its limit; he raised his hand ready to slap her and said, "Shut up, don't say another word, you ought to be ashamed of yourself."

Kamal stood up and raised his hand ready to intervene, but Said didn't hit his sister. Their two hands remained raised up in the air while they stared at each other. Then they heard a voice close to them saying, gently, "No, no, not like this gentlemen, is this the way brothers behave? Praise the Prophet Muhammad, people!"

Kamal saw the face of the grocer near him smiling wickedly, and saying, "No sir, not like this," then pulled him back.

He went on saying, "You are the eldest and the wisest, and this is your sister, if you do not mind my saying so, she is a woman after all, in other words, with all due respect, you should solve the problem among you two, do not let women interfere. Had she been my sister . . ."

Nahleh interrupted him, saying, "Who are you and what business is it of yours?"

"What business is it of mine, you say?" He shook his head and continued talking, "No madam, be nice and gentle. What business is it of mine, isn't it a shame, lady? Isn't it a shame, madam?"

Kamal moved back and stared at them, feeling trapped. He couldn't understand this dialogue and who was with whom and for whom. Said shouted at his sister, looking beyond Kamal's shoulders, "Anyone in your position ought to shut up and not say a word."

"Really!" replied Nahleh, hiding behind Kamal. She went on, addressing Said, "Why should I shut up? What business is it of yours? You are neither my husband nor my tutor. I have a husband whose name I still carry, I'm not divorced."

Kamal sighed and said to her, "I thought that . . ."

"It's enough my brother," She then exclaimed, sadly, "I've had it with all of you! One tells me come here, the other go there, and then you insist that I'm an adult."

Kamal was shocked, asking her, "What do you mean?"

He felt the blood rushing to his head and asked again, "What do you mean, I don't understand. Don't you want to go to Frankfurt?"

He turned to her, ignoring Said, and said sadly and painfully, as if she had betrayed him, "You mean that you don't want to go to Frankfurt?"

She shouted, wailing, "What Frankfurt? Am I the type to go to Frankfurt or such places?"

He held her, trying to bring her back to reality, and said, "I want to save you from this rotten place, from these people, I want you to live with dignity."

She stared at him, trying to make him understand and bring him back to reality, "My dignity is safe, my brother, what have I done? Thank God I'm honorable and I did nothing that displeases God. I have a man dearer to me than anything else in this world, and if it were not for these conditions he wouldn't have abandoned me. But that's how life is and, if it weren't for the lack of security here, he wouldn't have abandoned me. What can he do? Do you want him to wait for his children to kill him?"

He stared at her intensely and asked, "You mean you plan to stay with him?"

She then pointed at Said, who was standing behind him and tried to explain her position using her own logic, "If I'm insulted while married, what will you do when I'm divorced and single? He attacked me in my own house and tried to kill me. Each of you is trying to run my life though I don't need you; what would you do the moment I did need you? If I were divorced and went back home, you would use me as a doormat."

Kamal was shocked, he said, "But I had planned to . . . is it possible for you to remain here?"

He looked around him, at the blackened walls and the bulb dancing in the draft coming through the broken windowpane, while the grocer smiled meanly and Said's face dripped with hatred. He said to her, sadly, "I want you to live your life."

She moved away from him, walked a few steps, then turned to him and said, convinced and resigned, "This is my life, this is where I live and I have no other choice. Why can't you understand that? Who do you think I am? Who do you think you are?"

He bent his head and said, heartbroken, "It's my fault, I was wrong."

Said looked at him scornfully and said vindictively, "Do you see now? Just see, just see!"

Abu Salem's sons returned led by someone new, a young man, tall and big with a puckered face, with thick, loose veins and a bushy mustache. Nahleh hid behind Kamal and said to him, frightened, "This is the one, this one is the beast."

He walked like a wrestler entering the ring. He extended his hand and, using a language he had learned in the streets and the shady, underground world, he said rudely, "I am Saadu and they call me the hyena of the valleys. To make a long story short, children of Hamdan, we've had it with you, we've wasted time and we want to get this over with. If your sister signs the power of attorney we'll be done, otherwise we will have to resort to a different solution, one that will please neither you nor us. We're cornered and we've got to find a way out. We would like to end this standoff now, not tomorrow or the day after. My brother Salem has tried his best, and my brother Hamzeh has ideas, but I, personally, want action. Enough. We're fed up. Do you understand what I'm saying? Do you understand, my stepmother? Do you understand what I'm saying?"

She hid behind Kamal and mumbled, "Poor, wretched Nahleh."

He said, harshly, "Listen to me, woman, stepmother, we can't grant you a divorce because it doesn't depend on us. Moreover, and pardon me for saying so, what's happened, has happened; our father took a second wife, so let him get his fill. The man wants a younger wife and it's his right. God gave him wealth, what can we say? However, our assets are our right—the land, the villa, and the shares all belong to us. As for you, the shari'a law gives you what is rightfully yours, and we guarantee you your rights in the inheritance. You will get one sixteenth of his wealth after his death."

Said interrupted him, saying, "She gets one eighth."

He turned to him and said, "No sir, she is entitled to one sixteenth only and our mother the same amount. It amounts to a handsome sum, what do you say?"

Nahleh whispered in Kamal's ear, "No Kamal, don't accept, the shares were my dowry."

As soon as Kamal heard her words, his heart sank and his face turned pale. He couldn't believe what he had just heard. They were dividing the inheritance while the owner was still alive? His sister, despite being in this dump, this prison, under the threat of torture, was fighting over her inheritance like a man, like a dog, a hyena. Kamal and Said remained silent but Nahleh said with unusual audacity and boldness, "The shares in the company belong to me because they were my dowry."

"Well, well, well, your dowry, madam? Who do you think you are, Georgina Rizk?" replied Saadu.

Kamal, who still looked pale and frightened, intervened saying, "Wait, wait, I have a solution, take my shares in the company, I don't want this partnership anyhow."

A voice in the back said, "Careful Saadu, he's bluffing, his shares are worth nothing because he did not participate in the capital."

Kamal remembered that he hadn't contributed to the capital and that his shares were worth nothing without him. His presence would reinforce his position or hers, but he wondered whether her position was worth the effort. She wanted the shares and the company, what does this woman know about a sewage company, she has enough of that in her head. If she wants it, she'll have to do without him as a partner. He remained silent, observing them and growing paler and more disheartened.

"You talk about your father as if he were dead, he might live longer than you," said Nahleh to the sons.

Saadu smiled and said contemptuously, "No lady, he could die at any time, and when he does, my stepmother, what would you say?"

At those words, Kamal stood up suddenly, despite his dizziness. He said, fearful and disgusted, "I can't believe it, why have we come to this? What's happening in the world?"

The man nicknamed 'the hyena of the valleys' rebuked him saying, "Sit down, sire, sit down Mr. Engineer, Doctor, do you think that we're like you, that we speak a foreign language, walk straight, and eat cake? We, sir, have endured all sorts of hardships to get what we have now. Do you see these?" he asked Kamal, showing him his hands, "We stand in blood up to the elbow, and do you see this head?" he asked, uncovering a head as gray as fog. Then he described his life: "I am a young man whose life was hijacked early on. I endured humiliation for twenty-eight years and I was trampled underfoot, I've had my share of beatings. I spent my youth working in factories, ports, and restaurants, and now, dear engineer, if you want to know, I don't give a damn. Those assets belong to all of us, I worked for them, and so did Salem, Marwan, and Aziz, you'd better keep quiet. To make a long story short, I want to tell you that the assets belong to us and not to the old man, though he is in the lead position, but in a split second he could disappear into a thousand pieces. Do you think this is a game? We are too old to play games. We've left our youth and our life behind us, we thought the struggle was over, but it's not over and everyone gets what he strives for, do you hear me, sir? You are worth something if you have money, that's how life is and this is what we get from hard work. Don't ever believe what you're told, Abu Salem's sons are neither crooks nor thieves and no woman can fool us. How can a woman fool us, we are streetwise children, we worked with people and for people, we won't let anyone play games with us, do you hear me, sir? Do you hear me, Dr. Engineer? What do you say?"

Kamal wondered about the people who surrounded him, their logic and their way of thinking. Were these the persons he was about to do business with? Would he ever be able to reach an agreement with them, his future partners? Would he be able to deal with the hyena who has stood in blood up to his elbow and his knees? How would he be able to deal with such savvy dealers? They've been in the country all their lives and have never left. Their roots and ties with the street and with the people have never been broken. They understand the people well and speak their language. What does he know about his people? He was always different. He remembered Nahleh's words: "You've always been different." Therefore, his character hadn't been shaped by his life abroad or by Helga and Germany. He was different and he will stay different, he will never be able to understand them and they won't understand him. The sewage company is only an idea, a beautiful idea but difficult to execute. He won't stay, and if he does, he won't take a partner or partners, he'll work alone, just as he has since his childhood. He'll then return to loneliness and a life of exile inside his own country. Is this what he had dreamed of finding here, exile inside his own country? He turned to Nahleh and said, "Listen to me, sister, give them the shares and the company and I'll give you whatever you want."

She said, cautiously, "How many shares?"

He replied, sickened and dismayed, "All of them."

Said objected, "You would give her all the shares? Take it easy."

Someone standing behind Saadu shouted, "You fools!"

But Saadu rebuked him with a loud growl, saying, "What business is it of yours, they're brothers working things out among themselves, why do you interfere?"

"What do you mean this is not my business?"

The man who uttered those words moved forward and his face appeared in the circle of light. He was elegant with big eyes and silky hair. He said, "What do you mean it's not my business, if he leaves, who will be our partner?"

Said seized the opportunity of his brother's withdrawal and offered to replace him as a partner. There was no comment, so he continued, "I can be a partner. What do you need, machines? I have machines. Do you want experience? I have experience. Do you want someone who knows the market? I do. I also have a very successful factory and can hardly keep up with demand; even the Israelis buy my products. Ask my father about it, ask Samaan, tell them, Samaan, about the factory."

Samaan said, meanly and slyly, "Even the Israelis buy your products."

"What about the machines?" asked Said.

"As punctual as a watch," replied Samaan.

The elegant man interrupted again, "This is nonsense, a candy factory isn't a sewage factory. What are you talking about?"

Said objected, "Why, which one is better?"

The handsome man became irate and turned to his brothers to explain the consequence of the situation and its tragic aspect, "Do you understand what's happening? We would lose a scholar, a mind, and a project. Do you understand?"

His brother, 'the hyena of the valleys' rebuked him again, "Enough, Hamzeh, sweetheart, dearest. We can do without you. Let this morning go by peacefully and pronounce God's name, say that nothing would happen to you except what God willed, say that there might be good in what appears to be bad."

Hamzeh shouted in a voice that cracked with frustration, "Do you understand, do you realize the impact of what's happening?"

His brother, 'the hyena of the valleys,' growled, "Enough, Hamzeh, calm down and pronounce God's name. Why are you putting stones in the middle of the stream? Are you the only one who has studied overseas? It's Abu Salem's fault, he wanted his children to get university degrees, what degrees? In moments of crisis when knives are used and business shows huge losses, who helps you? When you were overseas, we were up to our elbows and knees in blood, do you understand what I'm saying? Let's stay friends. Let everyone mind his own business. You're worth what you have, whether in money or in power, and if you have nothing you're worth nothing, you can be blown away easily. And you Dr. Engineer, what do you have? If you have shares, you're worth shares, and your brother," addressing himself to Said, "You have a factory, then you are worth a factory and, you, madam, what do you have? You're worth nothing but this power of attorney, you either sign it or I'll make the birds in the sky hear your voice, by God I will."

At this moment Kamal lost his balance and fell to the ground, unconscious.

We spent hours discussing the meaning of exile and return, the meaning of growth and modernization. Kamal gave free voice to his pain. He couldn't understand what had changed people's attitudes and wondered whether in the face of such change, he should return home. He then turned to me and asked, "You, why did you come back?"

I said, with both doubt and understanding, "Because I'm hopeful."

He made fun of me while Violet objected to his comments, since she was torn between her decision to leave the country and her nostalgic attachment to her love for Mazen. But Mazen was busy with his companion, or comrade, or friend Abd al-Hadi. Both were planning to bring about a change of taste through education to pull us out of this low state of decay. Kamal's abandonment of the sewage project pushed the Bey away from the issue of the environment, which he replaced with my project, an Art and Culture Center. The Bey proposed that Violet sing, and that he read poetry. When he saw us whispering, however, he changed his plans and said in his usual courteous way, "Violet must leave her mark before she leaves."

Violet sat at the far end of the terrace, far from us, watching the horizon. She felt that the world was moving ahead, leaving her behind. Her enthusiasm for the activities of the Cultural Center and the events of the opening day moved in waves, sometimes she was as enthusiastic as Mazen, the Bey and I, and sometimes she sided with Kamal. He had become pessimistic and was greatly discouraged since he had lost his battle over Nahleh and had abandoned the project. Today however, as the Bey reminded her of her departure plans, she experienced the same distress that she had felt when she decided to forget her love for Mazen. He didn't seem to remember, but he probably did because he still had an inviting look. It was so unfair and irresponsible; as usual, he was playing with her feelings. He never uttered a word of blame, eluding promises and a misinterpretation of his intentions. She was looking for a commitment of some kind, but he had nothing to offer, and it was up to her to go on as they did before or leave.

Abd al-Hadi Bey was looking for an opportunity to convince her that she had everything a man could wish for. He, a man, wanted to have what she had because she was an artist, she was beautiful, and she shared some of his feelings, in other words, they were very much alike. He didn't tell her that in so many words but conveyed his thoughts to her indirectly, in a sweet, sticky way that angered and disgusted her. Was it because she played the guitar and openly expressed her feelings for the man she loved in her songs that he thought her easy and accessible to everybody? Or did he think, as he often implied, that a sensitive woman is doomed and would be unable to live without a lover?

Violet was not the passionate type and she didn't have a lover. She believed that love allowed her to fly across space, music, and the scents of April. Men didn't understand that, however, none of them, whether it was Guevara or this man. This situation made her long to immigrate, to become emotionless like the

Americans, or at least to have a foothold somewhere in a land that lives without dreams and illusions. If love meant humiliation and heartache, then let there be no love. Since this country didn't provide her with an opportunity to search and fulfill herself, why stay here?

The last time Violet had said those words and defended them passionately in my presence and Mazen's, the Bey had been observing her intently. He had tried to convince her that the environment was not arid, cold, or gloomy as she thought, the problem was with the observer, not the object observed. Had she looked carefully she would have seen that here was a man who had Hemingway's strength, an adventurer who liked hunting and danger. Had she been in Washington and had she seen him or heard about him, she would have immediately realized that at his hand she could experience the most beautiful emotions.

The Bey looked at her thighs from the corner of his eye as she sat beside him in the cafeteria drinking tea and listening to a light song. It reminded her of a delicate love that blows like a breath, a vision, willow leaves, and the whiteness of the horizon. She still hoped that Mazen would return to the table and order a mint tea for her and tell her that the homeland is all we have and that people are its most beautiful component and that she, of all people, is the dearest and the most gifted of them all, and it would be a pity for her to immigrate and leave the country. She was dreaming and looking for him across the terrace and the horizon, listening to Fairuz's voice when she suddenly felt an arm lean on her thigh, as if by chance. She was startled and held her breath in order to find out what was happening. A few minutes later the elbow was moving in circles and meaningful pressures, rising then falling and plunging in her flesh. She looked at the Bey puzzled and surprised, but he was smiling and shaking his head to me and Kamal, while his arm moved up and down under the table. We saw her suddenly freeze, her eyes stared at the void and at Mazen who was standing very far away, by the cash register. She was overcome with a feeling of hatred, resentment, and disgust for this environment, and for Mazen in particular, because had it not been for his story and the humiliation to which he subjected her, this weasel wouldn't have dared do what he was doing. Had it not been for his carelessness and his loss she would not have found herself in this situation. She felt the elbow tickle her, her intestines twitched and she had a strong urge to vomit. She stood suddenly, causing his elbow to fall free. He looked at her to make sure that she had understood and searched for a special message in her eyes but there was none. I said, puzzled, "What's happening, where to?"

She whispered in a voice that sounded like the whistling of the wind, "To hell."

It was clear and even certain, that America represented for Violet, as it did for many others, an escape from a world that hadn't changed while they had. Though Violet had never been a social scientist or a highly educated person, she was nevertheless a woman who had known life both in her country and outside of it. She came originally from Bethlehem and grew up in Jerusalem, and for her Wadi al-Rihan represented a bleak world, which brought her nothing. At her work she had seen women in their real condition under the hair dryers and men without halos or greatness. She knew that men looked at women as mere sex objects, at least that's how they saw Violet and those like her. Respectable women achieved respect only because they gave birth to a dozen children or because they covered their heads, sacrificed their spirits, and became colorless and tasteless, just bags stuffed with a strange substance, shapeless and senseless. They were looked at as mere sacks, similar to a sack of lentils, a sack of rice, a sack of potatoes, or a sack of barley, and barley eaters aren't human beings. The men of Wadi al-Rihan on the other hand were, according to Violet, like monkeys with half brains and long tails that helped them climb trees and pick fruits, and whatever they could not eat, they would urinate on.

This explains why American men such as Tom Selleck or Cary Grant seemed to her like saviors, though she was much younger than Cary Grant and those of his generation. She studied in a nuns' school, played guitar, and sang adolescent songs, seduced by the April breeze. She dreamed of the handsome young man, affectionate and pious, who would love a virgin, considering her a flower with beautiful eyes that reflected the light inside. She dreamed about a man who would tell her that she was an angel in the shape of a human being. She wanted to be a man's paradise, his rising sun, while he would be her shining moon.

Reality was different, however, and there was neither a full moon nor did she become famous like the singer Fairuz. The men in Wadi al-Rihan were not princes, they were simple workers and farmers that Israel's factories stole from barren, desolate farms. They too memorized the story of the revolution as they sang to the glorious leader, to the blood of the martyrs, to liberation accords, and to victory celebrations. Such were the people and the princes of Wadi al-Rihan, and this was victory in the age of television, which transformed shame into liberation and a semblance of victory.

That was the explanation that Mazen gave her when they were riding the tide, but he failed to tell her that he was one of them and that Violet was a naïve and misled girl. He offered no explanation but Violet understood everything when she took time to think. However, the mind sends a message different from that of the heart. She continuously reminded herself that men in this country were hopeless, and Mazen was like the rest of them, an extinguished flame, a mere illusion.

She still remembered her reply when someone had asked her about men; she had whispered, "No one among them is a human being, I must have been crazy to have fallen in love with one of them."

She told Mazen her story with this and that one, to his amazement. He commented in disbelief, "You, is it possible? How do you explain it? You must be either unlucky or stupid!"

She agreed with him, and said, "Yes, you're probably right."

Remembering the girls who had been with her and what had happened to them during the Jerusalem days in Salah al-Din Street, Violet realized that she was not stupid after all, since she had not slipped and fallen into the arms that were ready to receive her. Those were the hands of the politicians whose articles and poems stirred the crowds everywhere: on university campuses, in the theater, the halls of the National Hotel, and the YMCA. She was a member of that generation of the 1970s, when a girl would watch the leaders of the revolution with awe, listen to the roar of their voices resonating in the microphones, and hear people cheering them on. Then came the debates, the comments and strolling in the halls, listening to the praise of this leader and that poet, while she naïvely and stupidly saw everything through the lights and heard the voices through the uproar and the cheers of the people. She saw them as their nation's leaders, the geniuses of their time, uttering words of wisdom. She would follow them like their shadow, seeking their blessing, while they smiled and made her believe that she was the woman, the companion, and the friend, the hope, and the element of change. They would ask if they had heard of Rosa Luxembourg, Maya Chekova, and Maya Goldman, but she didn't know any of them, and embarrassed, she would remain silent and sweat heavily. Feeling sorry for her they would say, "Poor girl, how can you know so little! Come with me, come let me teach you how to live."

They would hold her hand and lead her from one meeting place to another, through shops and monasteries where people would come and go while she stood there, a mere presence. Then came the fall, nine girls she had known had traveled that road and fallen, becoming like prostitutes, with one major difference, that the prostitutes were paid for their services whereas the girls were cheap prey, the rewards of the revolution and the liberation. They were seduced the same night by a poet, a leader, or even an intruder to the revolution, and a would-be poet. They got nothing in return but talk about the revolution, an addiction to hashish or morphine, and an emotional affliction that crushed them. She had seen nine youthful girls reduced to decrepit women, like secondhand goods.

She stood there watching the sun set slowly behind the olive trees on the hill. She smelled the scent of a jasmine that Nahleh had brought from her garden and planted near the entrance. It had grown into a big tree. She wondered how many months had passed since Nahleh's incident, Zayna's arrival, and the day she had met Mazen. Time passed at an unbelievable speed and events happened like in a speeded-up film.

Two months ago, only two months ago, she was soaring and singing for Mazen as she sang in the past for the priest she had fallen in love with. She was a young girl then, and felt that life was like a beautiful film, filled with events, emotions, and music. She compared it to a Julie Andrews movie she saw years ago, a film that had a special place in her heart, one that reflected an experience she'd lived. She had imagined herself as Julie Andrews, with her baby face, her guitar and her love of an older man, a baron who fought the Nazis. But why weren't the men she met like the baron? Each one had a complex that brought him down from the position of a baron to that of an animal. How could a baron fall so fast? Why did it happen to her and so quickly as if there were a sign on her forehead that said to a man: "Help yourself." It was as if her clothes, her makeup, her name told them: "I'm easy." How many times had she looked in the mirror to understand their audacity toward her after the first handshake? Her clothes weren't revealing or low cut, they didn't expose armpits or cleavage like Futna's clothes. Her hair was short and simple, her conversation was elegant and polite, and she didn't laugh at dirty jokes and hidden meanings like Futna. Her laughter was decent, and she didn't guffaw or clap her hands and shake them the way Futna did. But Futna was protected by her name, her native city, Jerusalem, her family name and the Shayibs; hadn't they been trusted with the keys of the Aqsa Mosque!

Violet wondered whether people's attitude toward her was due to her profession as a hairdresser, her mother's work as a nurse, and her father's work in the post office. She wished they all had different professions. She wished she had a different name, one less inviting. Had her mother been like Amira with a commanding tone and a confident voice, he might not have dared to nudge her with his elbow, his elbow! What a beast, what a pig!

She was extremely angry and felt a blinding rage that transformed the world around her into a very strong storm. She wanted to go back to the cafeteria and throw her anger in his face, tell him that he was an animal and that his elbow and his face looked like an old shoe. Or worse, his face resembled the tail of a sheep with his double chin, a disgusting sight. Who does this pig think he is? She couldn't care less about his family name, his career as a diplomat, his palace, his English accent, and his cashmere sweaters. And Amira and her stupid daughter Futna meant nothing to her. The members of the Shayib family were nothing more than overblown balloons, nothing but hot air. Futna's pregnancy was nothing but an ugly scandal. She was more honorable than Futna and her mother because she earned her living honorably and didn't sell herself to a rich old man, as old as her father.

When Futna crossed the terrace she saw Violet. She asked, her voice hoarse from a cold she had caught and her pregnancy at this advanced age, "Hi Violet, are you writing poetry?"

But Violet turned her head toward the west and looked at the mountains and the valleys, filled with anger. She whispered, spitefully, "For whom and for what? I'm leaving soon."

The Bey had a history and a heritage as well. He was the son of wealthy ancestors who had lived life to the fullest. Some had owned land near the coast where they held parties and banquets, enjoying evenings of singing, dancing, and love. He would not have accepted the kind of love common during his father's generation. He didn't dream of a dancer or a musician, but he wished he could fall in love with a girl with special qualities, a girl who read books and spoke French and English. He wanted a girl who wore bold clothes, narrow around the waist with a large belt, a girl he would dance with at the Orient House.

During those days girls were like doves and dahlias. They had long necks with a small head like that of a finicky goldfinch, their eyes were large and almond-shaped like Audrey Hepburn's, and their long, silky black hair would be combed in a ponytail. Some wore their hair in a new style called 'à la garçon,' the style of choice for distinguished women but worn by all at present. The dress or the skirt at that time was very wide, like an umbrella with pleats and numerous layers. Whenever a girl sat down or her clothes were raised by the wind, one could see white layers like the transparent petals of a rose. During those days a girl was like a dream or a soft pure melody, like a moving song played on the piano or the guitar. The piano was fashionable then, every well-born girl played the piano at the nuns' school.

He was so lucky to have met yesterday's girl, today. He dreamed of her for years until he met her. Violet was that type of girl, from a nuns' school, gifted, sentimental, with short hair, a long neck, and high cheekbones like Audrey Hepburn. She was both yesterday's and today's girl, and like yesterday's girls she wasn't for him and didn't want him. It had so happened that every girl he had wanted during those days had slipped through his fingers, and he would see her the following day with another young man dancing in the Orient House or in Ramallah. He stopped searching for the delicate girls and contented himself with the sturdier type. He had an explanation for the situation: the goldfinch tends to fly high up above the clouds, above the Dome of the Rock and the bell towers, as for the sturdy types they were like hens and ducks, they did not fly and moved slowly without making much noise, they wouldn't run away. So he lived for three years with Sarah, a year and a half with Mary, then with Marika and Tumader and many others, then he stopped counting. A couple of times he'd been about to fall and tie his future to a duck but he'd been saved at the last minute.

He was over sixty now, single, and childless, with no one to inherit his name and his fortune, without a woman willing to live with him without marriage. Was it true that he didn't have a penis? The truth is that he behaved like someone who had more than one penis, always ready to perform the act. He went through periods of great activity when he exploded with desire and power, followed by periods of rest that gradually grew longer. It surprised and saddened him when all the passion he felt died and boredom settled in. He would then turn to his books, searching for the secret of the universe and the human being, the secret of love and human relations. For years he felt he was a Kafka or rather that Kafka was thinking for him. He then moved to Washington and there he became enamored with Hemingway and grew a beard similar to his, he took up fishing, traveled, made love to women, but his interest in them was always short-lived.

Now, however, after all those years and his long experience in life, he knew himself, or at least his type, and he understood that the human being was not endowed with a free will but was guided. This was reality and those who didn't know it were either stupid or ignorant. Had he ever chosen what had happened to him? In the past he had dreamed of this and that, both in his private and public life, but things didn't happen the way he'd wanted and he hadn't known how they had moved and whether he had received what he'd wished for. He had wanted to join the faculty of law but instead he found himself somehow, in the department of philosophy and psychology. He had wanted to be an ambassador in a Western country but found himself a consul in Turkey. He wanted to have the most beautiful and the brightest women but his wish was unfulfilled and he didn't resist what happened to him or even regret it. Why was he fighting now what had already happened and was over with? What was the point of resisting something and denying its benefit for the sake of something whose benefit was unknown to him? Things were in continuous motion—as a person changes, so do his mind and his heart. Since the mind moves in all directions, thoughts change shape. How can one bet on love knowing that feelings are like a balloon, inflated today and deflated tomorrow? How can he bet that emotions rushing like a rocket will not one day settle on earth and become a reality? Let whatever happens happen, hoping that he might get what he hopes for.

He stood like the others looking at the military post in Kiryat Raheel and he suddenly noticed the hill where the settlement was built, its trees and its roof tiles. It was a large settlement with a military camp, a fence, and forbidden roads. They were building a new checkpoint to mark the borders between the past and the present, between an occupation that had lasted years and an occupation that will last forever. He had become used to this sight and its depressing impact on him, but the problem, as he explained it, was bigger than us, bigger than them, bigger than a nation and even many nations. It was part of history, it was fate.

The soldier motioned the cars and said, "Go," so he moved fast toward his aim without thinking because his mind had shifted for a moment when he saw the soldiers and the checkpoint. But he regained his composure as he drove, surrounded by the olive trees, the scent of the evening, and the music. He concentrated on the aim of the day and his expectation of what was to happen.

He began planning and preparing the way for what he wanted. A small town like Wadi al-Rihan wasn't big enough for him. Moreover, sleeping in the upper room in the Hamdans' house, as he had done a few times before, wouldn't be suitable. It was not only a burden and a bother to them, but it would be impossible for him to lure his catch to a safe nest. It would be better to stay at a hotel in Nablus for a few days instead of traveling back and forth daily and lose the day on the road, and especially the nights, which are more important. He liked the idea and found it practical. Spending time with them would strengthen his position and keep him close to the two projects, the regressing environmental project and the progressing Art and Culture project. He stayed in touch with the organizers, keeping up with the events, without losing sight of developing situations and new details.

The Bey made arrangements to stay in a comfortable room at a nearby hotel. He rested a little, took a shower, smoothed his beard and watched the quiet city from his window. He realized that the place wouldn't suit the advanced stage of his project, when the fishhook catches the fish, and a permanent arrangement would have to be made. Later on, however, the dove would follow him to the diwan or any hotel in East or West Jerusalem, as peace was becoming a reality and the exchange of visitors and business was a fact. It was important to be organized and move carefully, one step at a time. He had no aim for his project, which complicated matters somewhat, he wondered how he would move ahead without an aim. He didn't know how Violet would feel about him, would she accept him or rebuff him, playing hard to get? Would she use her trip to America as an excuse, her involvement with the preparations and the arrangements to be made? Her travel plans didn't constitute an obstacle as once she sold the furniture and the house, she could leave immediately, he wouldn't hold her back. He hoped she wouldn't hang on to him, but what if she did? He didn't think that would be too bad. He couldn't have hoped for a better and sweeter conclusion to his project, especially in these surroundings where the accessible women are few. The indications were that it wouldn't be at all difficult to fulfill his dreams, judging from Mazen's experience.

He made up his mind and embarked on his project invoking God's help. On his way to Wadi al-Rihan he saw the settlement again, the army and the police checkpoint, and drove behind a long line of cars. None of this dissuaded him as it had in the past. The radio had been talking about a true peace and the end of problems and complications, and the gradual removal of checkpoints and settlements. This meant that one would finally be able to breathe and live a reasonable life, enjoy the usual pastimes, reading and engaging in discussions without a stick hanging over one's head. One would become a human being, a son of Adam. Let's then live free of worries, anxieties, and pain. Although pain was still eating away at the heart and the bones of Jerusalem, those were mere stages before peace prevails. Even if it ends up being a partial peace, what can one do? The issue is bigger than us or them, it is the responsibility of the Security Council, the Senate, the House of Lords, the United Nations, and similar bodies. It is the combined policy of nations and a new world order.

He arrived in Wadi al-Rihan early, as the night was just beginning to set in, the streets were still awake, the cars were moving and people's eyes were wide open. He would not, naturally, embarrass her or himself and arouse suspicion. Matters such as these are not to be publicized and what a person does in his private life is for himself and not for others to see. People wouldn't understand, and even if they did, they would make a mountain out of a molehill. What if he greeted her and went to visit her as a friend, like the others? Didn't Mazen visit her thousands of times and so did Kamal and the gray-haired man with the special look, wasn't he always with her wherever she went? Was he Violet's friend or her mother's? It was none of his business or anybody else's business, it was her private life. She was free to do whatever she wanted and so was he. Two independent individuals can play without hurting anybody.

It was not a convenient time to visit, however, he should wait an hour or two until the movement in the streets stopped and people either went to sleep or were watching television, then he would make his move.

He drove along the edge of Wadi al-Rihan, saw the Hamdan's farm on his right and noticed a light in the study and in the guard's room. It looked like a good opportunity to kill time and greet Abu Jaber, but the parked pickup was Mazen's. He slowed down, thinking that the car was here merely to transport vegetables the following morning. He locked his Mercedes and walked calmly toward the study. He heard voices in the room and recognized Kamal's voice. So, the pickup was then driven by Kamal, a pleasant and sociable person. He could have been an excellent and dependable partner had it not been for the turn of events. The political situation was not stable, however, and no one knew what the future might bring. How many times had he been surprised by the events and people's behavior, strange things had happened to him. He had had no choice but to accept them, as usual, after a period of reflection.

He knocked at the door but no one answered. The discussion inside appeared heated with very loud and emotional voices competing to be heard. There didn't seem to be an opportunity for a discussion or a break that would allow them to hear the Bey's delicate knock. He pushed the door and found himself before a large gathering. There was Kamal, Mazen, and their father Abu Jaber, in addition to another man, a dark, thin man with a sensitive face and large chestnut eyes. Abu Jaber stood up quickly to greet the Bey, while the others interrupted their discussion for half a minute and exchanged short greetings with the guest before returning to their business.

Abu Jaber said in a brief whisper, "We are talking about Abu Salem's son, the project, and Nahleh's shares."

Abd al-Hadi Bey shook his head and began to pay close attention to the conversation since he was very much concerned in the matter. He intended to join the project and had high hopes for it. Mazen turned to him suddenly and said, sharply, "Listen Bey, listen, listen, have you ever heard a wise person talk like this? We say it is a bull and he says milk it. We say it is a bull, a bull, man, can the bull become an engineer? What a story!"

The Bey intervened, calmly and politely, saying, "Please excuse me, I don't understand."

The dark skinned man was unsure of him, but Mazen reassured him saying, "Speak freely, don't worry, he's one of us."

It was a courteous gesture that the Bey appreciated, he smiled to the dark skinned man who turned to him and explained the situation, "After Kamal withdrew from the project it became garbage."

The man smiled at his own words and explained the joke to the others, "It's a project about garbage and it became garbage."

The Bey shook his head and replied politely, but without a smile, "I understand, I understand."

The young man went on, "In a word, the project hangs on Kamal. He invented it and we entrusted him with it. It will cost thousands of shekels and maybe millions, but Kamal has abandoned us."

Kamal objected loudly, "Isn't this what you wanted? In reality, the shares aren't yours, our father gave them to Nahleh and you took them by force."

186

The young man replied, "Then, dear sir, you give up a project that costs millions and leave the garbage where it is? Are you going to leave us lost between your brother's stupidity and a big, complex project that we don't understand, just for your sister's sake?"

Kamal looked at them vexed and angry, because the dark-skinned man knew very well that he did not give up the project merely because of Nahleh or their father, it was a more serious and more complicated matter. He sought only to provoke him or even defy him, to blackmail him in the name of the homeland, patriotism, his expertise, and modernization. Kamal refused to be pulled into this type of discussion, he was determined to avoid getting entangled in the war of blame because it would undoubtedly upset everybody including his father, who had whispered in his ear, at the beginning of the discussion, "Is it conceivable that you would leave a huge project in the hands of . . . you know who?" Kamal ignored his father's words and everybody else's, he had made up his mind. It wasn't because of Nahleh or the stupidity of Abu Salem's sons and that of his brother Said, it wasn't because of people's greed or their ignorance and the difficulties of life in this sick environment. It wasn't that at all, but something more serious than that, something he couldn't swallow or overcome, something graver than garbage. He was determined to avoid working in an atmosphere of fear, that was all. That was the reason, and nothing else.

He said, sharply, "Your tough brother was threatening us, let him run the project!"

The dark skinned man said regretfully, "Our brother Saadu is like your brother Said and that's why I'm here to beg you people of good will to cooperate with us and unite to save the money and the project. Are you willing to see millions of shekels and months of work go down the drain? Are you willing to go back empty handed and help the Germans instead of helping us? Are you willing to give your expertise to the West and not to us, your people, and all this for what, my brother and your sister! You're above all that, and God is great."

Kamal smiled and shook his head, wondering what this young man was up to. Was he trying with a few words to soften his heart and that of his brother and father? Or was he trying to make him forget his defeat and the night he'd spent imprisoned in the abandoned soap factory, his sister's painful experience, the threats to her legal rights and human rights that they had violated so blatantly, in front of him? The dark skinned man had seen this with his own eyes, and yet he dared ask for his help and support! For whom? For his brothers, one of whom is a gangster and the other a bull. God protect us from them. All this nonsense is happening at his age, to a man in his fifties, it was unbearable. The silence lasted a long time while Kamal stared at the dark skinned man without replying.

Mazen broke into the silence, saying, "I don't understand, when you returned from Germany you talked for hours about the bitter taste of exile in the West and how you felt like a branch cut from its tree. You talked about your love for your country, you told us that you'd returned in order to sharpen your emotions and your dreams, don't you remember?"

Kamal didn't reply, he felt a lump in his throat that spread to his head. Mazen was stirring painful memories and reminding him of his feeling of estrangement as he now came to the realization that his dream was a mirage and that life was, is, and will continue to be tasteless and meaningless, with no aim and without roots. He had dreamed of returning home at this time and this age, to devote himself to a new project, a new passion, something that would make up for the past and for life in a desolate land. In Germany he had felt that he was living a superficial, rootless life, but now, after discovering the state of his homeland, he felt like an orphan, the way he did when, as a child, Nahleh had come out of her mother's bedroom and exclaimed, "My mother is dying." He hadn't cried but had run to his books and his coloring pencils. He remembered that moment as if it had happened today, and he experienced the same feeling.

His father pleaded with him, "May you be blessed, my son, I beg you to reconsider. I've waited so long for you to return and stay with me to fulfill a dream of twenty years. Mazen has come back and many other people have as well, things might get better in our country."

He murmured sadly, "We will never amount to anything."

Mazen exclaimed, hitting his thigh, "We will amount to something! What if we were defeated a second time, we're used to defeats, but if we were smart we would stand up after the defeat, and we will do that. We will rise and become a nation. What's important is to act and not stop at words and pointless conversation. Life is work and commitment."

Kamal looked at him askance and couldn't hide his disgust. He wondered what world he was talking about and what commitment? Was it his commitment to his sister Nahleh, to Violet, or to his father's farm? Was it his commitment to his dream and to his great love, to Salma and to Jubran and all that he left in Lebanon? Life is commitment and it's work; the revolution gave us nothing but theories and poetry!

"Why are you silent, why are you looking at me like that? Don't you like what I'm saying?" asked Mazen. But Kamal just asked him to stop talking.

Mazen objected saying, "No, I won't stop talking. Is it conceivable that because of Nahleh and her well-being you've forgotten your country and your project? You've exchanged the well-being of the country for that of your sister. You've exchanged the good of the people and society for that of one individual! Suppose they stole her rights because they are ignorant and illiterate, isn't it your role to guide them and stretch a helping hand to them? The aim here is the company, not Nahleh, and regardless of the partners, the project belongs to the country."

Kamal motioned for him to stop talking and began to unbutton his shirt and feel his neck. He said, "Open a window, give us some air."

No one reacted, so he got up and opened the window himself; the evening air and the scent of lemon blossom and mint rushed into the room. He felt a new wave of sadness and sorrow, a dejection similar to what he usually experienced at the loss of a lover, a love that ends with separation, tears, and suffering. It was like those stories of the adolescent years, when the heart was still full of tenderness. Then the children grew up and those feelings were lost, whenever they went back looking for them, they found nothing but sorrow. Oh Nahleh, Oh Helga, Oh mother, what is this feeling of loneliness, this sorrow, this affliction? He had dreamed of meeting his family, discovering his people's precious emotions and their concerns. He had hoped to find love and sentiments and to recover his ability to feel. His colleague Hayk had told him after a visit to Syria, "People there are better than us, we in the West are mere machines, without the ability to dream and have emotions."

Where are you, Hayk, to see my condition and share my worries, my sadness, Nahleh's sadness, and that of all the others? You are like machines and we are individuals and each group turns on its head thinking otherwise. See what Mazen says and what he does, he talks about the individual and the group, but he is the master of lies because he is individualistic, the ultimate individualist.

Mazen asked angrily, "Why are you silent, don't you like us?"

Then he turned to his father and said to incite him, "Hey father! Weren't you dreaming of our return to unburden you? Didn't you dream of us growing up and becoming men to help the country rise from its slumber? Didn't you dream of all that?"

His father didn't reply but looked across the window, smelled the scent of lemon and felt the cold of the night. The trees outside seemed very dark that night, shapeless and confused. His old dream came back to him from behind the fog, but the fear of another disappointment strangled his wish to live a new dream and experience another disappointment he wouldn't be able to bear. His body couldn't take another disappointment. He wondered whether he were losing his role, if he were giving his children a model unworthy of emulating, the model of a broken-down person. He said in a conciliatory tone, "We, son, suffer when we dream and lose the dream. But we suffer more when we grow up and become bitter, don't become bitter."

Kamal choked, touched by his father's words, and said, "And, you father, are you bitter or haven't you reached that stage yet?"

He didn't say, "you have become" because the situation didn't allow it and he didn't say, "not yet" because he was already bitter. He had an ungrateful daughter, a billy goat of a son, a defeated and haughty son, a genius living in a foreign land, and two sons with no hope of ever entering the country. His farm was wilting before his eyes, while the settlement of Kiryat Raheel established around the valley was closing in on him. He had hoped for things to improve with the Oslo Accords, but nothing had changed, the settlement was still on top of the hill, surrounding the plain and his farm, crawling toward the valley and the neighboring villages. Was this the solution? Were those his children? The good fruit was falling and the rotten fruit was gaining importance, as one brother was betraying the other and taking over a project he had worked hard to establish. Was this what his generation had dreamed of and rushed to fulfill? Was this what Nasser had announced during the days of glory and the "Voice of the Arabs?" Was it, was it?

Mazen said with great energy, "Didn't you dream of our return in order to live in the country and undertake projects? Didn't you?"

His father shook his head and mumbled vaguely, "Of course, of course."

"Didn't you dream of seeing your children return to help you?" asked Mazen.

The father said again, "Of course, of course."

Mazen went on pressing him, "Haven't you been dreaming of the end of exile, and wished for each one of us to return to his country and bring with him his family, his knowledge and his money? Didn't you want us to settle down, help improve the homeland and change it to a beautiful paradise in people's eyes? Weren't those your dreams?"

His father had tears in his eyes, he repeated in a mournful voice, his head bent and his heart broken, "Of course, of course."

While Mazen was feeling elated by the sound of his own words that intoxicated him like poetry, Kamal saw tears in his father's eyes and felt his grief. He rushed to him, kneeled at his feet, hugged him, and placed his head on his lap. He whispered to him, deeply moved, "I feel your pain, by God I do."

The two burst into bitter tears, to Mazen's surprise. He stared at them and asked in total disbelief, "Why are they crying? Why are they crying?"

He looked at the Bey who lowered his gaze because his eyes were filled with tears as well. He turned to the dark skinned man, Abu Salem's son, and found him staring at this deeply touching scene and being totally affected by it. The sound of their crying was rising and breaking the silence of the night, echoing back to him. He suddenly realized how much he had changed and how, since the project of the Art and Culture Center, he had regained his energy and his fighting spirit, his hopes for the future. He had forgotten how a person who didn't understand the revolution and its theories, a simple man like his father would think, and how a man of science like Kamal, with a precise mathematical mind, thinks, and how a man like the Bey with a history and deep roots, thinks.

Mazen wondered how a young man returning from Budapest with an open mind and heart, and huge hopes for change, would think. In the heat of the battle to spread culture he had forgotten reality and how to see it through his father's eyes and farm work. He had forgotten to look at the world through the eyes of a sharp scientist who studied the weather and its implications in his lab. He had forgotten to look at the world through the eyes of the Shayib family, their past glory and their wealth. Was it possible that even a member of the Shayib family would cry like his father? But why not? Wasn't he a human being like any other, with feelings and pride, with a heritage and interests, how could he have forgotten that? How could he have overlooked the project and Saadu and Said, Nahleh, and her shares? How could he have forgotten Violet and her plans to immigrate? He mumbled in confusion and shock, his eyes moving between the weeping men, "Why are they crying? For what?"

He looked again at the Bey hoping he would come to his rescue, say something that would give his father some hope and consolation, and make Kamal stay. But the Bey was crying because he felt that history was moving ahead leaving people like him and Abu Jaber, the landowner, empty handed. He too was empty handed, but he wasn't like them because he was moving ahead without questioning life, without direction, like a ship in the sea navigating without a helm, without sails, and without a port.

There was an obvious difference between the attitude of two men facing the same situation and the same scene. Mazen became aware of his contradictions, his mistakes, and his excuses, while the Bey was carried away by the event and cried, moved and saddened. Mazen looked into himself searching for the reasons for his weakness while the Bey went to Violet to forget his sorrow, his fears, and his insecurities. He was hoping to find in her company answers to questions that were disturbing him, questions he had neither the courage nor the strength to probe with depth. He was too old to change, and the situation wasn't easy. His problem wasn't the sewage project because that was part of the environment. It wasn't concern about the situation and these people because people are history and we lost our history forever, and even if it could be restored, it wouldn't be through our own efforts and for us.

The Bey knocked at the door and the mother welcomed him politely and kindly. She explained that Violet had gone to the salon to show it to prospective buyers and that she would return in a few minutes. She asked whether he would like to eat some tabbouleh, which she had just finished preparing, assuring him that he had not tasted anything better in all his life. His smile indicated that he would not object to eating some tabbouleh and cucumber. When she brought the dish she asked him if he would like a glass of wine from a bottle she had brought back with her the last time she visited the Latrun monastery. He smiled again and began to relax after his tense encounter with the Hamdan family and the emotional experience he'd had there.

The mother recollected stories from the past and some from the present, then mentioned America and what was waiting for them there. She explained that the trip was still far in the future because neither the shop nor the house had yet been sold. Violet was dragging her feet, giving flimsy excuses and knowing very well though that nothing could be expected from Mazen.

Then she turned to the Bey and asked inquisitively, "And you, what do you think, is there any hope for this country to improve?"

He averted his face to avoid her question and hide the emotions and the humiliations it might provoke. What could they do? The others encircled the valley, climbed the mountains and took positions on the elevations as they had around the hills of Jerusalem. They encircled the city strangling and swallowing it. End of story. They had done the same with the mountains of the West Bank, the plains of Gaza, and those of Jericho. They are everywhere, and they take positions anywhere they want, expanding in all directions. And where is the Authority? Any authority? Can there be a country without authority?

She asked again, insistently, "Do you think that conditions will improve and that we'll be able to live a normal life, like the rest of the world?"

He shook his head and said to her, "Ya Umm Grace, what's the point of raising this painful subject. Let's stay with the wine, the tabbouleh, beautiful America, and Miami. You told me that Grace lives in Miami? It's a pretty city, paradise on earth. I spent five years in Boston."

He began telling her about his life in America, his memories there and how he had lived his life to the fullest. He had traveled from east to west in the U.S. and visited Canada and Mexico. He'd seen the Indian reservations, the Chinatowns, the Blacks, the Arabs, and the Jews, with their various traditions, each living as they wanted, without interfering in one another's lives and without spying on one another.

Umm Grace took a deep breath and said, "Alas! Here one hardly says a word before it spreads throughout the country."

He heeded her words well, measuring the consequences of his visit and the comments it might cause. He reaffirmed his decision to make all his visits under the cover of night, hiding them from everybody except Violet and her mother. What would people say if their story became known? They would say the old man goes out with a hairdresser, the honorable old man who inherited a name and the key of the Aqsa Mosque goes out with a Christian woman. They might say he goes out with a woman younger than his daughter. Nothing would be said, however. It would remain a secret.

Violet entered and was surprised to see him. She couldn't hide her displeasure at the sight of him, but out of courtesy and respect for his age she welcomed him and said flatly, looking away, "I can't wait to get rid of the salon, this country, and its calamities."

Her words didn't disturb him because he didn't believe he was included in them. Allusions in such situations are useless because the moment he began following his feelings, he left behind the acuity needed to understand them! When his instincts kicked in, they slowed down his logical thinking and possibly stopped it altogether. His feeling of relaxation might have reduced his alertness despite his intelligence, making it easy for him to start joking and talking about himself, bragging shamelessly.

The mother got up to prepare dinner because it was the suitable thing to do for a visitor at this hour. She had gotten used to friends' visits and to generously offering them food and drink, and she didn't find the Bey's visit out of place.

When the Bey found himself alone with Violet he went straight to the point, "I want my visits to remain a secret, people don't need to find out about us."

Violet felt a deep sense of revulsion and felt like vomiting, but she remained silent because she had lost the spark of life. She took a quick look at him, then turned her face away, muttering, "Oh merciful God."

Noticing that she was grave-faced, he tried to win her over by asking about her situation, the date of her departure, the sale of the salon and the house. He volunteered to find serious buyers for her, buyers who would pay a good price that would please her.

She mumbled a few harsh words, explaining that the market was at a standstill and people didn't want to invest their money in real estate because the situation was unstable, uncertain, and unpromising.

But he told her with determination that he would find a suitable buyer.

She asked, despondently, "A buyer from where, from here?"

He remembered that he didn't know anyone in Wadi al-Rihan apart from the Hamdan family, but who among them would want a salon and a house like this one? It was a charming house despite its small size, and it might find a modest buyer among those returning with the Authority, but who would buy the salon? He nevertheless assured, "Don't worry, I'll take care of the salon."

She gave him a meaningful look to let him know that she understood him and his game. She said again, somewhat shaken, "A buyer from where, from here?"

Possibly unused to lying, he said immediately and without thinking, "Of course not, but probably from Jerusalem."

She looked at him sideways, and mumbled, "From Jerusalem? Who in Jerusalem would buy a salon in Wadi al-Rihan? Is it possible that somebody would leave Jerusalem and come live here? Only a stupid person would do that."

He said to her impulsively, feeling a little embarrassed, "Why, Violet, what's wrong with Wadi al-Rihan? It's like paradise and paradise is beautiful with its people. I consider Wadi al-Rihan the most beautiful city because the most beautiful person lives there."

She turned her face away from him, rolled her eyes, and started jiggling the leg that was stretched in the air facing him. When she realized what she was doing she changed position and raised her right leg over her left one, away from him. He now saw only the beautiful side of her face with her short hair, her elongated neck like that of a goldfinch, and her marvelous body. He returned to his dreams and said, "When I was in Washington I met a woman who looked like you, but you're certainly younger and more beautiful. She was a famous writer and we met in a nightclub. I was standing at the bar having a drink and suddenly the barkeeper presented me with a drink offered by a woman surrounded by a group of men, sitting at another table, talking, drinking, and smoking. I asked the waiter to return the drink and tell the woman that an Arab man does not allow a woman to pay for his drink. The glass was returned, this time carried by one of the young men who were with her. He whispered in my ear, 'The lady wants you to join her.' We were introduced and I learned that she was the famous English writer Gloria Simons, have you heard of her?"

Violet shook her head and said listlessly, "No, I haven't heard of her."

He didn't pick up on the resentment in her voice because he was preoccupied with himself, his past memories, his future dreams, and the promises this visit held for him. He went back to casting his net through his story and the riddles it carried. She noticed that he laughed revoltingly, making noises similar to the bleating of a goat suffering from a cold.

He continued his story: "Gloria was angry because I had returned the drink she offered me and also because our horses had won the race. She said that she wouldn't forgive me unless I apologized in public for my behavior and for the race. But I told her that I was an Arab and I wasn't used to giving in to a woman and this was true too of our horses. I assured her that we would continue to win races."

Violet uttered something like a complaint and smiled disgustedly, saying, "Thank God we'll win the race."

He turned toward her for a second, then reverted to his memories and his story with Gloria, which ended in bed. Before reaching this stage, he told her in detail and with real pleasure how he had left Gloria with pride and haughtiness. He refused categorically to apologize, showing her that he was an Arab man who didn't give in to a woman whoever she might be, just as purebred Arab horses don't lose to Western horses. He explained how he had dealt Gloria's British pride a third blow.

He found out, however, that women like a strong man because when he returned to his hotel room two young men were waiting for him. They told him that Gloria swore that she wouldn't go to bed that night unless they brought her the proud Arab man. He went back and she took her revenge, but it was a revenge as sweet as sugar.

He turned to her and, whispered, "This is how women are, this is the way it is in life."

Feeling a shiver that froze all the pores in her body and settled in her stomach like a big rock, she was unable to utter a word. He interpreted her silence and calm as a sign of his success. He was convinced that the fish had taken the bait. This bolstered his confidence, and he went on talking with an impetuosity that was not in harmony with his appearance, his age, his position, and his family name.

"That's how I like women to be, open and knowing how to enjoy life. Our Arab women and Arab men as well, don't know how to enjoy life. I personally consider sex a need and something that has to be expressed and not suppressed. I don't understand why people complicate matters?"

She commented in a whisper, avoiding his eyes, "Is it because people complicate matters that you don't want anyone to know about your visit?"

He noticed the underlying irony in her words but ignored it because he believed that no matter how hard she tried Violet couldn't be more clever than he. After all, she was a hairdresser, with no culture or diplomas. She was also a woman of modest background, a little woman from Wadi al-Rihan, compared to him, the consul, the all-knowing, who had lived for five years in Washington and before that in Turkey, Spain, and other countries. She was no more than a limited woman, whereas he was a master.

He explained slowly, "I am an extremely open-minded person in the matter of needs and desires. I believe that a person must satisfy all his needs and express them any way he wants until he is satisfied. It doesn't matter how, what counts is personal satisfaction. As far as I'm concerned everything is acceptable, even homosexuality. Each person should do whatever he wants without restrictions."

She commented in a detached and ironic manner, "Do you mean they can parade in the streets?"

He lowered his gaze, shook his head slowly, and said with patience, "No, not parading in the streets."

He repeated his words a second time, but she didn't reply and continued to jiggle her leg in the air. He noticed how cold and unresponsive she was, finally! He was furious, but he remained calm because by nature he was patient and forgiving, and she was young and he was older.

He said to her, "Your problem is that you don't listen."

She stared into his face, saying with a chilling calm, "I don't have a problem!"

He corrected himself saying, "I mean that you only hear what you want to hear."

She looked at him again, but her respect for his age and his status as a guest was waning, and she asked him, defiantly, "Whom do I have to listen to?" She would have liked to add, "To your brain, to your loathsome words, you disgusting man?" But she didn't and went back to balancing her leg in the air.

He said, in an effort to save the situation but beginning to lose his patience, and stammering, "I mean that a person must satisfy his needs without complications and must eat until sated."

She smiled, amused by his stupid and obvious approach to show off and to reach his aim, "Without restrictions?"

He nodded, saying, "Without restrictions."

She asked, "Without rules?"

"Yes, without rules."

She asked again, "Without commitment?"

He replied, "Without commitment."

Her smile grew wider and she thought to herself: What a shit of a man, how dumb he is.

Encouraged by her smile, he continued, "The situation requires guts, however."

She looked him straight in the eyes and said in a clever manner, "Of course, of course, it requires courage and that's why no one must know about it, it must be done in secret."

His pupils hardened and he felt trapped despite his eloquence. He had the impression that he was naked in front of her perceptive eyes and he didn't know how to hide his feelings. His self-confidence shaken, he said to her, "It seems that the wine I've drunk has had an effect on me, I had two glasses before you came."

She didn't respond and continued to jiggle her leg in the air, carelessly. When she noticed that he had withdrawn into himself she did the same. She was sensitive to others' pain and their feelings. Many had the impression that she was weak and not as strong as she really was. Her extreme sensitivity led some people to take advantage of her. She always surprised them, however, reacting like a stubborn mule that rises suddenly, kicks, and throws its rider on the ground in seconds. Luckily, the Bey withdrew at the last minute, causing her anger to cool down before reaching its maximum and turning against him.

Violet tried to address him as a human being with a heart and a conscience, "I don't know why people always misunderstand me!"

He noticed her meditative tone and her well-spaced words, which he mistook for hesitation and weakness. He regained control and waited for a suitable opportunity to attack.

She said in a gentle tone that conveyed weakness, "I do not know why people think that I'm easy. What gives them the impression that I'm cheap?"

His eyes gleamed as he thought that the situation was improving because she was finally maneuvering. What about being easy and being cheap and giving the wrong impression, who was she fooling? Didn't Mazen Hamdan have his fill of her and Mazen is no better than the others.

She wondered modestly, "What's wrong with me: my clothes, my hair, or my makeup? Futna, however . . ."

She didn't continue as she remembered that Futna al-Shayib was his cousin or his cousin's daughter, a relative of sorts. It wouldn't be decent to mention her before him. She corrected herself and resumed saying, "Many girls dress like me and wear even shorter clothes. I don't wear short or revealing clothes, my makeup is simple, and my hair is its natural color, so why do people think as they do?"

He asked with great interest and pleasure because she was beginning to respond and open up to him, "What do they think?"

She moved her hand in a way that revealed her confusion and desperation, as she said, "I really don't know why, but I know that they think I'm cheap."

He smiled and asked, "What are you saying? That isn't possible."

She said bluntly, "Is it because I loved Mazen openly that people think I'm easy?"

He said, reflectively and looking at the wall facing him, "I think, Violet that the big mistake was that you loved openly and that you established a long-term relationship." He avoided looking at her, however, as he spoke.

She regained her composure and remembered that she was facing a man suffering from all kinds of illnesses. He despised women and people generally, and had no respect for beautiful love relationships and for truthful words. He offered nothing but words. As for his capacity to ponder deep emotions, face difficulties, or examine the secrets of the soul and its contradictions, those were things he couldn't do.

He came back to the same subject, "Your mistake was loving openly and believing that love is forever. But love is an infatuation, lasting only a second. You didn't have my experience, ask me. All women come and go and the soul remains confused because the feeling is never satisfied. What remains is the desire, only the desire."

She asked coldly, "You mean that love doesn't exist?"

He shut his eyes, appeared reflective, and said sincerely, "No, there is no love."

"And no feelings?" she asked.

He shook his head left and right, and said, "And no feelings, or rather temporary feelings, nothing more."

"And what remains is only desire, just that?" asked Violet.

He said, quite convinced, "Only the desire."

Her blood pressure rose, she regained her mule-like character, and began kicking.

"And you're visiting us because of such desire?" she asked him.

He didn't answer. She had guessed correctly, how could he lie and disprove her? Also, speaking directly is not agreeable and can be tactless.

She insisted, "Are you here because of that desire?"

Her voice was louder than necessary and people could hear her. He was concerned.

She went on addressing him in her direct manner, "This means that you want a prostitute, a clean and cute prostitute, and also one free of charge."

He was very scared, what if Umm Grace entered the room now? What if Violet's talk became louder? What if her voice reached the street and the neighbors heard? What if, what if? He wondered what had happened to her. She had seemed wise and reasonable, listening politely to him. She had even begun to yield. What had he said that caused her to react this way? She, a prostitute? Is there a respectable, educated, and dignified woman who would refer to herself as a prostitute? He hadn't realized that Violet could be impolite. He'd better escape before the situation deteriorated into a scandal. She might say more unpleasant things that would shock the ears of the polite gentleman he was. He'd better leave before the situation got worse!

He stood up without saying a word, quietly and calmly. He was hoping she would say something pleasant and polite to apologize for her words and show her regret and embarrassment at having said what she had. Instead, she stood up and said painfully and bitterly, "People always misunderstand."

He replied, sincerely and warmly, "I didn't misunderstand, I didn't."

She shook her head in a manner that expressed irony and bitterness and walked him to the door. As he was walking toward the stairs he seemed very short, shorter than he was, and she felt taller. She closed the door quietly and said to him from behind the door, "Abd al-Hadi Bey, you didn't misunderstand, you didn't."

Abd al-Hadi Bey ran away to Jerusalem early in the morning, leaving behind him the culture and Wadi al-Rihan. He took off in his Mercedes very early in the morning. Everyone wandered why. What had happened to cause this sudden departure? Wasn't he working with the organizing group planning the inauguration ceremony for the Center, looking for gifted performers, and trying to breathe life into this defeated people? Wasn't he the one who had said literally that a people cannot be counted and can't progress if they don't rebel against themselves and against their values, then rise culturally to erase the days of disarray and disgust and the crimes committed in the name of the homeland and in the name of patriotism? We said amen and didn't oppose him except when he suggested an evening where he would recite poetry and Violet would sing and play the guitar. Then everyone fell silent, offering no response. Mazen had an embarrassed smile as he visualized the Bey on the stage among the young people and those wearing jeans. He wondered how he would carry himself, what he would say, what he would wear. He imagined him standing under the lights in flesh and blood, with his double chin and his fat, wearing his tweed or cashmere suit and reading from a book. Would it be an English or an Arabic book; would he read Hemingway? No, not Hemingway since he isn't a poet. Whose book, then? Nizar Qabbani, undoubtedly. He would tell Violet while she played the guitar: your eyes are like the lamps of a temple.

My uncle asked whether anyone had upset the Bey.

No one replied, but Futna had a theory, "Maybe because he wanted to recite poetry and no one agreed?"

Mazen explained, "I don't think so, it wasn't a serious matter, even Violet knows that. Isn't that true Violet?"

But Violet looked at him coldly and said dryly, "You know best."

The sentence she had repeated many times that day finally caught his attention. He wanted to reconcile with her and bring things back to where they had been between them. He wanted to explain to her that he was finally willing to accept that life provides logical and reasonable things, while the extraordinary and the unusual existed only in his head. As for reality, his reality, the reality of the country, the reality of the people, the reality of women and love and feelings, those were the norm. Whatever was reasonable and available was the solution, the political line to follow, the Authority, the land, the people, this weakness, and this defeat. How can we achieve total liberation for a divided people, a people without heroes and lacking the proper support for their political measures? Had people been stronger and more solid, they would have achieved greater liberation. Is there a perfect liberation for an imperfect people, a defeated people? This is the interest due on the people's capital, this is its savings account. And he is no better than his people. What does he have to offer them that would entitle him to demand an extraordinary woman, a dream woman? He didn't even appreciate Salma Jubran, who was like a dream. He didn't remain faithful to her. He gave her nothing because his capital was meager, or rather nil. He demanded a great deal, and when it was time to pay back, his pockets were empty except for a rusted dime, like the remains of the English army, a useless niggardly inheritance, only a few dimes!

My uncle asked, bewildered, "Did he return to Jerusalem without saying anything?"

Amira said, clearly concerned, "He must have returned for a serious matter, may God protect us."

Violet smiled and looked beyond the horizon of the terrace, murmuring to herself, "A serious matter!"

She remembered yesterday's scene with mixed emotions of anger and pleasure. She was angry because the Bey had dared say what he'd said and because he'd treated her, at the beginning, like a child or a schoolgirl. He thought that she would bask in his magnificence and be honored to know him, he, the gray-haired man, and she, Violet. She felt a wonderful pleasure in her discovery that she was brighter than he expected and even more clever than he. She remembered how he had used the excuse of the two glasses of wine to hide the true reason for his failure or for his stupidity. He isn't stupid, definitely not, but he's stupider than he realized. Now he knows and that's why he ran away.

Futna asked her, "Why are you laughing? Let us laugh with you!"

Mazen seized the opportunity to butt into the conversation, saying, "Ms. Violet is not aware of things anymore and has forgotten those she knows, thinking only of America. Let's see, what in America is better than here?"

She gave him an oblique, angry look and wondered what he meant. Lately, he had been trying to get her attention, to curry favor with her, to say the beautiful words she wished he had said in the old days. She no longer cared about that; she had made up her mind to sell the house and the salon and immigrate to Florida. She wanted to live there like a queen, free to come and go, to swim, dance, and sing, to join a club or a band, then marry and have two or three children. She wanted to live in a nice house with a backyard and a garage she would open with a remote like Grace's. She wanted to lead a peaceful, comfortable life without problems, without struggle, and without worries.

Mazen said to her, defiantly, "If America is truly beautiful no one would have left, isn't that true, Zayna?"

He stood up and turned around himself, raised his arms in the direction of the hills and the length of the horizon all the way to Jaffa, and said, "Do you mean to say that America is more beautiful than here? More beautiful than our mountains and lands?"

I kept silent. What could I say? Of course America is more beautiful. America is a continent, it has all the colors of nature. In spring it becomes a paradise, cherry blossoms in Washington, lilac blossoms in Virginia and the Carolinas, the daffodils, azaleas, magnolias, and dogwoods. In the fall the leaves turn orange and yellow, leaves as light as feathers and soft to walk on. One never gets tired of looking at the colors. In winter there's the snow, snowflakes, and snowstorms. The houses exude tender warmth around the fireplace and the burning wood. Where was America? I was getting homesick.

Mazen said, boasting of the beauty of the country and the scents in the air, "Smell, smell the scent of the homeland. It's better than musk and amber."

Violet remained silent, and he went on, "I would defend the smallest of its weeds with my life. Look at the greenery and the beauty. Smell the scent."

She mocked him, purposely making light of his words, "Haven't you traveled to other countries and seen real green? Do you call this cream color and this brown, green?"

He faced her and said defiantly, "What's wrong with you? Now America is above everything and we're garbage? Let's see what you get from America. We know what those who went before you got."

Then he turned to me and said, "Look at Zayna. She has everything but she discovered that without her people she isn't worth anything."

Violet shook her head with bitterness but didn't argue with him. She would have told him: you are one of those people and so is the Bey and Abu Salem's daughter, bigmouthed and creating scandals. Before her there was Nahleh, the whole neighborhood, and the whole valley, this disgusting and destitute valley. Here even breath is repugnant. One does not breathe. One suffocates and dies, thanks to the people of Wadi al-Rihan. As if it weren't enough to put up with the Israelis, one has to put up with one's own people too!

He said proudly, "Whoever treats people with haughtiness isn't one of them."

She stared at him despite herself because she couldn't believe that he, of all people, would say those words. He was the one who continuously criticized Wadi al-Rihan. He swore at the people when he was drunk, when he was sober, and when he was depressed. He was the one who treated his family haughtily. He despised the farm and work and went from place to place sipping coffee and tea. He was the one who treated her and all the women he met with arrogance and justified his conduct by saying that he could not find the woman of his dreams. How often had she been fooled in the past by his logic, she a hairdresser and he a revolutionary! She adorned the brides, set the hair, dyed it, and cut it while all he did was recite poetry. She spoke a simple language and he used complex terms. He spoke about liberation and his country's problems. She turned on the television to see Sharihan and Ramadan riddles, whereas he flipped channels to watch the news from Jordan, Israel, and Syria. And then there was the satellite dish. Her mother had said then, grumbling, "If he likes the dish let him buy one, as if we don't have enough trouble."

But he never bought one and Umm Grace continued to complain.

Futna said, "People, I've heard some news but I'm afraid to tell you."

My uncle stared at her from under his glasses and said with controlled irony, "Are you referring to Abu Salem's return?"

"How did you know?" she asked.

Umm Grace sighed, I was shocked, and Mazen didn't say a word.

Violet commented, sad and fearful, "Things will soon heat up."

Mazen asked her, still watching her every move and word, "What do you mean when you say that things will heat up soon, with whom?"

She turned her head sideways and said, retreating, "I didn't mean anything, the expression just popped out of my mouth."

He said, defiantly, "No, you meant it, we want to understand what you intended by it."

She replied whispering, "No, I didn't mean anything. It's over, forget it."

He said provocatively, "You meant it and we want to understand what you meant."

She stood, suddenly fed up, and said, "Yes I did mean it and what is it to you? Leave me alone. Why are you on my case? You make an issue out of every word I say. I don't want you to understand and I don't want to understand. Leave me alone."

He said, stubbornly, "No, I won't leave you alone."

She stared at him with deep hatred, he seemed to enjoy making light of her anger. She had had some feeling for him up to yesterday evening, but now, after what had happened, he was nothing, simply nothing.

He continued, stubbornly, "We want to understand."

She jumped nervously out of her chair, slamming into the table, walking like a crazy woman.

He couldn't go to sleep and decided to wait for Kamal's return. Violet's antagonistic attitude had affected him deeply, her shouting at him in public had given him the impression that she truly didn't want him and that even she hated him. The fact that she had avoided him for days and her attitude today made him wonder whether their relationship had really come to an end, that it could not be salvaged. She had been preparing for her trip for weeks, holding farewell parties and attending some, but he thought that those had been mere games. As soon as he raised his finger and told her kindly, "forget it," she would forget America and remain here in this country and abandon the idea of immigration. Leaving one's country is no joke. It's even a crime and a sin. We struggle for the return and they leave? Kamal comes back from exile and Violet wants to immigrate, while he watches them both and does nothing! He decided to discuss the subject with both of them and to adopt a firmer position. He would tell them in no uncertain terms that leaving a weak homeland means abandoning one's duty and identity and hopes for the future.

Kamal returned in the evening with another man from Germany, his colleague Hayk, who worked with another company helping the Authority and developing the country. Hayk talked with great enthusiasm about his projects, development, and the power of construction. He explained how Germany came back to life after a true death because of the war, and in a few years it became a great power controlling the market, the price of gold and cars, rubbing everybody's nose in the mud. Where does the Ford stand in relation to the Mercedes, the dollar to the strong mark? Strength isn't only planes and rockets and propellers. Strength isn't only military bases, colonies, and fleets. It's the stock market, it's a market for one's products, it's Toyota and Mercedes. Had strength been only that, America would be the master of the world, but the dollar without the mark and the yen is nothing. Both currencies back the dollar. It isn't possible to explain the meaning of modern strength with an old concept.

Mazen stood behind the counter looking at Hayk as he carried on his discussions with the people, moving among the visitors, speaking French and English, playing the guitar and the piano, and trying to learn to play the drums. He advised his father about the use of some organic pesticides, free of poison and gentle to the environment. He explained that killing the insects doesn't require the use of chemicals but only raising a kind of insect that eats the harmful ones. He explained how to raise cattle and livestock without grains and how to plant zucchini and strawberries without soil.

Violet said, as they sat in the cafeteria drinking tea and coffee, "I'm very happy, very happy."

Mazen looked her in the eye but she shifted her gaze away from him, as if to discard the ghost of the past, and the remains of yesterday. He had a funny feeling, and for the first time he felt the humiliation of love. All women, including Violet, had given themselves to him totally and he had never felt threatened. Now, however, as she placed him face to face with a choice with which he could not compete, he felt the humiliation of loss. Where did his youth go, his attractiveness, his charm, and the power of his gaze? In the past, Mazen had only to ask and women would acquiesce to his demands, but now he tries in vain. He speaks no French, English, German, or Spanish; he doesn't play the piano or sing; he doesn't talk about the environment. He says nothing and does nothing and there is nothing left for him but what has been said before and proved useless. In the sixties Guevara was the man of his time, it was the time of progress and modernization, the time of excess and change, but now, what does he have? Only useless old words, a name that died with yesterday's dawn. Guevara died, Castro is aging, and Moscow is disintegrating from the inside and will soon collapse. The revolution defeated him inside and out and he has grown old like secondhand goods in a market full of new items. At that moment he wished that Violet and Kamal would leave as quickly as possible, without returning and without regret.

part three

And Then, The Inheritance

Weeks passed and the news of the sewage project spread, amid opposition and disapproval. People went to the municipality, to the mayors, to the governor, and the notables to complain, but the mayors said "Amen" and the notables washed their hands of it, leaving everything in God's hands. They left the meetings and the deals and went east, seeking open spaces and the oil fields. It's true that oil fields have a smell that can cause headaches, but they're bearable headaches compared to the ones they faced in Wadi al-Rihan and its municipality. The headache caused by the oil fields is at least beneficial and doesn't impact the environment and the nostrils the way sewage does. It doesn't stink like sewage, which attracts rats and wasps. Then there was the lassitude that spread in the region like a summer cloud and fell over people's heads, sparing no one from the bites of mosquitoes, bugs, and fleas.

My uncle like many others rushed to complain about the impact of the sewage factory when Kamal told him that he was no longer involved in the project, and that it was now Said and Abu Salem's sons' responsibility. Abu Salem had returned to Wadi al-Rihan a few weeks ago, despite the threats. His return had given Kamal some hope and could have convinced him to run the project, but he had been quickly disillusioned by Abu Salem's poor management and the pressure exerted by his sons. They convinced their father that Said would cost them less to run the project, that Said would be better than his pretentious brother, a philosopher who thought he understood the work he was doing. They told him that he was a German, an immigrant who had lived most of his life abroad, far from their world, and that he'd better get rid of him for his peace of mind.

The project failed, and the stench filled the air and people's nostrils, reaching the inhabitants of the neighboring villages and the wheat fields. The area was covered with rats, frogs, blue flies, and snakes. A sense of desolation and disgust spread among the people, who fell silent, discouraged after their numerous complaints and sit-ins in the halls of the municipality and in front of the police stations and the security forces. A journalist who wrote that there were cases of plague was arrested on the pretext that he was spreading rumors and causing unrest. People learned of the matter and said that what the journalist had written was true, citing the names of the numerous plague victims. Then they went back to whispering, complaining, and pleading with the notables and the relatives, including Abu Jaber, the closest to them and the first witness to the project.

I rode in the station wagon with my uncle to visit the sewage station. It was my uncle's first visit to a sewage station, but I had seen some in the United States and in Europe, and they were truly wonderful, with public parks, fertilizer factories, and water purification centers. But this one was ugly and disgusting, a real catastrophe.

I stood with my uncle on top of the hill looking from a distance, saddened and grieving. The cinchona trees and the beautiful oleander flowers projected an air of refinement, reminding us of Kamal's taste and delicate touch. He had done a lot to transform the sewage project into a garden like those in Frankfurt and Berlin. He had planted shrubs and white poplars, cinchona trees, oleander, mallow, and petunias. After he left the project, the wild weeds grew tall between the trees and the mallow flowers wilted from neglect. Most of the delicate petunias died, leaving nothing in their place but long stems with thorns and wild flowers. The wind blew from the west, carrying droplets of sewage and bacteria raised higher by huge fans turning over the surface of the ponds. As for the ponds, what a mess! What a crime! Something one never could have dreamed of even in their worst nightmares, they were filled with a liquid similar to molasses, but as hard as cement and as black as mud.

My uncle sighed deeply at the sight and had an asthma attack, while I jumped a few meters into the air when I saw a large rat as big as a wild rabbit looking at me defiantly from among the weeds and the petunias. We quickly got into the car and drove away to escape the bug bites and a flock of wasps. My uncle said breathlessly, "What a catastrophe! What a sewage station! I wish it had collapsed before it was completed."

The people were divided into two and even three groups, one saying that the project had become a curse, a detested environmental catastrophe. The second group said that the project was a great achievement because it protected the environment, purified it, and provided it with water and manure. The third group was torn between the two sides seeing the project as a huge blessing when considered from the angle of knowledge and history. This group was represented by Mazen Hamdan Guevara whose knowledge of the street, of the milieu, and the action, his life in Beirut, in Tunis, in Moscow, and finally here in Wadi al-Rihan had given him an edge. He knew himself, the others, the past, and the future. He was convinced that it was impossible to do any better in a Third World country and providing cheap labor. He believed that the political, economic, and social conditions had led to an imbalance in jobs, in the ranks of the leaders, and in the results; in other words, he knew that the situation was not healthy.

Mazen wondered how we were expected to produce a civilized project in a poor environment, one lacking the basics for development and change. We were in Wadi al-Rihan and not in Frankfurt or Berlin. Here we copy them, we imitate them, and the dilemma lay in the concept of imitation. The imitator is not an innovator, no matter how much he tries, he cannot reproduce the original. He isn't gifted and he suffers from complexes. The imitator's hand, his mind, his character, and his feeling that he is responsible for himself or for others according to obscure universal measures that he doesn't comprehend, constitute a handicap in his life. Take Said, for example—was he qualified to run the project? Abu Salem said that with God's will Said was qualified because his sons told him so.

They disliked Kamal who didn't say yes and amen to Abu Salem and the rest of the shareholders who were, naturally, Abu Salem's sons.

Mazen's father said, "I don't understand, you used to say that the project without Kamal wouldn't take, because he was the specialist and the origintator of the idea. You also used to say that the project couldn't be run by a bull. Now you tell me that the project is working well and the odor isn't too strong and doesn't affect the people! I don't understand you!"

Mazen remained silent and motionless, but Kamal sighed and said, disgusted, "Change the subject, please. We're here to eat; shall we Nahleh?"

"Whatever you say," replied Nahleh. She got up to help her stepmother in the kitchen. Violet and her mother left and only Futna stayed.

My uncle said, quite insistent, "Do you really not smell the odor or are you telling us stories?"

Mazen remembered the discussions he had engaged in, in the past about the organization and its composition, and wondered whether there could be an organization without order, and order without administration, and administration without qualifications and capability. The revolution started and people followed, the educated and the crooks, the successful and the failures. It led people to this stage. Before that it guided them and squeezed out the best of them. It created an unqualified and lazy generation that slept till noon and stayed up till the morning, meeting on planes and in airports. That generation was living in a dream that had lost its luster and its myth. It had returned to the same thing it had once opposed and has become a tribe that split into many tribes. The head of the tribe has become the center of power. When we sifted the tribes we were left with one head, one leader, while the rest became a herd, a herd of heads and heads in a herd. Can an organization be built with the heads of a herd? Can a company or a factory be established that way? In this case in particular, who is the head, Kamal, the engineer, or Salem, who provided the capital, or Said, the technician with a queue of heirs standing behind him?

Mazen said to his father categorically, "This project needs time. Give it time and it will succeed."

214

My uncle turned to Kamal and asked him, "And you intend to leave?"

Kamal replied calmly, while continuing to eat, "I'm leaving and so is Hayk, and Violet will follow suit. Would you like to come with us?"

My uncle was silent and ate his food mechanically while looking at his two sons, the freedom fighter who had changed so much, and the genius he couldn't keep. He was wondering about his farm and who would inherit it. He had pawned his house, his car, and Umm Jaber's jewelry and had never sold a parcel. Here are his sons each in a different place. None of them was interested in the farm or aspired to own it. They didn't even have plans to build a little cottage on it to spend their summer vacations there. He wondered who would inherit it! He said, bent over his plate, "This year the season is very good and the land was very giving. Tomorrow we'll pick the mulberry before it rots on the branches."

No one replied, and he raised his voice and said firmly, "On Friday we'll all go to the farm and eat the mulberry from the tree."

Kamal apologized, saying, "No father, I'm leaving on Friday morning."

The food stuck in my uncle's throat when he heard that. He said to Kamal, "On Friday? I thought that you were staying for two or three more months."

Kamal didn't reply and continued to eat as if unconcerned, but his heart was torn as he thought about life and how it doesn't give a person all he wants. He found his fulfillment in the West and it gave to him generously, but what did he get from here? What did he give—an abominable project that will be remembered for generations to come. People will say that his son cheated them, they will tell his father that God gave him three sons, one like a bull, a stupid son, and a go-getter who limps.

My uncle said, "On Friday? You mean there's no way you can postpone your departure date?"

Kamal said, tersely, "I received an interesting offer."

Mazen snorted derisively revealing his sarcasm and his understanding of his brother's true nature. He was convinced that someone who was trained in the West, shaped in the West, and married in the West, would never come back to his people.

Futna asked him in a hoarse voice, "Is it possible that you'll leave before the festival and my delivery?"

He turned to her and looked at her belly. He smiled but didn't comment. He pondered on women who think that their delivery is an important event and a great achievement, a victory for them and for us. He was leaving a more important project and a failed achievement, a terrible failure, a huge one.

Nahleh asked with veiled sarcasm, "When are you due?"

Futna touched her belly and said, proudly, "I'm entering my delivery month in a few days," then she turned to Nahleh and told her, "Well, Nahleh, what gift will you give the baby and me?"

Nahleh replied, laughing sarcastically, as if reminding Futna of what she was trying to forget, "I offer you a sincere wish, from the bottom of my heart, for a safe delivery."

"How generous you are!" said Futna.

Nahleh said wickedly, laughing, "Dear Futna, a woman your age and in your situation shouldn't think of gifts. The best gift from God is for you to have a safe delivery and a healthy and normal child."

Futna glared at her, controlling her anger. She was reminding her for the one thousand and tenth time that she was old and that her son might not be normal, that she might encounter difficulties. There wouldn't be difficulties or surprises, both she and her son were safe and everything was fine. Her doctor in Hadassa had said that everything was normal and that there was nothing to worry about. She didn't care what her mother, Nahleh, or the heirs thought—the baby was a boy, and the boy protects the inheritance.

Mazen asked his sister, "How many invitations do you need?" But Nahleh continued to eat as if the matter didn't concern her. Futna said, "I need four or five invitations, for my mother and my brother and the Bey, of course, can I get them?"

He didn't reply but continued to stare at Nahleh eating slowly and pensively; he asked her, "Well Nahleh, are Abu Salem's sons coming?"

She replied sternly, "How would I know? Ask their father. It's none of my business."

Her father commented, trying to win her over, "What do you mean, it's not your business? You're better than they are and the crown jewel of the family."

She twisted her lips and smiled at her father's words, but only Kamal noticed her expression; their eyes met, yet in the dim light of the place he couldn't tell if her smile was meant for him. It didn't matter anyhow, everything was over and things were clear now, she was the child of this milieu, the outcome of Kuwait and Wadi al-Rihan, she lived in both places and nowhere else, she saw nothing of the rest of the world. Would she have remained silent had she been like him, in a similar situation, with a similar mind and similar experience and thinking? Would she have accepted this midget, this illiterate, backward man, with his heirs, a bunch of mafiosos? And then this Mazen, what a creature, he wasn't any different, or if he were, the difference was insignificant.

Mazen asked her again, "How many invitations do you want, how many seats?"

Kamal smiled reflecting on his brother's question, and how he was taking into consideration Abu Salem's sons. He was concerned about their seats, not mine, not ours. I will be in Frankfurt, Jaber is in Dubai, and Jamal is in Morocco. You, count Abu Salem's sons but you forget me and Jaber and Jamal, we have neither invitation cards nor seats, we aren't part of the celebration, just photos on the shelf, as if we weren't part of the family, just photos.

The father said, "You can't leave before the festival. Attend the festival and then go."

Mazen commented, sarcastically, "Do you want him to attend the festival and miss out on the offer? Is that possible? The offer is much more important than the festival."

Kamal didn't reply and smiled to him kindly. He knew that Mazen was jealous of him. One evening when he was drunk Mazen had opened up to him, saying, "You're lucky, Kamal, that you didn't squander your life. I squandered mine over nonsense and there's nothing left in me but a breath of life. I used to swear at you and Jaber, calling you merchants and slaves. I used to call you opportunists, upstarts, and bourgeois. I used to tell myself that even Said was better than you because he stuck to the land, and I thought, naturally, that Guevara was the master of the world because he was the freedom fighter with the belt of death around his waist. I was the one whose life was in the balance for my homeland. Now there is no life left and no homeland, I lost the torch and I'm lost in a dark souq of stolen goods. There's darkness from Mauritania to the Iranian borders, and from Cairo to Dhahran. I found out that all was useless, the belt of death, the candle that we carried, and the generations that melted away, the million and more martyrs, who was counting? Now that I'm wounded and exhausted and have come out of the feast empty-handed, I'm beginning to regret having squandered my life. I wish I'd done something meaningful in my life, something valuable, a small project, like you. I wanted to be larger than myself, bigger than the world and the limits of the wind, but I ended up like a paper kite tossed in the wind!"

My uncle said, "What's wrong Kamal, why aren't you eating? Nahleh, serve your brother."

Nahleh looked at him in the darkness of the place and saw a tear in his eyes. She bit her lip and shivered, deeply moved. This man, this human being, this honest person had given her a lot, he had given her all he could. He had stood by her in difficult moments but she had moved away from him and ridiculed his honesty and his generosity. He had said words that hurt her but those were only words. He must know that a woman has no one but her husband, and though Abu Salem's sons are a huge burden, it was the only solution. He was her husband and the husband's children are always a source of trouble. She wondered whether Kamal's tears were for her, for Said, or for the project.

Mazen asked Abu Salem, "Abu Salem, how many seats do you want me to keep for you?"

Abu Salem said, evasive, "As many as you'd like."

My uncle said, annoyed, "What a meaningless answer. Tell him how many invitations you need—five, ten, how many?"

He looked at Nahleh sideways and said, "As many as Nahleh wants."

She replied, indifferent, "It isn't my business. I don't interfere between you and your sons, I've learned my lesson."

He looked at her and smiled cunningly, he said to himself: the sly girl hasn't forgotten, her words have been as cutting as the edge of a knife. She had constantly repeated: Your sons, Abu Salem, did this and that, your sons imprisoned me and frightened me. They claimed the lands of Makhfiyeh,

Sabastiya, Zwata, and Qalqilya, while you ran away from trouble and didn't care what would happen to me. You ran away alone and left me to face them.

Mazen said, "The governor will be inaugurating the Center and will be accompanied by the scouts. The flags will fly high and the sound of music and songs will reach Jerusalem."

Futna announced, "My mother will be coming to attend the festivities and will be staying a few days. She'll be elated when she learns what's happening."

My uncle commented, sarcastic and indifferent, "What's going to happen? Something good, I hope."

She explained with childish enthusiasm, "I mean the presence of the governor, the scouts, and the flags. My mother likes national songs and such matters, she has memorized all the songs dedicated to Abd al-Nasser and one of Umm Kulthum's songs whose title I've forgotten. My mother sings very beautiful national songs all the time."

My uncle turned to her and asked, in a deep, sarcastic tone, "Your mother sings?"

He said those words and visualized her mother, a petite, thin woman with brittle bones and sinking cheeks, singing. He smiled and said, "With God's blessings."

Futna continued as enthusiastic as a child, "Don't you believe me? Ask Violet and Umm Grace. My mother attended a nuns' school, she plays the piano very well."

My uncle repeated, "Very well?" and she confirmed, "Very well."

He blew out the smoke from his cigarette and said, "Well Mazen, what's the matter with you, why do you bring in outside talent when you have local talent?"

Everyone laughed, angering Futna. She said that her mother was quite a lady, a graduate of a nuns' school. Her grandfather was the protector of the Haram al-Sharif and had the key to the Aqsa Mosque. She said that her mother knits and did crochet and she had been lately busy preparing the baby's trousseau, all blue because it is certainly a boy.

Nahleh said with obvious envy, "It doesn't matter, Futna, whether it's a boy or a girl, what's important is to have a safe delivery and a normal, healthy baby."

Futna replied while smacking her lips, "When my mother comes to attend the festival you will see that all the wool she's knitting is blue."

Nahleh whispered, envious and mocking, "It's all blue!"

Futna kept bragging, adding oil to the fire of Nahleh's jealousy, "My mother is known, she comes from a notable family and I'm sure that the governor knows her."

Nahleh approved, laughing sarcastically, "Of course, of course, he'll recognize her."

Futna said, addressing Mazen, "Surely, surely, when he shakes her hand he will recognize her and he'll invite her to sit beside him, in the first row."

Mazen smiled and so did Kamal, while Nahleh guffawed, but my uncle said seriously, "Why shouldn't she sit in the first row? Who is better than her or us?"

Mazen laughed and Kamal smiled, and both agreed on the following: Sitt Amira would sit in the first row near the consuls and the journalists to engage them in polite conversation in English, while all the others would sit in the second row. They didn't want the foreigners to say that the family took the front rows and gave them the back seats.

A few days before the festival things suddenly changed in the street. The inhabitants of Wadi al-Rihan became very active. An air of rejoicing dominated the place, helping the inhabitants to forget their oppression and the nauseating odors. They got involved in the action and seemed in the highest of spirits for no specific reason, in other words, they were happy without reason. The streets were filled with journalists and foreigners, and television cameras. The loudspeakers energized the vendors and the shopkeepers, forcing them to abandon their benches and their water pipes to check what was happening. They were curious about the male and female journalists roaming around in the streets, wearing shorts, taking pictures of children holding photos of the citadel, surrounded by dancers, singers, and ads for companies. There were ads describing Pepsi Cola as the favorite drink of the festival. Benetton made the same claim for its clothes and warned against imitations. There were ads for Toyota, Mercedes, Kolinos, and Cutex, among many others.

The publicity, the ads, and the foreigners made the inhabitants of Wadi al-Rihan feel the winds of change. They anticipated great benefits since, according to their thinking, the cameras, the publicity, the groups of tourists, and the journalists hadn't come for nothing, there must be something worthwhile happening. This valuable thing is the citadel. How could people have forgotten throughout the centuries that they had a great citadel and valuable heritage on top of the hill, right before their eyes, but no one saw it. How could this great monument have been abandoned and forgotten when it was a piece of art and the pride of civilization and history?All the cameras, the journalists, the local newspapers, and the newsletters confirm that, so how could they have forgotten that here, in Wadi al-Rihan, there was a historical ruin like Petra and the pyramids? Why had no one ever exploited this lofty, imposing structure? Do you know what this meant? It meant tourists, hotels, restaurants, amusement parks, and money. Do you know what Petra's income is from tourists and tourism? Do you know how many tourists visit the sphinx and the pyramids every year? Do you know the number of tourists who go to Granada, Carthage, and Jerash?

How could it have escaped our attention that we were sitting on an oil well, on money and a great source of revenue? Why had we wasted time with insignificant and silly incidents and considered them to be quite dramatic? Why had we demonstrated in front of the project and the municipality, complaining about a few rats and odors that would soon dissipate? This is history while those were innovations, this is a heritage for life and those were everyday, passing trivialities. How could we have forgotten this and remembered that? Had we been guided by awareness and ruled by glory, had there been revival and sacrifice, eternity and nobility of birth, had we been far-sighted, we wouldn't have paid attention to insignificant words and events.

The citadel is therefore a symbol of the world because we discovered the world and the world discovered us through an invincible heritage. This is what history, civilization, and culture are all about.

The young boys rode around on their bicycles, distributing fliers, programs, and pictures of the citadel. People were so excited and enthusiastic that they printed the picture of the citadel on tee shirts and purses. Others made stickers to put on cars, shop windows, and mirrors, expressing their love for and affiliation with the citadel. This is how Mazen with me behind him became the true heroes of the citadel revival. People greeted us everywhere we went. Being a foreigner and aloof by nature, I stayed in the background and watched Mazen run the show. He changed Wadi al-Rihan into an oasis of friendly relations and love, visited by total strangers and family members. Anyone walking in the street would see Arabian robes from the Gulf, hats from Europe, saris from Pakistan, and straw baskets and shell lamps from Vietnam. We sold merchandise from all over the world at the expense of our own products, which we've forsaken, having decided to import what we like. We soon discovered that we had truly hurt our products, as candy, toffee, and the 'Honey of the West' could not compete with the imported items. We ended up eating them but their taste didn't satisfy us, though we praised them in the local press and said that they tasted as sweet as chocolate and as delicious as dates.

Mazen explained that it wasn't our fault, rather it was history's fault because history was younger than us and modernization required time, patience, and work. The populace didn't know anymore whether we had a history on which to build or no history at all. They said that the citadel was a symbol of history, but then they asked how it was possible to modernize without history? My uncle wondered what to do with his strawberries, whether he had to export them or eat them? Said offered to take them to make a new kind of toffee for the festivities. This is why, on the day of the celebration, we ate a new toffee with a new cover showing the name of Wadi al-Rihan and the image of the citadel , and we thanked God.

The citadel was bathed in flags, lights, and boy scouts. It looked like a bride on her wedding day. Pedestrians pointed it out proudly, saying, "Tonight is the night for our citadel." My uncle was concerned, however, and said, "Please God, do not reveal our weaknesses and let this end well."

Mazen, on the other hand, declared anxiously that the weather report announced westerly winds, and asked for God's protection. As for Futna, her mother, Nahleh, Abu Salem, and Umm Grace, they were overjoyed and ecstatic because Violet was scheduled to sing before the governor, the notables, and the consuls. She would thus prove to them that in Wadi al-Rihan, we could compete in whatever we wanted, with world summits and superstars.

Giving in to the pressure of the family and his own curiosity, Kamal postponed his trip to Frankurt till after the festivities. He didn't want to abandon us on a great day of celebration, festivities, and the display of our gifts, but more important, he had heard the weather report and was concerned and curious about the outcome of events. He wondered what would happen if the westerly winds brought the odors, the mosquitoes, and the flies, and if the rats of the station came out, how the governor and the consuls would react. What would his brother Mazen, the man in charge, say about the arrangements and the success of the festivities?

The success of this celebration would mean continuous cultural activity at the citadel, visits from intellectuals, the arrival of tourists, modernity, and setting the foundations of change. Though the sewage project had failed to get rid of the garbage, purify the water, and improve the environment, Mazen might succeed in generating light from the citadel. Though it is true that culture cannot replace the needs of the street or children's food, it is still considered the nourishment of the soul. No people could rise without culture and intellectual activities. It was, therefore, his duty to provide art and food for the soul of each member of this population, he owed it to them. In other words, culture was for everybody and this celebration was for everybody, and so was the citadel, it belonged to all and everybody had a right to it.

Mazen distributed thousands of invitations, fliers, and programs. Everyone in town and in the villages of the North was getting ready to attend this festivity, together with the children, friends, and relatives. They came in groups, they came by the busload, in trucks and taxis, early in the morning, and filled the streets of Wadi al-Rihan. My uncle went back home for lunch, breathing heavily from the heat, the noise, and the crowded streets and shops. He said to his wife, breathlessly, "Hordes of people are coming in huge numbers."

She was happy and optimistic and said, "Mazen must be very happy."

Contrary to people's expectations and those of my uncle's wife, Mazen was not happy or proud, because he had never thought that all those people would come, and such numbers meant overcrowding, suffocation, and chaos. He thought about the dancers, the microphones, the program, and electricity. As he had been busy making contacts with the consulates, the journalists, the unions, the associations, and foreigners, he hadn't arranged to provide large-scale security for the festivities. He was wondering who would organize the people's entrance to the theater, and who would guarantee the security of the officials and where they would be seated, especially since the invitations weren't numbered. No matter how many additional seats they brought, there would never be enough for each guest to sit down or even to stand inside the theater or on the terrace. It occurred to him that the boy scouts accompanying the governor might help to keep order and maintain security. But the boy scouts had brought drums, trumpets, and whistles and insisted on doing what they had come to do: participate in the show and entertain the audience with a song dedicated to the citadel and its past glory. They paraded in the streets of our town the whole morning like soldiers. They played music that everybody liked, exciting the children of the city who followed them everywhere, carrying drums or tin boxes on which they played the tune they liked.

Despite our happiness with the joyous atmosphere of the festivities, the activities at the market, the balloons, the candy and the ice cream, the overcrowded shops and public places made us extremely anxious. We were concerned about people rushing to the gates of the citadel. It was barely five in the evening and hours before opening time, and the lines already stretched all the way to the hills of Nablus.

There were checkpoints on the Arab side and on the Israeli side, those of the Authority and those of its authority. On one side we heard "salam," and on the other side "shalom." The car drivers were concerned about traffic and wanted to drive through without delays. But the traffic wasn't moving smoothly. It was blocked between the Arab and the Israeli checkpoints. One was concerned with security and another was preoccupied with ensuring security; in other words, we became the concern of the security, but there was no security for us. The situation created a traffic jam that extended all the way to Hawara, on the east side. We tried in vain to intervene to facilitate the traffic but we failed. The governor said that he had no control over it and the municipal director claimed that he was responsible for the sewers not the traffic. As for the mayors of the nearby villages, they arrived through VIP channels, passed without any problem and sat in the front rows—those reserved for the consuls and the journalists. We had to cajole and flatter them to get back some of the seats they occupied for the sponsoring countries and the priests.

We didn't know where to seat the nuns until my uncle intervened. He gave up his seat to make room for them. Futna sat first in the front row claiming that she was keeping the seat for her mother who was arriving from Jerusalem, with the French and the Spanish consuls. But Mazen pursuaded her to give up the seat, upsetting her terribly. She considered the move almost an insult and withdrew with Nahleh and Umm Grace to the backstage area. There, they watched the dancers, the music players, the electrician, and the sound engineer preparing the stage and testing the microphones, saying hello, hello. At this exact moment Futna felt something sticky between her legs, but she didnt pay much attention to it and got carried away with the atmosphere of the festivities.

When the consuls, the journalists, and the notables arrived, the spectators were present in large numbers but the festivities were delayed due to sudden confusion, shouting, and fighting at the gates. One person was heard saying, "Allahu Akbar," and another said, "Get out of my way," while a third one yelled, "Shame on you, it isn't acceptable to behave this way in public, in front of foreigners."

Saadu was shouting loudly and pushing the crowd, followed by Said. He said, "Who deserves to be here, the foreigners or us?"

Said agreed with him, saying, "Of course, us."

He pushed the people on his left and on his right causing them to fall, some were trampled under the feet.

A young boy was bleeding from the eye and shouting, "My eye, my eye," but no one stopped to help him. The workers rushed to Mazen and told him that the boy had lost his eye and needed an ambulance. Lying at people's feet and waiting for an ambulance that was taking its time to arrive, the boy lost consciousness.

The ambulance wasn't allowed to go through without being thoroughly searched, to make sure that no bombs or machine guns were hidden in the midst of glucose and syringes. No one knew whether the delay happened at the Arab or the Israeli checkpoint.

Mazen stood at the top of the stairs watching the pushing, the shoving, the fighting, saying to himself, "God almighty, what kind of people are they!" He saw Said pushing the crowds, preceded by Saadu who was making his way through the spectators and shouting, "Move, move!"

Mazen was concerned about this confusion and cried to his brother, "Hey, Said, fear God."

But Said pushed a sweaty Saadu and told him, "We've arrived, enter from here, go on, go on."

When both arrived at the stage entrance they found no room to stand, so they jumped over people's shoulders until they reached their seats. When Kamal saw them moving toward the consuls, he thanked God for the plane ticket that was in his pocket for the return trip to Germany. Mazen tried to block their way and whispered to them to stop and move away, but Said squeezed between the nuns and told his brother to leave him alone. His comportment shocked the nuns and made even me appeal to the Virgin Mary for her protection. Saadu moved through the rows and sat directly behind Sitt Amira and beside Abd al-Hadi Bey al-Shayib. He inadvertently hit her in the back with his elbow, making her turn and scold him angrily, saying, "Shame on you young man, respect people."

Mazen's eyes caught Kamal's eyes from a distance from his location behind the curtain. Kamal smiled spontaneously, either from embarrassment or possibly to encourage Mazen, but his brother misunderstood his intention and interpreted the smile differently, seeing it as his way of gloating. He was sure that Kamal had seen Said and Saadu push their way through the crowds and sit behind the consuls, in the midst of the nuns and the notables. He was boiling inside as he saw Kamal standing near the ticket window, watching people as if they were part of an experiment in his lab. His anger against Saadu and Said was redirected toward Kamal's perceived arrogance. Mazen wondered whether his brother felt himself above these creatures? They are our people, our family, our friends, and the inhabitants of this land. They are tired of martyrdom and funerals, they've come to have fun and forget their worries. The Germans are not our people, what do we get from them, even if they stand in line and are organized! What if their government is the best in the world and their country the most advanced, with the cleanest air! What if their streets are impeccably clean and their garbage divided into five categories in five different barrels! What if their sewage is as sweet as sugar, are you one of them or one of us?

Mazen suddenly heard a familiar laugh and turned his head to find Futna with her round belly sitting on the drummer's seat, beating the drum, while Nahleh was playing the organ and Umm Grace was laughing and clapping. He was mesmerized by the sight and marveled at Wadi al-Rihan and its transformation, amazed by its inhabitants, who had become like children in a wedding party. If he had had security forces and a large army he would have controlled the crowds, but he was alone, how could he impose order! This was the worst and biggest mistake of his life. Was it his luck or this eager milieu, people's psychology, the lights, the fliers, the programs, and the boy scouts? There were the invitation cards as well, thousands of them. He wondered who had printed so many? Who had distributed them? And the ice cream stands and the sugar candy. Who had excited the inhabitants of Wadi al-Rihan? Who had forgotten to include seat numbers on the invitation cards? How could a small mistake, a simple mistake affect everything? We had been concerned about the weather and had taken a million precautions but how could we have anticipated what was happening now?

Suddenly, he heard the boy scouts' drums and the tune of the festival shaking the stage. The words went as follows:

I am from the Citadel, dear
Spread the good news and meet me here.
Doves fly and doves land,
Peace is at hand,
Dreams are coming true
In Wadi al-Rihan, for me and you.
O God, O God, O God,

Let the wronged rejoice,
And in one voice,
Our efforts applaud.

The song excited the spectators, who joined in, singing very loudly, their voices reaching all the way to the closest police station. It reached the other checkpoint by wireless and ordered it to get ready. In their enthusiasm, they were not aware that the citadel had been isolated from the rest of the world and from Wadi al-Rihan, surrounded by security forces.

The wind blew in from the west and carried with it the odors we had feared, but the confusion outside, the crowds inside, and the spectators' happiness with the boy scouts, the music and the stomping of the dabkeh dancers on the stage made it a lesser evil than we had expected. Most people attributed the odor to the crowds and the summer sweat rather than to the sewage and the station's malfunction. The show went on, the audience dancing and shouting without anyone inside the citadel noticing the military presence outside, the increased number of security forces, and the invasion of rats brought by the westerly winds.

We probably had exaggerated when we attributed the agitation of the insects and the rats inside and outside the citadel to the blowing of the wind and the sewage station, because in reality, they were an integral part of the environment. In this wild region the garbage rats were abundant, especially in the quarries, the villages, and the settlement of Kiryat Rahil. They might have been stirred up by the blowing winds, which might have drawn them out of their holes in search of spoils. So, as soon as it was Violet's turn to sing, she ran out shouting, "A rat in the guitar, a rat in the guitar!"

The women backstage ran to help her but Futna stumbled, got caught in the electric wires and fell heavily on the floor, causing her water to break and her labor to begin.

Mazen was shocked by the sight and the sounds he was hearing, he wondered whether it was a celebration or a nightmare, an educational activity, or a silly carnival. He heard the workers calling for an ambulance, but no one approached the woman lying on the floor surrounded by a small pool of water. Nahleh was kneeling beside her, shouting, "This is no time for this kind of behavior, Sitt Futna!"

The ambulance was waiting behind the checkpoint where it was searched meticulously. But the siege was tightened because the voices coming from the citadel threatened trouble and great excitement that might lead to a confrontation with the police or the security forces or even between the people and the settlers of Tal al-Rihan.

Tal al-Rihan was not very far away, just a few kilometers. In the past, in the good old days, the days of freedom, the inhabitants of Wadi al-Rihan used to go to that hill to celebrate the feast of the Nayruz, the Thursday of the dead, the Thursday of the eggs, and the feast of the Prophet Moses. People during those days still observed traditions and feast rituals, but now, after thirty years of occupation, the confiscation of the hill where the Kiryat Rahil settlement had been established was surrounded by a thick fence, a checkpoint, and guards; people have grown used to the situation. They look beyond the horizon so they can forget that foreigners live on top of this hill, foreigners with sideburns who carry arms and swear that the valley and the hill were originally Wadi Rahil and Solomon's Hill. Just as they had taken Tal al-Rihan in the seventies, they had hoped to regain the rest of the plateau and the valley in the eighties.

Years went by however, and the inhabitants of Wadi al-Rihan didn't recover the hill nor did the settlers of Kiryat Rahil seize the wadi. Both groups, however, watch each other hoping to mark a point or win a goal. This explains the violence of the last years, the killings and the looting on both sides. But naturally, the inhabitants of Wadi al-Rihan, less favored by circumstances, marked only a few thefts, a stolen car, some cement, old metal pieces, a sack of flour and hay. In return, and due to favorable circumstances, the inhabitants of Tal al-Rihan, whenever an opportunity arose, whether by day or by night, launched armed attacks on the Wadi, with machine guns and bombs, under the watchful eye of the security forces. On this day, the day of the citadel, because of the chaos and the enthusiasm of the people, the security measures were reinforced.

No one knows exactly why the festivities got out of hand and people rushed out and fought with the police, and the security forces, causing the most violent confrontation that had ever taken place between weapons and stones. Later on, when the press wrote about the event many stories were told, someone stated that the checkpoint had refused to let the ambulance through to transport Futna to Hadassa hospital. The driver and the medics became involved in a very heated discussion with the police, which ended in shouting and calls for help, making the public leave the theater to take part in the fight. Another version of the story reported that the rats became excited and started running among the public and between the chairs, chasing the spectators out. There, they saw what was happening with the medics, went to their rescue and took part in the fight. A third version was reported in the paper *Akhbar al-yom*, based on an eyewitness account. He said that someone saw men from the Tal al-Rihan settlement carrying lit torches and weapons. He shouted "Fire, fire," to warn people. Some however, denied that version considering it an inflammatory exaggeration. The panic was the result of the misunderstanding caused by the phonetic similarity between *far* and *nar* in Arabic.

Whatever the cause and the motivation, it was clear that the festivities in Wadi al-Rihan were influenced by various intrinsic factors that predisposed the situation to an explosion. On the one hand, there was the confusion due to poor planning, a large number of tickets, the flyers, and the programs. There was also the growing enthusiasm of hearts discontented with martyrdom and sad stories, who had come to rejoice despite history. When they saw the dabkeh dancing group rumbling, and heard the boy scouts' drum, they were overwhelmed with nostalgia. They sung for the homeland, the citadel, and finally for sacrifice and martyrdom. The mayhem was caused by a multitude of factors, a situation that went out of hand, the effect of a failed sewage project, the confrontation between the security forces and the medics, and Futna's delivery behind the stage in front of the workers, the singers, and the dabkeh dancers. Most of the workers were patriotic young men who had spent bitter years in detention, quarries, and vicious chases in the valleys and the narrow alleys. They became emotional and shouted proudly, "*Tar*, revenge." What was heard then was certainly either "fire," or "revenge," or "rat." There wasn't a big difference between the way they sounded in Arabic; as for their impact and their result, that was a different matter.

When the festivities exploded Mazen found himself in an unenviable situation. He had failed to steer the celebration in the right direction and he was responsible for the situation turning upside down. He was responsible for a large number of consuls, journalists, and the governor. What could he do for all those people without security, a police force, or even guards? All he had at his disposal were a group of scouts, dabkeh dancers, and a band of singers. What could those people wearing ribbons, red berets, and gold-trimmed waistcoats do in the face of confrontations with stones, bullets, and bombs?

A shell hit the window and began emitting tear gas, forcing Mazen to jump to his feet and ask people to close the windows. But nobody moved, their despondency rendered them speechless and motionless. Some stood behind the windows watching what was happening in the streets below the citadel, between the people and the security forces. Others gathered around the governor, who was trying to contact the police and the security forces. They were busy with more important matters. They feared a collective movement of angry people rushing toward the settlers who were standing watch near the barricade and on top of the hill. This explained why the governor was incessantly shouting, "Hello police, hello security," but no one from the outside answered him.

Mazen's eyes caught the confused look of the governor. He was a man in his sixties who had spent his youth in camps and exile in other people's countries. He had devoted his whole life to the revolution and had paid a high price, and later, retired. Then, unexpectedly he was told that he had a country, a people, a solution, a peace, and consuls. Placed in a position of responsibility, this bright man knew that he would be walking a tightrope, would never know a moment of peace and quiet. Here he was now, like Mazen and the others, surrounded inside the citadel, with consuls, journalists , priests, nuns, and a woman who had given birth backstage and was in dire need of medical assistance. But where would he get an ambulance?

He discussed the matter with Mazen, trying to find a way out of the citadel, out of this trap. He was new to the area although it was his birthplace. Years of occupation and life in exile and an absence that had lasted decades had made him a visitor and a tourist among people who had lived for generations connected to their roots in the land. That's why they didn't feel that he was one of them, or in other words, they didn't know whether he was one of them or one of "them." One of us, one of them, or us and them, or you and us, and this meant speaking another language, taking a different action, and dealing with a different people and another exile, a new exile he had never heard of or experienced. You are in your country without being in it, you are with your people, but your people are outside and you are here, in this citadel. Inside and outside, there was a police and security force, an Authority, a system, and a government, and a dazed people, an unlucky people who had come to have some fun but for no apparent reason the fun had turned into a funeral in the blink of an eye. There might be multiple reasons, but what mattered now was finding a way out of this trap.

Mazen told the governor that the usual road was not passable because of checkpoints and confrontations. The longer road behind the citadel was not practicable or safe because it ran through Kiryat Rahil, in the middle of the settlement of Tal al-Rihan. He wondered whether the governor would be willing to be seen by the inhabitants of Wadi al-Rihan and the journalists driving through an Israeli settlement. It was a major question, a loaded question for a government official. His choice would not be interpreted casually or as necessity of the moment. It was bound to be judged in the context of history, politics, and a semblance of a government and streets that the Authority does not control. They

232

were roundabout roads imposed on people by force and impacting their livelihood. Those were lands they had inherited with deeds from the time of Moses and even Muhammad. And here there was this solution, this occupation that took whatever it wanted without accountability, as the people were told this was liberation, it was the way to peace, a way around the past to reach the future. They were told that the present was not theirs. That explained its name, *eltifafiyyeh*, wrapping around.

People wondered about the eltifafiyyeh concept. They understood it, however, and they even interpreted it this way: it was a noun derived from the verb *laffa*, and *laffa* did not mean to move in circles, but it meant to wrap something up and take it away, in other words, it meant to swallow something or sleep on it. This was, naturally, an exaggeration because the intermediary was not the person gulping, but was gulped himself. They drew their conclusion in those words, "Then, did he come to gulp, to wrap?" They wondered, shouted, threw stones and said, "Go away."

The governor had a bright idea. He thought of asking people in power about their position in the matter. He would tell them, "This is our position: we are responsible for unarmed guests, a woman who has just given birth, a citadel isolated from the rest of the world, surrounded by a confrontation between the people and the security forces. We are trapped, caught between bullets, stones, and gas bombs, what should we do?"

Mazen would say that we had a bus and a way around the citadel. The road went through Kiryat Rahil, which presented a problem. The governor would wonder if that meant boarding a bus that would drive through the settlement of Tal al-Rihan? But wasn't Tal al-Rihan ours, after all, and what belongs to us does not belong to them; was there any doubt about it? If someone says, "There is doubt," he would say, "Wrong!" If they approved, he would say, "You're right, let's board." Where was Mazen?

Mazen's father looked at his son in disbelief, and said, "Kiryat Rahil? Did you say Kiryat Rahil?"

Mazen replied quickly and determinedly, "We need to maneuver, maneuver, maneuver. Do you want us to die in this citadel?"

His father responded sullenly, "Is that it, you've lost patience? Let's wait until things calm down and take the regular road like everybody else."

Mazen pointed to the stage and asked, "Dad, what about Futna?"

The father turned back and said disgusted, "Take Futna and go, I'm not leaving."

He then walked slowly toward the window, mumbling, "Kiryat Rahil! By God, Kiryat Rahil, is this what we've come to?"

Mazen was watching Amira busy with her daughter and her grandson. She was surrounded by the boy scouts who were eager to help. One was asking, "Aunt, what do you want?"

Another told her, "I got you a pillow."

And a third scout brought her water. Amira answered each one of them calmly, saying, "May God bless you. You are the best men in the world, give me, give me."

Mazen felt somewhat guilty and embarrassed vis-à-vis those youngsters who stayed with Futna and her mother all the time and paid no attention to the others, the consuls, the journalists, the priests, and the nuns. Their only concern was this baby. At this age a person is still pure and innocent, at this age the birth of a baby is the secret of the universe and its miracle and other things do not matter. At this age a baby is more important than all the consuls, the journalists, the clerics, and the politicians.

He was in a position of responsibility, however, trusted with important people; what would happen if any one of them were hurt? What if a consul, a priest, or a even a journalist were hurt? Would the situation in Wadi al-Rihan be compared to life in Algeria in the nineties?

He overheard the words Kiryat Rahil in a conversation between the governor and one of the consuls. A journalist asked, "Kiryat Rahil?"

Then the governor asked, nervously, "Tell me what should I do? It is Kiryat Rahil despite you and me. If you were the man in charge, what would you do?"

The journalist was dumfounded and stared at him from behind his eye glasses, repeating, "Kiryat Rahil?"

"Yes sir, Kiryat Rahil," reiterated the governor, with controlled anger, as if the journalist was responsible for the situation and its complications. He went on cornering him with his questions, "Do you have any objection? Do you have an alternative?"

234

The journalist was trying to get out of the situation repeating the name Kiryat Rahil. The governor became even angrier and shouted at him, "What do you suggest? Do you have an alternative?"

The journalist turned around and left, mumbling, "Why should I interfere, you're the one in a position of responsibility."

The governor shouted, trying to stop him, "Listen brother, what I say is not to be published, do you understand what I'm telling you?"

The journalist muttered as he moved away, "Of course I understand."

He stood near the window watching the action.

Futna said smiling, but exhausted, "I was afraid he would be a Mongoloid."

Her mother said comfortingly, "Your son is normal, but he weighs so little. He's very thin and needs an ambulance, he does."

Amira looked left and right and saw Mazen. She begged him for assistance, "Mazen, isn't there an ambulance?"

He looked at her, then at her daughter, then at the child and said confused, "What do you want me to say? You know the situation."

She saw his confusion and hesitation, and said to encourage him, "This difficulty will pass, we've seen worse."

She smiled to herself then to him, and said whispering, "At least it's not in Hadassa."

Not in Hadassa? He wondered what she meant with those words. What if he had mentioned Kiryat Rahil, what would she have said? He was peeking behind the curtain as if looking for something, but that thing was in his head or in his heart or in both—what was it?

He saw Kamal standing near the window and joined him, seeking an explanation. Kamal made no reply as if he hadn't heard him. Mazen repeated the word Kiryat Rahil, provoking Kamal to respond in a loud whisper, "The problem is not with Kiryat Rahil but with you, Mazen Hamdan, boarding a bus alone and leaving the people waiting for a way out of here."

His words upset Mazen, who asked him, "What do you mean?"

He turned to him and pointed at the outside, saying, "You were always there, all your life, what brought you here? What changed you?"

His eyes bulged, his heart sank as a result of this attack, and he prepared to defend himself. He said angrily, "You were there all your life as well and you didn't care."

Then he left quickly to get away from his brother. He felt his legs give way due to a very sharp pain like a knife stab. He turned to Kamal and shouted under the effect of pain, "Stay there and never come back."

He took a few more steps, his head buzzing with questions and reactions, his father's questions, Amira's questions, and those of his brother. He moved in circles looking for something, when suddenly a question popped into his mind, a new question, born at this instant. He stood still, turned back again and shouted to his brother, "Which is better, a bus or a plane?"

But his question remained unanswered.

Sitt Amira refused to board the bus which carried the consuls and the journalists. She objected strongly and categorically to the very idea of crossing Kiryat Rahil to reach the hospital in Nablus. The governor changed his mind as well and felt that staying in the citadel with the people in these circumstances was a must. It was a matter of duty, for history and for people's judgement. What would they have said had he left, that he had followed the consuls and the paying purses, leaving them alone? What would the journalists have said? And the Hamdan and Shayib families? Would they have said that he had left a woman bleeding on the floor and run for his life? He wouldn't run away, he would stay with them to the last man and the last breath.

Mazen came begging the governor to board the ambulance with them to cross the two checkpoints, the Arab and the Israeli. Futna was bleeding and she could well die, while the child was weak and needed medical assistance quickly. Mazen sat in the front and Amira stayed with her daughter and the grandson in the back of the car. They crossed the Arab checkpoint without delay or complications, but the disaster was the required stop in the main street in front of the Kiryat Rahil checkpoint. While they were enduring the long and tiring wait, Mazen noticed the Bey in his Mercedes, with the yellow license plate of Jerusalem. He crossed the checkpoint without stopping and without being searched. He went by like lightning. Mazen was surprised and turned his head to confirm what he had seen but his position between the governor and the driver blocked his view. The governor asked him whether something was the matter with him. He explained, still surprised and dazed:

"Was Abd al-Hadi Bey al-Shayib at the party?"

The governor said, casually, "He was sitting behind his sister and I greeted him.".

Mazen asked, "Behind what sister?"

The governor explained casually, as he was watching the soldiers dragging their feet while a long line of cars was forming each waiting its turn, patiently and apprehensively, "The sister sitting in the back of the ambulance."

"Do you mean Amira?"

The governor didn't answer him and continued to watch the soldiers, the cars, and two young men standing against the wall, as if in a punishment position. They faced the wall, holding their hands above their heads. He whispered, "By God, what have we done to be treated like this?" wondered the governor.

Mazen, who had become accustomed to this sight, wasn't moved or scared, or even surprised. He didn't comment on the governor's words or pay attention to him; he was thinking instead of the Bey and how he had passed through the checkpoint thanks to his Jerusalem license plate. He wondered how he had arrived at the checkpoint and whether he truly had been at the festivities? Why had no one seen him? Was it because of the crowds and the chaos, or had he arrived with the consuls and left with them? Why had no one seen him? He turned to look back from the small window and saw Amira carrying the baby, while Futna was lying on the stretcher holding a glucose bottle in her hand. He shouted to them, "The Bey passed through the checkpoint in his car without stopping."

Amira looked at him with her big eyes but didn't comment. He repeated, "He crossed the checkpoint with his Jerusalem license plate."

She didn't say a thing and continued to stare without uttering a word, but Futna said in a weak voice, "He went and left us? That's not possible, you're certainly mistaken, it can't have been him."

The mother continued to stare without saying a word. Mazen turned his head and continued to watch the action around him.

The governor stepped out of the car and tried to approach one of the soldiers, but one of them shouted at him in a thundering voice, "Stop, stop!"

The governor stretched his hand to explain to him that he meant well, and wanted only to talk to him. But the soldier repeated, "Stop, stop."

But the governor insisted and raised his voice saying, "Just a word, one word."

The soldier thundered, "Not even half a word, go back."

When the soldier felt that the governor was dragging his feet and unwilling to obey immediately and quickly, he raised his weapon and pointed it at him, saying sharply, "Return to your place."

The governor returned to the ambulance and sat in his place.

Futna said in a weak voice, "Maybe if you say that we're going to Hadassa they would let us go."

The mother didn't answer her and kept staring through the small window, her arms unconsciously squeezing the baby, repeating: Hadassa, Hadassa, son of Hadassa, the ticket to cross the checkpoint, by God! She continued to stare through the small window.

The governor said, pensive, "I used to dream, I often dreamed, but for what!"

He stopped suddenly and turned his eyes toward the hill on which Kiryat Rahil was built. He saw the red brick, the barbed wire, various buildings, the playgrounds, strange stairs, and huge water pipes cutting through the rocks and the ground. The homeland had become strange, it has become an exile, he thought to himself. The land of dreams was devoid of dreams. The liberation dream has become a mere slogan that doesn't relate to the land, a nightmare. How much had he dreamed while in Dhahran, and in Lebanon and Tunisia? He used to dream of a genie coming out of a bottle, offering him his services, saying, "Shubbayk, lubbayk." He would ask the genie to carry him and throw him under an olive tree, give him a loaf of bread, olives, an onion, and salt. Here he was now, in front of an olive tree, on a road filled with checkpoints and facing a high fence. This is where the dream ended.

Mazen said with painful embarrassment, "The festivities were a scandal, all our work and efforts were for nothing."

The governor shook his head without commenting and recalled the past, the long years, the many martyrs and sacrifices. Then came Madrid and Oslo, then Tal al-Rihan and Kiryat Rahil.

Mazen was watching a familiar sight, a checkpoint, soldiers, young men with their hands raised above their heads, a long line of cars, while whistling bullets were heard in the distance. The wind carried the smoke of bombs and gases, he said, "I sometimes feel my head is like a barrel full of gun powder. What's wrong with us, brother? What have we done and how can we face the tragedies and protect ourselves? Our people aren't up to the challenge and neither are we up to the plan. No small spot in the world would give us hope or even the flicker of a light, what have we done?"

He then remembered Kamal, what he had said and how he was running away from these circumstances. Did he blame him? In the depth of his heart he did but in a remote corner of his mind a question kept nagging him, "Had Wadi al-Rihan embraced him? Even we, his family, had we embraced him, had we understood him, had we listened to him, had we given to him so that he would give back to us?" Mazen had told him that leadership was giving, but Kamal had yelled back, "I'm not a leader and I don't have leadership qualities. I'm only a scientist, ready to work, give me work."

But the work moved away from him and was picked up by Said, who changed the purification station into a pollution station.

Mazen suddenly remembered his brother and said, "Kamal is leaving tonight I wonder how he'll manage."

The governor asked him casually, while taking in the sight of the growing number of young people lined against the wall and the street full of cars, "Who are you talking about?"

Mazen replied, saddened, "My eldest brother, he's a scientist who works for the Germans."

The governor said in a monotonous tone, "For the Germans? What Germans? He must return and work with us. The country needs its sons' brains, he must come back."

Mazen muttered, feeling twice as depressed as before he had heard the empty reply of the governor who spoke meaningless words, "It's difficult for him to return."

But the governor repeated thoughtlessly, "He must come back."

Mazen repeated somewhat angrily, "It's difficult for him to return."

The governor repeated the usual words, "Give me his papers and I'll bring him back."

But Mazen didn't reply and remained silent. The governor turned to him and said, sincerely, "I can bring him back. I can get him an identity card and a national number."

Mazen wanted to take a deep breath, to shout, to beat his cheeks, to rip his shirt and get out of his clothes. He wanted to tell him: is Kamal a national number? Is that what we are, just numbers? Is that the difficulty? Is that the secret of his refusal to return? Doesn't this man understand that the most difficult thing in this case was not the number, but numbers? We are the difficult part because we are the numbers, we are the leaders, we are the environment, we are the street. He then remembered the conversation they had had about Kamal and Nahleh's experience in old Nablus, and the ordeal with the Black Tigers. They had been held at a national detention center, and it was therefore more dangerous. It wouldn't have been so frightening had Kamal been detained by the Israelis. What could Mazen say? He had asked his brother vigorously to be patient, to understand, and to make sacrifices because the true leader must be generous. Kamal had shouted at him, having lost all patience, "I am neither a leader nor an administrator, just give me work." But the work had disappeared and Said had caught it.

Futna said in a weak voice, "Mother why do you always react like this, what would happen if we said Hadassa? They might let us go through if we say that we're going to Hadassa."

The mother didn't reply and continued to stare at the sight from the small window behind Mazen's head. Although the window was too small to reveal the whole scene, she knew what was happening there. She had memorized the events, as familiar to her as the various districts of Jerusalem, all its corners and its paths. She was a young woman in her thirties when they had entered the city with their machine guns, and she was over sixty now. She was a mother, Nasser's mother then and she was a grandmother now, for this one!

She looked at her daughter, felt sad and remembered her son Abd al-Nasser. She found it strange that the present generation of the Shayib children lacked enthusiasm, ambition, and intelligence. In the past, they had been lighting flames, strong like a rock and a dome, their radiance had lit Jerusalem. One could recognize them in a crowd. There were famous leaders, religious scholars, historians, and thinkers in the family. At that time, Jerusalem was the greatest city in the world and the members of the Shayib family were the jewels of the world.

There were prestigious schools and colleges in Jerusalem at that time. Its graduates were geniuses, lawyers, teachers, scientists, and religious scholars. Religion was a shining subject then, it pulled one up toward the skies, lit the public squares, and the centers of learning. Now religion is heard through loudspeakers and the shouting from the top of the minarets every Friday, rather every day, five times a day. The voices were hoarse and raucous, lacking tenderness. They sounded like drums and aroused fear in people's hearts. It had been so different in the past, the morning adhan had been like a glass of milk scented with the fragrance of flowers, drunk in the morning it brought a feeling of peace and serenity to the drinker and warmed his heart and insides.

Futna's father, may he rest in peace, used to tell the judge and the court cleric that "the adhan has to be as soft as the breeze, and as tender as basil because the adhan is the breeze of paradise, the scent of paradise and God's whisper inviting us to submit to him."

Amira didn't submit now because the adhan woke her up like the sound of a cannon and reminded her of the present situation, of the sounds of cannons, of machine guns and tanks. Can this be God's voice? Or was it the sound of the tanks crossing the valley and climbing over the hill to reach the citadel?

If Futna only understood this difference, if she had understood it in the past she would understand the present situation. But Futna didn't listen to the morning, noon, and evening adhan, she only listened to her music. She loved dancing and wearing beautiful clothes, looking attractive in her short dresses and getting pregnant from over there, then giving birth. Was this today's generation? Was this what the old generation had given birth to?

Futna said to her mother, "Mother, I'm bleeding heavily. When will we get there?"

Amira remembered her daughter and found her very pale, her lips were as white as cotton. She put the baby down and knocked very hard on the windowpane. When Mazen looked back she said, begging, "Can you talk to them and tell them that she has just given birth and is bleeding? If we continue at this rate we'll never get there, we won't."

The governor turned to her and said, "We'll get there, but as you see the line is long, you must be patient."

Mazen felt uneasy sitting between the governor and the driver. He wanted to ask him to make way for him so that he could tell the soldiers that she had just given birth and was bleeding, and the child needed medical attention. But he was embarrassed as he remembered the governor's humiliation when he tried to talk to the soldiers. He said, "Sometimes I feel as if I were suffocating and I wish I could get out of my skin and run away to Frankfurt or Berlin like Kamal, who ran off to save his skin. But I stayed inside my skin and my own skin is too tight for me. I'm ashamed of myself, sometimes I look in the mirror and I say to myself, you're Mazen? You are Hamdan Guevara? You are Hamdan's son?"

The governor said with mounting anxiety, "Leave it to God, what can we say? One must be patient and look beyond the present. If we paid attention to every word where would we be today?"

Mazen turned to him and asked angrily, "Well, where are we now?"

The governor smiled with the expression of those who know, the mature, experienced men, those scoured by time. He said quietly, "We must be patient and look beyond the horizon."

Mazen was deeply irate and wanted to shout at the governor. How could he tell him to be patient, to wait, to look beyond the horizon? Did he have a date? Did he have a deadline, a year, two years, ten years, fifty years? He wished they could understand each other, but Mazen wasn't sure that the man understood.

242

The governor mumbled in a low voice, "We dreamed a lot but to no avail!"

A few years earlier he had been living in Tunis, in a palace near the sea. The visitors, the journalists, an Arab minister and one from the European Union had said that it would be solved. But he hadn't believed them because the solution had been suggested many times before. It had been mentioned in Tunis, in Beirut, in Amman, in Baghdad, and in Moscow, but it had never materialized. He had gotten used to living without a solution. He had grown older and became more and more removed from his past and his activities. He had begun his professional life as a story writer, then as a playwright. One of his plays had been performed on stage but it hadn't achieved much success because it hadn't appealed to the people. It promoted the spirit of struggle and patriotic feelings. It contained speeches glorifying heroes, martyrdom, and suffering. The play ended with the ululations of a tearless mother who had lost her son. People left the theater without crying, without emotions, and without feelings.

His stories had been quite successful because they were about real people he had dug from the past and his memories, when he lived in the village. He had read avidly and spent long hours silent, observing people's lives, listening to them talk under the mulberry tree, and the vine trellis, in the cafés, and during Monday's market. The peasants' voices filled the pages of his stories and the reader felt them budding with life, with the day's concerns, and the hopes of the future. Then came the present and his present was removed from that of the people, from their streets, and their simple daily stories, their marriages and their divorces, the fights between neighbors stealing from each other, or fighting over a basket of figs.

Futna said in a faint voice, "Mother, I'm bleeding heavily."

Amira knocked at the window and Mazen turned his head toward the governor, then toward her and didn't say a thing. But the governor said, very slowly, "What can we say, the line is long."

Four persons were trapped in this long line between the citadel and the road block. There was Sitt Amira, Futna's mother and the baby's grandmother, Mazen

Hamdan Guevara sitting between the governor and the driver, and the governor predicting a quick resolution to the situation. There was also a bleeding woman and a newborn baby in dire need of medical attention.

Mazen was getting extremely anxious and began moving his legs in a fast, nervous, and annoying way. Even the governor was beginning to lose his patience after an hour and a half waiting in this line. Amira had recourse to religion for help. She recited the al-Falaq chapter three times, then al-Kursi followed by Yasin, but none of them resulted in opening the way for their passage. Strangely enough it was the daughter who felt least threatened, possibly because of her silliness, her mental limitations, or the bleeding and her will to live. She was the calmest of them all, the most reassured and relaxed. She was sure of crossing the road block, and didn't think that the bleeding would lead to her death. Her major concern was staining her clothes with blood and her good appearance. She feared that sleeping on her back would spoil her hairdo, and continually interrupted her mother's recitation of Qur'anic verses to ask if she were presentable. Her mother would reassure her with a nod of the head to avoid interrupting her recitation of the holy verses. Futna asked her mother to bring her the blue nightgown, her slippers, and the baby's clothes after they arrive at the hospital. Amira's response to her daughter's request was to raise her voice, occasionally stressing some meaningful words. But only the word envy attracted Futna's attention. She asked her mother, "Mother dear, do you think that all this happened to us because of Nahleh's envious eyes?"

The mother didn't reply and continued to pray in the darkness and the silence of the night. It was almost ten in the evening but the line had not moved. The floodlights were blinding, but the soldiers at the road bloc were relaxed and the number of young men lined against the wall was growing. The long wait had exhausted the governor, he felt depressed and bored, and tried to kill time telling stories and evoking memories of his life in Tunis, Beirut, Dharan, and even his childhood in the village. He related that he used to study under the light of the street lamp until the morning. He had read Eliya Abu Madi, Maxim Gorki, and Hasanayn Haykal among other authors whose books could only be smuggled in.

He said to Mazen, smiling as he remembered his past victories, "We used to snatch the books and read them over and over again. Whenever a book was confiscated we would laugh, because we knew it by heart. It was stored in our brains and couldn't be confiscated."

Mazen asked him, in a covert irony, having reached his wit's end, "Are the words still stored in your memory?"

He didn't turn to Mazen to answer his question, but went on talking in a monotonous voice, almost whispering, "Of course they're stored, and will be to the day I die. Do you think that words can be confiscated? A ruler can confiscate a book but not its words. They are the concrete embodiment of ideas. Do you understand what I'm saying?"

Mazen was extremely bored, but he confirmed his understanding of the governor's words.

The governor smiled in the darkness and said to Mazen, "Oh my God, we've endured and suffered so much! No people in the world has endured what we've endured, more than the Jews, more than the American Indians and the blacks."

Mazen turned to him and asked, curious, "The blacks?"

The governor paid no attention to him and continued to sift through his memories, "I saw them in America and in Africa. By God they are good people and they like us. They like the Arabs and the Muslims and some of them have converted to Islam. They invited us to speak in their mosque and after the sermon they began singing, they held hands and began to move as if they were dancing an African dance and I found myself dancing with them. From that time on, Jackson never left us. He visited us seven times in Tunis and according to him things were beginning to turn in our favor."

Mazen muttered surprised and curious, "In our favor?"

The governor said joyfully, "Naturally, naturally, you know that the number of blacks is increasing in America, it's unbelievable, and so is the number of Spanish and Mexicans and all those who come from overseas. I mean all those described as colored. Their number is increasing very fast, while the number of whites is decreasing daily. The equation is predictable and its result means that the colored peoples, led by the blacks, will rule America without a revolution, without a coup d'état, without bloodshed and all that nonsense. It will be done through elections, they will rule through the elections!"

Mazen turned to him and asked, furiously, "Are you sure?"

The governor exclaimed in reply, "Of course I'm sure. Jackson said so and Jackson backs his arguments with polls, and the polls say that the number of whites in America in the year 2055 will literally be one-third of the whole population. At that time what would America become?"

Mazen said, "A third world country."

The governor seemed to agree with him, saying, "It's possible, it's possible, and then America will be different."

Mazen stopped balancing his legs and said begging, "Let me pass because I'm squeezed in here and I must get out. Can I, would you please? Excuse me?"

He went out in the dark to pee.

Futna said, "Nahleh didn't believe that the baby would be a boy. I told her twenty times that a doctor in Hadassa confirmed it to me. He saw it on the screen and said it was a boy. But Nahleh refused to believe me. She would have liked the baby to be a girl or a Mongoloid. When she saw me give birth she lost her mind and gave us both the evil eye."

Her mother raised her voice while reciting the Qur'anic verses to silence her daughter, but Futna didn't stop talking, as usual. She went on, "It's also possible that Abu Salem's daughter is the cause, God only knows."

The mother stopped praying to figure out what her daughter was inventing. Futna explained, "I mean the curse of Abu Salem's daughter when we went to their house. Do you remember how insolent she was? Do you remember what she said and did? Do you remember how she touched her belly and said vulgar words that only a vagabond would utter? Maybe she felt that I was happy and very lucky because the baby I was carrying was the only heir. In other words, my son was an only child and a male and had only one sister. His sister isn't even interested in the inheritance. This means that he will inherit everything, unlike Abu Salem's daughter, who has ten brothers and two unmarried sisters, not counting Nahleh.

246

I am sure she thought of all this while she was sitting there staring at my belly, her hands resting on her own belly. Isn't that true mother?"

Her mother did not reply but she stopped praying. She fell into a total silence that covered her brain like an endless white fog. She didn't see any use in praying for a woman who could think like this. But Futna was her daughter after all, whatever she said and whatever she did, she was still her daughter. She was kind and pleasant, and very amusing. She couldn't deny, however, that sometimes she got on her nerves. She loved her mother dearly and sincerely and always inquired about her whenever she was sick. She gave to her generously whenever she asked for money and even when she didn't. She gave to her father and brother, as well, showering them with her wealth. She even opened a souvenir shop for her brother with her late husband's money, before his death. If anything serious should happen to her daughter, she would lose her consolation and her support in this world. Futna was indeed the best of daughters, the prettiest and the dearest daughter, and this baby was after all her baby, despite his problems.

The governor continued talking in the same monotonous voice, "I thought that misery existed only in Beirut but it seems to follow us everywhere. How can the wealthiest revolution become so poor? Was it conceivable that the oil rich countries would ever become indebted? And you still say that America will never change! It has to change despite itself, it must change. America is responsible for our misery and when America becomes like all other countries in the world you could say that we are free."

He then turned toward Mazen and asked hastily, "Do you want to get in?"

Mazen was standing in the dark, leaning against the door. He shook his head and said dryly, "I'd better stay here."

The governor went on saying, "The problem with our people is their eagerness for a quick solution, one delivered on a rocket, at no cost to them. Is it conceivable to have a solution without paying a price? Look at Japan, Germany, and even China."

Mazen muttered, "Look at Mandela."

The governor didn't seem to hear him, or maybe he heard him and didn't stop, to avoid losing his train of thought. He went on, "Look at China, opium was destroying the people and hunger was eating away at their bodies. See where they are now. They're as active as ants, riding bicycles, every member of the family rides a bicycle, even the ministers ride a bicycle. They're a united people, a patient people, and a people with a vision for the future. If we could only look far enough! But our people want immediate solutions delivered on a rocket."

Mazen objected, whispering, "No, in a Mercedes."

The governor did not seem to have heard him or he heard him but did not pay much attention because the focus of his conversation was the bicycles. He continued his reflections on this topic, "People used to say silly and stupid things about the Chinese, that they wore khaki clothes like prisoners and police officers, that they were all dressed alike. What's wrong with that? I wish we wore identical khaki clothes like them, rode in carts and bicycles, and could become a great nation like them. If we imitated them we would become like them and even better, don't you agree?"

Mazen didn't reply. He was thinking about Kamal's project that had turned into a catastrophe. The purification station had become a problem, the festival was a scandal, and this man whose help he had sought to go through the roadblock did nothing but talk. He cited examples from Japan, Germany, and China where the people run and ride bicycles, unlike the Arabs, who ride donkeys and travel in Mercedes cars.

He turned his face away from the ambulance and saw the young men lined against the wall with their arms still raised above their heads. Then he saw the long line of cars shining under the floodlights. He remembered Kamal, his father, the crowds, Saad and Said, and Abd al-Hadi al-Shayib. He also thought about the consuls and the journalists who had left in the bus while they were still waiting in the ambulance, at the roadblock. Who was to blame, he or the governor? Neither one. The governor could do nothing but dispense words from his past readings in a remote village. China runs on bicycles and how do we run? We run on dilapidated coffins!

Futna said, her voice weakening, "Mother, I must be sleepy. I'm dizzy, I can't keep my eyes open, is it alright to sleep?"

The mother became aware of the seriousness of her daughter's condition and said, "No, don't sleep, you might lose consciousness."

Amira remembered how she used to advise her to be strong, solid, and courageous. She repeated the same recommendation, "I've always told you to be tough. Don't sleep or close your eyes, do you understand me?"

Futna replied, in a weak voice, "Alright mother," then she fell asleep.

The mother knocked at the small window and asked in a harsh, determined voice, "You, in front, what's happening with you?"

The governor turned to her and said calmly, "Sitt Amira the line is long, we cannot jump over the other cars. We must be patient, we have to wait for God's help."

She said, angrily, "Honorable governor we can't wait anymore. My daughter is losing all her blood and she is about to die as I watch her. Is this acceptable? And you Mazen, where is Mazen?"

The governor called him, smiling, "Answer her Mazen, answer."

Mazen moved closer to the window and said with frustration, "Yes, aunt, your orders?"

She said angrily, "I don't understand, both of you are important people in the country and you're unable to talk to them? Talk to them in English."

The governor said, defending his position, "Believe me, I tried, didn't you see me?"

She replied angrily, "I want results, not efforts. Try again, a second time. My daughter has delivered a baby and is bleeding heavily, she might die while you are sitting here telling stories and talking nonsense. Don't you know English?"

The governor smiled and said, politely, "No, I don't."

She said dryly, "How did you talk with them, then? You said you've tried, what language did you use? And you Mazen, do you know how to talk to them?"

Mazen replied, weary and embarrassed, "Of course, I do."

"In what language?" she asked.

"I know a little English and Russian. But they understand our Arabic. It's not a question of language however, the fact is that they're upset."

She grumbled angrily, "By God! Aren't we all upset? My daughter is about to die and they don't want me to be upset?"

She then turned to her daughter and shook her by the shoulder saying, "Futna, Futna, get up dear. I think that we should step out and talk with them. Open the door."

Mazen hesitated and said in a low voice, "No aunt, what are you saying?"

She replied, firmly, "Open the door I tell you. Do you think that I'm not able to talk to them? I know French and English and also a little German. I can talk eloquently and say words that would make anyone proud. I can make them listen to me and respect me. Go ahead, open up."

He lowered his voice even more, saying, "Sitt Amira, the Israelis do not acknowledge anyone, listen to anybody, or respect anyone, have you forgotten that?"

She said stubbornly, "No, I haven't forgotten, neither have I forgotten that I am Amira the daughter of Shayib, whose father fought with the revolutionaries against the British, and whose grandfather protected the Aqsa Mosque. Are you trying to intimidate me with a bunch of soldiers gathered from all over the world? I can't sit still while my daughter is dying before my eyes. Go ahead, open up, open up I tell you."

She then turned to her daughter and shook her, "Get up Futna, get up my daughter, let them see what we can do. One knows no English and the other is afraid of the soldiers. Get up daughter, get up sweetheart."

But Futna didn't move, throwing her mother in a state of panic. She shouted, "Futna get up. Futna! Futna!"

Mazen rushed to the back of the car and opened the door, but Futna had gone to her Creator while they were arguing.

Two soldiers moved toward Mazen and the ambulance, pointing their weapons and shouting, "Stop, stop!"

One of the two soldiers hit him on the head with the handle of the machine gun, causing him to fall to the ground. The baby woke up and cried as they shouted. The grandmother looked at the soldiers, then at her daughter, and when the floodlights shined on her, her eyes were glassy and tearless. The soldiers shouted again and the baby cried. One of them said pointing the machine gun at her, "I said stop."

She said, calmly, "Alright, alright."

She then handed them the crying baby, and said calmly and proudly, in English: "Thank you very much, this is your share."

My uncle drove me to the airport and said, reproachfully, "It isn't acceptable that you're going away and leaving us."

I wiped away my tears for the first time in many years; I had recovered my ability to feel. I said affectionately, "I'll be back, I'll return, by God I will."

He said in guise of a reminder, "And your little brother, for whom are you leaving him?"

I said, a little embarrassed, "You and Amira are up to the responsibility."

He said, hoping to influence my decision, "Although the inheritance of the boy is double that of the girl, your part will be saved for you."

I shook my head without commenting, and I walked toward the plane.

GLOSSARY

adhan: the call to prayer.

Amaneh ya Layl: 'I trust you, O night!' part of the *mawwal*, a sung colloquial Arabic poem.

'Antar and 'Abla: a famous couple from the pre-Islamic period. The poet Antar declared his love to his cousin Abla in memorable poems.

araq: known as 'uzzo' in the West. An alcoholic drink made from raisins.

al-Atlal: literally 'the ruins;' the title of a famous song interpreted by the well-known Egyptian singer, Umm Kalthum.

Avicenna: Western name for the Muslim philosopher Ibn Sina (980–1037).

awwameh: a type of Arab sweet, similar to doughnuts.

Bab al-Khalil: one of the gates of the old city in East Jerusalem.

balouza: a milk custard.

Bilal the Stupid: the author may be deliberately recalling the name 'Bilal,' the name of a historical figure, the freed black slave, a convert to Islam, who was the first person to make the call to prayers, the adhan.

bisarah: Egyptian dish made of ground fava beans, onions, and garlic, with appropriate spices.

bushnaq: a term used to refer to someone who is fair-skinned and good-looking; from the name of a family, 'Bushnaq,' that emigrated from Bosnia to Palestine and Jordan in the late nineteenth century.

dabkeh: a Levantine folk dance.

dhikr: prayers consisting of the invocation of God's name.

diwan: gathering place for either formal or informal meetings.

dunum: a measure of land. One dunum is equal to 1,000 square meters.

Eliya Abu Madi: twentieth-century Lebanese poet (1894–1957), a member of the Mahjar school established by the immigrant poets in New York, and made famous by Khalil Gibran.

Fairuz: Contemporary female Lebanese singer, born in 1935, popular throughout the Arab world.

falafel: deep fried bean cakes made with broad beans, herbs, sesame seeds, and spices.

al-Falaq, al-Kursi, and Yasin: titles of chapters (suras) in the Qur'an.

far/nar/tar: the phonetic similarity between far ('rat'), nar ('fire'), and tar ('revenge') is very close and justifies the confusion of the three words.

al-Fatiha: the opening chapter (sura) in the Qur'an.

fidai: freedom or guerilla fighter.

ful: specially cooked fava beans eaten for breakfast.

Georgina Rizk: Lebanese winner of the 1971 Miss Universe beauty contest (b. 1943).

ha' (haq): the colloquial Palestinian word for a (legal or moral) right, also meaning 'price' or 'cost.' Hence the play on words in the novel.

hajj/hajjeh: term used to refer to or directly address men and women who have performed the pilgrimage to Mecca.

al-Hamd: the opening word of the Fatiha, the first chapter (sura) in the Qur'an.

al-Haram al-Sharif: name used to refer to the compound that includes both the Dome of the Rock mosque and the Aqsa Mosque, in Jerusalem.

Haykal, Muhammad Hasanayn: well-know Egyptian political journalist, writer, and editor, who served as editor-in-chief of the Egyptian daily newspaper, *al-Ahram*, and later served as adviser to, and was a close confidant of Gamal Abd al-Nasser. Also the author of numerous books about Egyptian politics (b. 1923).

ka'ek: pretzel-like bread, covered with sesame seeds and eaten with either za'tar, cheese, or hard boiled eggs.

Khaled Muhammad Khaled: contemporary Egyptian intellectual and journalist.

khatma: recitation of the entire Qur'an for a specific intention.

kirdan: a large necklace, part of country women's jewelry.

knafeh: dough shaped like shredded wheat, stuffed with walnuts or sweet cheese, and baked in syrup and melted butter.

kufiyeh: a long scarf worn under the 'i'qal as a headdress; also a black and white checkered scarf used by Palestinians as a national symbol.

al-Ma'arri, Abu al-'Ala': blind poet (973–1057) of the Abbasid period.

madhahib: schools of Islamic jurisprudence or law.

mahaleb: a kind of cheese, made from goat's milk.

Makhfiyeh: residential, middle-class neighborhood located on the mountain of Jersim, in Nablus.

mansaf: a dish of rice, meat, and yogurt.

maramiyeh: verbena.

mashallah: literally 'what God wills;' an expression uttered as an expression of appreciation for God's gifts. Also a piece of gold jewelry worn as a trinket on a chain around the neck as a means of protection.

mawwal: see *Amaneh ya Layl* above.

msakhkhan: a traditional Palestinian dish of chicken, onions, sumac, and olive oil. Eaten with thin country bread.

mulukhiya: pronounced 'mlukhiyeh' by Palestinians, a thick soup-sauce made of Jew's mallow, especially prized in Egypt.

Musrareh: a neighborhood in West Jerusalem.

Muwashshah: a stanzaic Arabic poem put to music and sung.

al-Nakba: 'catastrophe;' the name that Palestinians use to describe the events surrounding the loss of their homeland in 1948. The year of the creation of the State of Israel, 1948 is seen by Palestinians as a disastrous year in their history, turning them into a refugee people.

Nizar Qabbani: modern Syrian poet and diplomat, famous for his love poems (1923–98).

owl: the sight of an owl is a bad omen in Arab tradition.

Qays wa Layla: proverbial couple famous for their platonic love, which Qays ibn al-Mulawah, an Umayyad poet, described in his poetry.

qazha: nigella seeds. Pronounced 'azha' in colloquial Palestinian. The seeds are highly prized for their medicinal value and taste-enhancing effect. Often sprinkled on goat's cheese.

qirat: carat, a gold weight measure.

al-Ram, al-Tireh, and Abu Dees: Palestinian villages close to Jerusalem.

Rose al-Yusuf: a late-nineteenth-century female Egyptian journalist. She founded a weekly magazine that carries her name and is published to the present day.

salam: an Arabic word of greeting meaning 'peace.'

shalom: a Hebrew word of greeting meaning 'peace.'

shari'a: Islamic law.

al-Shatir Hassan: a hero of Egyptian folk tales who carries off great feats of cunning and bravery.

shawirma: slow-roasted meat or chicken.

shubbayk, lubbayk: magical terms equivalent to the familiar magical expression, Abracadabra. 'Lubbayk' is derived from the verb 'labbayka' meaning 'I am at your service.'

Sidna'l-Sheikh: term of respect used to address an Imam, a man in charge of religious duties in a mosque.

sitt: Term of address meaning 'Mrs.' or 'lady.'

sukkar qalil: 'small amount of sugar.'

Sunna: the traditions of the Prophet Muhammad, one of the sources of the Shari'a law.

tabbouleh: Levantine salad consisting of burgul, parsley, tomatoes, and onions.

tabliyeh: a traditional low round table, which requires people to sit on the floor when eating around it.

tala'a al-badru: literally, 'the full moon has appeared,' the title of a religious song referring to the Prophet Muhmmad, sung by Umm Kulthum.

tarawih: nightly prayers carried out during the month of Ramadan.

tamriyeh: Arabic sweet made of flour and clarified butter and sweetened with a sugar syrup.

tarbush: a fez.

Umm Kulthum: iconic twentieth-century female Egyptian singer, arguably the most famous in the Arab world (1904–75).

'umra: The name given to the lesser pilgrimage in Islam. The greater pilgrimage is called the Haj.

Wadi al-Joz: a neighborhood in East Jerusalem.

Wadi al-Rihan: literally 'the valley of basil;' an imaginary location in Palestine.

waqf: plural awqaf. A form of religious endowment in Islam, assigned only for charitable use.

ya: familiar vocative, equivalent in meaning to 'hey,' in English. It is also an exclamatory particle.

za'tar: powder consisting of dried thyme leaves, salt, sumac, and sesame seeds, eaten, usually for breakfast, with bread dipped in olive oil.

zunud al-sitt: a type of Arab sweet.

Modern Arabic Literature
from the American University in Cairo Press

Ibrahim Abdel Meguid *The Other Place*
No One Sleeps in Alexandria • *Birds of Amber*
Yahya Taher Abdullah *The Mountain of Green Tea*
Leila Abouzeid *The Last Chapter*
Ibrahim Aslan *Nile Sparrows* • *The Heron*
Alaa Al Aswany *The Yacoubian Building*
Hala El Badry *A Certain Woman*
Salwa Bakr *The Wiles of Men*
Hoda Barakat *The Tiller of Waters*
Mourid Barghouti *I Saw Ramallah*
Mohamed El-Bisatie *A Last Glass of Tea*
Houses Behind the Trees • *Clamor of the Lake*
Fathy Ghanem *The Man Who Lost His Shadow*
Randa Ghazy *Dreaming of Palestine*
Gamal al-Ghitani *Zayni Barakat*
Tawfiq al-Hakim *The Prison of Life*
Yahya Hakki *The Lamp of Umm Hashim*
Bensalem Himmich *The Polymath* • *The Theocrat*
Taha Hussein *A Man of Letters* • *The Sufferers* • *The Days*
Sonallah Ibrahim *Cairo: From Edge to Edge* • *Zaat* • *The Committee*
Yusuf Idris *City of Love and Ashes*
Denys Johnson-Davies *Under the Naked Sky: Short Stories
from the Arab World*
Said al-Kafrawi *The Hill of Gypsies*
Sahar Khalifeh *The Inheritance*
Edwar al-Kharrat *Rama and the Dragon* • *Stones of Bobello*

Betool Khedairi • *Absent*

Ibrahim al-Koni *Anubis*

Naguib Mahfouz *Adrift on the Nile* • *Akhenaten, Dweller in Truth*
Arabian Nights and Days • *Autumn Quail*
The Beggar • *The Beginning and the End*
The Cairo Trilogy: Palace Walk, Palace of Desire, Sugar Street
Children of the Alley • *The Day the Leader Was Killed* • *The Dreams*
Echoes of an Autobiography • *The Harafish*
The Journey of Ibn Fattouma • *Khufu's Wisdom*
Midaq Alley • *Miramar* • *Naguib Mahfouz at Sidi Gaber*
Respected Sir • *Rhadopis of Nubia* • *The Search* • *The Seventh Heaven*
Thebes at War • *The Thief and the Dogs* • *The Time and the Place*
Wedding Song • *Voices from the Other World*

Selim Matar *The Woman of the Flask*

Ahlam Mosteghanemi *Memory in the Flesh* • *Chaos of the Senses*

Buthaina Al Nasiri *Final Night*

Haggag Hassan Oddoul *Nights of Musk*

Abd al-Hakim Qasim *Rites of Assent*

Somaya Ramadan *Leaves of Narcissus*

Lenin El-Ramly *In Plain Arabic*

Ghada Samman *The Night of the First Billion*

Rafik Schami *Damascus Nights*

Miral al-Tahawy *The Tent* • *Blue Aubergine*

Bahaa Taher *Love in Exile*

Fuad al-Takarli *The Long Way Back*

Latifa al-Zayyat *The Open Door*